TIME TRADERS II
THE DEFIANT AGENTS
KEY OUT OF TIME

BAEN BOOKS BY ANDRE NORTON:

Time Traders
Time Traders II

TIME TRADERS II

THE DEFIANT AGENTS
KEY OUT OF TIME

ANDRE NORTON

BAEN

TIME TRADERS II: THE DEFIANT AGENTS & KEY OUT OF TIME

The Defiant Agents copyright © 1962 by The World Publishing Co. *Key Out of Time* copyright © 1963 by The World Publishing Co.

A Baen Books Original Omnibus

Baen Publishing Enterprises
P.O. Box 1403
Riverdale, NY 10471
www.baen.com

ISBN: 0-671-31968-X

Cover art by Stephen Hickman

First Baen printing, February 2001

Library of Congress Cataloging-in-Publication Data

Norton, Andre.
  [Defiant agents]
  Time traders II / by Andre Norton.
    p.   cm.
  "A Baen Books original omnibus"—T.p. verso.
  Contents: The defiant agents — Key out of time.
  Summary: In two related adventures, Travis Fox and Ross Murdock are stranded on two separate planets where they discover that the fate of those worlds, and possibly the galaxy itself, will be determined by their actions.
  ISBN 0-671-31968-X
  1. Science fiction, American. [1. Time travel—Fiction. 2. Science fiction.] I. Norton, Andre. Key out of time. II. Title.

PZ7.N82   Tj   2001
[Fic]—dc21   00-049426

Distributed by Simon & Schuster
1230 Avenue of the Americas
New York, NY 10020

Production by Windhaven Press, Auburn, NH
Printed in the United States of America

10   9   8   7   6   5   4   3   2   1

Contents

TIME TRADERS II
THE DEFIANT AGENTS
KEY OUT OF TIME

The Defiant Agents

1

No windows broke the four plain walls of the office; no sunlight shone on the desk there. Yet the five disks set out on its surface appeared to glow—perhaps the heat of the mischief they could cause . . . had caused . . . blazed in them.

But fanciful imaginings did not change cold, hard fact. Dr. Gordon Ashe, one of the four men peering unhappily at the display, shook his head slightly as if to free his mind of such cobwebs.

His neighbor to the right, Colonel Kelgarries, leaned forward to ask harshly: "No chance of a mistake?"

"You saw the detector." The thin gray man behind the desk answered with chill precision. "No, no possible mistake. These five have definitely been snooped."

"And two choices among them," Ashe murmured. That was the important point now.

"I thought these were under maximum security," Kelgarries challenged the gray man.

Florian Waldour's remote expression did not change.

3

"Every possible precaution was in force. There was a sleeper—a hidden agent—planted—"

"Who?" Kelgarries demanded.

Ashe glanced around at his three companions—Kelgarries, colonel in command of one sector of Project Star, Florian Waldour, the security head on the station, Dr. James Ruthven . . .

"Camdon!" he said, hardly able to believe this answer to which logic had led him.

Waldour nodded.

It was the first time since he had known and worked with Kelgarries that Ashe saw him display open astonishment.

"Camdon? But he was sent by—" The colonel's eyes narrowed. "He must have been sent. . . . There were too many cross checks to fake that!"

"Oh, he was sent, all right." For the first time there was a note of emotion in Waldour's voice. "He was a sleeper, a very deep sleeper. They must have planted him a full twenty-five or thirty years ago. He's been just what he claimed to be as long as that."

"Well, he certainly was worth their time and trouble, wasn't he?" James Ruthven's voice was a growling rumble. He sucked in thick lips, continuing to stare at the disks. "How long ago were these snooped?"

Ashe's thoughts turned swiftly from the enormity of the betrayal to that important point. The time element—that was the primary concern now that the damage was done, and they knew it.

"That's one thing we don't know." Waldour's reply came slowly as if he hated the admission.

"We'll be safer, then, if we presume the very earliest period." Ruthven's statement was as ruthless in its implications as the shock they had had when Waldour announced the disaster.

"Eighteen months ago?" Ashe protested.

But Ruthven was nodding. "Camdon was in on this from the very first. We've had the tapes in and out for study all that time, and the new detector against snooping was not put in service until two weeks ago. This case came up on the first check, didn't it?" he asked Waldour.

"First check," the security man agreed. "Camdon left the base six days ago. But he has been in and out on his liaison duties from the first."

"He had to go through those search points every time," Kelgarries protested. "Thought nothing could get through those." The colonel brightened. "Maybe he got his snooper films and then couldn't take them off base. Have his quarters been turned out?"

Waldour's lips lifted in a grimace of exasperation. "Please, Colonel," he said wearily, "this is not a kindergarten exercise. In confirmation of his success, listen . . ." He touched a button on his desk and out of the air came the emotionless chant of a newscaster.

"Fears for the safety of Lassiter Camdon, space expeditor for the Western Alliance Space Council, have been confirmed by the discovery of burned wreckage in the mountains. Mr. Camdon was returning from a mission to the Star Laboratory when his plane lost contact with Ragnor Field. Reports of a storm in that vicinity immediately raised concern—" Waldour snapped off the voice.

"True—or a cover for his escape?" Kelgarries wondered aloud.

"Could be either. They may have deliberately written him off when they had all they wanted," Waldour acknowledged. "But to get back to our troubles—Dr. Ruthven is right to assume the worst. I believe we can only insure the recovery of our project by thinking that these tapes were snooped anywhere from eighteen months ago to last week. And we must work accordingly!"

The room fell silent as they all considered that. Ashe slipped down in his chair, his thoughts enmeshed in memories. First there had been Operation Retrograde, when specially trained "time agents" had shuttled back and forth in history, striving to locate and track down the mysterious source of alien knowledge which Greater Russia had suddenly—and ominously—begun to use.

Ashe himself and a younger partner, Ross Murdock, had been part of the final action which had solved the mystery, having traced that source of knowledge not to an earlier and forgotten human civilization but to wrecked spaceships from an eon-old galactic empire—an empire which had flourished when glacial ice covered most of Europe and northern America and humans were cave-dwelling primitives. Murdock, trapped by the Russians in one of those wrecked ships, had inadvertently summoned its original owners. They had descended to trace—through the Russian time stations—the looters of their wrecks, destroying the whole Russian time-travel system.

But the aliens had not chanced on the parallel western system. And a year later that had been put into Project Folsom One. Again Ashe, Murdock, and a newcomer, the Apache Travis Fox, had gone back into time to the Arizona of the Folsom hunters, discovering what they wanted—two ships, one wrecked, the other intact. And when the project had attempted to bring the intact ship back into the present, chance had triggered controls set by the dead alien commander. A party of four, Ashe, Murdock, Fox, and a technician, had then made an involuntary space voyage, touching three worlds on which the galactic civilization of the far past had left ruins.

Voyage tape fed into the controls of the ship had taken the men, and, when rewound, it had almost miraculously returned them to Earth with a cargo of similar tapes found on a world which might have been the capital for a government comprised of whole solar systems. Tapes—each one was the key to another planet.

And that ancient galactic knowledge was treasure such as humans had never dreamed of possessing, though many rightly feared that such discoveries could be weapons in hostile hands. Tapes chosen at random had been shared with other nations at a great drawing. But each nation secretly remained convinced that, in spite of the untold riches it might hold as a result of chance, its rivals had done better. Right at this moment, Ashe knew there were Western agents trying to do at the Russian project just what Camdon had done there. However, that did not help in solving their present dilemma about Operation Cochise, now perhaps the most important part of their plan.

Some of the tapes were duds, either too damaged to be useful, or set for worlds hostile to humans lacking the special equipment the earlier star-traveling race had had at its command. Of the five tapes they now knew had been snooped, three would be useless to the enemy.

But one of the remaining two . . . Ashe frowned. One was the goal toward which they had been working feverishly for a full twelve months. Their assignment was to plant a colony across the gulf of space—a successful colony—later to be used as a steppingstone to other worlds . . .

"So we have to move faster." Ruthven's comment reached Ashe through his stream of memories.

"I thought you required at least three more months to conclude personnel training," Waldour observed.

Ruthven lifted a fat hand, running the nail of a broad thumb back and forth across his lower lip in a habitual gesture Ashe had learned to mistrust. As the latter stiffened, bracing for a battle of wills, he saw Kelgarries come alert too. At least the colonel more often than not was able to counter Ruthven's demands.

"We test and we test," said the fat man. "Always we test. We move like turtles when it would be better to race like greyhounds. There is such a thing as overcaution, as I have said from the first. One would think"—his accusing glance included Ashe and Kelgarries—"that there had never been any improvising in this project, that all had always been done by the book. I say that this is the time we must take the big gamble, or else we may find we have been outbid for space entirely. Let those others discover even one alien installation they can master and—" his thumb shifted from his lip, grinding down on the desk top as if it were crushing some venturesome but entirely unimportant insect—"and we are finished before we really begin."

There were a number of men in the project who would agree with that, Ashe knew. And a greater number in the country and Alliance at large. The public was used to reckless gambles which paid off, and there had been enough of those in the past to give an impressive argument for that point of view. But Ashe, himself, could not agree to a speed-up. He had been out among the stars, shaved disaster too closely because the proper training had not been given.

"I shall report that I advise a take-off within a week," Ruthven was continuing. "To the council I shall say that—"

"And I do not agree!" Ashe cut in. He glanced at Kelgarries for the quick backing he expected, but instead there was a lengthening moment of silence. Then the colonel spread out his hands and said sullenly:

"I don't agree either, but I don't have the final say-so. Ashe, what would be needed to speed up any take-off?"

It was Ruthven who replied. "We can use the Redax, as I have said from the start."

Ashe straightened, his mouth tight, his eyes hard and angry.

"And I'll protest that . . . to the council! Man, we're dealing with human beings—selected volunteers, men who trust us—not with laboratory animals!"

Ruthven's thick lips pouted into what was close to a smile of derision. "Always the sentimentalists, you experts in the past! Tell me, Dr. Ashe, were you always so thoughtful of your men when you sent agents back into time? And certainly a voyage into space is less risky than time travel. These volunteers know what they have signed for. They will be ready—"

"Then you propose telling them about the use of Redax—what it does to a man's mind?" countered Ashe.

"Certainly. They will receive all necessary instructions."

Ashe was not satisfied. He would have spoken again, except that Kelgarries interrupted:

"If it comes to that, none of us here has any right to make final decisions. Waldour has already sent in his report about the snoop. We'll have to await orders from the council."

Ruthven levered himself out of his chair, his solid bulk stretching his uniform coveralls. "That is correct, Colonel. In the meantime I would suggest we all check to see what can be done to speed up each one's portion of labor." Without another word, he tramped to the door.

Waldour eyed the other two with mounting impatience. It was plain he had work to do and wanted them to leave. But Ashe was reluctant. He had a feeling that matters were slipping out of his control, that he was about to face a crisis which was somehow worse than just a major security leak. Was the enemy always on the other side of the world? Or could he wear the same uniform, even pretend to share the same goals?

In the outer corridor he still hesitated. Kelgarries, a step or so in advance, looked back over his shoulder impatiently.

"There's no use fighting—our hands are tied." His words were slurred, almost as if he wanted to disown them.

"Then you'll agree to use the Redax?" For the second time within the hour Ashe felt as if he had taken a step only to have firm earth turn into slippery, shifting sand underfoot.

"It isn't a matter of my agreeing. It may be a matter of getting through or not getting through—now. If they've had eighteen months, or even twelve . . . !" The colonel's fingers balled into a fist. "And *they* won't be delayed by any humanitarian reasoning—"

"Then you believe Ruthven will win the council's approval?"

"When you are dealing with frightened men, you're talking to ears closed to anything except what they want to hear. After all, we can't prove that the Redax will be harmful."

"But we've only used it under rigidly controlled

conditions. To speed up the process would mean a total disregard of those controls. Snapping a party of men and women back into their racial past and holding them there for too long a period . . ." Ashe shook his head.

"You have been in Operation Retrograde from the start, and we've been remarkably successful—"

"Operating in a different way, educating picked men to return to certain points in history where their particular temperaments and characteristics fitted the roles they were selected to play, yes. And even then we had our percentage of failures. But to try this—returning people not physically into time, but *mentally and emotionally* into prototypes of their ancestors—that's something else again. The Apaches have volunteered, and they've been passed by the psychologists and the testers. But they're Americans of today, not tribal nomads of two or three hundred years ago. If you break down some barriers, you might just end up breaking them all."

Kelgarries was scowling. "You mean—they might revert utterly, have no contact with the present at all?"

"That's just what I do mean. Education and training, yes, but full awakening of racial memories, no. The two branches of conditioning should go slowly and hand in hand, otherwise—real trouble!"

"Only we no longer have the time to go slow. I'm certain Ruthven will be able to push this through—with Waldour's report to back him."

"Then we'll have to warn Fox and the rest. They must be given a choice in the matter."

"Ruthven said that would be done." The colonel did not sound convinced.

Ashe snorted. "If I hear him telling them, I'll believe it!"

"I wonder whether we can . . ."

Ashe half turned and frowned at the colonel. "What do you mean?"

"You said yourself that we had our failures in time travel. We expected those, accepted them, even when they hurt. When we asked for volunteers for this project we had to

make them understand that there was a heavy element of
risk involved. Three teams of recruits—the Eskimos from
Point Barren, the Apaches, and the Islanders—all picked
because their people had a high survival rating in the past,
to be colonists on widely different types of planets. Well,
the Eskimos and the Islanders aren't matched to any of the
worlds on those snooped tapes, but Topaz is waiting for the
Apaches. And we may have to move them there in a hurry.
It's a rotten gamble any way you see it!"

"I'll appeal directly to the council."

Kelgarries shrugged. "All right. You have my backing."

"But you believe such an effort hopeless?"

"You know the red-tape merchants. You'll have to move
fast if you want to beat Ruthven. He's probably on a
direct line now to Stanton, Reese, and Margate. This is
what he has been waiting for!"

But if we contacted the media, public opinion would
back us—"

"You don't mean that, of course." Kelgarries was suddenly coldly remote.

Ashe flushed under the heavy brown which overlay his
regular features. To threaten a silence break was near
blasphemy here. He ran both hands down the fabric
covering his thighs as if to rub away some soil on his
palms.

"No," he replied heavily, his voice dull. "I guess I don't.
I'll contact Hough and hope for the best."

"Meanwhile," Kelgarries spoke briskly, "we'll do what
we can to speed up the program as it now stands. I
suggest you take off for New York within the hour—"

"Me? Why?" Ashe asked with a trace of suspicion.

"Because I can't leave without acting directly against
orders, and that would put us wrong immediately. You
see Hough and talk to him personally—put it to him
straight. He'll have to have all the facts if he's going to
counter any move from Stanton before the council. You
know every argument we can use and all the proof on
our side, and you're authority enough to make it count."

"If I can do all that, I will." Ashe was alert and eager. The colonel, seeing his change of expression, felt easier.

But Kelgarries stood a moment watching Ashe as he hurried down a side corridor, before he moved on slowly to his own box of an office. Once inside he sat for a long time staring at the wall and seeing nothing but the pictures produced by his thoughts. Then he pressed a button and read off the symbols which flashed on a small viewscreen set in his desk. Punching a code, he relayed an order which might postpone trouble for a while. Ashe was far too valuable a man to lose, and his emotions could boil him straight into disaster over this.

"Bidwell—reschedule Team A. They are to go to the Hypno-Lab instead of the reserve in ten minutes."

Releasing the mike, he again stared at the wall. No one dared interrupt a hypno-training period, and this one would last three hours. Ashe could not possibly see the trainees before he left for New York. And that would remove one temptation from his path—he would not talk at the wrong time.

Kelgarries' mouth twisted sourly. He took no pride in what he was doing. And he was perfectly certain that Ruthven would win and that Ashe's fears of Redax were well founded. It all came back to the old basic tenet of the service: the end justified the means. They must use every method and man under their control to make sure that Topaz would remain a Western possession, even though that strange planet now swung far beyond the sky which covered both Western Alliance and Greater Russia. Time had run out too fast; they were being forced to play what cards they held, even though those might be low ones. Ashe would be back, but not, Kelgarries hoped, until this had been decided one way or another. Not until this was finished.

Finished! Kelgarries blinked at the wall. Perhaps *they* were finished, too. No one would know until the transport ship landed on that other world, that jewellike disk of gold-brown they had named Topaz.

2

There were an even dozen of the air-borne guardians. Each swung in its own orbit just beyond the atmosphere of a bronze-gold planet in the four-world system of a yellow star. The globes had been launched to form a protective web around Topaz six months earlier. Just as contact mines sown in a harbor could close that landfall to ships not knowing the secret channel, so was this world supposedly closed to any spaceship lacking the signal to ward off the missiles the spheres could summon. This system for protecting the new human settlers had been tested as well as possible, but not as yet put to the ultimate proof. Still, the small bright globes spun undisturbed across a two-mooned sky at night and made reassuring blips on an installation screen by day.

Then a thirteenth object winked into being and began the encircling, closing spiral of descent. A sphere resembling the warden-globes, it was a hundred times their size, and its orbit was controlled by instruments under the eye and hand of a human pilot.

Four men were strapped down on cushioned sling-seats

13

in the control cabin of the Western Alliance ship, two hanging where their fingers might reach buttons and levers. The two others were merely passengers, their own labor waiting for the time when they would set down on the alien soil of Topaz. The planet hung there in their viewscreen, richly beautiful in its amber gold, growing larger, nearer, so that they could pick out features of seas, continents, mountain ranges, which had been studied on tape until they were familiar—or as familiar as a world not Earth could be.

One of the warden-globes came alert and oscillated in its set path. It whirled faster as its delicate interior mechanisms responded to the signal that would send it on its mission of destruction. A relay clicked, but imperceptibly slow in setting the proper course. On the instrument, far below, which checked the globe's new course the mistake was not noted.

The screen of the ship spiraling toward Topaz registered a path which would bring it into violent contact with the globe. They were still some hundreds of miles apart when the alarm rang. The pilot's hand clawed out at the bank of controls; under the almost intolerable pressure of their descent, there was so little he could do. His crooked fingers fell back powerlessly from the buttons and levers; his mouth was a twisted grimace of bleak acceptance as the beat of the signal increased.

One of the passengers forced his head around on the padded rest, fought to form words, to speak to his companion. The other was staring ahead at the screen, his thick lips wide and flat against his teeth in a snarl of rage.

"They . . . are . . . here. . . ."

Ruthven paid no attention to the obvious as stated by his fellow scientist. His fury was a red, pulsing thing inside him, fed by his own helplessness. To be pinned here so near his goal, set up as a target for a mere machine, ate into him like a stream of deadly acid. His big gamble would puff out in a blast of fire to light up

Topaz's sky, with nothing left—nothing. On the armrest of his sling-seat his nails scratched deep.

The four men in the control cabin could only sit and watch, waiting for the rendezvous which would blot them out. Ruthven's flaming anger was a futile blaze. His companion in the passenger seat had closed his eyes, his lips moving soundlessly. The pilot and his assistant divided their attention between the screen, with its appalling message, and the controls they could not effectively use, feverishly seeking a way out in these last moments.

Below them in the bowels of the ship were those who would not know the end consciously—save in one compartment. In a padded cage a prick-eared head stirred where it rested on forepaws, slitted eyes blinked, aware not only of familiar surroundings, but also of the tension and fear generated by human minds and emotions levels above. A pointed nose raised, and growling rose from a throat covered with thick buff-gray hair.

The growl aroused another similar captive. Knowing yellow eyes met yellow eyes. An intelligence, which was not natural to the animal body which contained it, fought down instinct raging to send both those bodies hurtling at the fastenings of the twin cages. Curiosity and the ability to adapt had been bred into these creatures from time immemorial. Then something else had been added to sly and cunning brains. A step up had been taken—to weld intelligence to cunning, connect thought to instinct.

More than a generation earlier mankind had chosen barren desert—the "white sands" of New Mexico—as a testing ground for atomic experiments. Humankind could be barred, warded out of the radiation limits. The natural desert dwellers, four-footed and winged, could not be so controlled.

Thousands of years earlier, the first southward roving Amerindian tribes had met with their kind, a hunter of the open country, a smaller cousin of the wolf, whose natural abilities had made an indelible impression on the human mind. He appeared in countless Indian legends

as the Shaper or the Trickster, sometimes friend, sometimes enemy. Godling for some tribes, father of all evil
for others. In the wealth of tales the coyote, above all
other animals, held pride of place.

Driven by the press of civilization into the badlands
and deserts, fought with poison, gun, and trap, the coyote
had survived, adapting to new ways with all his legendary
cunning. Those who had reviled him as vermin had
unwillingly added to the folklore which surrounded him,
telling their own tales of robbed traps, skillful escapes.
He continued to be a trickster, laughing on moonlit nights
from the tops of ridges at those who would hunt him
down.

Then, in the early twenty-first century, when myths were
scoffed at, the stories of the coyote's slyness began once
more on a fantastic scale. And finally scientists were
sufficiently intrigued to seek out this creature that seemed
to display in truth all the abilities credited to his immortal
namesake by pre-Columbian tribes.

What they discovered was indeed shattering to certain
closed minds. For the coyote had not only adapted to the
country of the white sands; he had evolved into something
which could not be dismissed as an animal, clever and
cunning, but limited to beast range. Six cubs had been
brought back on the first expedition, coyote in body, their
developing minds different. The descendants of those cubs
were now in the ship's cages, their mutated senses alert,
ready for the slightest chance of escape. Sent to Topaz as
eyes and ears for less keenly endowed humans, they were
not completely under the domination of man. The range of
their mental powers was still uncomprehended by those who
had bred, trained, and worked with them from the days their
eyes had opened and they had taken their first wobbly steps
away from their dams.

The male growled again, his lips wrinkling back in a
snarl as the emanations of fear from the men he could
not see reached panic peak. He still crouched, belly flat,
on the protecting pads of his cage; but he strove now

to wriggle closer to the door, just as his mate made the same effort.

Between the animals and those in the control cabin lay the others—forty of them. Their bodies were cushioned and protected with every ingenious device known to those who had placed them there so many weeks earlier. Their minds were free of the ship, roving into places where men had not trod before, a territory potentially more dangerous than any solid earth could ever be.

Operation Retrograde had returned men bodily into the past, sending agents to hunt mammoths, follow the roads of the Bronze Age traders, ride with Attila and Genghis Khan, pull bows among the archers of ancient Egypt. But Redax returned men in mind to the paths of their ancestors, or this was the theory. And those who slept here and now in their narrow boxes, lay under its influence. The men who had arbitrarily set them on this course could only assume they were actually reliving the lives of Apache nomads in the wide southwestern wastes of the late eighteenth and early nineteenth centuries.

Above, the pilot's hand pushed out again, fighting the pressure to reach one particular button. That, too, had been a last-minute addition, an experiment which had only received partial testing. To use it was the final move he could make, although he was already half convinced of its uselessness.

With no faith and only a wan hope, he depressed that round of metal flush with the board. What followed no one ever lived to explain.

At the planetside installation that tracked the missiles, a screen flared brightly enough to blind momentarily the man on watch, and the warden-globe was shaken off course. When it jiggled back into line it was no longer the efficient eye-in-the-sky it had been, though its tenders were not to realize that for an important minute or two.

While the ship, now out of control, sped in dizzy whirls toward Topaz, engines fought blindly to stabilize, to re-establish their functions. Some succeeded, some wobbled in and out of the danger zone, two failed. And in the control cabin three dead men spun imprisoned in their seats.

Dr. James Ruthven, blood bubbling from his lips with every shallow breath he could draw, fought the stealthy tide of blackness which crept up his brain, his stubborn will holding to rags of consciousness, refusing to acknowledge the pain of his fatally injured body.

The orbiting ship spun on an erratic path. Slowly its mechanisms were correcting, relays clicking, striving to bring it to a landing under auto-pilot. All the ingenuity built into its computer was now centered in landing the globe.

It was not a good landing. The sphere touched a mountain side, scraped down rocks, shearing away a portion of its outer bulk. But the mountain barrier was now between it and the base from which the missiles had been launched, and the crash had not been recorded. As far as the watchers several hundred miles away knew, the warden in the sky had performed as promised. Their first line of defense had proven satisfactory. There had been no unauthorized landing on Topaz.

In the wreckage of the control cabin Ruthven pawed at the fastenings of his sling-chair. He no longer tried to suppress the moans every effort tore out of him. Time held the whip, drove him. He rolled from his seat to the floor, lay there gasping, as again he fought doggedly to remain above the waves—those frightening, fast-coming waves of darkness.

Somehow he was crawling, crawling along a tilted surface until he gained the well where the ladder to the lower section hung, now at an acute angle. That angle made it possible for him to reach the next level.

He was too dazed to realize the meaning of the crumpled bulkheads. There was a spur of bare rock under his hands as he edged over and around twisted metal. The moans were now a gobbling, burbling, almost continuous cry as he reached his goal—a small cabin still intact.

For long moments of anguish he paused by the chair there, afraid that he could not make the last effort, raise his almost inert bulk up to the point where he could reach the Redax release. For a second of unusual clarity he wondered if there was any reason for this supreme ordeal, whether any of the sleepers could be aroused. This might now be a ship of the dead.

His right hand, his arm, and finally his bulk over the seat, he braced himself and brought his left hand up. He could not use any of the fingers; it was like lifting numb, heavy weights. But he lurched forward, swept the unfeeling cold flesh down against the release in a gesture which he knew must be his final move. And, as he fell back to the floor, Dr. Ruthven could not be certain whether he had succeeded or failed. He tried to twist his head around, to focus his eyes upward at that switch. Was it down or still stubbornly up, locking the sleepers into confinement? But fog drifted between; he could not see it— or anything else.

The light in the cabin flickered and went out as another circuit in the broken ship failed. It was dark, too, in the small cubby below which housed the two cages. Chance, which had snuffed out nineteen lives in the space globe, had missed ripping open that cabin on the mountain side. Five yards down the corridor the outside fabric of the ship was split wide open, the crisp air native to Topaz entering, sending a message to two keen noses through the combination of odors now pervading the wreckage.

And the male coyote went into action. Days ago he had managed to work loose the lower end of the mesh which fronted his cage, but his mind had told him that a sortie inside the ship was valueless. The odd rapport he'd had with the human brains, unknown to them, had operated to keep him to the old role of cunning deception, which in the past had saved countless of his species from sudden and violent death. Now with teeth and paws he went diligently to work, urged on by the whines of his mate, that tantalizing smell of an outside world tickling their nostrils—a wild world, lacking the taint of man-places.

He slipped under the loosened mesh and stood up to paw at the front of the female's cage. One forepaw caught in the latch and pressed it down, and the weight of the door swung against him. Together they were free now to reach the corridor and see ahead the subdued light of a strange moon beckoning them on into the open.

The female, always more cautious than her mate, lingered behind as he trotted forward, his ears a-prick with curiosity. Their training had been the same since cubhood—to range and explore, but always in the company and at the order of man. This was not according to the pattern she knew, and she was suspicious. But to her sensitive nose the smell of the ship was offensive and the puffs of breeze from outside enticing. Her mate had already slipped through the break. Now he barked with excitement and wonder, and she trotted on to join him.

Above, the Redax, which had never been intended to stand rough usage, proved to be a better survivor of the crash than most of the other installations. Power purred along a network of lines, activated beams, turned off and on a series of fixtures in those coffin-beds. For five of the sleepers—nothing. The cabin which had held them was a flattened smear against the mountain side. Three more half-roused, choked, fought for life and breath in a nightmare that was mercifully short, and succumbed.

But in the cabin nearest the rent through which the coyotes had escaped, a young man sat up abruptly, staring into the dark with wide-open, terror-haunted eyes. He clawed for purchase against the smooth edge of the box in which he had lain and somehow got to his knees. Weaving weakly back and forth, he half fell, half pushed to the floor where he could stand only by keeping his hold on the box.

Dazed, sick, weak, he swayed there, aware only of

himself and his own sensations. There were small sounds in the dark, a stilled moan, a gasping sigh. But that meant nothing. Within him grew a compulsion to be out of this place, his terror making him lurch forward.

His flailing hand rapped painfully against an upright surface which his questing fingers identified hazily as an exit. Unconsciously he fumbled along the surface of the door until it gave under that weak pressure. Then he was out, his head swimming, drawn by light behind the rent wall.

He scrabbled towards it at a crawl, making his way over the splintered skin of the globe. Then he dropped with a jarring thud onto the mound of earth the ship had pushed before it during its downward slide. Limply he tumbled on in a small cascade of clods and sand, hitting a less movable rock with enough force to land him on his back and stun him again.

The second and smaller moon of Topaz swung brightly through the sky, its greenish light making the blood-streaked face of the explorer an alien mask. It had passed well on to the horizon, and its large yellow companion had risen, when yapping broke the small sounds of the night.

As the *yipp, yipp, yipp* arose in a crescendo, the man stirred, putting one hand to his head. His eyes opened, he looked vaguely about him and sat up. Behind him was the torn and ripped ship, but he did not look back at it.

Instead, he got to his feet and staggered out into the moonlight. Inside his brain there was a whirl of thoughts, memories, emotions. Perhaps Ruthven or one of his assistants could have sorted that chaotic mixture. But for all practical purposes Travis Fox—Amerindian Time Agent, member of Team A, Operation Cochise—was far less of a thinking animal now than the two coyotes paying their ritual addresses to a moon which was not the one of their vanished homeland.

Travis wavered on, drawn somehow by that howling.

It was familiar, a thread of something real through all the broken clutter in his head. He stumbled, fell, crawled up again, but he kept on.

Above, the female coyote lowered her head, drew a test sniff of a new scent. She recognized that as part of the proper way of life. She yapped once at her mate, but he was absorbed in his night song, his muzzle pointed moonward as he voiced a fine wail.

Travis tripped, pitched forward on his hands and knees, and felt the jar of such a landing shoot up his stiffened forearms. He tried to get up, but his body only twisted, so he landed on his back and lay looking up at the moon.

A strong, familiar odor . . . then a shadow looming above him. Hot breath against his cheek, and the swift sweep on an animal tongue on his face. He flung up his hand, gripped thick fur, and held on as if he had found one anchor of sanity in a world gone completely mad.

3

Travis, one knee braced against the red earth, blinked as he parted a screen of tall rust-brown grass with cautious fingers. He looked out into a valley where golden mist clouded most of the landscape. His head ached with dull persistence, the pain amplified by his own bewilderment. To study the land ahead was like trying to see through one picture interposed over another and far different one. He knew what ought to be there, but what was before him was very dissimilar.

A buff-gray shape flitted through the tall cover grass, and Travis tensed. *Mba'a*—coyote? Or were his companions actually *ga-n*, spirits who could choose their shape at will and had, oddly, this time assumed the bodies of man's tricky enemy? Were they *ndendai*—enemies—or *dalaanbiyat'i*, allies? In this mad world he did not know.

Ei'dik'e? His mind formed a word he did not speak: Friend?

Yellow eyes met his directly. Dimly he had been aware, ever since awakening in this strange wilderness with the coming of morning light, that the four-footed ones trotting with him as he walked aimlessly had unbeastlike traits. Not only did they face him eye-to-eye, but in some ways they appeared able to read his thoughts.

He had longed for water to ease the burning in his throat, the ever-present pain in his head, and the creatures had nudged him in another direction, bringing him to a pool where he had drunk liquid with a strangely sweet, but not unpleasant taste.

Now he had given them names, names which had come out of the welter of dreams which shadowed his stumbling journey across this weird country.

Nalik'ideyu (Maiden-Who-Walks-Ridges) was the female who continued to shepherd him along, never venturing too far from his side. Naginlta (He-Who-Scouts-Ahead) was the male who did just that, disappearing at long intervals and then returning to face the man and his mate as if conveying some report necessary to their journey.

It was Nalik'ideyu who sought Travis now, her red tongue lolling from her mouth as she panted. Not from exertion, he was certain of that. No, she was excited and eager . . . on the hunt! That was it—a hunt!

Travis' own tongue ran across his lips as an impression hit him with feral force. There was meat—rich, fresh—just ahead. Meat that lived, waiting to be killed. Inside him his own avid hunger roused, shaking him farther out of the crusting dream.

His hands went to his waist, but the groping fingers did not find what vague memory told him should be there—a belt, heavy with knife in sheath.

He examined his own body with attention to find he was adequately covered by breeches of a smooth, dull brown material which blended well with the vegetation about him. He wore a loose shirt, belted in at the narrow waist by a folded strip of cloth, the ends of which fluttered free. On his feet were tall moccasins, the leg pieces extending some distance up his calves, the toes turned up in rounded points.

Some of this he found familiar, but these were fragments of memory; again his mind fitted one picture above another. One thing he did know for sure—he had no weapons. And that realization struck home with a thrust of real and terrible fear which tore away more of the bewilderment cloaking his mind.

Nalik-ideyu was impatient. Having advanced a step or two, she now looked back at him over her shoulder, yellow eyes slitted, her demand on him as instant and real as if she had voiced understandable words. Meat was waiting, and she was hungry. Also she expected Travis to aid in the hunt—at once.

Though he could not match her fluid grace in moving through the grass, Travis followed her, keeping to cover. He shook his head vigorously, in spite of the stab of pain the motion cost him, and paid more attention to his surroundings. It was apparent that the earth under him, the grass around, the valley of the golden haze, were all real, not part of a dream. Therefore that other countryside which he kept seeing in a ghostly fashion was a hallucination.

Even the air which he drew into his lungs and expelled again, had a strange smell, or was it taste? He could not be sure which. He knew that hypno-training could produce odd side effects, but . . . this . . .

Travis paused, staring unseeingly before him at the grass still waving from the coyote's passage. Hypno-training! What was that? Now three pictures fought to focus in his mind: the two landscapes which did not match and a shadowy third. He shook his head again, his hands to his temples. This—this only was real: the ground, the grass, the valley, the hunger in him, the hunt waiting . . .

He forced himself to concentrate on the immediate present and the portion of world he could see, feel, scent, which lay here and now about him.

The grass grew shorter as he proceeded in Nalik'ideyu's wake. But the haze was not thinning. It seemed to hang in patches, and when he ventured through the edge of a patch it was like creeping through a fog of golden, dancing motes. Here and there a glittering speck whirled and darted like a living thing. Masked by the stuff, Travis reached a line of brush and sniffed.

It was a warm scent, a heavy odor he could not identify and yet one he associated with a living creature. Flat to earth, he pushed head and shoulders under the low limbs of the bush to look ahead.

Here was a space where the fog did not hold, a pocket of earth clear under the morning sun. And grazing there were three animals. Again shock cleared a portion of Travis' bemused brain.

They were about the size, he thought, of antelopes, and they had a general resemblance to those beasts in that they had four slender legs, a rounded body, and a head. But they had alien features, so alien as to hold him in open-mouthed amazement.

The bodies had bare spots here and there, and patches of creamy—fur? Or was it hair which hung in strips, as if the creatures had been partially plucked in careless fashion? The necks were long and moved about in a serpentine motion, as though their spines were as limber as reptiles'. On the end of those long and twisting necks were heads which also appeared more suitable to another species—broad, rather flat, with a singular toadlike look—but furnished with horns set halfway down the nose, horns which began in a single root and then branched into two sharp points.

They were unearthly! Again Travis blinked, brought his hand up to his head as he continued to view the browsers. There were three of them: two larger ones with horns, the other a smaller beast with less of the ragged fur and only the beginning button of a protuberance on the nose. It was probably a calf.

One of those mental alerts from the coyotes broke his absorption. Nalik'ideyu was not interested in the odd appearance of the grazing creatures. She was intent upon their usefulness in another way—as a full and satisfying meal—and she was again impatient with him for his dull response.

His examination took a more practical turn. An antelope's defense was speed, though it could be tricked into hunting range through its inordinate curiosity. The slender legs of these beasts suggested a like degree of speed, and Travis had no weapons at all.

Those nose horns had an ugly look; this thing might be a fighter rather than a runner. But the suggestion which had flashed from coyote to him had taken root. Travis was hungry, he was a hunter, and here was meat on the hoof, strange as it looked.

Again he received a message. Naginlta was on the opposite side of the clearing. If the creatures depended on speed, then Travis believed they could probably outrun not only him but the coyotes as well—which left cunning and some sort of plan.

Travis glanced at the cover where he knew Nalik'ideyu crouched and from which had come that flash of agreement. He shivered. These were truly no animals, but *ga-n, ga-n* of power! And as *ga-n* he must treat them, accede to their will. Spurred by that, the Apache gave only flicks of attention to the browsers while at the same time he studied the part of the landscape uncovered by mist.

Without weapons or speed, they must conceive a trap. Again Travis sensed agreement from the *ga-n,* and with it a strong impression urging him to the right. He was making progress with skill he did not even recognize and which he had never been conscious of learning.

The bushes and small, droop-limbed trees, had branches not clothed with leaves from proper twigs but with a reddish bristly growth protruding directly from their surfaces. The trees screened the pocket-sized meadow, reaching a rocky cleft where the mist curled in a long tongue through a wall twice Travis' height. If the browsers could be maneuvered into taking the path through that cleft . . .

Travis searched about him, and his hands closed upon the oldest weapon of his species, a stone pulled from the earth and balanced neatly in the palm of his hand. It was a long chance but his best one.

The Apache took the first step on a new and fearsome road. These *ga-n* had put their thoughts—or their desires—into his mind. Could he so contact them in return?

With the stone clenched in his fist, his shoulders pressed against the wall not too far from the cleft opening, Travis strove to think out, clearly and simply, his poor plan. He did not know that he was reacting the way scientists light years away had hoped he might. Nor did Travis guess that at this point he had already traveled far beyond the expectations of the men who had bred and trained the two mutant coyotes. He only believed that he was obeying the wishes of two spirits he thought far more powerful than any man. So he pictured in his mind the cleft, the running creatures, and the part the *ga-n* could play if they so willed.

Assent—in its way as loud and clear as if shouted. The man fingered the stone, weighed it. There would probably be just one moment when he could use it to effect, so he must be ready.

From this point he could no longer see the small meadow where the grazers were. But Travis knew, as well as if he watched the scene, that the coyotes were creeping in, belly flat to earth, adding a feline stealth and patience to their own cunning.

There! Travis' head jerked, the alert had come, the drive was beginning. He tensed, gripping his stone.

A yapping bark was answered by a sound he could not describe, a noise midway between a cough and a grunt. Again a yap-yap . . .

A toad-head burst through the screen of brush, the double horn on its nose festooned with grass torn up by the roots. Wide eyes—milky and seeming to be without pupils—fastened on Travis, but he could not be sure the thing saw him, for it kept on, picking up speed as it approached the cleft. Behind it ran the calf, and that guttural cry was bubbling from its broad flat lips.

The long neck of the adult writhed, the frog-head swung closer to the ground so that the twin points of the horn were at a slant—aimed now at Travis. He had been right to suspect their deadliness, but he had only a fleeting chance to recognize that fact as the thing bore down, clearly intent on goring him.

He hurled his stone and then flung his body to one side, tumbling and rolling into the brush where he fought madly to regain his feet, expecting at any moment to feel trampling hoofs and thrusting horns. There was a crash to his right, as the bushes and grass were wildly shaken.

On his hands and knees the Apache retreated, his head turned to watch behind him. He saw the flirt of a triangular flap-tail in the mouth of the cleft. The calf had escaped. And now the threshing in the bushes stilled.

Was the thing stalking him? He got to his feet, for the first time hearing clearly the continued yapping, as if a battle was in progress. Then the second of the adult beasts came into view, backing and turning, trying to keep its lowered head with menacing double horn always pointed to the coyotes as they danced a teasing, worrying circle about it.

One of the coyotes flung up its head, looked upslope, and barked. Then, as one, both rushed the fighting beast, but for the first time from the same side, leaving it a clear path to retreat. It made a rush before which they fled easily. Then it whirled with a speed and grace, which did not fit its ungainly, ill-proportioned body, and jumped toward the cleft, the coyotes making no effort to hinder its escape.

Travis came out of cover, approaching the brush which had concealed the crash of the other animal. The actions of the coyotes had convinced him that there was no danger now; they would never have allowed the escape of their prey had the first beast not been downed.

His shot with the stone, the Apache decided as he stood moments later surveying the twitching crumpled body, must have hit the thing in the head, stunning it. Then the momentum of its charge had carried it full force against the rock to kill it. Blind luck—or the power of the *ga-n?* He pulled back as the coyotes came padding up shoulder to shoulder to inspect the kill. It was truly more theirs than his.

Their prey yielded not only food but a weapon for Travis. Instead of the belt knife he had remembered having, he was now equipped with two. The double horn had been easy to free from the shattered skull, and some careful work with stones had broken off one prong at just the angle he wanted. So now he had a short and a longer tool, defense. At least they were better than the stone with which he had entered the hunt.

Nalik-ideyu pushed past him to lap daintily at the water. Then she sat up on her haunches, watching Travis as he smoothed the horn with a stone.

"A knife," he said to her, "this will be a knife. And—" he glanced up, measuring the value of the wood represented by trees and bushes—"then a bow. With a bow we shall hunt better."

The coyote yawned, her yellow eyes half closed, a study in satisfaction and content.

"A knife," Travis repeated, "and a bow." He needed weapons; he had to have them!

Why? His hand stopped scraping. Why? The toad-faced double horn had been quick to attack, but Travis could have avoided it, and it had not hunted him first. Why was he ridden by this fear that he must not be unarmed?

He dipped his hand into the pool of the spring and lifted the water to cool his sweating face. The coyote moved, turned around in the grass, crushing down the growth into a nest in which she curled up, head on paws. But Travis sat back on his heels, his now idle hands hanging down between his knees, and forced himself to the task of sorting out jumbled memories.

This landscape was wrong—totally unlike what it should be—but it was real. He had helped kill this alien creature. He had eaten its meat, raw. Its horn lay within touch now. All that was real and unchangeable. Which meant that the rest of it, that other desert world in which he had wandered with his kind, ridden horses, raided invading men of another race, that was not real—or else far, far removed from where he now sat.

Yet there had been no dividing line between those two worlds. One moment he had been in the desert place, returning from a successful foray against the Mexicans. Mexicans! Travis caught at that identification, tried to use it as a thread to draw closer to the beginning of his mystery.

Mexicans . . . And he was an Apache, one of the Eagle people, one who rode with Cochise. No!

Sweat again beaded his face where the water had cooled it. He was not of that past. He was Travis Fox, of the early twenty-first century, not a nomad of the middle nineteenth! He was of Team A of the project!

The Arizona desert and then this! From one to the other in an instant. He looked about him in rising fear. Wait! He had been in the dark when he got out of the desert, lying in a box. Getting out, he had crawled down a passage to reach moonlight, strange moonlight.

A box in which he had lain, a passage with smooth metallic walls, and an alien world at the end of it.

The coyote's ears twitched, her head came up, she was staring at the man's drawn face, at his eyes with their core of fear. She whined.

Travis caught up the two pieces of horn, thrust them into his sash belt, and got to his feet. Nalik'ideyu sat up, her head cocked a little to one side. As the man turned to seek his own back trail she padded along in his wake and whined for Naginlta. But Travis was more intent now on what he must prove to himself than he was on the actions of the two animals.

It was a wandering trail, and now he did not question his skill in being able to follow it so unerringly. The sun was hot. Winged things buzzed from the bushes, small scuttling things fled from him through the tall grass. Once Naginlta growled a warning which led them all to a detour, and Travis might not have picked up the proper trace again had not the coyote scout led him to it.

"Who are you?" he asked once, and then guessed it would have better been said, "What are you?" These were not animals, or rather they were more than the animals he had always known. And one part of him, the part which remembered the desert rancherias where Cochise had ruled, said they were spirits. Yet that other part of him . . . Travis shook his head, accepting them now for what they were—welcome company in an alien place.

The day wore on close to sunset, and still Travis followed that wandering trail. The need which drove him kept him going through the rough country of hills and ravines. Now the mist lifted above towering walls of mountains very near him, yet not the mountains of his memory. These were dull brown, with a forbidding look, like sun-dried skulls baring teeth in warning against all comers.

With great difficulty, Travis topped a rise. Ahead against the skyline stood both coyotes. And, as the man joined them, first one and then the other flung back its head and sounded the sobbing, shattering cry which had been a part of that other life.

The Apache looked down. His puzzle was answered in part. The wreckage crumpled on the mountain side was identifiable—a spaceship! Cold fear gripped him and his own head went back; from between his tight lips came a cry as desolate as the one the animals had voiced.

4

Fire, mankind's oldest ally, weapon, tool, leaped high before the naked stone of the mountain side. Men sat cross-legged about it, fifteen of them. And behind, guarded by the flames and that somber circle, were the women. There was a uniformity in this gathering. The members were plainly all of the same racial stock, of medium height, stocky yet fined down to the peak of stamina and endurance, their skin brown, their shoulder-length hair black. And they were all young—none over thirty, some still in their late teens. Alike, too, was a certain drawn look in their faces, a tenseness of the eyes and mouth as they listened to Travis.

"So we must be on Topaz. Do any of you remember boarding the ship?"

"No. Only that we awoke within it." Across the fire one chin lifted; the eyes which caught Travis' held a deep, smoldering anger. "This is more trickery of the Pinda-lick-o-yi, the White Eyes. Between us there has never been fair dealing. They have broken their promise as a man breaks a rotten stick, for their words are

33

as rotten. And it was you, Fox, who brought us to listen to them."

A stir about the circle, a murmur from the women.

"And do I not also sit here with you in this strange wilderness?" he countered.

"I do not understand," another of the men held out his hand, palm up, in a gesture of asking—"what has happened to us. We were in the old Apache world . . . I, Jil-Lee, was riding with Cuchillo Negro as we went down to the taking of Ramos. And then I was here, in a broken ship and beside me a dead man who was once my brother. How did I come out of the past of our people into another world across the stars?"

"Pinda-lick-o-yi tricks!" The first speaker spat into the fire.

"It was something called Redax, I think," Travis replied. "I heard Dr. Ashe speak of this. A new machine which could make a man remember not his own past, but the past of his ancestors. While we were on that ship we must have been under its influence, so we lived as our people lived a hundred years or more ago—"

"And the purpose of such a thing?" Jil-Lee asked.

"To make us more like our ancestors perhaps. It is part of what they told us at the project. To venture into these new worlds requires a different type of man than lives on Earth today. Traits we have forgotten are needed to face the dangers of wild places."

"You, Fox, have been beyond the stars before, and you found there were such dangers to face?"

"It is true. You have heard of the three worlds I saw when the ship from the old days took us off, unwilling, to the stars. Did you not all volunteer to pioneer in this manner so you could also see strange and new things?"

"But we did not agree to be returned to the past in medicine dreams and be sent unknowingly into space!"

Travis nodded. "Deklay is right. But I know no more than you why we were so sent, or why the ship crashed. We have found Dr. Ruthven's body in the cabin, only we have discovered nothing else which tells us why we were brought here. With the ship broken, we must stay."

They were silent now, men and women alike. Behind them lay several days of activity, nights of exhausted slumber. Against the cliff wall lay the packs of supplies they have salvaged from the wreck. By mutual consent they had left the vicinity of the broken globe, following their old custom of speedily withdrawing from a place of death.

"This is a world empty of men?" Jil-Lee wanted to know.

"So far we have found only animals signs, and the *ga-n* have not warned us of anything else—"

"Those devil ones!" Again Deklay spat into the fire. "I say we should have no dealings with them. The *mba'a* is no friend to the People."

Again a murmur which seemed one of agreement answered that outburst. Travis stiffened. Just how much influence had the Redax had over them? He knew from his own experience that sometimes he had an odd double reaction—two different feelings which almost sickened him when they struck simultaneously. And he was beginning to suspect that with some of the others the return to the past had been far more deep and lasting. Now Jil-Lee was actually to reason out what had happened. While Deklay had reverted to an ancestor who had ridden with Victorio or Mangas Coloradas! Travis had a flash of premonition, a chill which made him half foresee a time when the past and the present might well split them apart—fatally.

"Devil or *ga-n*." A man with a quiet face, rather deeply sunken eyes, spoke for the first time. "We are in two minds because of this Redax, so let us not do anything in haste. Back in the desert world of the People I have seen the *mba'a*, and he was very clever. With the badger he went hunting, and when the badger had dug up the rat's nest, so did the *mba'a* wait on the other side of the thorny bush and catch those who would escape that way. Between him and the badger there was no war. These two who sit over yonder now—they are also hunters and they seem friendly to us. In a strange place a man needs all the help he can find. Let us not call names out of old tales, which may mean nothing in fact."

"Buck speaks straightly," Jil-Lee agreed. "We seek a camp which can be defended. For perhaps there are men here whose hunting territory we have invaded, though we have not yet seen them. We are a people small in number and alone. Let us walk softly on trails which are strange to our feet."

Inwardly Travis sighed in relief. Buck, Jil-Lee . . . for the moment their sensible words appeared to swing the opinions of the party. If either of them could be established as *haldzil*, or clan leader, they would all be safer. He himself had no aspirations in that direction and dared not push too hard. It had been his initial urging which had brought them as volunteers into the project. Now he was doubly suspect, and especially by those who thought as Deklay, he was considered too alien to their old ways.

So far their protests had been fewer than he anticipated. Although brothers and sisters had followed each other into the team after the immemorial desire of Apaches to cling to family ties, they were not a true clan with solidity of that to back them, but representatives of half a dozen.

Basically, back on Earth, they had all been among the most progressive of their people—progressive, that is, in the white man's sense of the word. Travis had a fleeting recognition of his now oblique way of thinking. He, too, had been marked by the Redax. They had all been educated in the modern fashion and all possessed a spirit of adventure which marked them over their fellows. They had volunteered for the team and successfully passed the tests to weed out the temperamentally unfit or faint-hearted. But all that was before Redax. . . .

Why had they been submitted to that? And why this flight? What had pushed Dr. Ashe and Murdock and Colonel Kelgarries, time agents he knew and trusted, into dispatching them without warning to Topaz? Something had happened, something which had given Dr. Ruthven ascendancy over those others and had started them on this wild trip.

Travis was conscious of a stir about the firelit circle. The men were rising, moving back into the shadows, stretching out on the blankets they had found among other stores on the ship. They had discovered weapons there— knives, bows, quivers of arrows, all of which they had been trained to use in the intensive schooling of the project and which needed no more repair than they themselves could give. And the rations they carried were field supplies, few of them. Tomorrow they must begin hunting in earnest. . . .

"Why has this thing been done to us?" Buck was beside Travis, those quiet eyes sliding past him to seek the fire once more. "I do not think you were told when the rest of us were not—"

Travis seized upon that. "There are those who say that I knew, agreed?"

"That is so. Once we stood at the same place in time— in our thoughts, our desires. Now we stand at many places, as if we climbed a stairway, each at his own speed—a stairway the Pinda-lick-o-yi has set us upon. Some here, some there, some yet farther above . . ." He sketched a series of step outlines in the air. "And in this there is trouble—"

"The truth," Travis agreed. "Yet it is also true that I knew nothing of this, that I climb with you on these stairs."

"So I believe. But there comes a time when it is best not to be a woman stirring a pot of boiling stew but rather one who stands quietly at a distance—"

"You mean?" Travis pressed.

"I say that alone among us you have crossed the stars before, therefore new things are not so hard to understand. And we need a scout. Also the coyotes run in your footsteps, and you do not fear them."

It made good sense. Let him scout ahead of the party, taking the coyotes with him. Stay away from the camp for a while and speak small—until the people on Buck's stairway were most closely united.

"I go in the morning," Travis agreed. He could slip away tonight, but just now he could not force himself away from the fire, from the companionship.

"You might take Tsoay with you," Buck continued.

Travis waited for him to enlarge on that suggestion. Tsoay was one of the youngest of their group, Buck's own cross-cousin and near-brother.

"It is well," Buck explained, "that we learn this land, and it has always been our custom that the younger walk in the footprints of the older. Also, not only should trails be learned, but also men."

Travis caught the thought behind that. Perhaps by taking the younger men as scouts, one after another, he could build up among them a following of sorts. Among the Apaches, leadership was wholly a matter of personality. Until the reservation days, chieftains had gained their position by force of character alone, though they might come successively from one family clan over several generations.

He did not want the chieftainship here. No, but neither did he want growing whispers working about him to cut him off from his people. To every Apache severance from the clan was a little death. He must have those who would back him if Deklay, or those who thought like Deklay, turned grumbling into open hostility.

"Tsoay is one quick to learn," Travis agreed. "We go at dawn—"

"Along the mountain range?" Buck inquired.

"If we seek a protected place for the rancheria, yes. The mountains have always provided good strongholds for the People."

"And you think there is need for a fort?"

Travis shrugged. "I have been one day's journey out into this world. I saw nothing but animals. But that is no promise that elsewhere there are no enemies. The planet was on the tapes we brought back from that other world, and so it was known to the others who once rode between star and star as we rode between ranch and town. If they had this world set on a journey tape, it was for a reason; that reason may still be in force."

"Yet it was long ago that these star people rode so . . ." Buck mused. "Would the reason last so long?"

Travis remembered two other worlds, one of weird desert inhabited by beast things—or had they once been human, human to the point of possessing intelligence?—that had come out of sand burrows at night to attack a space-ship. And the second world where the ruins of a giant city had stood choked with jungle vegetation, where he had made a blowgun from tubes of rustless metal as a weapon gift for small winged men—but were they men? Both had been remnants of that ancient galactic empire.

"Some things could so remain," he answered soberly. "If we find them, we must be careful. But first a good site for the rancheria."

"There is no return to home for us," Buck stated flatly.

"Why do you say that? There could be a rescue ship later—"

The other raised his eyes again to Travis. "When you slept under the Redax how did you ride?"

"As a warrior—raiding . . . living . . ."

"And I—I was one with *go'ndi*," Buck returned simply.

"But—"

"But the white man has assured us that such power— the power of the chief—does not exist? Yes, the Pinda-lick-o-yi has told us so many things. He is busy, busy with his tools, his machines, always busy. And those who think in another fashion cannot be measured by his rules, so they are foolish dreamers. Not all white men think so. There was Dr. Ashe—he was beginning to understand a little.

"Perhaps I, too, am standing still, halfway up the stairway of the past. But of this I am very sure: For us,

there will be no return to our own place. And the time
will come when something new shall grow from the seed
of the past. Also it is necessary that you be one of the
tenders of that growth. So I urge you, take Tsoay, and
the next time, Lupe. For the young who may be swayed
this way and that by words—as the wind shakes a small
tree—must be given firm roots."

In Travis education warred with instinct, just as the picture Redax' had planted in his mind had warred with his
awaking to this alien landscape. Yet now he believed he
must be guided by what he felt. And he knew that no
man of his race would claim *go'ndi*, the power of spirit
known only to a great chief, unless he had actually felt
it swell within him. It might have been fostered by hallucination in the past, but the aura of it carried into the
here and now. And Travis had no doubts that Buck
believed implicitly in what he said, and that belief carried credulity to others.

"This is wisdom, *Nantan*—"

Buck shook his head. "I am no *nantan*, no chief. But
of some things I am sure. You also be sure of what lies
within you, younger brother!"

On the third day, ranging eastward along the base of
the mountain range, Travis found what he believed would
be an acceptable camp site. There was a canyon with a
good spring of water cut round by well-marked game trails.
A series of ledges brought him up to a small plateau
where scrub wood could be used to build the wickiups.
Water and food lay within reach, and the ledge approach
was easy to defend. Even Deklay and his fellow malcon-
tents were forced to concede the value of the site.

His duty to the clan accomplished, Travis returned to
his own concern, one which had haunted him for days.
Topaz had been taped by men of the vanished star empire.
Therefore, the planet was important, but why? As yet he
had found no indication that anything above the intelligence level of the split horns was native to this world.
But he was gnawed by the certainty that there *was*

something here, waiting. . . . And the desire to learn what it was became an ever-burning ache.

Perhaps he was what Deklay had accused him of being, one who had come to follow the road of the Pinda-lick-o-yi too closely. For Travis was content to scout with only the coyotes for company, and he did not find the loneliness of the unknown planet as intimidating as most of the others.

He was checking his small trail pack on the fourth day after they had settled on the plateau when Buck and Jil-Lee hunkered down beside him.

"You got to hunt—?" Buck broke the silence first.

"Not for meat."

"What do you fear? That *ndendai*—enemy people—have marked this as their land?" Jil-Lee questioned.

"That may be true, but now I hunt for what this world was at one time, the reason why the ancient star men marked it as their own."

"And this knowledge may be of value to us?" Jil-Lee asked slowly. "Will it bring food to our mouths, shelter for our bodies—mean life for us?"

"All that is possible. It is the unknowing which is bad."

"True. Unknowing is always bad," Buck agreed. "But the bow which is fitted to one hand and strength of arm, may not be suited to another. Remember that, younger brother. Also, do you go alone?"

"With Naginlta and Nalik'ideyu I am not alone."

"Take Tsoay with you also. The four-footed ones are indeed *ga-n* for the service of those they like, but it is not good that man walks alone from his kind."

There it was again, the feeling of clan solidarity which Travis did not always share. On the other hand, Tsoay would not be a hindrance. On other scouts the boy had proved to have a keen eye for the country and a liking for experimentation which was not a universal attribute even among those of his own age.

"I would go to find a path through the mountains; it may be a long trail," Travis half protested.

"You believe what you seek may lie to the north?"

Travis shrugged. "I do not know. How can I? But it will be another way of seeking."

"Tsoay shall go. He keeps silent before older warriors as is proper for the untried, but his thoughts fly free as do yours," Buck replied. "It is in him also, this need to see new places."

"There is this," Jil-Lee got to his feet, "—do not go so far, brother, that you may not easily find a way to return. This is a wide land, and within it we are but a handful of men alone—"

"That, too, I know." Travis thought he could read more than one kind of warning in Jil-Lee's words.

They were the second day away from the plateau camp, and climbing, when they chanced upon the pass Travis had hoped might exist. Before them lay an abrupt descent to what appeared to be open plains country cloaked in a dusky amber Travis now knew was the thick grass found in the southern valleys. Tsoay pointed with his chin.

"Wide land—good for horses, cattle, ranches . . ."

But all those lay far beyond the black space surrounding them. Travis wondered if there was any native animal which could serve man in place of the horse.

"Do we go down?" Tsoay asked.

From this point Travis could sight no break far out on the amber plain, no sign of any building or any disturbance of its smooth emptiness. Yet it drew him. "We go," he decided.

Close as it had looked from the pass, the plain was yet a day and a night, spent in careful watching by turns, ahead of them. It was midmorning of the second day that they left the foothill breaks, and the grass of the open country was waist high about them. Travis could see it rippling where the coyotes threaded ahead. Then he was conscious of a persistent buzzing, a noise which irritated faintly until he was compelled to trace it to its source.

The grass had been trampled flat for an irregular patch, with a trail of broken stalks out of the heart of the plain.

At one side was a buzzing, seething mass of glitter-winged insects which Travis already knew as carrion eaters. They arose reluctantly from their feast as he approached.

He drew a short breath which was close to a grunt of astounded recognition. What lay there was so impossible that he could not believe the evidence of his eyes. Tsoay gave a sharp exclamation, went down on one knee for a closer examination, then looked at Travis over his shoulder, his eyes wide, more than a trace of excitement in his voice.

"Horse dung—and fresh!"

5

"There was one horse, unshod but ridden. It came here from the plains and it had been ridden hard, going lame. There was a rest here, maybe shortly after dawn." Travis sorted out what they had learned by a careful examination of the ground.

Nalik'ideyu, Naginlta, and Tsoay, watched and listened as if the coyotes as well as the boy could understand every word.

"There is that also—" Tsoay indicated the one trace left by the unknown rider, an impression blurred as if some attempt had been made to conceal it.

"Small and light, the rider is both. Also in fear, I think—"

"We follow?" Tsoay asked.

"We follow," Travis assented. He looked to the coyotes, and as he had learned to do, thought out his message. This trail was the one to be followed. When the rider was sighted they were to report back if the Apaches had not yet caught up.

There was no visible agreement; the coyotes simply vanished through the wall of grass.

"Then there are others here," Tsoay said as he and Travis began their return to the foothills. "Perhaps there was a second ship—"

"That horse," Travis said, shaking his head. "There was no provision in the project for the shipping of horses."

"Perhaps they have always been here."

"Not so. To each world its own species of beasts. But we shall know the truth when we look upon that horse—and its rider."

It was warmer this side of the mountains, and the heat of the plains beat at them. Travis thought that the horse might well be seeking water if allowed his head. Where did he come from? And why had his rider gone in haste and fear?

This was rough, broken country and the tired, limping horse seemed to have picked the easiest way through it, without any hindrance from the man with him. Travis spotted a soft patch of ground with a deep-set impression. This time there had been no attempt at erasure; the boot track was plain. The rider had dismounted and was leading the horse—yet he was moving swiftly.

They followed the tracks around the bend of a shallow cut and found Nalik-ideyu waiting for them. Between her forefeet was a bundle still covered with smears of soft earth, and behind her were drag marks from a hole under the overhang of a bush. The coyote had plainly just disinterred her find. Travis squatted down to examine it, using his eyes before his hands.

It was a bag made of hide, probably the hide of one of the split horns by its color and the scraps of long hair which had been left in a simple decorative fringe along the bottom. The sides had been laced together neatly by someone used to working in leather, the closing flap lashed down tightly with braided thong loops.

As the Apache leaned closer to it he could smell a mixture of odors—the hide itself, horse, wood smoke, and other scents—strange to him. He undid the fastenings and pulled out the contents.

There was a shirt, with long full sleeves, of a gray wool undyed after the sheep. Then a very bulky short jacket which, after fingering it doubtfully, Travis decided was made of felt. It was elaborately decorated with highly colorful embroidery, and there was no mistaking the design—a heavy antlered kind of deer in mortal combat with what might be a puma. It was bordered with a geometric pattern of beautiful, oddly familiar work. Travis smoothed it flat over his knee and tried to remember where he had seen its like before . . . a book! An illustration in a book! But which book, when? Not recently, and it was not a pattern known to his own people.

Twisted into the interior of the jacket was a silklike scarf, clear, light blue—the blue of Earth's cloudless skies on certain days, so different from the yellow shield now hanging above them. A small case of leather, with sil-houetted designs cut from hide and affixed to it, designs as intricate and complex as the embroidery on the jacket— art of a high standard. In the case a knife and spoon, the bowl and blade of dull metal, the handles of horn carved with horse heads, the tiny wide open eyes set with glittering stones.

Personal possessions dear to the owner, so that when they must be abandoned for flight they were hidden with some hope of recovery. Travis slowly repacked them, trying to fold the garments into their original creases. He was still puzzled by those designs.

"Who?" Tsoay touched the edge of the jacket with one finger, his admiration for it plain to read.

"I don't know. But it is of our own world."

"That is a deer, though the horns are wrong," Tsoay agreed. "And the puma is very well done. The one who made this knows animals well."

Travis pushed the jacket back into the bag and laced it shut. But he did not return it to the hiding place. Instead, he made it a part of his own pack. If they did not succeed in running down the fugitive, he wanted an opportunity for closer study, a chance to remember just where he had seen that picture before.

The narrow valley where they had discovered the bag sloped upward, and there were signs that their quarry found the ground harder to cover. The second discard lay in open sight—again a leather bag which Nalik-ideyu sniffed and than began to lick eagerly, thrusting her nose into its flaccid interior.

Travis picked it up, finding it damp to the touch. It had an odd smell, like that of sour milk. He ran a finger around inside, brought it out wet; yet this was neither water bag nor canteen. And he was completely mystified when he turned it inside out, for though the inner surface was wet, the bag was empty. He offered it to the coyote, and she took it promptly.

Holding it firmly to the earth with her forepaws, she licked the surface, though Travis could see no deposit which might attract her. It was clear that the bag had once held some sort of food.

"Here they rested," Tsoay said. "Not too far ahead now—"

But now they were in the kind of country where a man could hide in order to check on his back trail. Travis studied the terrain and then made his own plans. They would leave the plainly marked trace of the fugitive, strike out upslope to the east and try to parallel the other's route. It was tricky going in that maze of rock outcrops and wood copses.

Nalik-ideyu gave a last lick to the bag as Travis signaled her. She regarded him, then turned her head to survey the country before them. At last she trotted on, her buff coat melting into the vegetation. With Naginlta she would scout the quarry and keep watch, leaving the men to take the longer way around.

Travis pulled off his shirt, folding it into a packet and tucking it beneath the folds of his sash-belt, just as his ancestors had always done before a fight. Then he cached his pack and Tsoay's. As they began the stiff climb they carried only their bows, the quivers slung on their shoulders, and the long-bladed knives. But they flitted like shadows and, like the coyotes, their red-brown bodies became indistinguishable against the bronze of the land.

They should be, Travis judged, not more than an hour away from sundown. And they had to locate the stranger before the dark closed in. His respect for their quarry had grown. The unknown might have been driven by fear, but he held to a good pace and headed intelligently for just the kind of country which would serve him best. If Travis could only remember where he had seen the like of that embroidery! It had a meaning which might be important now. . . .

Tsoay slipped behind a wind-gnarled tree and disappeared. Travis stooped under a line of bush limbs. Both were working their way south, using the peak ahead as an agreed landmark, pausing at intervals to examine the landscape for any hint of a man and horse.

Travis squirmed snake fashion into an opening between two rock pillars and lay there, the westering sun hot on his bare shoulders and back, his chin propped on his forearm. In the band holding back his hair he had inserted some concealing tufts of wiry mountain grass, the ends of which drooped over his rugged features.

Only seconds earlier he had caught that fragmentary warning from one of the coyotes. What they sought was very close, it was right down there. Both animals were in ambush, awaiting orders. And what they found was familiar, another confirmation that the fugitive was human, not native to Topaz.

With searching eyes, Travis examined the site indicated by the coyotes. His respect for the stranger was raised another notch. In time either he or Tsoay might have sighted that hideaway without the aid of the animal scouts; on the other hand, they might have failed. For the fugitive had truly gone to earth, using some pocket or crevice in the mountain wall.

There was no sign of the horse, but a branch here and there had been pulled out of place, the scars of their removal readable when one knew where to look. Odd,

Travis began to puzzle over what he saw. It was almost as if whatever pursuit the stranger feared would come not at ground level but from above; the precautions the stranger had taken were to veil his retreat to the reaches of the mountain side.

Had he expected any trailer to make a flanking move from up that slope where the Apaches now lay? Travis' teeth nipped the weathered skin of his forearm. Could it be that at some time during the day's journeying the fugitive had doubled back, having seen his trackers? But there had been no traces of any such scouting, and the coyotes would surely have warned them. Human eyes and ears could be tricked, but Travis trusted the senses of Naginlta and Nalik-ideyu far above his own.

No, he did not believe that the rider expected the Apaches. But the man did expect someone or something which would come upon him from the heights. The heights . . . Travis rolled his head slightly to look at the upper reaches of the hills about him—with suspicion.

In their own journey across the mountains and through the pass they had found nothing threatening. Dangerous animals might roam there. There had been some paw marks, one such trail the coyotes had warned against. But the type of precautions the stranger had taken were against intelligent, thinking beings, not against animals more likely to track by scent than by sight.

And if the stranger expected an attack from above, then Travis and Tsoay must be alert. Travis analyzed each feature of the hillside, setting in his mind a picture of every inch of ground they must cross. Just as he had wanted daylight as an ally before, so now was he willing to wait for the shadows of twilight.

He closed his eyes in a final check, able to recall the details of the hiding place, knowing that he could reach it when the conditions favored, without error. Then he edged back from his vantage point, and raising his fingers to his lips, made a small angry chittering, three times repeated. One of the species inhabiting these heights, as they had noted earlier, was a creature about as big as the palm of a man's hand, resembling nothing so much as a round ball of ruffled feathers, though its covering might actually have been a silky, fluffy fur. Its short legs could cover ground at an amazing speed, and it had the bold impudence of a creature with few natural enemies. This was its usual cry.

Tsoay's hand waved Travis on to where the younger man had taken position behind the bleached trunk of a fallen tree.

"He hides," Tsoay whispered.

"Against trouble from above." Travis added his own observation.

"But not us, I think."

So Tsoay had come to that conclusion too? Travis tried to gauge the nearness of twilight. There was a period after the passing of Topaz' sun when the dusky light played odd tricks with shadows. That would be the first time for their move. He said as much, and Tsoay nodded eagerly. They sat with their backs to a boulder, the tree trunk serving as a screen, and chewed methodically on rations. There was energy and sustenance in the tasteless squares which would support men, even though their stomachs continued to demand the satisfaction of fresh meat.

Taking turns, they dozed a little. But the last banners of Topaz' sun were still in the sky when Travis judged the shadows cover enough. He had no way of knowing how the stranger was armed. Though he used a horse for transportation, he might well carry a rifle and the most modern sidearms.

The Apaches' bows were little use for infighting, but they had their knives. However, Travis wanted to take the fugitive unharmed if he could. There was information he must have. So he did not even draw his knife as he started downhill.

When he reached a pool of violet dusk at the bottom of the small ravine Naginlta's eyes regarded him knowingly. Travis signaled with his hand and thought out what would be the coyotes' part in this surprise attack. The prick-eared silhouette vanished. Uphill the chitter of a fluff-fur sounded twice—Tsoay was in position.

A howl . . . wailing . . . sobbing . . . was heard, one of the keening songs of the *mba'a*. Travis darted forward. He heard the nicker of a frightened horse, a clicking which could have marked the pawing of hoof on gravel, saw the brush hiding the stranger's hole tremble, a portion of it fall away.

Travis sped on, his moccasins making no sound on the ground. One of the coyotes gave tongue for the second time, the eerie wailing rising to a yapping which ech-oed from the rocks about them. Travis poised for a dive.

Another section of those artfully heaped branches had given way and a horse reared, its upflung head plainly marked against the sky. A blurred figure weaved back and forth before it, trying to control the mount. The stranger had his hands full, certainly no weapon drawn—this was it!

Travis leaped. His hands found their mark, the shoulders of the stranger. There was a shrill cry from the other as he tried to turn in the Apache's hold, to face his attacker. But Travis bore them both on, rolling almost under the feet of the horse, sliding downhill, the unknown's writhing body pinned down by the Apache's weight and his clasp, tight as an iron grip, about the other's chest and upper arms.

He felt his opponent go limp, but was suspicious enough not to release that hold, for the heavy breathing of the stranger was not that of an unconscious man. They lay so, the unknown still tight in Travis' hold but no longer fighting. The Apache could hear Tsoay soothing the horse with the purring words of a practiced horseman.

Still the stranger did not resume the struggle. They could not lie in this position all night, Travis thought with a wry twist of amusement. He shifted his hold, and got the lightning-quick response he had expected. But it was not quite quick enough, for Travis had the other's hands behind his back, cupping slender, almost delicate wrists together.

"Throw me a cord!" he called to Tsoay.

The younger man ran up with an extra bow cord, and in a moment they had bonds on the struggling captive. Travis rolled their catch over, reaching down for a fistful of hair to pull the head into a patch of clearer light.

In his grasp that hair came loose, a braid unwinding. He grunted as he looked down into the stranger's face. Dust marks were streaked now with tear runnels, but the gray eyes which turned fiercely on him said that their owner cried more in rage than fear.

His captive might be wearing long trousers tucked into curved, toed boots, and a loose overblouse, but she was certainly not only a woman, but a very young and attractive one. Also, at the present moment, an exceedingly angry one. And behind that anger was fear, the fear of one fighting hopelessly against insurmountable odds. But as she eyed Travis now her expression changed.

He felt that she had expected another captor altogether and was astounded at the sight of him. Her tongue touched her lips, moistening them, and now the fear in her was another kind—the wary fear of one facing a totally new and perhaps dangerous thing.

"Who are you?" Travis spoke in English, for he had no doubts that she was from Earth.

Now she sucked in her breath with a gasp of pure astonishment.

"Who are *you?*" she parroted his question in a marked accent. English was not her native tongue, he was sure.

Travis reached out, and again his hands closed on her shoulders. She started to twist and then realized he was merely pulling her up to a sitting position. Some of the fear had left her eyes, an intent interest taking its place.

"You are not Sons of the Blue Wolf," she stated in her heavily accented speech.

Travis smiled. "I am the Fox, not the Wolf," he returned. "And the Coyote is my brother." He snapped his fingers at the shadows, and the two animals came noiselessly into sight. Her gaze widened even more at

Naginlta and Nalik'ideyu, and she deduced the bond which must exist between her captor and the beasts.

"This woman is also of our world." Tsoay spoke in Apache, looking over their prisoner with frank interest. "Only she is not of the People."

Sons of the Blue Wolf? Travis thought again of the embroidery designs on the jacket. Who had called themselves by that picturesque title—where—and when in time?

"What do you fear, Daughter of the Blue Wolf?" he asked.

And with that question he seemed to touch some button activating terror. She flung back her head so that she could see the darkening sky.

"The flyer!" Her voice was muted as if more than a whisper would carry to the stars just coming into brilliance above them. "They will come . . . tracking. I did not reach the inner mountains in time."

There was a despairing note in that which cut through to Travis, who found that he, too, was searching the sky, not knowing what he looked for or what kind of menace it promised, only that the danger was real.

6

"The night comes," Tsoay spoke slowly in English. "Do those you fear hunt in the dark?"

She shook her head to free her forehead from a coil of braid, pulled loose in her struggle with Travis.

"They do not need eyes or such noses as those four-footed hunters of yours. They have a machine to track—"

"Then what purpose is this brush pile of yours?" Travis raised his chin at the disturbed hiding place.

"They do not constantly use the machine, and one can hope. But at night they can ride on its beam. We are not far enough into the hills to lose them. Bahatur went lame, and so I was slowed. . . ."

"And what lies in these mountains that those you fear dare not invade them?" Travis continued.

"I do not know, save if one can climb far enough inside, one is safe from pursuit."

"I ask it again: Who are you?" The Apache leaned forward, his face in the fast-fading light now only inches away from hers. She did not shrink from his close scrutiny but met him eye to eye. This was a woman of proud independence, truly a chief's daughter, Travis decided.

"I am of the People of the Blue Wolf. We were brought across the star lanes to make this world safe for . . . for . . . the . . ." She hesitated, and now there was a shade of puzzlement on her face. "There is a reason—a dream. No, there is the dream and there is reality. I am Kaydessa of the Golden Horde, but sometimes I remember other things—like this speech of strange words I am mouthing now—"

"The Golden Horde!" Travis knew now. The embroidery, Sons of the Blue Wolf, all fitted into a special pattern. But what a pattern! Scythian art, the ornament that the warriors of Genghis Khan bore so proudly. Tatars, Mongols—the barbarians who had swept from the fastness of the steppes to change the course of history, not only in Asia but across the plains of middle Europe and in old Russia where the Golden Horde had once ruled. The men of the Great Khans who had ridden behind the yak-tailed standards of Genghis Khan, Kublai Khan, Tamerlane—!

"The Golden Horde," Travis repeated once again. "That lies far back in the history of another world, Wolf Daughter."

She stared at him, a sad and lost expression on her dust-grimed face.

"I know." Her voice was so muted he could hardly distinguish the words. "My people live in two times, and many do not realize that."

Tsoay had crouched down beside them to listen. Now he put out his hand, touching Travis' shoulder.

"Redax?"

"Or its like." For Travis was sure of one point. The project, which had been training three teams for space colonization—one of Eskimos, one of the Pacific Islanders, and one of his own Apaches—had no reason or chance to select Mongols from the wild past of the raiding Hordes. There was only one nation on Earth which could have picked such colonists.

"You are Russian." He studied her carefully, intent on noting the effect of his words.

But she did not lose that lost look. "Russian . . . Russian . . ." she repeated, as if the very word was strange.

Travis was alarmed. Any Greater Russian colony planted here could well possess technicians with machines capable of tracking a fugitive, and if mountain heights were protection against such a hunt, he intended to gain them, even by night traveling. He said this to Tsoay, and the other emphatically agreed.

"The horse is too lame to go on," the younger man reported.

Travis hesitated for a long second. Since the time they had stolen their first mounts from the encroaching Spanish, horses had always been wealth to his people. To leave an animal which could well serve the clan was not right. But they dared not waste time with a lame beast.

"Leave it here, free," he ordered.

"And the woman?"

"She goes with us. We must learn all we can of these people and what they do here. Listen, Wolf Daughter," again Travis leaned close to make sure she was listening to him as he spoke with emphasis—"you will travel with us into these high places, and there will be no trouble from you." He drew his knife and held the blade warningly before her eyes.

"It was already in my mind to go to the mountains," she told him evenly. "Untie my hands, brave warrior, you have surely nothing to fear from a woman."

His hand made a swift sweep and plucked a knife as long and keen as his from the folds of the sash beneath her loose outer garment.

"Not now, Wolf Daughter, since I have drawn your fangs."

He helped her to her feet and slashed the cord about her wrists with her knife, which he then fastened to his own belt. Alerting the coyotes, he dispatched them ahead; and the three started on, the Mongol girl between the two Apaches. The abandoned horse nickered lonesomely and then began to graze on tufts of grass, moving slowly to favor his foot.

The two moons rode the sky as the hours advanced, their beams fighting the shadows. Travis felt reasonably safe from any attack at ground level, depending upon the coyotes for warning. But he held them all to a steady pace. And he did not question the girl again until all three of them hunkered down at a small mountain spring, to dash icy water over their faces and drink from cupped hands.

"Why do you flee your own people, Wolf Daughter?"

"My name is Kaydessa," she corrected him.

He chuckled with laughter at the prim tone of her voice. "And you see here Tsoay of the People—the Apaches—while I am Fox." He was giving her the English equivalent of his tribal name.

"Apaches." She tried to repeat the word with the same accent he had used. "And what are Apaches?"

"Indians—Amerindians," he explained. "But you have not answered my question, Kaydessa. Why do you run from your own people?"

"Not from my people," she said, shaking her head determinedly. "From those others. It is like this—Oh, how can I make you understand rightly?" She spread her wet hands out before her in the moonlight, the damp patches on her sleeves clinging to her arms. "There are my people of the Golden Horde, though once we were different and we can remember bits of that previous life. Then there are also the men who live in the sky ship and use the machine so that we think only the thoughts they would have us think. Now why," she looked at Travis intently— "do I wish to tell you all this? It is strange. You say you are Indian—American—are we then enemies? There is a part memory which says that we are . . . were . . ."

"Let us rather say," he corrected her, "that the Apaches and the Horde are not enemies here and now, no matter what was before." That was the truth, Travis recognized.

By all accounts his people had come out of Asia in the very dim beginnings of migrating peoples. For all her dark-red hair and gray eyes, this girl who had been arbitrarily returned to a past just as they had been by Redax, could well be a distant clan-cousin.

"You—" Kaydessa's fingers rested for a moment on his wrist—"you, too, were sent here from across the stars. Is this not so?"

"It is so."

"And there are those here who govern you now?"

"No. We are free."

"How did you become free?" she demanded fiercely.

Travis hesitated. He did not want to tell of the wrecked ship, the fact that his people possessed no real defenses against the Russian-controlled colony.

"We went to the mountains," he replied evasively.

"Your governing machine failed?" Kaydessa laughed. "Ah, they are so great, those men of the machines. But they are smaller and weaker when their machines cannot obey them."

"It is so with your camp?" Travis probed gently. He was not quite sure of her meaning, but he dared not ask more detailed questions without dangerously revealing his own ignorance.

"In some manner their control machine—it can only work upon those within a certain distance. They discovered that in the days of the first landing, when hunters went out freely and many of them did not return. After that when hunters were sent out to learn how lay this land, they went along in the flyer with a machine so that there would be no more escapes. But we knew!" Kaydessa's fingers curled into small fists. "Yes, we knew that if we could get beyond the machines, there was freedom for us. And we planned—many of us—planned. Then nine or ten sleeps ago those others were very excited. They gathered in their ship, watching their machines. And something happened. For a while all those machines went dead.

"Jagatai, Kuchar, my brother Hulagur, Menlik . . ." She

was counting the names off on her fingers. "They raided the horse herd, rode out . . ."

"And you?"

"I, too, should have ridden. But there was Aljar, my sister—Kuchar's wife. She was very near her time and to ride thus, fleeing far and fast, might kill her and the child. So I did not go. Her son was born that night, but the others had the machine at work once more. We might long to go here," she brought her fist up to her breast, and then raised it to her head—"but there was that *here* which kept us to the camp and their will. We only knew that if we could reach the mountains, we might find our people who had already gained their freedom."

"But you are here. How did you escape?" Tsoay wanted to know.

"They knew that I would have gone had it not been for Aljar. So they said they would make her ride out with them unless I played guide to lead them to my brother and the others. Then I knew I must take up the sword of duty and hunt with them. But I prayed that the spirits of the upper air look with favor upon me, and they granted aid. . . ." Her eyes held a look of wonder. "For when we were out on the plains and well away from the settlement, a grass devil attacked the leader of the searching party, and he dropped the mind control and so it was broken. Then I rode. Blue Sky Above knows how I rode. And those others have not the skill with horses as have the people of the Wolf."

"When did this happen?"

"Three suns ago."

Travis counted back in his mind. Her date for the failure of the machine in the Russian camp seemed to coincide with the crash landing of the American ship. Had one thing any connection with the other? It was very possible. The planeting spacer might have fought some kind of weird duel with the other colony before it plunged to earth on the other side of the mountain range.

"Do you know where in these mountains your people hide?"

Kaydessa shook her head. "Only that I must head south, and when I reach the highest peak make a signal fire on the north slope. But that I cannot do now, for those in the flyer may see it. I know they are on my trail, for twice I have seen it. Listen, Fox, I ask this of you— I, Kaydessa, who am eldest daughter to the Khan—for you are like unto us, a warrior and a brave man, that I believe. It may be that you cannot be governed by their machine, for you have not rested under their spell, nor are of our blood. Therefore, if they come close enough to send forth the call, the call I must obey as if I were a slave dragged upon a horse rope, then do you bind my hands and feet and hold me here, no matter how much I struggle to follow that command. For that which is truly me does not want to go. Will you swear this by the fires which expel demons?"

The utter sincerity of her tone convinced Travis that she was pleading for aid against a danger she firmly believed in. Whether she was right about his immunity to the Russian mental control was another matter, and one he would rather not put to the test.

"We do not swear by your fires, Blue Wolf Maiden, but by the path of the Lightning." His fingers moved as if to curl about the sacred charred wood his people had once carried as "medicine." "So do I promise!"

She looked at him for a long moment and then nodded in satisfaction.

They left the pool and pushed on toward the mountain slopes, working their way back to the pass. A low growl out of the dark brought them to an instant halt. Naginlta's warning was sharp; there was danger ahead, acute danger.

The moonlight from the moons made a weird pattern of light and dark on the stretch ahead. Anything from a slinking four-footed hunter to a war party of intelligent beings might have been lying in wait there.

A flitting shadow out of shadows. Nalik'ideyu pressed against Travis' legs, making a barrier of her warm body, attracting his attention to a spot at the left perhaps a hundred yards on. There was a great splotch of dark there, large enough to hide a really formidable opponent; that wordless communication between animal and man told Travis that such an opponent was just what was lurking there.

Whatever lay in ambush beside the upper track was growing impatient as its destined prey ceased to advance, the coyotes reported.

"Your left—beyond that pointed rock—in the big shadow—"

"Do you see it?" Tsoay demanded.

"No. But the *mba'a* do."

The men had their bows ready, arrows set to the cords. But in this light such weapons were practically useless unless the enemy moved into the path of the moon.

"What is it?" Kaydessa asked in a half whisper.

"Something waits for us ahead."

Before he could stop her, she set her fingers to her lips and gave a piercing whistle.

There was answering movement in the shadow. Travis shot at that, his arrow followed instantly by one from Tsoay. There was a cry, scaling up in a throat-scalding scream which made Travis flinch. Not because of the sound, but because of the hint which lay behind it—could it have been a human cry?

The thing flopped out into a patch of moonlight. Its four-limbed, silvery body was as big as a man's. But the worst was that it had been groveling on all fours when it fell, and now it was rising on its hind feet, one forepaw striking madly at the two arrows dancing head-deep in its upper shoulder. Man? No! But something sufficiently manlike to chill the three downtrail.

A whirling four-footed hunter dashed in, snapped at the creature's legs. It squalled again, aiming a blow with a forepaw; but the attacking coyote was already gone. Together Naginlta and Nalik'ideyu were harassing the creature, just as they had fought the split horn, giving the hunters time to shoot. Travis, although he again felt that touch of horror and disgust he could not account for, shot again.

Between them the Apaches must have sent a dozen arrows into the raving beast before it went to its knees and Naginlta sprang for its throat. Even then the coyote yelped and flinched, a bleeding gash across its head from the raking talons of the dying thing. When it no longer moved, Travis approached to see more closely what they had brought down. That smell . . .

Just as the embroidery on Kaydessa's jacket had awakened memories from his past on Earth, so did this stench remind him of something. Where—when—had he smelled it before? Travis connected it with dark, dark and danger. Then he gasped in a half exclamation.

Not on this world, no, but on two others: two worlds of that broken stellar empire where he had been an involuntary explorer two planet years ago! The beast things which had lived in the dark of the desert world the humans' wandering galactic derelict had landed upon. Yes, the beast things whose nature they had never been able to deduce. Were they the degenerate dregs of a once intelligent species? Or were they animals, akin to man, but still animals?

The ape-things had controlled the night of the desert world. And they had been met again—also in the dark—in the ruins of the city which had been the final goal of the ship's taped voyage. So they were a part of the vanished civilization. And Travis' own vague surmise concerning Topaz was proven correct. This had not been an empty world for the long-gone space people. This planet had a purpose and a use, or else this beast would not have been here.

"Devil!" Kaydessa made a face of disgust.

"You know it?" Tsoay asked Travis. "What is it?"

"That I do not know, but it is a thing left over from the star people's time. And I have seen it on two other of their worlds."

"A man?" Tsoay surveyed the body critically. "It wears no clothes, has no weapons, but it walks erect. It looks like an ape, a very big ape. It is not a good thing, I think."

"If it runs with a pack—as they do elsewhere—this could be a very bad thing." Travis, remembering how these creatures had attacked in force on the other worlds, looked about him apprehensively. Even with the coyotes on guard, they could not stand up to such a pack closing in through the dark. They had better hole up in some defendable place and wait out the rest of the night.

Naginlta brought them to a cliff overhang where they could set their backs to the hard rock of the mountain, face outward to a space they could cover with arrow flight if the need arose. And the coyotes, lying before them with their noses resting on paws, would, Travis knew, alert them long before the enemy could close in.

They huddled against the rock, Kaydessa between them, alert at first to every sound of the night, their hearts beating faster at a small scrape of gravel, the rustle of a bush. Slowly, they began to relax.

"It is well that two sleep while one guards," Travis observed. "By morning we must push on, out of this country."

So the two Apaches shared the watch in turn, the Tatar girl at first protesting, and then falling exhausted into a slumber which left her breathing heavily.

Travis, on the dawn watch, began to speculate about the ape-thing they had killed. The two previous times he had met this creature it had been in ruins of the old empire. Were there ruins somewhere here? He wanted to make sure about that. On the other hand, there was the problem of the Tatar-Mongol settlement controlled by the Russians. There was no doubt in his mind that, were the Russians to suspect the existence of the Apache camp, they would make every attempt to hunt down and kill or capture the survivors from the American ship. A warning must be carried to the rancheria as quickly as they could make the return trip.

Beside him the girl stirred, raising her head. Travis glanced at her and then watched with attention. She was looking straight ahead, her eyes as fixed as if she were in a trance. Now she inched forward from the mountain wall, wriggling out of its shelter.

"What—?" Tsoay had awakened again. But Travis was already moving. He pushed on, rushing up to stand beside her, shoulder to shoulder.

"What is it? Where do you go?" he asked.

She made no answer, did not even seem aware of his voice. He caught at her arm and she pulled to free herself. When he tightened his grip she did not fight him actively as during their first encounter, but merely pulled and twisted as if she were being compelled to go ahead.

Compulsion! He remembered her plea the night before, asking his help against recapture by the machine. Now he deliberately tripped her, twisted her hands behind her back. She swayed in his hold, trying to win to her feet, paying no attention to him save as a hindrance against her answering that demanding call he could not hear.

7

"What happened?" Tsoay took a swift stride, stood over the writhing girl whose strength was now such that Travis had to exert all his efforts to control her.

"I think that the machine she spoke about is holding her. She is being drawn to it out of hiding as one draws a calf on a rope."

Both coyotes had arisen and were watching the struggle with interest, but there was no warning from them. Whatever called Kaydessa into such mindless and will-less answer did not touch the animals. And neither Apache felt it. So perhaps only Kaydessa's people were subject to it, as she had thought. How far away was that machine? Not too near, for otherwise the coyotes would have traced the man or men operating it.

"We cannot move her," Tsoay brought the problem into the open—"unless we bind and carry her. She is one of their kind. Why not let her go to them, unless you fear she will talk." His hand went to the knife in his belt, and Travis knew what primitive impulse moved in the younger man.

In the old days a captive who was likely to give trouble was briskly eliminated. In Tsoay that memory was awake now. Travis shook his head.

"She has said that others of her kin are in these hills. We must not set two wolf packs hunting us," Travis said, giving the more practical reason which might better appeal to that savage instinct for self-preservation. "But you are right, since she has tried to answer this summons, we cannot force her with us. Therefore, do you take the back trail. Tell Buck what we have discovered and have him make the necessary precautions against either these Mongol outlaws or a Russian thrust over the mountains."

"And you?"

"I stay to discover where the outlaws hide and learn all I can of this settlement. We may have reason to need friends—"

"Friends!" Tsoay spat. "The People need no friends! If we have warning, we can hold our own country! As the Pinda-lick-o-yi have discovered before."

"Bows and arrows against guns and machines?" Travis inquired bitingly. "We must know more before we make any warrior boasts for the future. Tell Buck what we have discovered. Also say I will join you before," Travis calculated—"ten suns. If I do not, send no search party; the clan is too small to risk more lives for one."

"And if these Russians take you—?"

Travis grinned, not pleasantly. "They shall learn nothing! Can their machines sort out the thoughts of a dead man?" He did not intend his future to end as abruptly as that, but also he would not be easy meat for any Russian hunting party.

Tsoay took a share of their rations and refused the company of the coyotes. Travis realized that for all his seeming ease with the animals, the younger scout had little more liking for them than Deklay and the others back at the rancheria. Tsoay went at dawn, aiming at the pass.

Travis sat down beside Kaydessa. They had bound her

to a small tree, and she strove incessantly to free herself, turning her head at an acute and painful angle, only to face the same direction in which she had been tied. There was no breaking the spell which held her. And she would soon wear herself out with that struggling. Then he struck an expert blow.

The girl sagged limply, and he untied her. It all depended now on the range of the beam or broadcast of that diabolical machine. From the attitude of the coyotes, he assumed that those using the machine had not made any attempt to come close. They might not even know where their quarry was; they would simply sit and wait in the foothills for the caller to reel in a helpless captive.

Travis thought that if he moved Kaydessa farther away from that point, sooner or later they would be out of range and she would awake from the knockout, free again. Although she was not light, he could manage to carry her for a while. So burdened, Travis started on, with the coyotes scouting ahead.

He speedily discovered that he had set himself an ambitious task. The going was rough, and carrying the girl reduced his advance to a snail-paced crawl. But it gave him time to make certain plans.

As long as the Russians held the balance of power on this side of the mountain range, the rancheria was in danger. Bows and knives against modern armament was no contest at all. And it would only be a matter of time before exploration on the part of the northern settlement— or some tracking down of Tatar fugitives—would bring the enemy across the pass.

The Apaches could move farther south into the unknown continent below the wrecked ship, thus prolonging the time before they were discovered. But that would only postpone the inevitable showdown. Whether Travis could make his clan believe that, was also a matter of concern.

On the other hand, if the Russian overlords could be

met in some practical way . . . Travis' mind fastened on
that more attractive idea, worrying it as Naginlta worried a prey, tearing out and devouring the more delicate
portions. Every bit of sense and prudence argued against
such an approach, whose success could rest only between
improbability and impossibility; yet that was the direction in which he longed to move.

Across his shoulder Kaydessa stirred and moaned. The
Apache doubled his efforts to reach the outcrop of rock
he could see ahead, chiseled into high relief by the winds.
In its lee they would have protection from any sighting
from below. Panting, he made it, lowering the girl into
the guarded cup of space, and waited.

She moaned again, lifted one hand to her head. Her
eyes were half open, and still he could not be sure
whether they focused on him and her surroundings intelligently or not.

"Kaydessa!"

Her heavy eyelids lifted, and he had no doubt she could
see him. But there was no recognition of his identity in
her gaze, only surprise and fear—the same expression she
had worn during their first meeting in the foothills.

"Daughter of the Wolf," he spoke slowly. "Remember!"
Travis made that an order, an emphatic appeal to the mind
under the influence of the caller.

She frowned, the struggle she was making naked on
her face. Then she answered:

"You—Fox—"

Travis grunted with relief, his alarm subsiding. Then
she *could* remember.

"Yes," he responded eagerly.

But she was gazing about, her puzzlement growing.
"Where is this—?"

"We are higher in the mountains."

Now fear was pushing out bewilderment. "How did I
come here?"

"I brought you." Swiftly he outlined what had happened
at their night camp.

The hand which had been at her head was now pressed tight across her lips as if she were biting furiously into its flesh to still some panic of her own, and her gray eyes were round and haunted.

"You are free now," Travis said.

Kaydessa nodded, and then dropped her hand to speak. "You brought me away from the hunters. You did not have to obey them?"

"I heard nothing."

"You do not hear—you feel!" She shuddered. "Please." She clawed at the stone beside her, pulling up to her feet. "Let us go—let us go quickly! They will try again—move farther in—"

"Listen," Travis had to be sure of one thing—"have they any way of knowing that they had you under control and that you have again escaped?"

Kaydessa shook her head, some of the panic again shadowing her eyes.

"Then we'll just go on—" his chin lifted to the wastelands before them—"try to keep out of their reach."

And away from the pass to the south, he told himself silently. He dared not lead the enemy to that secret. So he must travel west or hole up somewhere in this unknown wilderness until they could be sure Kaydessa was no longer susceptible to that call, or that they were safely beyond its beamed radius. There was the chance of contacting her outlaw kin, just as there was the chance of stumbling into a pack of the ape-things. Before dark they must discover a protected camp site.

They needed water, food. He had a bare half dozen ration bars. But the coyotes could locate water.

"Come!" Travis beckoned to Kaydessa, motioning her to climb ahead of him so that he could watch for any indication of her succumbing once again to the influence of the enemy. But his burdened early morning flight had told on Travis more than he thought, and he discovered he could not spur himself on to a pace better than a walk. Now and again one of the coyotes, usually Nalik'ideyu, would come into view, express impatience in both stance and mental signal, and then be gone again. The Apache was increasingly aware that the animals were disturbed, yet to his tentative gropings at contact they did not reply. Since they gave no warning of hostile animal or man, he could only be on constant guard, watching the countryside about him.

They had been following a ledge for several minutes before Travis was aware of some strange features of that path. Perhaps he had actually noted them with a trained eye before his archaeological studies of the recent past gave him a reason for the faint marks. This crack in the mountain's skin might have begun as a natural fault, but afterward it had been worked with tools, smoothed, widened to serve the purpose of some form of intelligence!

Travis caught at Kaydessa's shoulder to slow her pace. He could not have told why he did not want to speak aloud here, but he felt the need for silence. She glanced around, perplexed, more so when he went down on his knees and ran his fingers along one of those ancient tool marks. He was certain it was very old. Inside of him anticipation bubbled. A road made with such labor could only lead to something of importance. He was going to make the discovery, the dream which had first drawn him into these mountains.

"What is it?" Kaydessa knelt beside him, frowning at the ledge.

"This was cut by someone, a long time ago," Travis half whispered and then wondered why. There was no reason to believe the road makers could hear him when a thousand years or more lay between the chipping of that stone and this day.

The Tatar girl looked over her shoulder. Perhaps she too was troubled by the sense that here time was subtly telescoped, that past and present might be meeting. Or was that feeling with them both because of their enforced conditioning?

"Who?" Now her voice sank in turn.

"Listen—" he regarded her intently—"did your people

or the Russians ever find any traces of the old civilization here—ruins?"

"No." She leaned forward, tracing with her own finger the same almost-obliterated marks which had intrigued
Travis. "But I think they have looked. Before they discovered that we could be free, they sent out parties—to
hunt, they said—but afterward they always asked many
questions about the country. Only they never asked about
ruins. Is that what they wished us to find? But why? Of
what value are old stones piled on one another?"

"In themselves, little, save for the knowledge they may
give us of the people who piled them. But for what the
stones might contain—much value!"

"And how do you know what they might contain, Fox?"

"Because I have seen such treasure houses of the star
men," he returned absently. To him the marks on the
ledge were a pledge of greater discoveries to come. He
must find where that carefully constructed road ran—to
what it led. "Let us see where this will take us."

But first he gave the chittering signal in four sharp
bursts. And the tawny-gray bodies came out of the tangled
brush, bounding up the ledge. Together the coyotes faced
him, their attention all for his halting communication.

Ruins might lie ahead; he hoped that they did. But on
another planet such ruins had twice proved to be deadly
traps, and only good fortune had prevented their closing on the human explorers. If the ape-things or any other
dangerous form of life had taken up residence before them,
he wanted good warning.

Together the coyotes turned and loped along the now
level way of the ledge, disappearing around a curve fitted to the mountain side while Travis and Kaydessa followed.

They heard it before they saw its source—a waterfall.
Probably not a large one, but high. Rounding the curve,
they came into a fine mist of spray where sunlight made
rainbows of color across a filmy veil of water.

For a long moment they stood entranced. Kaydessa then

gave a little cry, held out her hands to the purling mist and brought them to her lips again to suck the gathered moisture.

Water slicked the surface of the ledge, and Travis pushed her back against the wall of the cliff. As far as he could discern, their road continued behind the out-flung curtain of water, and footing on the wet stone was treacherous. With their backs to the solid security of the wall, facing outward into the solid drape of water, they edged behind it and came out into rainbowed sunlight again.

Here either provident nature or ancient art had hollowed a pocket in the stone which was filled with water. They drank. Then Travis filled his canteen while Kaydessa washed her face, holding the cold freshness of the moisture to her cheeks with both palms.

She spoke, but he could not hear her through the roar. She leaned closer and raised her voice to a half shout:

"This is a place of spirits! Do you not also feel their power, Fox?"

Perhaps for a space out of time he did feel something. This was a watering place, perhaps a never-ceasing watering place—and to his desert-born-and-bred race all water was a spirit gift never to be taken for granted. The rainbow—the Spirit People's sacred sign—old beliefs stirred in Travis, moving him. "I feel," he said, nodding in emphasis to his agreement.

They followed the ledge road to a section where a landslide of an earlier season had choked it. Travis worked a careful way across the debris, Kaydessa obeying his guidance in turn. Then they were on a sloping downward way which led to a staircase—the treads weather-worn and crumbling, the angle so steep Travis wondered if it had ever been intended for beings with a physique approximating the humans'.

They came to a cleft where an arch of stone was chiseled out as a roofing. Travis thought he could make out a trace of carving on the capstone, so worn by years and weather that it was now only a faint shadow of design.

The cleft was a door into another valley. Here, too, golden mist swirled in tendrils to disguise and cloak what stood there. Travis had found his ruins. Only the structures were intact, not breached by time.

Mist flowed in lapping tongues back and forth, confusing outlines, now shuttering, now baring oval windows which were spaced in diamonds of four on round tower surfaces. There were no visible cracks, no cloaking of climbing vegetation, nothing to suggest age and long roots in the valley. Nor did the architecture he could view match any he had seen on those other worlds.

Travis strode away from the cleft doorway. Under his moccasins was a block pavement, yellow and green stone set in a simple pattern of checks. This, too, was level, unchipped and undisturbed, save for a drift or two of soil driven in by the wind. And nowhere could he see any vegetation.

The towers were of the same green stone as half the pavement blocks, a glassy green which made him think of jade—if jade could be mined in such quantities as these five-story towers demanded.

Nalik'ideyu padded to him, and he could hear the faint click of her claws on the pavement. There was a deep silence in this place, as if the air itself swallowed and digested all sound. The wind which had been with them all the day of their journeying was left beyond the cleft.

Yet there was life here. The coyote told him that in her own way. She had not made up her mind concerning that life—wariness and curiosity warred in her now as her pointed muzzle lifted toward the windows overhead.

The windows were all well above ground level, but there was no opening in the first stories as far as Travis could see. He debated moving into the range of those windows to investigate the far side of the towers for doorways. The mist and the message from Nalik'ideyu nourished his suspicions. Out in the open he would be too good a target for whatever or whoever might be standing within the deep-welled frames.

The silence was shattered by a boom. Travis jumped, slewed half around, knife in hand.

Boom-boom . . . a second heavy beat-beat . . . then a clangor with a swelling echo.

Kaydessa flung back her head and called, her voice rising up as if funneled by the valley walls. She then whistled as she had done when they fronted the ape-thing and ran on to catch at Travis' sleeve, her face eager.

"My people! Come—it is my people!"

She tugged him on before breaking into a run, weaving fearlessly around the base of one of the towers. Travis ran after her, afraid he might lose her in the mist.

Three towers, another stretch of open pavement, and then the mist lifted to show them a second carved doorway not two hundred yards ahead. The boom-boom seemed to pull Kaydessa. Travis could do nothing but trail her, the coyotes now trotting beside him.

8

They burst through a last wide band of mist into a wilderness of tall grass and shrubs. Travis heard the coyotes give tongue, but it was too late. Out of nowhere whirled a leather loop, settling about his chest, snapping his arms tight to his body, taking him off his feet with a jerk to be dragged helplessly along the ground behind a galloping horse.

A tawny fury sprang in the air to snap at the horse's head. Travis kicked fruitlessly, trying to regain his feet as the horse reared, and fought against the control of his shouting rider. All through the melee the Apache heard Kaydessa shrilly screaming words he did not understand.

Travis was on his knees, coughing in the dust, exerting the muscles in his chest and shoulders to loosen the lariat. On either side of him the coyotes wove a snarling pattern of defiance, dashing back and forth to present no target for the enemy, yet keeping the excited horses so stirred up that their riders could use neither ropes nor blades.

Then Kaydessa ran between two of the ringing horses

to Travis and jerked at the loop about him. The tough, braided leather eased its hold, and he was able to gasp in full lungfuls of air. She was still shouting, but the tone had changed from one of recognition to a definite scolding.

Travis won to his feet just as the rider who had lassoed him finally got his horse under rein and dismounted. Holding the rope, the man walked hand over hand toward them, as Travis back on the Arizona range would have approached a nervous, unschooled pony.

The Mongol was an inch or so shorter than the Apache, and his face was young, though he had a drooping mustache bracketing his mouth with slender spear points of black hair. His breeches were tucked into high red boots, and he wore a loose felt jacket patterned with the same elaborate embroidery Travis had seen on Kaydessa's. On his head was a hat with a wide fur border—in spite of the heat—and that too bore touches of scarlet and gold design.

Still holding his lariat, the Mongol reached Kaydessa and stood for a moment, eyeing her up and down before he asked a question. She gave an impatient twitch to the rope. The coyotes snarled, but the Apache thought the animals no longer considered the danger immediate.

"This is my brother Hulagur." Kaydessa made the introduction over her shoulder. "He does not have your speech."

Hulagur not only did not understand, he was also impatient. He jerked at the rope with such sudden force that Travis was almost thrown. Then Kaydessa dragged as fiercely on the lariat in the other direction and burst into a soaring harangue which drew the rest of the men closer.

Travis flexed his upper arms, and the slack gained by Kaydessa's action made the lariat give again. He studied the Tatar outlaws. There were five of them beside Hulagur, lean men, hard-faced, narrow-eyed, the ragged clothing of three pieced out with scraps of hide. Besides the swords with the curved blades, they were armed with bows, two to each man, one long, one shorter. One of the riders carried a lance, long tassels of woolly hair streaming from below its head. Travis saw in them a formidable array of barbaric fighting men, but he thought that man for man the Apaches could not only take on the Mongols with confidence, but might well defeat them.

The Apache had never been a hot-headed, ride-for-glory fighter like the Cheyenne, the Sioux, and the Comanche of the open plains. He estimated the odds against him, used ambush, trick, and every feature of the countryside as weapon and defense. Fifteen Apache fighting men under Chief Geronimo had kept five thousand American and Mexican troops in the field for a year and had come off victorious for the moment.

Travis knew the tales of Genghis Khan and his formidable generals who swept over Asia into Europe, unbeaten and seemingly undefeatable. But they had been a wild wave, fed by a reservoir of manpower from the steppes of their homeland, utilizing driven walls of captives to protect their own men in city assaults and attacks. He doubted if even that endless sea of men could have won the Arizona desert defended by Apaches under Cochise, Victorio, or Mangas Coloradas. The white man had done it—by superior arms and attrition; but bow against bow, knife against sword, craft and cunning against craft and cunning—he did not think so. . . .

Hulagur dropped the end of the lariat, and Kaydessa swung around, loosening the loop so that the rope fell to Travis' feet. The Apache stepped free of it, turned and passed between two of the horsemen to gather up the bow he had dropped. The coyotes had gone with him and when he turned again to face the company of Tatars, both animals crowded past him to the entrance of the valley, plainly urging him to retire there.

The horsemen had faced about also, and the warrior with the lance balanced the shaft of the weapon in his hand as if considering the possibility of trying to spear Travis. But just then Kaydessa came up, towing Hulagur by a firm hold on his sash-belt.

"I have told this one," she reported to Travis, "how it is between us and that you also are enemy to those who hunt us. It is well that you sit together beside a fire and talk of these things."

Again that boom-boom broke her speech, coming from farther out in the open land.

"You will do this?" She made of it a half question, half statement.

Travis glanced about him. He could dodge back into the misty valley of the towers before the Tatars could ride him down. However, if he could patch up some kind of truce between his people and the outlaws, the Apaches would have only the Russians from the settlement to watch. Too many times in the human past had war on two fronts been disastrous.

"I come—carrying this—and not pulled by your ropes." He held up his bow in an exaggerated gesture so that Hulagur could understand.

Coiling the lariat, the Mongol looked from the Apache bow to Travis. Slowly, and with obvious reluctance, he nodded agreement.

At Hulagur's call the lancer rode up to the waiting Apache, stretched out a booted foot in the heavy stirrup, and held down a hand to bring Travis up behind him riding double. Kaydessa mounted in the same fashion behind her brother.

Travis looked at the coyotes. Together the animals stood in the door to the tower valley, and neither made any move to follow as the horses trotted off. He beckoned with his hand and called to them.

Heads up, they continued to watch him go in company with the Mongols. Then without any reply to his coaxing, they melted back into the mists. For a moment Travis was tempted to slide down and run the risk of taking a lance point between the shoulders as he followed Naginlta and Nalik'ideyu into retreat. He was startled, jarred by the new awareness of how much he had come to depend on the animals. Ordinarily, Travis Fox was not one to be governed by the wishes of a *mba'a*, intelligent and un-animallike as it might be. This was an affair of men, and coyotes had no part in it!

Half an hour later Travis sat in the outlaw camp. There were fifteen Mongols in sight, a half dozen women and two children adding to the count. On a hillock near their yurts, the round brush-and-hide shelters—not too different from the wickiups of Travis' own people—was a crude drum, a hide stretched taut over a hollowed section of log. And next to that stood a man wearing a tall pointed cap, a red robe, and a girdle from which swung a fringe of small bones, tiny animal skulls, and polished bits of stone and carved wood.

It was this man's efforts which sent the boom-boom sounding at intervals over the landscape. Was this a signal—part of a ritual? Travis was not certain, though he guessed that the drummer was either medicine man or shaman, and so of some power in this company. Such men were credited with the ability to prophesy and also to communicate between man and spirit in the old days of the great Hordes.

The Apache evaluated the rest of the company. Like his own party, these men were much the same age—young and vigorous. And it was also apparent that Hulagur held a position of some importance among them—if he were not their chief.

After a last resounding roll on the drum, the shaman thrust the sticks into his girdle and came down to the fire at the center of the camp. He was taller than his fellows, pole thin under his robes, his face narrow, clean-shaven, with brows arched by nature to give him an unchanging expression of skepticism. He strode along, his tinkling collection of charms providing a not unmusical accompaniment, and came to stand directly before Travis, eyeing him carefully.

Travis copied his silence in what was close to a duel of wills. There was that in the shaman's narrowed green eyes which suggested that if Hulagur did in fact lead these fighting men, he had an advisor of determination and intelligence behind him.

"This is Menlik." Kaydessa did not push past the men to the fireside, but her voice carried.

Hulagur growled at his sister, but his admonition made no impression on her, and she replied in as hot a tone. The shaman's hand went up, silencing both of them.

"You are—who?" Like Kaydessa, Menlik spoke a heavily accented English.

"I am Travis Fox, of the Apaches."

"The Apaches," the shaman repeated. "You are of the West, the American West, then."

"You know much, man of spirit talk."

"One remembers. At times one remembers," Menlik answered almost absently. "How does an Apache find his way across the stars?"

"The same way Menlik and his people did," Travis returned. "You were sent to settle this planet, and so were we."

"There are many more of you?" countered Menlik swiftly.

"Are there not many of the Horde? Would one man, or three, or four, be sent to hold a world?" Travis fenced. "You hold the north, we the south of this land."

"But *they* are not governed by a machine!" Kaydessa cut in. "They are free!"

Menlik frowned at the girl. "Woman, this is a matter for warriors. Keep your tongue silent between your jaws!"

She stamped one foot, standing with her fists on her hips.

"I am a Daughter of the Blue Wolf. And we are all warriors—men and women alike—so shall we be as long as the Horde is not free to ride where we wish! These men have won their freedom; it is well that we learn how."

Menlik's expression did not change, but his lids drooped over his eyes as a murmur of what might be agreement came from the group. More than one of them must have

understood enough English to translate for the others.
Travis wondered about that. Had these men and women
who had outwardly reverted to the life of their nomad
ancestors once been well educated in the modern sense,
educated enough to learn the basic language of the nation
their rulers regarded as their principal enemy?

"So you ride the land south of the mountains?" the
shaman continued.

"That is true."

"Then why did you come hither?"

Travis shrugged. "Why does anyone ride or travel into
new lands? There is a desire to see what may lie
beyond—"

"Or to scout before the march of warriors!" Menlik
snapped. "There is no peace between your rulers and
mine. Do you ride now to take the herds and pastures
of the Horde—or to try to do so?"

Travis turned his head deliberately from side to side,
allowing them all to witness his slow and openly contemptuous appraisal of their camp.

"*This* is your Horde, Shaman? Fifteen warriors? Much
has changed since the days of Temujin, has it not?"

"What do you know of Temujin—you, who are a man
of no ancestors, out of the West?"

"What do I know of Temujin? That he was a leader
of warriors and became Genghis Khan, the great lord of
the East. But the Apaches had their warlords also, rider
of the barren lands. And I am of those who raided over
two nations when Victorio and Cochise scattered their enemies as a man scatters a handful of dust in the wind."

"You talk bold, Apache. . . ." There was a hint of threat
in that.

"I speak as any warrior, Shaman. Or are you so used
to talking with spirits instead of men that you do not
realize that?"

He might have been alienating the shaman by such a
sharp reply, but Travis thought he judged the temper of
these people. To face them boldly was the only way to

impress them. They would not treat with an inferior, and he was already at a disadvantage coming on foot, without any backing in force, into a territory held by horsemen who were suspicious and jealous of their recently acquired freedom. His only chance was to establish himself as an equal and then try to convince them that Apache and Tatar-Mongol had a common cause against the Russians who controlled the settlement on the northern plains.

Menlik's right hand went to his sash-girdle and plucked out a carved stick which he waved between them, muttering phrases Travis could not understand. Had the shaman retreated so far along the road to his past that he now believed in his own supernatural powers? Or was this to impress his watching followers?

"You call upon your spirits for aid, Menlik? But the Apache has the companionship of the *ga-n*. Ask of Kaydessa: Who hunts with the Fox in the wilds?" Travis' sharp challenge stopped that wand in mid-air. Menlik's head swung to the girl.

"He hunts with wolves who think like men." She supplied the information the shaman would not openly ask for. "I have seen them act as his scouts. This is no spirit thing, but real and of this world!"

"Any man may train a dog to his bidding!" Menlik spat.

"Does a dog obey orders which are not said aloud? These brown wolves come and sit before him, look into his eyes. And then he knows what lies within their heads, and they know what he would have them do. This is not the way of a master of hounds with his pack!"

Again the murmur ran about the camp as one or two translated. Menlik frowned. Then he rammed his sorcerer's wand back into his sash.

"If you are a man of power—such powers," he said slowly, "then you may walk alone where those who talk with spirits go—into the mountains." He then spoke over his shoulder in his native tongue, and one of the women reached behind her into a hut, brought out a skin bag and a horn cup. Kaydessa took the cup from her and held it while the other woman poured a white liquid from the bag to fill it.

Kaydessa passed the cup to Menlik. He pivoted with it in his hand, dribbling expertly over its brim a few drops at each point of the compass, chanting as he moved. Then he sucked in a mouthful of the contents before presenting the vessel to Travis.

The Apache smelled the same sour scent that had clung to the emptied bag in the foothills. And another part of memory supplied him with the nature of the drink. This was kumiss, a fermented mare's milk which was the wine and water of the steppes.

He forced himself to swallow a draft, though it was alien to his taste, and passed the cup back to Menlik. The shaman emptied the horn and, with that, set aside ceremony. With an upraised hand he beckoned Travis to the fire again, indicating a pot set on the coals.

"Rest . . . eat!" he bade abruptly.

Night was gathering in. Travis tried to calculate how far Tsoay must have backtracked to the rancheria. He thought that he could have already made the pass and be within a day and a half from the Apache camp if he pushed on, as he would. As to where the coyotes were, Travis had no idea. But it was plain that he himself must remain in this encampment for the night or risk rousing the Mongols' suspicion once more.

He ate of the stew, spearing chunks out of the pot with the point of his knife. And it was not until he sat back, his hunger appeased, that the shaman dropped down beside him.

"The Khatun Kaydessa says that when she was slave to the caller, you did not feel its chains," he began.

"Those who rule you are not my overlords. The bonds they set upon your minds do not touch me." Travis hoped that that was the truth and his escape that morning had not been just a fluke.

"This could be, for you and I are not of one blood," Menlik agreed. "Tell me—how did you escape your bonds?"

"The machine which held us so was broken," Travis replied with a portion of the truth, and Menlik sucked in his breath.

"The machines, always the machines!" he cried hoarsely. "A thing which can sit in a man's head and make him do what it will against his will; it is demon sent! There are other machines to be broken, Apache."

"Words will not break them," Travis pointed out.

"Only a fool rides to his death without hope of striking a single blow before he chokes on the blood in his throat," Menlik retorted. "We cannot use bow or tulwar against weapons which flame and kill quicker than any storm lightning! And always the mind machines can make a man drop his knife and stand helplessly waiting for the slave collar to be set on his neck!"

Travis asked a question of his own. "I know that they can bring a caller part way into this mountain, for this very day I saw its effect upon the maiden. But there are many places in the hills well set for ambushes, and those unaffected by the machine could be waiting there. Would there be many machines so that they could send out again and again?"

Menlik's bony hand played with his wand. Then a slow smile curved his lips into the guise of a hunting cat's noiseless snarl.

"There is meat in that pot, Apache, rich meat, good for the filling of a lean belly! So men whose minds the machine could not trouble—such men to be waiting in ambush for the taking of the men who use such a machine—yes. But here would have to be bait, very good bait for such a trap, Lord of Wiles. Never do those others come far into the mountains. Their flyer does not lift well here, and they do not trust traveling on horseback. They were greatly angered to come so far in to reach Kaydessa, though they could not have been too close, or you would not have escaped at all. Yes, strong bait."

"Such bait as perhaps the knowledge that there were strangers across the mountains?"

Menlik turned his wand about in his hands. He was no longer smiling, and his glance at Travis was sharp and swift.

"Do you sit as Khan in your tribe, Lord?"

"I sit as one they will listen to." Travis hoped that was so. Whether Buck and the moderates would hold clan leadership upon his return was a fact he could not count upon as certain.

"This is a thing which we must hold council over," Menlik continued. "But it is an idea of power. Yes, one to think about, Lord. And I shall think . . ."

He got up and moved away. Travis blinked at the fire. He was very tired, and he disliked sleeping in this camp. But he must not go without the rest his body needed to supply him with a clear head in the morning. And not showing uneasiness might be one way of winning Menlik's confidence.

9

Travis settled his back against the spire of rock and raised his right hand into the path of the sun, cradling in his palm a disk of glistening metal. Flash . . . flash . . . he made the signal pattern just as his ancestors a hundred and fifty years earlier and far across space had used trade mirrors to relay war alerts among the Chiricahua and White Mountain ranges. If Tsoay had returned safely, and if Buck had kept the agreed lookout on that peak a mile or so ahead, then the clan would know that he was coming and with what escort.

He waited now, rubbing the small metal mirror absently on the loose sleeve of his shirt, waiting for a reply. Mirrors were best, not smoke fires which would broadcast too far the presence of men in the hills. Tsoay must have returned. . . .

"What is it that you do?"

Menlik, his shaman's robe pulled up so that his breeches and boots were dark against the golden rock, climbed up beside the Apache. Menlik, Hulagur, and Kaydessa were riding with Travis, offering him one of their

small ponies to hurry the trip. He was still regarded warily
by the Tatars, but he did not blame them for their
cautious attitude.

"Ah—" A flicker of light from the point ahead. One . . .
two . . . three flashes, a pause, then two more together.
He had been read. Buck had dispatched scouts to meet
them, and knowing his people's skill at the business,
Travis was certain the Tatars would never suspect their
flanking unless the Apaches purposefully revealed themselves. Also the Tatars were not to go to the rancheria,
but would be met at a mid-point by a delegation of
Apaches. This was no time for the Tatars to learn just
how few the clan numbered.

Menlik watched Travis flash an acknowledgment to the
sentry ahead. "In this way you speak to your men?"

"This way I speak."

"A thing good and to be remembered. We have the
drum, but that is for the ears of all with hearing. This
is for the eyes only of those on watch for it. Yes, a good
thing. And your people—they will meet with us?"

"They wait ahead," Travis confirmed.

It was close to midday and the heat, gathered in the
rocky ways, was like a heaviness in the air itself. The
Tatars had shucked their heavy jackets and rolled the fur
brims of their hats far up their heads away from their
sweat-beaded faces. And at every halt they passed from
hand to hand the skin bag of kumiss.

Now even the ponies shuffled on with drooping heads,
picking a way in a cut which deepened into a canyon.
Travis kept a watch for the scouts. And not for the first
time he thought of the disappearance of the coyotes.
Somehow, back in the Tatar camp, he had counted con-
fidently on the animals' rejoining him once he had started
his return over the mountains.

But he had seen nothing of either beast, nor had he
felt that unexplainable mental contact with them which
had been present since his first awakening on Topaz. Why
they had left him so unceremoniously after defending him

from the Mongol attack, and why they were keeping themselves aloof now, he did not know. But he was conscious of a thread of alarm for their continued absence, and he hoped he would find they had gone back to the rancheria.

The ponies thudded dispiritedly along a sandy wash which bottomed the canyon. Here the heat became a leaden weight and the men were panting like four-footed beasts running before hunters. Finally Travis sighted what he had been seeking, a flicker of movement on the wall well above. He flung up his hand, pulling his mount to a stand. Apaches stood in full view, bows ready, arrows on cords. But they made no sound.

Kaydessa cried out, booted her mount to draw equal with Travis.

"A trap!" Her face, flushed with heat, was also stark with anger.

Travis smiled slowly. "Is there a rope about you, Wolf Daughter?" he inquired softly. "Are you now dragged across this sand?"

Her mouth opened and then closed again. The quirt she had half raised to slash at him, flopped across her pony's neck.

The Apache glanced back at the two men. Hulagur's hand was on his sword hilt, his eyes darting from one of those silent watchers to the next. But the utter hopelessness of the Tatar position was too plain. Only Menlik made no move toward any weapon, even his spirit wand. Instead, he sat quietly in the saddle, displaying no emotion toward the Apaches save his usual self-confident detachment.

"We go on." Travis pointed ahead.

Just as suddenly as they had appeared from the heart of the golden cliffs, so did the scouts vanish. Most of them were already on their way to the point Buck had selected for the meeting place. There had been only six men up there, but the Tatars had no way of knowing just how large a portion of the whole clan that number was.

Travis' pony lifted his head, nickered, and achieved a stumbling trot. Somewhere ahead was water, one of those oases of growth and life which pocked the whole mountain range—to the preservation of animals and men.

Menlik and Hulagur pushed on until their mounts were hard on the heels of the two ridden by the girl and Travis. Travis wondered if they still waited for some arrow to strike home, though he saw that both men rode with outward disregard for the patrolling scouts.

A grass-leaf bush beckoned them on and again the ponies quickened pace, coming out into a tributary canyon which housed a small pool and a good stand of grass and brush. To one side of the water Buck stood, his arms folded across his chest, armed only with his belt knife. Grouped behind him were Deklay, Tsoay, Nolan, Manulito—Travis tabulated hurriedly. Manulito and Deklay were to be classed together— or had been when he was last in the rancheria. On Buck's stairway from the past, both had halted more than halfway down. Nolan was a quiet man who seldom spoke, and whose opinion Travis could not foretell. Tsoay would back Buck.

Probably such a divided party was the best Travis could have hoped to gather. A delegation composed entirely of those who were ready to leave the past of the Redax— a collection of Bucks and Jil-Lees—was outside the bounds of possibility. But Travis was none too happy to have Deklay in on this.

Travis dismounted, letting the pony push forward by himself to dip nose into the pool.

"This is," Travis pointed politely with his chin—"Menlik, one who talks with spirits. . . . Hulagur, who is son to a chief . . . and Kaydessa, who is daughter to a chief. They are of the horse people of the north." He made the introduction carefully in English.

Then he turned to the Tatars. "Buck, Deklay, Nolan, Manulito, Tsoay," he named them all, "these stand to listen, and to speak for the Apaches."

But sometime later when the two parties sat facing each other, he wondered whether a common decision could come from the clansmen on his side of that irregular circle. Deklay's expression was closed; he had even edged a short way back, as if he had no desire to approach the strangers. And Travis read into every line of Deklay's body his distrust and antagonism.

He himself began to speak, retelling his adventures since they had followed Kaydessa's trail, sketching in the situation at the Tatar-Mongol settlement as he had learned it from her and from Menlik. He was careful to speak in English so that the Tatars could hear all he was reporting to his own kind. And the Apaches listened blankfaced, though Tsoay must already have reported much of this. When Travis was done it was Deklay who asked a question:

"What have we to do with these people?"

"There is this—" Travis chose his words carefully, thinking of what might move a warrior still conditioned to riding with the raiders of more than a hundred years earlier, "the Pinda-lick-o-yi (whom we call Russians) are not willing to live side by side with any who are not of their mind. And they have weapons such as make our bow cords bits of rotten string, our knives slivers of rust. They do not kill; they enslave. And when they discover that we live, then they will come against us—"

Deklay's lips moved in a wolf grin. "This is a large land, and we know how to use it. The Pinda-lick-o-yi will not find us—"

"With their eyes maybe not," Travis replied. "With their machines—that is another matter."

"Machines!" Deklay spat. "Always these machines . . . Is that all you can talk about? It would seem that you are bewitched by these machines, which we have not seen— none of us!"

"It was a machine which brought you here," Buck observed. "Go you back and look upon the spaceship and remember, Deklay. The knowledge of the Pinda-lick-o-yi is greater than ours when it deals with metal and wire and things which can be made with both. Machines brought us along the road of the stars, and there is no tracker in the clan who could hope to do the same. But now I have this to ask: Does our brother have a plan?"

"Those who are Russians," Travis answered slowly, "they do not number many. But more may later come from our own world. Have you heard of such arriving?" he asked Menlik.

"Not so, but we are not told much. We live apart and no one of us goes to the ship unless he is summoned. For they have weapons to guard them, or long since they would have been dead. It is not proper for a man to eat from the pot, ride in the wind, sleep easy under the same sky with him who has slain his brother."

"They have then killed among your people?"

"They have killed," Menlik returned briefly.

Kaydessa stirred and muttered a word or two to her brother. Hulagur's head came up, and he exploded into violent speech.

"What does he say?" Deklay demanded.

The girl replied: "He speaks of our father who aided in the escape of three and so afterward was slain by the leader as a lesson to us—since he was our 'white beard,' the Khan."

"We have taken the oath in blood—under the Wolf Head Standard—that they will also die," Menlik added. "But first we must shake them out of their ship-shell."

"That is the problem," Travis elaborated for the benefit of his clansmen. "We must get these Russians away from their protected camp—out into the open. When they now go they are covered by this 'caller' which keeps the Tatars under their control, but it has no effect on us."

"So, again I say: What is all this to us?" Deklay got to his feet. "This machine does not hunt us, and we can make our camps in this land where no Pinda-lick-o-yi can find them—"

"We are not *dobe-gusndhe-he*—invulnerable. Nor do we know the full range of machines they can use. It does no one well to say '*doxa-da*'—this is not so—when he does not know all that lies in an enemy's wickiup."

To Travis' relief he saw agreement mirrored on Buck's face, Tsoay's, Nolan's. From the beginning he had had little hope of swaying Deklay; he could only trust that the verdict of the majority would be the accepted one. It went back to the old, old Apache institution of prestige. A *nantan*-chief had the *go'ndi*, the high power, as a gift from birth. Common men could possess horse power or cattle power; they might have the gift of acquiring wealth so they could make generous gifts—be *ikadntl'izi*, the wealthy ones who spoke for their family groups within the loose network of the tribe. But there was no hereditary chieftainship or even an undivided rule within a rancheria. The *nagunlka-dnat'an*, or war chief, often led only on the warpath and had no voice in clan matters save those dealing with a raid.

And to have a split now would fatally weaken their small clan. Deklay and those of a like mind might elect to withdraw and not one of the rest could deny him that right.

"We shall think on this," Buck said. "Here is food, water, pasturage for horses, a camp for our visitors. They will wait here." He looked at Travis. "You will wait with them, Fox, since you know their ways."

Travis' immediate reaction was objection, but then he realized Buck's wisdom. To offer the proposition of alliance to the Apaches needed an impartial spokesman. And if he himself did it, Deklay might automatically oppose the idea. Let Buck talk and it would be a statement of fact.

"It is well," Travis agreed.

Buck looked about, as if judging time from the lie of sun and shadow on the ground. "We shall return in the morning when the shadow lies here." With the toe of his high moccasin he made an impression in the soft earth. Then, without any formal farewell, he strode off, the others fast on his heels.

"He is your chief, that one?" Kaydessa asked, pointing after Buck.

"He is one having a large voice in council," Travis replied. He set about building up the cooking fire, bringing out the body of a split-horn calf which had been left them. Menlik sat on his heels by the pool, dipping up drinking water with his hand. Now he squinted his eyes against the probe of the sun.

"It will require much talking to win over the short one," he observed. "That one does not like us or your plan. Just as there will be those among the Horde who will not like it either." He flipped water drops from his fingers. "But this I do know, man who calls himself Fox, if we do not make a common cause, then we have no hope of going against the Russians. It will be for them as a man crushing fleas." He brought his hand down on his knee in emphatic slaps. "So . . . and so . . . and so!"

"This do I think also," Travis admitted.

"So let us both hope that all men will be as wise as we," Menlik said, smiling. "And since we can take a hand in that decision, this remains a time for rest."

The shaman might be content to sleep the afternoon away, but after he had eaten, Hulagur wandered up and down the valley, making a lengthy business of rubbing down their horses with twists of last season's grass. Now and then he paused beside Kaydessa and spoke, his uneasiness plain to Travis although he could not understand the words.

Travis had settled down in the shade, half dozing, yet alert to every movement of the three Tatars. He tried not to think of what might be happening in the rancheria by switching his mind to that misty valley of the towers. Did any of those three alien structures contain such a grab bag of the past as he, Ashe, and Murdock had found on that other world where the winged people had gathered together for them the artifacts of an older civilization? At that time he had created for their hosts a new weapon of defense, turning metal tubes into blowguns. It had been there, too, where he had chanced upon the library of tapes, one of which had eventually landed Travis and his people here on Topaz.

Even if he did find racks of such tapes in one of those towers, there would be no way of using them—with the ship wrecked on the mountain side. Only—Travis' fingers itched where they lay quiet on his knees—there might be other things waiting. If he were only free to explore!

He reached out to touch Menlik's shoulder. The shaman half turned, opening his eyes with the languid effort of a sleepy cat. But the spark of intelligence awoke in them quickly.

"What is it?"

For a moment Travis hesitated, already regretting his impulse. He did not know how much Menlik remembered of the present. Remember of the present—one part of the Apache's mind was wryly amused at that snarled estimate of their situation. Men who had been dropped into their racial and ancestral pasts until the present time was less real than the dreams conditioning them had a difficult job evaluating any situation. But since Menlik had clung to his knowledge of English, he must be less far down that stairway.

"When we met you, Kaydessa and I, it was outside that valley." Travis was still of two minds about this questioning, but the Tatar camp had been close to the towers and there was a good chance the Mongols had explored them. "And inside were buildings . . . very old . . ."

Menlik was fully alert now. He took his wand, played with it as he spoke:

"That is, or was, a place of much power, Fox. Oh, I know that you question my kinship with the spirits and the powers they give. But one learns not to dispute what one feels here—and here—" His long, somewhat grimy fingers went to his forehead and then to the bare brown chest where his shirt fell open. "I have walked the stone path in that valley, and there have been the whispers—"

"Whispers?"

Menlik twirled the wand. "Whispers which are too low for many ears to distinguish. You can hear them as one

hears the buzzing of an insect, but never the words—
no, never the words! But that is a place of great power!"

"A place to explore!"

But Menlik watched only his wand. "That I wonder,
Fox, truly do I wonder. This is not our world. And here
there may be that which does not welcome us."

Tricks-in-trade of a shaman? Or was it true recognition
of something beyond human description? Travis could not
be sure, but he knew that he must return to the valley
and see for himself.

"Listen," Menlik said, leaning closer, "I have heard your
tale, that you were on that first ship, the one which
brought you unwilling along the old star paths. Have you
ever seen such a thing as this?"

He smoothed a space of soft earth and with the narrow tip of his wand began to draw. Whatever role Menlik
had played in the present before he had been recondi-
tioned into a shaman of the Horde, he had had the ability
of an artist, for with a minimum of lines he created a
figure in that sketch.

It was a man or at least a figure with general human
outlines. But the round, slightly oversized skull was bare,
the clothing skintight to reveal unnaturally thin limbs.
There were large eyes, small nose and mouth, rather
crowded into the lower third of the head, giving an
impression of an over-expanded brain case above. And
it was familiar.

Not the flying men of the other world, certainly not
the nocturnal ape-things. Yet for all its alien quality Travis
was sure he had seen its like before. He closed his eyes
and tried to visualize it apart from the lines in the soil.

Such a head, white, almost like the bone of a skull laid
bare, such a head lying face down on a bone-thin arm clad
in a blue-purple skintight sleeve. Where had he seen it?

The Apache gave a sharp exclamation as he remembered fully. The derelict spaceship as he had first found
it—the dead alien officer had still been seated at its
controls! The alien who had set the tape which took them

out into that forgotten empire—he was the subject of Menlik's drawing!

"Where? When did you see such a one?" The Apache bent down over the Tatar.

Menlik looked troubled. "He came into my mind when I walked the valley. I thought I could almost see such a face in one of the tower windows, but of that I am not sure. Who is it?"

"Someone from the old days—those who once ruled the stars," Travis answered. But were they still here then, the remnant of a civilization which had flourished ten thousand years ago? Were the Baldies, who centuries ago had ruthlessly hunted down the Russians who had dared to loot their wrecked ships, still on Topaz?

He remembered Ross Murdock's escape from those aliens in the far past of Europe, and he shivered. Murdock was tough, steel tough, yet his own description of that epic chase and the final meeting had carried with it his terror. What could a handful of primitively armed and almost primitively minded humans do now if they had to dispute Topaz with the Baldies?

10

"Beyond this—" Menlik worked his way to the very lip of a drop, raising a finger cautiously—"beyond this we do not go."

"But you say that the camp of your people lies well out in the plains—" Jil-Lee was up on one knee, using the field glasses they had brought from the stores of the wrecked ship. He passed them along to Travis. There was nothing to be sighted but the rippling amber waves of the tall grasses, save for an occasional break of a copse of trees near the foothills.

They had reached this point in the early morning, threading through the pass, making their way across the section known to the outlaws. From here they could survey the debatable land where their temporary allies insisted the Russians were in full control.

The result of the conference in the south had been this uneasy alliance. From the start Travis realized that he could not hope to commit the clan to any set plan, that even to get this scouting party to come against the stubborn resistance of Deklay and his reactionaries was a major achievement. There was now an opening wedge of six Apaches in the north.

"Beyond this," Menlik repeated, "they keep watch and can control us with the caller."

"What do you think?" Travis passed the glasses to Nolan.

If they were ever to develop a war chief, this lean man, tall for an Apache and slow to speak, might fill that role. He adjusted the lenses and began a detailed study-sweep of the open territory. Then he stiffened. His mouth, below the masking of the glasses, was tight.

"What is it?" Jil-Lee asked.

"Riders—two . . . four . . . five . . . Also something else—in the air."

Menlik jerked back and grabbed at Nolan's arm, dragging him down by the weight of his body.

"The flyer! Come back—back!" He was still pulling at Nolan, prodding at Travis with one foot, and the Apaches stared at him with amazement.

The shaman sputtered in his own language, and then, visibly regaining command of himself, spoke English once more.

"Those are hunters, and they carry a caller. Either some others have escaped or they are determined to find our mountain camp."

Jil-Lee looked at Travis. "You did not feel anything when the woman was under that spell?"

Travis shook his head. Jil-Lee nodded and then said to the shaman: "We shall stay here and watch. But since it is bad for you—do you go. And we shall meet you near this place of the towers. Agreed?"

For a moment Menlik's face held a shadowy expression Travis tried to read. Was it resentment—resentment that he was forced to retreat when the others could stand their ground? Did the Tatar believe that he lost face this way? But the shaman gave a grunt of what they took as assent and slipped over the edge of the lookout point. A moment later they heard him speaking the Mongol tongue, warning Hulagur and Lotchu, his companions on the scout. Then came the clatter of pony hoofs as they rode their mounts away.

The Apaches settled back in the cup, which gave them a wide view over the plains. Soon it was not necessary to use the glasses in order to sight the advancing party of hunters—five riders, four wearing Tatar dress. The fifth had such an odd outline that Travis was reminded of Menlik's sketch of the alien. Under the sharper vision of the glasses he saw that the rider was equipped with a pack strapped between his shoulders and a bulbous helmet covering most of his head. Specialized equipment for communication, Travis guessed.

"That is a 'copter up above," Nolan said. "Different shape from ours."

They had been familiar with helicopters back on Earth. Ranchers used them for range inspection, and all of the Apache volunteers had flown in them. But Nolan was correct; this one possessed several unfamiliar features.

"The Tatars say they don't bring those very far into the mountains," Jil-Lee mused. "That could explain their man on horseback; he gets in where they don't fly."

Nolan fingered his bow. "If these Russians depend upon their machine to control what they seek, then they may be taken by surprise—"

"But not yet!" Travis spoke sharply. Nolan frowned at him.

Jil-Lee chuckled. "The way is not so dark for us, younger brother, that we need your torch held for our feet!"

Travis swallowed back any retort, accepting the fairness of that rebuke. He had no right to believe that he alone knew the best way of handling the enemy. Biting on the sourness of that realization, he lay quietly with the others, watching the riders enter the foothills perhaps a quarter of a mile to the west.

The helicopter was circling now over the men riding into a cut between two rises. When they were lost to view, the pilot made wider casts, and Travis thought the flyer's crew were probably in communication with the helmeted one of the quintet on the ground.

He stirred. "They are heading for the Tatar camp, just as if they know exactly where it is—"

"That also may be true," Nolan replied. "What do we know of these Tatars? They have freely said that the Russians can hold them in mind ropes when they wish. Already they may be so bound. I say—let us go back to our own country." He added to the decisiveness of that by handing Jil-Lee the glasses and sliding down from their perch.

Travis looked at the other. In a way he could understand the wisdom of Nolan's suggestion. But he was sure that withdrawal now would only postpone trouble. Sooner or later the Apaches would have to stand against the Russians, and if they could do it now while the enemy was occupied with trouble from the Tatars, so much the better.

Jil-Lee was following Nolan. But something in Travis rebelled. He watched the circling helicopter. If it was overhanging the action area of the horsemen, they had either reined in or were searching a relatively small section of the foothills.

Reluctantly Travis descended to the hollow where Jil-Lee stood with Nolan. Tsoay and Lupe and Rope were a little to one side as if the final orders would come from their seniors.

"It would be well," Jil-Lee said slowly, "if we saw what weapons they have. I want a closer look at the equipment of that one in the helmet. Also," he smiled straight at Nolan—"I do not think that they can detect the presence of warriors of the People unless we will it so."

Nolan ran a finger along the curve of his bow, shot a measuring glance right and left at the general contours of the country.

"There is wisdom in what you say, elder brother. Only this is a trail we shall take alone, not allowing the men

with fur hats to know where we walk." He looked point-
edly in Travis' direction.

"That is wisdom, *Ba'is'a*," Travis promptly replied, giving
Nolan the old title accorded the leader of a war party.
Travis was grateful for that much of a concession.

They swung into action, heading southeast at an angle
which should bring them across the track of the enemy
hunting party. The path was theirs at last, only moments
after the passing of their quarry. None of the five riders was taking any precautions to cover his trail. Each
moved with the confidence of one without fear of attack.

From cover the Apaches looked aloft. They could hear
the faint hum of the helicopter. It was still circling, Tsoay
reported from a higher check point, but those circles
remained close over the plains area—the riders had already
passed beyond the limits of that aerial sentry.

Three to a side, the Apaches advanced with the trail
between them. They were carefully hidden when they
caught up with the hunters. The four Tatars were grouped
together; the fifth man, heavily burdened by his pack,
had climbed from the saddle and was sitting on the
ground, his hands busy with a flat plate which covered
him from upper chest to belt.

Now that he had a chance to see them closely, Travis
noted the lack of expression on the broad Tatar faces.
The four men were blank of eye, astride their mounts
with no apparent awareness of their present surroundings.
Then as one, their heads swung around to the helmeted
leader before they dismounted and stood motionless for
a long moment in a way which reminded Travis of the
coyotes' attitude when they endeavored to pass some
message to him. But these men even lacked the signs
of thinking intelligence the animals had.

The helmeted man's hand moved across his chest plate,
and instantly his followers came into a measure of life.
One put his hand to his forehead with an odd, half-dazed
gesture. Another half crouched, his lips wrinkling back
in a snarl. And the leader, watching him, laughed. Then

he snapped an order, his hand poised over his control plate.

One of the four took the horse reins, made the mounts fast to near-by bushes. Then as one they began to walk forward, the Russian bringing up the rear several paces behind the nearest Tatar. They were going upslope to the crest of a small ridge.

The Tatar who first reached the crest put his hands to cup his mouth, sent a ringing cry southward, and the faint "hu-hu-hu" echoed on and on through the hills.

Either Menlik had reached the camp in time, or his people were not to be so easily enticed. For though the hunters waited for a long time, there was no answer to that hail. At last the helmeted man called his captives, bringing them sullenly down to mount and ride again— a move which suited the Apaches.

They could not tell how close was the communication between the rider and the helicopter. And they were still too near the plains to attack unless it was necessary for their own protection. Travis dropped back to join Nolan.

"He controls them by that plate on his chest," he said. "If we would take them, we must get at that—"

"These Tatars use lariats in fighting. Did they not rope you as a calf is roped for branding? Then why do they not so take this Russian, binding his arms to his sides?" The suspicion in Nolan's voice was plain.

"Perhaps in them is some conditioned control making it so that they cannot attack their rulers—"

"I do not like this matter of machines which can play this way and that with minds and bodies!" flared Nolan. "A man should only *use* a weapon, not be one!"

Travis could agree to that. Had they by the wreck of their own ship and the death of Ruthven, escaped just such an existence as these Tatars now endured? If so, why? He and all the Apaches were volunteers, eager and willing to form new world colonies. What had happened back on Earth that they had been so ruthlessly sent out without warning and under Redax? Another small piece

of that puzzle, or maybe the heart of the whole picture
snapped into place. Had the project learned in some way
of the Tatar settlement on Topaz and so been forced to
speed up that translation from early twenty-first-century
Americans to primitives? That would explain a lot!

Travis returned abruptly to the matter now at hand as
he saw a peak ahead. The party they were trailing was
heading directly for the outlaw hide-out. Travis hoped
Menlik had warned them in time. There—that wall of cliff
to his left must shelter the valley of the towers, though
it was still miles ahead. Travis did not believe the hunters
would be able to reach their goal unless they traveled
at night. They might not know of the ape-things which
could menace the dark.

But the enemy, whether he knew of such dangers or
not, did not intend to press on. As the sun pulled away,
leaving crevices and crannies shadow dark, the hunters
stopped to make camp. The Apaches, after their custom
on the war trail, gathered on the heights above.

"This Russian seems to think that he shall find those
he seeks sitting waiting for him, as if their feet were
nipped tight in a trap," Tsoay remarked.

"It is the habit of the Pinda-lick-o-yi," Lupe added, "to
believe they are greater than all others. Yet this one is
a stupid fool walking into the arms of a she-bear with
a cub." He chuckled.

"A man with a rifle does not fear a man armed only
with a stick," Travis cut in quickly. "This one is armed
with a weapon which he has good reason to believe
makes him invulnerable to attack. If he rests tonight, he
probably leaves his machine on guard."

"At least we are sure of one thing," Nolan said in half
agreement. "This one does not suspect that there are any
in these hills save those he can master. And his machine
does not work against us. Thus at dawn—" He made a
swift gesture, and they smiled in concert.

At dawn—the old time of attack. An Apache does not
attack at night. Travis was not sure that any of them could

break that old taboo and creep down upon the camp before the coming of new light.

But tomorrow morning they would take over this confident Russian, strip him of his enslaving machine.

Travis' head jerked. It had come as suddenly as a blow between his eyes—to half stun him. What . . . what was it? Not any physical impact—no, something which was dazing but still immaterial. He braced his whole body, awaiting its return, trying frantically to understand what had happened in that instant of vertigo and seeming disembodiment. Never had he experienced anything like it—or had he? Two years or more ago when he had gone through the time transfer to enter the Arizona of the Folsom Men some ten thousand years earlier—that moment of transfer had been something like this, a sensation of being awry in space and time with no stable footing to be found.

Yet he was lying here on very tangible rock and soil, and nothing about him in the shadow-hung landscape of Topaz had changed in the slightest. But that blow had left behind it a quivering residue of panic buried far inside him, a tender spot like an open wound.

Travis drew a deep breath which was almost a sob, levered himself up on one elbow to stare down intently into the enemy camp. Was this some attack from the other's unknown weapons? Suddenly he was not at all sure what might happen when the Apaches made that dawn rush.

Jil-Lee was in station on his right. Travis must compare notes with him to be sure that this was not indeed a trap. Better to retreat now than to be taken like fish in a net. He crept out of his place, gave the chittering signal call of the fluff-ball, and heard Jil-Lee's answer in a cleverly mimicked trill of a night insect.

"Did you feel something just now—in your head?" Travis found it difficult to put that sensation into words.

"No so. But you did?"

He had—of course, he had! The remains of it were still in him, that point of panic. "Yes."

"The machine?"

"I don't know." Travis' confusion grew. It might be that he alone of the party had been struck. If so, he could be a danger to his own kind.

"This is not good. I think we had better hold council, away from here." Jil-Lee's whisper was the merest ghost of sound. He chirped again to be answered from Tsoay upslope, who passed on the signal.

The first moon was high in the sky as the Apaches gathered together. Again Travis asked his question: Had any of the others felt that odd blow? He was met by negatives.

But Nolan had the final word: "This is not good," he echoed Jil-Lee's comment. "If it was the Russian machine at work, then we may all be swept into his net along with those he seeks. Perhaps the longer one remains close to that thing, the more influence it gains over him. We shall stay here until dawn. If the enemy would reach the place they seek, then they must pass below us, for that is the easiest road. Burdened with his machine, that Russian has ever taken the easiest way. So, we shall see if he also has a defense against these when they come without warning." He touched the arrows in his quiver.

To kill from ambush meant that they might never learn the secret of the machine, but after his experience Travis was willing to admit that Nolan's caution was the wise way. Travis wanted no part of a second attack like that which had shaken him so. And Nolan had not ordered a general retreat. It must be in the war chief's thoughts as it was in Travis' that if the machine could have an influence over Apaches, it must cease to function.

They set their ambush with the age-old skill the Redax had grafted into their memories. Then there was nothing to do but wait.

It was an hour after dawn when Tsoay signaled that the enemy was coming, and shortly after, they heard the thud of ponies' hoofs. The first Tatar plodded into view, and by the stance of his body in the saddle, Travis knew

the Russian had him under full control. Two, then three
Tatars passed between the teeth of the Apache trap. The
fourth one had allowed a wider gap to open between
himself and his fellows.

Then the Russian leader came. His face below the bulge
of the helmet was not happy. Travis believed the man
was not a horseman by inclination. The Apache set arrow
to bow cord, and at the chirp from Nolan, fired in concert
with his clansmen.

Only one of those arrows found a target. The Russian's
pony gave a shrill scream of pain and terror, reared,
pawing at the air, toppled back, pinning its shouting rider
under it.

The Russian had had a defense right enough, one which
had somehow deflected the arrows. But he neither had
protection against his own awkward seat in the saddle
nor the arrow which had seriously wounded the now
thrashing pony.

Ahead the Tatars twisted and writhed, mouthed tortured
cries, then dropped out of their saddles to lie limply on
the ground as if the arrows aimed at the master had
instead struck each to the heart.

11

Either the Russian was lucky, or his reactions were quick. He had somehow rolled clear of the struggling horse as Lupe leaped from behind a boulder, knife out and ready. To the eyes of the Apaches the helmeted man lay easy prey to Lupe's attack. Nor did he raise an arm to defend himself, though one hand lay free across the plate on his chest.

But the young Apache stumbled, rebounding back as if he had run into an unseen wall—when his knife was still six inches away from the other. Lupe cried out, shook under a second impact as the Russian fired an automatic with his other hand.

Travis dropped his bow, returned to the most primitive weapon of all. His hand closed around a stone and he hurled the fist-sized oval straight at the helmet so clearly outlined against the rocks below.

But even as Lupe's knife had never touched flesh, so was the rock deflected; the Russian was covered by some protective field. This was certainly nothing the Apaches had seen before. Nolan's whistle summoned them to draw back.

The Russian fired again, the sharp bark of the hand gun harsh and loud. He did not have any real target, for with the exception of Lupe, the Apaches had gone to earth. Between the rocks the Russian was struggling to his feet, but he moved slowly, favoring his side and one leg; he had not come totally unharmed from his tumble with the pony.

An armed enemy who could not be touched—one who knew there were more than outlaws in this region. The Russian leader was far more of a threat to the Apaches now than he had ever been. He must not be allowed to escape.

He was holstering his gun, moving along with one hand against the rocks to steady himself, trying to reach one of the ponies that stood with trailing reins beside the inert Tatars.

But when the enemy reached the far side of that rock he would have to sacrifice either his steadying hold, or his touch on the chest plate where his other hand rested. Would he, then, for an instant be vulnerable?

The pony!

Travis put an arrow on bow cord and shot. Not at the Russian, who had released his hold of the rock, preferring to totter instead of lose control of the chest plate—but into the air straight before the nose of the mount.

The pony neighed wildly, tried to turn, and its shoulder caught the free, groping hand of the Russian and spun the man around and back, so that he flung up both hands in an effort to ward himself off the rocks. Then the pony stampeded down the break, its companions catching the same fever, trailing in a mad dash which kept the Russian hard against the boulders.

He continued to stand there until the horses, save for the wounded one still kicking fruitlessly, were gone. Travis felt a sense of reprieve. They might not be able to get at the Russian, but he was hurt and afoot, two strikes which might yet reduce him to a condition the Apaches could handle.

Apparently the other was also aware of that, for now he pushed out from the rocks and stumbled along after the ponies. But he went only a step or two. Then, settling back once more against a convenient boulder, he began to work at the plate on his chest.

Nolan appeared noiselessly beside Travis. "What does he do?" His lips were very close to the younger man's ear, his voice hardly more than a breath.

Travis shook his head slightly. The Russian's actions were a complete mystery. Unless, now disabled and afoot, he was trying to summon aid. Though there was no landing place for a helicopter here.

Now was the time to try and reach Lupe. Travis had seen a slight movement in the fallen Apache's hand, the first indication that the enemy's shot had not been as fatal as it had looked. He touched Nolan's arm, pointed to Lupe; and then, discarding bow and quiver beside the war leader, he stripped for action. There was cover down to the wounded Apache which would aid him. He must pass one of the Tatars on the way, but none of the tribesmen had shown any signs of life since they had fallen from their saddles at the first attack.

With infinite care, Travis lowered himself into a narrow passage, took a lizard's way between brush and boulder, pausing only when he reached the Tatar for a quick check on the potential enemy.

The lean brown face was half turned, one cheek in the sand, but the slack mouth, the closed eyes were those, Travis believed, of a dead man. By some action of his diabolic machine the Russian must have snuffed out his four captives—perhaps in the belief that they were part of the Apache attack.

Travis reached the rock where Lupe lay. He knew that Nolan was watching the Russian and would give him warning if he suddenly showed an interest in anything but his machine. The Apache reached out, his hands closing on Lupe's ankles. Beneath his touch, flesh and muscle tensed. Lupe's eyes were open, focused now on

Travis. There was a bleeding furrow above his right ear. The Russian had tried a difficult head shot, failing in his aim by a mere fraction of an inch.

Lupe made a swift move for which Travis was ready. His grip on the other's body helped to tumble them both around a rock which lay between them and the Russian. There was the crack of another shot and dust spurted from the side of the boulder. But they lay together, safe for the present, as Travis was sure the enemy would not risk an open attack on their small fortress.

With Travis' aid Lupe struggled back up to the site where Nolan waited. Jil-Lee was there to make competent examination of the boy's wound.

"Creased," he reported. "A sore head, but no great damage. Perhaps a scar later, warrior!" He gave Lupe an encouraging thump on the shoulder, before plastering an aid pack over the cut.

"Now we go!" Nolan spoke with emphatic decision.

"He saw enough of us to know we are not Tatars."

Nolan's eyes were cold, his mouth grim as he faced Travis.

"And how can we fight him—?"

"There is a wall—a wall you cannot see—about him," Lupe broke in. "When I would strike at him, I could not!"

"A man with invisible protection and a gun," Jil-Lee took up the argument. "How would you deal with him, younger brother?"

"I don't know," Travis admitted. Yet he also believed that if they withdrew, left the Russian here to be found by his own people, the enemy would immediately begin an investigation of the southern country. Perhaps, pushed by their need for learning more about the Apaches, they would bring the helicopter in over the mountains. The answer to all Apache dangers, for now, lay in the immediate future of this one man.

"He is hurt, he cannot go far on foot. And even if he calls the 'copter, there is no landing place. He will have to move elsewhere to be picked up." Travis thought aloud, citing the thin handful of points in their favor.

Tsoay nodded toward the rim of the ravine. "Rocks up there and rocks can roll. Start an earthslide . . ."

Something within Travis balked at that. From the first he had been willing enough to slug it out with the Russian, weapon to weapon, man to man. Also, he had wanted to take a captive, not stand over a body. But to use the nature of the country against the enemy, that was the oldest Apache trick of all and one they would have to be forced to employ.

Nolan had already nodded in assent, and Tsoay and Jil-Lee started off. Even if the Russian did possess a protective wall device, could it operate in full against a landslide? They all doubted that.

The Apaches reached the cliff rim without exposing themselves to the enemy's fire. The Russian still sat there calmly, his back against the rock, his hands busy with his equipment as if he had all the time in the world.

Then suddenly came a scream from more than one throat.

"Dar-u-gar!" The ancient war cry of the Mongol Hordes.

Then over the lip of the other slope rose a wave of men—their curved swords out, a glazed set to their eyes—heading for the Amerindians with utter disregard for any personal safety. Menlik in the lead, his shaman's robe flapping wide below his belt like the wings of some oversized predatory bird. Hulagur . . . Jagatai . . . men from the outlaws' camp. And they were not striving to destroy their disabled overlord in the vale below, but to wipe out the Apaches!

Only the fact that the Apaches were already sheltered behind the rocks they were laboring to dislodge gave them a precious few moments of grace. There was no time to use their bows. They could only use knives to meet the swords of the Tatars, knives and the fact that they could fight with unclouded minds.

"He has them under control!" Travis pawed at Jil-Lee's shoulder. "Get him—they'll stop!"

He did not wait to see if the other Apache understood. Instead, he threw the full force of his own body against the rock they had made the center stone of their slide. It gave and rolled, carrying with it the rest of the piled rubble. Travis stumbled, fell flat, and then a body thudded down upon him, and he was fighting for his life to keep a blade from his throat. Around him were the shouts and cries of embroiled warriors; then all was silenced by a roar from below.

Glazed eyes in a face only a foot from his own, the twisted panting mouth sending gusts of breath into his nostrils. Suddenly there was reason back in those eyes, a bewilderment which became fear . . . panic . . . The Tatar's body twisted in Travis' hold, striving now not to attack, but to win free. As the Apache loosened his grip the other jerked away, so that for a moment or two they lay gasping, side by side.

Men sat up to look at men. There was a spreading stain down Jil-Lee's side and one of the Tatars sprawled near him, both his hands on his chest, coughing violently.

Menlik clawed at the trunk of a wind-twisted mountain tree, pulled himself to his feet, and stood swaying as might a man long ill and recovering from severe exertion.

Insensibly both sides drew apart, leaving a space between Tatar and Apache. The faces of the Amerindians were grim, those of the Mongols bewildered and then harsh as they eyed their late opponents with dawning reason. What had begun in compulsion for the Tatars might well flare now into rational combat—and from that to a campaign of extermination.

Travis was on his feet. He looked over the lip of the drop. The Russian was still in his place down there, a pile of rubble about him. His protection must have failed, for his head was back at an unnatural angle and the dent in his helmet could be easily seen.

"That one is dead—or helpless!" Travis cried out. "Do you still wish to fight for him, Shaman?"

Menlik came away from the tree and walked to the edge of the drop. The others, too, were moving forward. After the shaman looked down he stooped, picked up a small stone, and flung it at the motionless Russian. There was a crack of sound. They all saw the tiny spurt of flame, a curl of smoke from the plate on the Russian's chest. Not only the man, but his control was finished now.

A wolfish growl and two of the Tatars swung over, started down to the Russian. Menlik shouted and they slackened pace.

"We want that," he cried in English. "Perhaps so we can learn—"

"The learning is yours," Jil-Lee replied. "Just as this land is yours, Shaman. But I warn you, from this day do not ride south!"

Menlik turned, the charms on his belt clicking. "So that is the way it is to be, Apache?"

"That is the way it shall be, Tatar! We do not ride to war with allies who may turn their knives against our backs because they are slaves to a machine the enemy controls."

The Tatar's long, slender-fingered hands opened and closed. "You are a wise man, Apache, but sometimes more than wisdom alone is needed—"

"We are wise men, Shaman, let it rest there," Jil-Lee replied somberly.

Already the Apaches were on their way, putting two cliff ridges behind them before they halted to examine and cover their wounds.

"We go." Nolan's chin lifted, indicating the southern route. "Here we do not come again; there is too much witchcraft in this place."

Travis stirred, saw that Jil-Lee was frowning at him.

"Go—?" he repeated.

"Yes, younger brother? You would continue to run with these who are governed by a machine?"

"No. Only, eyes are needed on this side of the mountains."

"Why?" This time Jil-Lee was plainly on the side of the conservatives. "We have now seen this machine at work. It is fortunate that the Russian is dead. He will carry no tales of us back to his people as you feared. Thus, if we remain south from now on, we are safe. And this fight between Tatar and Russian is none of ours. What do you seek here?"

"I must go again to the place of the towers," Travis answered with the truth. But his friends were facing him with heavy disapproval—now a full row of Deklays.

"Did you not tell us that you felt this strange thing during the night we waited above the camp? What if you become one with these Tatars and are also controlled by the machine? Then you, too, can be made into a weapon against us—your clansmen!" Jil-Lee was almost openly hostile.

Sense was on his side. But in Travis was this other desire of which he was becoming more conscious by the minute. There was a reason for those towers, perhaps a reason important enough for him to discover and run the risk of angering his own people.

"There may be this—" Nolan's voice was remote and cold, "you may already be a piece of this thing, bound to the machines. If so, we do not want you among us."

There it was—an open hostility with more power behind it than Deklay's motiveless disapproval had carried. Travis was troubled. The family, the clan—they were important. If he took the wrong step now and was outlawed from that tight fortress, then as an Apache he would indeed be a lost man. In the past of his people there had been renegades from the tribe—men such as the infamous Apache Kid who had killed and killed again, not only white men but his own people. Wolf men living wolves' lives in the hills. Travis was threatened with that. Yet—up the ladder of civilization, down the ladder—why did this feverish curiosity ride him so cruelly now?

"Listen," Jil-Lee, his side padded with bandages, stepped closer—"and tell me, younger brother, what is it that you seek in these towers?"

"On another world there were secrets of the old ones to be found in such ancient buildings. Here that might also be true."

"And among the secrets of those old ones," Nolan's voice was still harsh—"were those which brought us to this world, is that not so?"

"Did any man drive you, Nolan, or you, Tsoay, or you, Jil-Lee, or any of us, to promise to go beyond the stars? You were told what might be done, and you were eager to try it. You were all volunteers!"

"Save for this voyage when we were told nothing," Jil-Lee answered, cutting straight to the heart of the matter. "Yet, Nolan, I do not believe that it is for more voyage tapes that our younger brother now searches, nor would those do us any good—as our ship will not rise again from here. What is it that you do seek?"

"Knowledge—weapons, maybe. Can we stand against these machines of the Russians? Yet many of the devices they now use are taken from the star ships they have looted through time. To every weapon there is a defense."

Nolan blinked and for the first time a hint of interest touched the mask of his face. "To the bow, the rifle," he said softly, "to the rifle, the machine gun, to the cannon, the bomb. The defense can be far worse than the first weapon. So you think that in these towers there may be things which shall be to the Russian's machines as the bomb is to the cannon of the Horse Soldiers?"

Travis had an inspiration. "Did not our people lay aside the bow for the rifle when we went up against the Bluecoats?"

"We do not so go up against these Russians!" protested Lupe.

"Not now. But what if they come across the mountains, perhaps driving the Tatars before them to do their fighting—?"

"And you believe that if you find weapons in these towers, you will know how to use them?" Jil-Lee asked. "What will give you that knowledge, younger brother?"

"I do not claim such knowledge," Travis countered. "But this much I do have: Once I studied to be an archaeologist and I have seen other storehouses of these star people. Who else among us can say as much as that?"

"That is the truth," Jil-Lee acknowledged. "Also there is good sense in this seeking out of the tower things. Let the Russians find such first—if they exist at all—and then we may truly be caught in a box canyon with only death at our heels."

"And you would go to these towers now?" Nolan demanded.

"I can cut across country and then rejoin you on the other side of the pass!" The feeling of urgency which had been mounting in Travis was now so demanding that he wanted to race ahead through the wilderness. He was surprised when Jil-Lee put out his palm up as if to warn the younger man.

"Take care, younger brother! This is not a lucky business. And remember, if one goes too far down a wrong trail, there is sometimes no returning—"

"We shall wait on the other side of the pass for one day," Nolan added. "Then—" he shrugged—"where you go will be your own affair."

Travis did not understand that promise of trouble. He was already two steps down his chosen path.

12

Travis had taken a direct cross route through the heights, but not swiftly enough to reach his objective before night-fall. And he had no wish to enter the tower valley by moonlight. In him two emotions now warred. There was the urge to invade the towers, to discover their secret, and flaring higher and higher the beginnings of a new fear. Was he now a battlefield for the superstitions of his race reborn by the Redax and his modern education in the Pinda-lick-o-yi world—half Apache brave of the past, half modern archaeologist with a thirst for knowledge? Or was the fear rooted more deeply and for another reason?

Travis crouched in a hollow, trying to understand what he felt. Why was it suddenly so overwhelmingly impor-tant for him to investigate the towers? If he only had the coyotes with him. . . . Why and where had they gone?

He was alive to every noise out of the night, every scent the wind carried to him. The night had its own life, just as the daylight hours held theirs. Only a few of those sounds could he identify, even less did he see.

117

There was one wide-winged, huge flying thing which passed across the green-gold plate of the nearer moon. It was so large that for an instant Travis believed the helicopter had come. Then the wings flapped, breaking the glide, and the creature merged in the shadows of the night—a hunter large enough to be a serious threat, and one he had never seen before.

Relying on his own small defense, the strewing of brittle sticks along the only approach to the hollow, Travis dozed at intervals, his head down on his forearm across his bent knees. But the cold cramped him and he was glad to see the graying sky of pre-dawn. He ate two rations bars and swallowed a couple of mouthfuls of water from his canteen and started on.

By sunup he had reached the ledge of the waterfall, and he hurried along the ancient road at a pace which increased to a run the closer he drew to the valley. Deliberately he slowed, his native caution now in control, so that he was walking as he passed through the gateway into the swirling mists which alternately exposed and veiled the towers.

There was no change in the scene from the time he had come there with Kaydessa. But now, rising from a comfortable sprawl on the yellow-and-green pavement, was a welcoming committee—Nalik'ideyu and Naginlta showing no more excitement at his coming than if they had parted only moments before.

Travis went down on one knee, holding out his hand to the female, who had always been the more friendly. She advanced a step or two, touched a cold nose to his knuckles, and whined.

"Why?" He voiced that one word, but behind it was a long list of questions. Why had they left him? Why were they here where there was no hunting? Why did they meet him now as if they had calmly expected his return?

Travis glanced from the animals to the towers, those windows set in diamond pattern. And again he was visited by the impression that he was under observation. With the mist floating across those openings, it would be easy for a lurker to watch him unseen.

He walked slowly on into the valley, his moccasins making no sound on the pavement, but he could hear the faint click of the coyotes' claws as they paced beside him, on each hand. The sun did not penetrate here, making merely a gilt fog of the mist. As he approached within touching distance of the first tower, it seemed to Travis that the mist was curling about him; he could no longer see the archway through which he had entered the valley.

"Naye-nezyani—Slayer of Monsters—give strength to the bow arm, to the knife wrist!" Out of what long-buried memory did that ancient plea come? Travis was hardly aware of the sense of the words until he spoke them aloud. "You who wait—*shi inday to-dah ishan*—an Apache is not food for you! I am Fox of the Itca-tcudnde'yu— the Eagle People; and beside me walk *ga'ns* of power . . ."

Travis blinked and shook his head as one waking. Why had he spoken so, using words and phrases which were not part of any modern speech?

He moved on, around the base of the first tower, to find no door, no break in its surface below the second-story windows—to the next structure and the next, until he had encircled all three. If he were to enter any, he must find a way of reaching the lowest windows.

On he went to the other opening of the valley, the one which gave upon the territory of the Tatar camp. But he did not sight any of the Mongols as he hacked down a sapling, trimmed, and smoothed it into a blunt-pointed lance. His sash-belt, torn into even strips and knotted together, gave him a rope which he judged would be barely long enough for his purpose.

Then Travis made a chancy cast for the lower window of the nearest tower. On the second try the lance slipped in, and he gave a quick jerk, jamming the lance as a bar across the opening. It was a frail ladder but the best he could improvise. He climbed until the sill of the window was within reach and he could pull himself up and over.

The sill was wide, at least a twenty-four-inch span between the inner and outer surface of the tower. Travis sat there for a minute, reluctant to enter. Near the end of his dangling scarf-rope the two coyotes lay on the pavement, their heads up, their tongues lolling from their mouths, their expressions ones of detached interest.

Perhaps it was the width of the outer wall that subdued the amount of light in the room. The chamber was circular, and directly opposite him was a second window, the lowest of the matching diamond pattern. He took the four-foot drop from the sill to the floor but lingered in the light as he surveyed every inch of the room. There were no furnishings at all, but in the very center sank a well of darkness. A smooth pillar, glowing faintly, rose from its core. Travis' adjusting eyes noted how the light came in small ripples—green and purple, over a foundation shade of dark blue.

The pillar seemed rooted below and it extended up through a similar opening in the ceiling, providing the only possible exit up or down, save for climbing from window to window outside. Travis moved slowly to the well. Underfoot was a smooth surface overlaid with a velvet carpet of dust which arose in languid puffs as he walked. Here and there he sighted prints in the dust, strange triangular wedges which he thought might possibly have been made by the claws of birds. But there were no other footprints. This tower had been undisturbed for a long, long time.

He came to the well and looked down. There was dark there, dark in which the pulsations of light from the pillar shone the stronger. But that glow did not extend beyond the edge of the well through which the thick rod threaded. Even by close examination he could detect no break in the smooth surface of the pillar, nothing remotely resembling hand- or footholds. If it did serve the purpose of a staircase, there were no treads.

At last Travis put out his hand to touch the surface of the pillar. And then he jerked back—to no effect. There was no breaking contact between his fingers and an unknown material which had the sleekness of polished metal but—and the thought made him slightly queasy—the warmth and very slight give of flesh!

He summoned all his strength to pull free and could not. Not only did that hold grip him, but his other hand and arm were being drawn to join the first! Inside Travis primitive fears awoke full force, and he threw back his head, voicing a cry of panic as wild as that of a hunting beast.

An instant later, his left palm was as tight a prisoner as his right. And with both hands so held, his whole body was suddenly snapped forward, off the safe foundation of the floor, tight to the pillar.

In this position he was sucked down into the well. And while unable to free himself from the pillar, he did slip along its length easily enough. Travis shut his eyes in an involuntary protest against this weird form of capture, and a shiver ran through his body as he continued to descend.

After the first shock had subsided the Apache realized that he was not truly falling at all. Had the pillar been horizontal instead of vertical, he would have gauged its speed that of a walk. He passed through two more room enclosures; he must already be below the level of the valley floor outside. And he was still a prisoner of the pillar, now in total darkness.

His feet came down against a level surface, and he guessed he must have reached the end. Again he pulled back, arching his shoulders in a final desperate attempt at escape, and stumbled away as he was released.

He came up sideways against a wall and stood there panting. The light, which might have come from the pillar but which seemed more a part of the very air, was bright enough to reveal that he was in a corridor running into greater dark both right and left.

Travis took two strides back to the pillar, fitted his palms once again to its surface, with no result. This time his flesh did not adhere and there was no possible way for him to climb that slick pole. He could only hope that at some point the corridor would give him access to the surface. But which way to go—?

At last he chose the right-hand path and started along it, pausing every few steps to listen. But there was no sound except the soft pad of his own feet. The air was fresh enough, and he thought he could detect a faint current coming toward him from some point ahead— perhaps an exit.

Instead, he came into a room and a small gasp of astonishment was wrung out of him. The walls were blank, covered with the same ripples of blue-purple-green light which colored the pillar. Just before him was a table and behind it a bench, both carved from the native yellow-red mountain rock. And there was no exit except the doorway in which he now stood.

Travis walked to the bench. Immovable, it was placed so that whoever sat there must face the opposite wall of the chamber with the table before him. And on the table was an object Travis recognized immediately from his voyage in the alien star ship, one of the tape-readers through which the involuntary explorers had learned what little they knew of the older galactic civilization.

A reader—and beside it a box of tapes. Travis touched the edge of that box gingerly, half expecting it to crumble into nothingness. This was a place long deserted. Stone table, bench, the towers could survive through centuries of abandonment, but these other objects . . .

The substance of the reader was firm under the film of dust; there was less dust here than had been in the upper tower chamber. Hardly knowing why, Travis threw one leg over the bench and sat down behind the table, the reader before him, the box of tapes just beyond his hand.

He surveyed the walls and then looked away hurriedly.

The rippling colors caught at his eyes. He had a feeling that if he watched that ebb and flow too long, he would be captured in some subtle web of enchantment just as the Russians' machine had caught and held the Tatars. He turned his attention to the reader. It was, he believed, much like the one they had used on the ship.

This room, table, bench, had all been designed with a set purpose. And that purpose—Travis' fingers rested on the box of tapes he could not yet bring himself to open—that purpose was to use the reader, he would swear to that. Tapes so left must have had a great importance for those who left them. It was as if the whole valley was a trap to channel a stranger into this underground chamber.

Travis snapped open the box, fed the first disk into the reader, and applied his eyes to the vision tube at its apex.

The rippling walls looked just the same when he looked up once more, but the cramp in his muscles told Travis that time had passed—perhaps hours instead of minutes— since he had taken out the first disk. He cupped his hands over his eyes and tried to think clearly. There had been sheets of meaningless symbol writing, but also there had been many clear, three-dimensional pictures, accompanied by a singsong commentary in an alien tongue, seemingly voiced out of thin air. He had been stuffed with ragged bits and patches of information, to be connected only by guesses, and some wild guesses, too. But this much he did know—these towers had been built by the bald space-men, and they were highly important to that vanished stellar civilization. The information in this room, as disjointed as it had been for him, led to a treasure trove on Topaz greater than he had dreamed.

Travis swayed on the bench. To know so much and yet so little! If Ashe were only here, or some other of the project technicians! A treasure such as Pandora's box had been, peril for one who opened it and did not understand. The Apache studied the three walls of blue-purple-green in turn and with new attention. There were ways through those walls; he was fairly sure he could unlock at least one of them. But not now—certainly not now!

And there was another thing he knew: The Russians must *not* find this. Such a discovery on their part would not only mean the end of his own people on Topaz, but the end of Earth as well. This place might hold new and alien knowledge that could destroy whole nations at a time!

If he could—much as his archaeologist's training would argue against it—he would blot out this whole valley above and below ground. But while the Russians might possess a means of such destruction, the Apaches did not. No, he and his people must prevent its discovery by the enemy by doing what he had seen as necessary from the first—wiping out the Russian leaders! And that must be done before they chanced upon the tower!

Travis arose stiffly. His eyes ached, his head felt stuffed with pictures, hints, speculations. He wanted to get out, back into the open air where perhaps the clean winds of the heights would blow some of this frightening half knowledge from his benumbed mind. He lurched down the corridor, puzzled now by the problem of getting back to the window level.

Here, before him, was the pillar. Without hope, but still obeying some buried instinct, Travis again set his hands to its surface. There was a tug at his cramped arms; once more his body was sucked to the pillar. This time he was rising!

He held his breath past the first level and then relaxed. The principle of this weird form of transportation was entirely beyond his understanding, but as long as it worked in reverse he didn't care to find out. He reached the windowed chamber, but the sunlight had left it; instead, the clean cut of moon sweep lay on the dusty floor. He must have been hours in that underground place.

Travis pulled away from the embrace of the pillar. The bar of his wooden lance was still across the window and he ran for it. To catch the scouting party at the pass he must hurry. The report they would make to the clan now had to be changed radically in the face of his new discoveries. The Apaches dared not retreat southward and withdraw from the fight, leaving the Russians to use what treasure lay here.

As he hit the pavement below he looked about for the coyotes. Then he tried the mind call. But as mysteriously as they had met him in the valley, so now were they gone again. And Travis had no time to hunt for them. With a sigh, he began his race to the pass.

In the old days, Travis remembered, Apache warriors had been able to cover forty-five or fifty miles a day on foot and over rough territory. But perhaps his modern breeding had slowed him. He had been so sure he could catch up before the others were through the pass. But he stood now in the hollow where they had camped, read the sign of overturned stone and bent twig left for him, and knew they would reach the rancheria and report the decision Deklay and the others wanted before he could head them off.

Travis slogged on. He was so tired now that only the drug from the ration bars he mouthed at intervals kept him going at a dogged pace, hardly more than a swift walk. And always his mind was haunted by fragments of pictures, pictures he had seen in the reader. The big bomb had been the nightmare of his own world for so long, and what was that against the forces the bald star rovers had been able to command?

He fell beside a stream and slept. There was sunshine about him as he arose to stagger on. What day was this? How long had he sat in the tower chamber? He was not sure of time any more. He only knew that he must reach the rancheria, tell his story, somehow win over Deklay and the other reactionaries to prove the necessity for invading the north in force.

A rocky point which was a familiar landmark came into focus. He padded on, his chest heaving, his breath whistling through parched, sun-cracked lips. He did not know that his face was now a mask of driven resolution.

"Hahhhhhh—"

The cry reached his dulled ears. Travis lifted his head, saw the men before him and tried to think what that show of weapons turned toward him could mean.

A stone thudded to earth only inches before his feet, to be followed by another. He wavered to a stop.

"*Ni'ilgac—!*"

Witch? Where was a witch? Travis shook his head. There was no witch.

"*Do ne'ilka da'!*"

The old death threat, but why—for whom?

Another stone, this one hitting him in the ribs with force enough to send him reeling back and down. He tried to get up again, saw Deklay grin widely and take aim— and at last Travis realized what was happening.

Then there was a bursting pain in his head and he was falling—falling into a well of black, this time with no pillar of blue to guide him.

13

The rasp of something wet and rough, persistent against his cheek; Travis tried to turn his head to avoid the contact and was answered by a burst of pain which trailed off into a giddiness, making him fear another move, no matter how minor. He opened his eyes and saw the pointed ears, the outline of a coyote head between him and a dull gray sky, was able to recognize Nalik'ideyu.

A wetness other than that from the coyote's tongue slid down his forehead now. The dull clouds overhead had released the first heavy rain Travis had experienced since their landing on Topaz. He shivered as the chill damp of his clothes made him aware that he must have been lying out in the full force of the downpour for some time.

It was a struggle to get to his knees, but Nalik'ideyu mouthed a hold on his shirt, tugging and pulling so that somehow he crept into a hollow beneath the branches of a tree where the spouting water was lessened to a few pattering drops.

There the Apache's strength deserted him again and he could only hunch over, his bent knees against his chest, trying to endure the throbbing misery in his head, the awful floating sensation which followed any movement. Fighting against that, he tried to remember just what had happened.

The meeting with Deklay and at least four or five others . . . then the Apache accusation of witchcraft, a serious thing in the old days. Old days! To Deklay and his fellows, these *were* the old days! And the threat that Deklay or some other had shouted at him—*"Do ne'ilka da'"*—meant literally: "It won't dawn for you—death!"

Stones, the last thing Travis remembered were the stones. Slowly his hands went out to explore his body. There was more than one bruised area on his shoulder and ribs, even on his thighs. He must still have been a target after he had fallen under the stone which had knocked him unconscious. Stoned . . . outlawed! But why? Surely Deklay's hostility could not have swept Buck, Jil-Lee, Tsoay, even Nolan, into agreeing to that? Now he could not think straight.

Travis because aware of warmth, not only of warmth and the soft touch of a furred body by his side, but a comforting communication of mind, a feeling he had no words to describe adequately. Nalik'ideyu was sitting crowded against him, her nose thrust up to rest on his shoulder. She breathed in soft puffs which stirred the loose locks of his rain-damp hair. And now he flung one arm about her, a gesture which brought a whisper of answering whine.

He was past wondering about the actions of the coyotes, only supremely thankful for Nalik'ideyu's present companionship. And a moment later when her mate squeezed under the low loop of a branch and joined them in this natural wickiup, Travis held out his other hand, drew it lovingly across Naginlta's wet hide.

"Now what?" he asked aloud. Deklay could only have taken such a drastic action with the majority of the clan solidly behind him. It could well be that this reactionary was the new chief, this act of Travis' expulsion merely adding to Deklay's growing prestige.

The shivering which had begun when Travis recovered consciousness, still shook him at intervals. Back on Earth, like all the others in the team, he had had every inoculation known to the space physicians, including several experimental ones. But the cold virus could still practically immobilize a man, and this was no time to give body room to chills and fever.

Catching his breath as his movements touched to life the pain in one bruise after another, Travis peeled off his soaked clothing, rubbed his body dry with handfuls of last year's leaves culled from the thick carpet under him, knowing there was nothing he could do until the whirling in his head disappeared. So he burrowed into the leaves until only his head was uncovered, and tried to sleep, the coyotes curling up one on either side of his nest.

He dreamed but later could not remember any incident from those dreams, save a certain frustration and fear. When he awoke, again to the sound of steady rain, it was dark. He reached out—both coyotes were gone. His head was clearer and suddenly he knew what must be done. As soon as his body was strong enough, he, too, would return to instincts and customs of the past. This situation was desperate enough for him to challenge Deklay.

In the dark Travis frowned. He was slightly taller, and three or four years younger than his enemy. But Deklay had the advantage in a stouter build and longer reach. However, Travis was sure that in his present life Deklay had never fought a duel—Apache fashion. And an Apache duel was not a meeting anyone entered into lightly. Travis had the right to enter the rancheria and deliver such a challenge. Then Deklay must meet him or admit himself in the wrong. That part of it was simple.

But in the past such duels had just one end, a fatal one for at least one of the fighters. If Travis took this trail, he must be prepared to go the limit. And he didn't want to kill Deklay! There were too few of them here on Topaz to make any loss less than a real catastrophe. While he had no liking for Deklay, neither did he nurse any hatred. However, he must challenge the other or remain a tribal outcast; and Travis had no right to gamble with time and the future, not after what he had learned in the tower. It might be his life and skill, or Deklay's, against the blotting out of them all—and their home world into the bargain.

First, he must locate the present camp of the clan. If Nolan's arguments had counted, they would be heading south away from the pass. And to follow would draw him farther from the tower valley. Travis' battered face ached as he grinned bitterly. This was another time when a man could wish he were two people, a scout on sentry duty at the valley, the fighter heading in the opposite direction to have it out with Deklay. But since he was merely one man he would have to gamble on time, one of the riskiest bets of all.

Before dawn Nalik'ideyu returned, carrying with her a bird—or at least birds must have been somewhere in the creature's ancestry, but the present representative of its kind had only vestigial remnants of wings, its trailing feet and legs well developed and far more powerful.

Travis skinned the corpse, automatically putting aside some spine quills to feather future arrows. Then he ate slivers of dusky meat raw, throwing the bones to Nalik'ideyu.

Though he was still stiff and sore, Travis was determined to be on his way. He tried mind contact with the coyote, picturing the Apaches, notably Deklay, as sharply as he could by mental image. And her assent was clear in return. She and her mate were willing to lead him to the tribe. He gave a light sigh of relief.

As he slogged on through the depressing drizzle, the Apache wondered again why the coyotes had left him before and waited in the tower valley. What link was there between the animals of Earth and the remains of the long-ago empire of the stars? For he was certain it was not by chance that Nalik'ideyu and Naginlta had lingered in that misty place. He longed to communicate with them directly, to ask questions and be answered.

Without their aid, Travis would never have been able to track the clan. The drizzle alternated with slashing bursts of rain, torrential enough to drive the trackers to the nearest cover. Overhead the sky was either dull bronze or night black. Even the coyotes paced nose to ground, often making wide casts for the trail while Travis waited.

The rain lasted for three days and nights, filling watercourses with rapidly rising streams. Travis could only hope that the others were having the same difficulty traveling that he was, perhaps the more so since they were burdened with packs. The fact that they kept on meant that they were determined to get as far from the northern mountains as they could.

On the fourth morning the bronze of the clouds slowly thinned into the usual gold, and the sun struck across hills where mist curled like steam from a hundred bubbling pots. Travis relaxed in the welcome warmth, feeling his shirt dry on his shoulders. It was still a waterlogged terrain ahead which should continue to slow the clan. He had high expectations of catching up with them soon, and now the worst of his bruises had faded. His muscles were limber, and he had worked out his plan as best he could.

Two hours later he sat in ambush, waiting for the scout who was walking into his hands. Under the direction of the coyotes, Travis had circled the line of march, come in ahead of the clan. Now he needed an emissary to state his challenge, and the fact that the scout he was about to jump was Manulito, one of Deklay's supporters, suited Travis' purpose perfectly. He gathered his feet under him as the other came opposite, and sprang.

The rush carried Manulito off his feet and face down on the sod while Travis made the best of his advantage and pinned the wildly fighting man under him. Had it been one of the older braves he might not have been so successful, but Manulito was still a boy by Apache standards.

"Lie still!" Travis ordered. "Listen well—so you can say to Deklay the words of the Fox!"

The frenzied struggles ceased. Manulito managed to wrench his head to the left so he could see his captor. Travis loosened his grip, got to his feet. Manulito sat up, his face darkly sullen, but he did not reach for his knife.

"You will say this to Deklay: The Fox says he is a man of little sense and less courage, preferring to throw stones rather than meet knife to knife as does a warrior. If he thinks as a warrior, let him prove it—his strength against my strength—after the ways of the People!"

Some of the sullenness left Manulito's expression. He was eager, excited.

"You would duel with Deklay after the old custom?"

"I would. Say this to Deklay, openly so that all men may hear. Then Deklay must also give answer openly."

Manulito flushed at that implication concerning his leader's courage, and Travis knew that he would deliver the challenge openly. To keep his hold on the clan the latter must accept it, and there would be an audience of his people to witness the success or defeat of their new chief and his policies.

As Manulito disappeared Travis summoned the coyotes, putting full effort into getting across one message. Any tribe led by Deklay would be hostile to the mutant animals. They must go into hiding, run free in the wilderness if the gamble failed Travis. Now they withdrew into the bushes but not out of reach of his mind.

He did not have too long to wait. First came Jil-Lee, Buck, Nolan, Tsoay, Lupe—those who had been with him on the northern scout. Then the others, the warriors first, the women making a half circle behind, leaving a free space in which Deklay walked.

"I am the Fox," Travis stated. "And this one has named me witch and *natdahe*, outlaw of the mountains. Therefore do I come to name names in my turn. Hear me, People: This Deklay—he would walk among you as *'izesnantan*, a great chief—but he does not have the *go'ndi,* the holy power of a chief. For this Deklay is a fool, with a head filled by nothing but his own wishes, not caring for his clan brothers. He says he leads you into safety; I say he leads you into the worst danger any living man can imagine—even in peyote dreams! He is one twisted in his thoughts, and he would make you twisted also—"

Buck cut in sharply, hushing the murmur of the massed clan.

"These are bold words, Fox. Will you back them?"

Travis' hands were already peeling off his shirt. "I will back them," he stated between set teeth. He had known since his awakening after the stoning that this next move was the only one left for him to make. But now that the testing of his action came, he could not be certain of the outcome, of anything save that the final decision of this battle might affect more than the fate of two men. He stripped, noting that Deklay was doing the same.

Having stepped into the center of the glade, Nolan was using the point of his knife to score a deep-ridged circle there. Naked except for his moccasins, with only his knife in his hand, Travis took the two strides which put him in the circle facing Deklay. He surveyed his opponent's finely muscled body, realizing that his earlier estimate of Deklay's probable advantages was close to the mark. In sheer strength the other outmatched him. Whether Deklay was skillful with his knife was another question, one which Travis would soon be able to answer.

They circled, eyes intent upon each move, striving to weigh and measure each other's strengths and weaknesses. Knife dueling among the Pinda-lick-o-yi, Travis remembered, had once been an art close to finished swordplay, with two evenly matched fighters able to engage for a long time without seriously marking each other. But this was a far rougher and more deadly game, with none of the niceties of such a meeting.

He evaded a vicious thrust from Deklay.

"The bull charges," he laughed. "And the Fox snaps!"

By some incredible stroke of good fortune, the point of his weapon actually grazed Deklay's arm, drawing a thin, red inch-long line across the skin.

"Charge again, bull. Feel once more the Fox's teeth!"

He strove to goad Deklay into a crippling loss of temper, knowing how the other could explode into violent rage. It was dangerous, that rage, but it could also make a man blindly careless.

There was an inarticulate sound from Deklay, a dusky swelling in the man's face. He spat, as might an enraged puma, and rushed at Travis who did not quite manage to avoid the lunge, falling back with a smarting slash across the ribs.

"The bull gores!" Deklay bellowed. "Horns toss the Fox!"

He rushed again, elated by the sight of the trickling wound on Travis' side. But the slighter man slipped away.

Travis knew he must be careful in such evasions. One foot across the ridged circle and he was finished as much as if Deklay's blade had found its mark. Travis tried a thrust of his own, and his foot came down hard on a sharp pebble. Through the sole of his moccasin pain shot upward, caused him to stumble. Again the scarlet flame of a wound, down his shoulder and forearm this time.

Well, there was one trick he knew. Travis tossed the knife into the air, caught it with his left hand. Deklay was now facing a left-handed fighter and must adjust to that.

"Paw, bull, rattle your horns!" Travis cried. "The Fox still shows his teeth!"

Deklay recovered from his instant of surprise. With a cry which was indeed like the bellow of an old range bull, he rushed in to grapple, sure of his superior strength against a younger and already wounded man.

Travis ducked, one knee thumping the ground. He groped out with his right hand, caught up a handful of earth, and flung it into the dusky brown face. Again it seemed that luck was on his side. That handful could not be as blinding as sand, but some bit of the shower landed in Deklay's eye.

For a space of seconds Deklay was wide open—open for a blow which would rip him up the middle, the blow Travis could not and would not deliver.

Instead, he took the offensive recklessly, springing straight for his opponent. As the earth-grimed fingers of one hand clawed into Deklay's face, he struck with the other, not with the point of the knife but with its shaft. But Deklay, already only half conscious from the blow, had his own chance. He fell to the ground, leaving his knife behind, two inches of steel between Travis' ribs.

Somehow—he didn't know from where he drew that strength—Travis kept his feet and took one step and then another, out of the circle until the comforting brace of a tree trunk was against his bare back. Was he finished—?

He fought to nurse his rags of consciousness. Had he summoned Buck with his eyes? Or had the urgency of what he had to say reached somehow from mind to mind? The other was at his side, but Travis put out a hand to ward him off.

"Towers—" He struggled to keep his wits through the pain and billowing weakness beginning to creep through him. "Russians mustn't get to the towers! Worse than the bomb . . . end us all!"

He had a hazy glimpse of Nolan and Jil-Lee closing in about him. The desire to cough tore at him, but they had to know, to believe . . .

"Russians get to the towers—everything finished. Not only here . . . maybe back home too . . ."

Did he read comprehension on Buck's face? Would Nolan and Jil-Lee and the rest believe him? Travis could not suppress the cough any longer, and the ripping pain which followed was the worst he had ever experienced. But still he kept his feet, tried to make them understand.

"Don't let them get to the towers. Find that storehouse!"

Travis stood away from the tree, reached out to Buck his earth- and bloodstained hand. "I swear . . . truth . . . this must be done!"

He was going down, and he had a queer thought that

once he reached the ground everything would end, not only for him but also for his mission. Trying to see the faces of the men about him was like attempting to identify the people in a dream.

"Towers!" He had meant to shout it, but he could not even hear for himself that last word as he fell.

14

Travis' back was braced against blanketed packs as he steadied a piece of light-yellow bark against one bent knee scowling at the lines drawn on it in faint green.

"We are here then . . . and the ship there—" His thumb was set on one point of the crude map, forefinger on the other. Buck nodded.

"That is so. Tsoay, Eskelta, Kawaykle, they watch the trails. There is the pass, two other ways men can come on foot. But who will watch the air?"

"The Tatars say the Russians dare not bring the 'copter into the mountains. After they first landed they lost a flyer in a tricky air-current flow up there. They have only one left and won't risk it. If only they aren't reinforced before we can move!" There it was again, that constant gnawing fear of time, time shortening into a rope to strangle them all.

"You think that the knowledge of our ship will bring them into the open?"

"That—or information about the towers would be the only things important enough to pull out their experts.

They could send a controlled Tatar party to explore the ship, sure. But that wouldn't give them the technical reports they need. No, I think if they knew a wrecked Western Alliance ship was here, it would bring them—or enough of them to lessen the odds. We have to catch them in the open. Otherwise, they can hole up forever in that ship-fort of theirs."

"And just how do we let them know our ship is here? Send out another scouting party and let them be trailed back?"

"That's our last resource." Travis continued to frown at the map. Yes, it would be possible to let the Russians sight and trail an Apache party. But there was none in the clan who were expendable. Surely there was some other way of laying the trap with the wrecked ship for bait. Capture one of the Russians, let him escape again, having seen what they wanted him to see? Again a time-wasting business. And how long would they have to wait and what risks would they take to pick up a Russian prisoner?

"If the Tatars were dependable . . ." Buck was thinking aloud.

But that "if" was far too big. They could not trust the Tatars. No matter how much the Mongols wanted to aid in pulling down the Russians, as long as they could be controlled by the caller they were useless. Or were they?

"Thought of something?" Buck must have caught Travis' change of expression.

"Suppose a Tatar saw our ship and then was picked up by a Russian hunting patrol and they got the information out of him?"

"Do you think any outlaw would volunteer to let himself be picked up again? And if he did, wouldn't the Russians also be able to learn that he had been set up for the trap?"

"An escaped prisoner?" Travis suggested.

Now Buck was plainly considering the possibilities of such a scheme. And Travis' own spirits rose a little. The idea was full of holes, but it could be worked out. Suppose they capture, say, Menlik, bring him here as a prisoner, let him think they were about to kill him because of that attack back in the foothills. Then let him escape, pursue him northward to a point where he could be driven into the hands of the Russians? Very chancy, but it just might work. Travis was favoring a gamble now, since his desperate one with the duel had paid off.

The risk he had accepted then had cost him two deep wounds, one of which might have been serious if Jil-Lee's project-sponsored medical training had not been to hand. But it had also made Travis one of the clan again, with his people willing to listen to his warning concerning the tower treasury.

"The girl—the Tatar girl!"

At first Travis did not understand Buck's ejaculation.

"We get the girl," the other elaborated, "let her escape, then hunt her to where they'll pick her up. Might even imprison her in the ship to begin with."

Kaydessa? Though something within him rebelled at that selection for the leading role in their drama, Travis could see the advantage of Buck's choice. Woman-stealing was an ancient pastime among primitive cultures. The Tatars themselves had found wives that way in the past, just as the Apache raiders of old had taken captive women into their wickiups. Yes, for raiders to steal a woman would be a natural act, accepted as such by the Russians. For the same woman to endeavor to escape and be hunted by her captors also was reasonable. And for such a woman, cut off from her outlaw kin, to eventually head back toward the Russian settlement as the only hope of evading her enemies—logical all the way!

"She would have to be well frightened," Travis observed with reluctance.

"That can be done for us—"

Travis glanced at Buck with sharp annoyance. He would not allow certain games out of their common past to be played with Kaydessa. But Buck had something very different from old-time brutality in mind.

"Three days ago, while you were still flat on your back, Deklay and I went back to the ship—"

"Deklay?"

"You beat him openly, so he must restore his honor in his own sight. And the council has forbidden another duel or challenge," Buck replied. "Therefore he will continue to push for recognition in another way. And now that he has heard your story and knows we must face the Russians, not run from them, he is eager to take the war trail—too eager. So we returned to the ship to make another search for weapons—"

"There were none there before except those we had . . ."

"Nor now either. But we discovered something else." Buck paused and Travis was shaken out of his absorption with the problem at hand by a note in the other's voice. It was as if Buck had come upon something he could not summon the right words to describe.

"First," Buck continued, "there was this dead thing there, near where we found Dr. Ruthven. It was something like a man . . . but all silvery hair—"

"The ape-things! The ape-things from the other worlds! What else did you see?" Travis had dropped the map. His side gave him a painful twinge as he caught at Buck's sleeve. The bald space rovers—did they still exist here somewhere? Had they come to explore the ship built on the pattern of their own but manned by humans?

"Nothing except tracks, a lot of them, in every open cabin and hole. I think there must have been a sizable pack of the things."

"What killed the dead one?"

Buck wet his lips. "I think—fear . . ." His voice dropped a little, almost apologetically, and Travis stared.

"The ship is changed. Inside, there is something wrong. When you walk the corridors your skin crawls, you think there is something behind you. You hear things, see things from the corners of your eyes. . . . When you turn, there's nothing, nothing at all! And the higher you climb into the ship, the worse it is. I tell you, Travis, never have I felt anything like it before!"

"It was a ship of many dead," Travis reminded him. Had the age-old Apache fear of the dead been activated by the Redax into an acute phobia—to strike down such a level-headed man as Buck?

"No, at first that, too, was my thought. Then I discovered that it was worst not near that chamber where we lay our dead, but higher, in the Redax cabin. I think perhaps the machine is still running, but running in a wrong way—so that it does not awaken old memories of our ancestors now, but brings into being all the fears which have ever haunted us through the dark of the ages. I tell you, Travis, when I came out of that place Deklay was leading me by the hand as if I were a child. And he was shivering as a man who will never be warm again. There is an evil there beyond our understanding. I think that this Tatar girl, were she only to stay there a very short time, would be well frightened—so frightened that any trained scientist examining her later would know there was a mystery to be explored."

"The ape-things—could they have tried to run the Redax?" Travis wondered. To associate machines with the creatures was outwardly pure folly. But they had been discovered on two of the planets of the old civilization, and Ashe had thought that they might represent the degenerate remnants of a once intelligent species.

"That is possible. If so, they raised a storm which drove them out and killed one of them. The ship is a haunted place now."

"But for us to use the girl . . ." Travis had seen the logic in Buck's first suggestion, but now he differed. If the atmosphere of the ship was as terrifying as Buck said, to imprison Kaydessa there, even temporarily, was still wrong.

"She need not remain long. Suppose we should do this: We shall enter with her and then allow the disturbance we would feel to overcome us. We could run, leave her alone. When she left the ship, we could then take up the chase, shepherding her back to the country she knows. Within the ship we would be with her and could see she did not remain too long."

Travis could see a good prospect in that plan. There was one thing he would insist on—if Kaydessa was to be in that ship, he himself would be one of the "captors." He said as much, and Buck accepted his determination as final.

They dispatched a scouting party to infiltrate the territory to the north, to watch and wait their chance of capture. Travis strove to regain his feet, to be ready to move when the moment came.

Five days later he was able to reach the ridge beyond which lay the wrecked ship. With him were Jil-Lee, Lupe, and Manulito. They satisfied themselves that the globe had had no visitors since Buck and Deklay; there was no sign that the ape-things had returned.

"From here," Travis said, "the ship doesn't look too bad, almost as if it might be able to take off again."

"It might lift," Jil-Lee gestured to the mountaintop behind the curve of the globe—"about that far. The tubes on this side are intact."

"What would happen were the Russians to get inside and try to fly again?" Manulito wondered aloud.

Travis was struck by a sudden idea, one perhaps just as wild as the other inspirations he had had since landing on Topaz, but one to be studied and explored—not dismissed without consideration. Suppose enough power remained to lift the ship partially and then blow it up? With the Russian technicians on board at the time . . . But he was no engineer, he had no idea whether any part of the globe might or might not work again.

"They are not fools; a close look would tell them it is a wreck," Jil-Lee countered.

Travis walked on. Not too far ahead a yellow-brown shape moved out of the brush, stood stiff-legged in his path, facing the ship and growling in a harsh rumble of sound. Whatever moved or operated in that wreck was picked up by the acute sense of the coyote, even at this distance.

"On!" Travis edged around the snarling animal. With one halting step and then another, it followed him. There was a sharp warning yelp from the brush, and a second coyote head appeared. Naginlta followed Travis, but Nalik'ideyu refused to approach the grounded globe.

Travis surveyed the ship closely, trying to remember the layout of its interior. To turn the whole sphere into a trap—was it possible? How had Ashe said the Redax worked? Something about high-frequency waves stimulating certain brain and nerve centers.

What if one were shielded from those rays? That tear in the side—he himself must have climbed through that the night they crashed. And the break was not too far from the space lock. Near the lock was a storage compartment. And if it had not been jammed, or its contents crushed, they might have something. He beckoned to Jil-Lee.

"Give me a hand—up there."

"Why?"

"I want to see if the space suits are intact."

Jil-Lee regarded Travis with open bewilderment, but Manulito pushed forward. "We do not need those suits to walk here, Travis. This air we can breathe—"

"Not for the air, and not in the open." Travis advanced at a deliberate pace. "Those suits may be insulated in more ways than one—"

"Against a mixed-up Redax broadcast, you mean!" Jil-Lee exclaimed. "Yes, but you stay here, younger brother. This is a risky climb, and you are not yet strong."

Travis was forced to accede to that, waiting as Manulito and Lupe climbed up to the tear and entered. At least Buck and Deklay's experience had forewarned them and they would be prepared for the weird ghosts haunting the interior.

But when they returned, pulling between them the limp

space suit, both men were pale, the shiny sheen of sweat on their foreheads, their hands shaking. Lupe sat down on the ground before Travis.

"Evil spirits," he said, giving to this modern phenomenon the old name. "Truly ghosts and witches walk in there."

Manulito had spread the suit on the ground and was examining it with a care which spoke of familiarity.

"This is unharmed," he reported. "Ready to wear."

The suits were all tailored for size, Travis knew. And this fitted a slender, medium-sized man. It would fit him, Travis Fox. But Manulito was already unbuckling the fastenings with practiced ease.

"I shall try it out," he announced. And Travis, seeing the awkward climb to the entrance of the ship, had to agree that the first test should be carried out by someone more agile at the moment.

Sealed into the suit, with the bubble helmet locked in place, the Apache climbed back into the globe. The only form of communication with him was the rope he had tied about him, and if he went above the first level, he would have to leave that behind.

In the first few moments they saw no twitch of alarm running along the rope. After counting fifty slowly, Travis gave it a tentative jerk, to find it firmly fastened within. So Manulito had tied it there and was climbing to the control cabin.

They continued to wait with what patience they could muster. Naginlta, pacing up and down a good distance from the ship, whined at intervals, the warning echoed each time by his mate upslope.

"I don't like it—" Travis broke off when the helmeted figured appeared again at the break. Moving slowly in his cumbersome clothing, Manulito reached the ground, fumbled with the catch of his head covering and then stood, taking deep, lung-filling gulps of air.

"Well?" Travis demanded.

"I see no ghosts," Manulito said, grinning. "This is

ghost-proof!" He slapped his gloved hand against the covering over his chest. "There is also this—from what I know of these ships—some of the relays still work. I think this could be made into a trap. We could entice the Russians in and then . . ." His hand moved in a quick upward flip.

"But we don't know anything about the engines," Travis replied.

"No? Listen—you, Fox, are not the only one to remember useful knowledge." Manulito had lost his cheerful grin. "Do you think we are just the savages those big brains back at the project wished us to be? They have played a trick on us with their Redax. So, we can play a few tricks, too. Me—? I went to M.I.T., or is that one of the things you no longer remember, Fox?"

Travis swallowed hastily. He really had forgotten that fact until this very minute. From the beginning, the Apache team had been carefully selected and screened, not only for survival potential, which was their basic value to the project, but also for certain individual skills. Just as Travis' grounding in archaeology had been one advantage, so had Manulito's technical training made a valuable, though different, contribution. If at first the Redax, used without warning, had smothered that training, perhaps the effects were now fading.

"You can do something, then?" he asked eagerly.

"I can try. There is a chance to booby trap the control cabin at least. And that is where they would poke and pry. Working in this suit will be tough. How about my trying to smash up the Redax first?"

"Not until after we use it on our captive," Jil-Lee decided. "Then there would be some time before the Russians come—"

"You talk as if they *will* come," cut in Lupe. "How can you be sure?"

"We can't," Travis agreed. "But we can count on this much, judging from the past. Once they know that there is a wrecked ship here, they will be forced to explore it. They cannot afford an enemy settlement on this side of the mountains. That would be, according to their way of thinking, an eternal threat."

Jil-Lee nodded. "That is true. This is a complicated plan, yes, and one in which many things may go wrong. But it is also one which covers all the loopholes we know of."

With Lupe's aid Manulito crawled out of the suit. As he leaned it carefully against a supporting rock he said:

"I have been thinking of this treasure house in the towers. Suppose we could find new weapons there. . . ."

Travis hesitated. He still shrank from the thought of opening the secret places behind those glowing walls, to loose a new peril.

"If we took weapons from there and lost the fight . . ." He advanced his first objection and was glad to see the expression of comprehension on Jil-Lee's face.

"It would be putting the weapons straight into Russian hands," the other agreed.

"We may have to chance it before we're through," Manulito warned. "Suppose we do get some of their technicians into this trap. We may need a bigger nutcracker than we've ever seen."

With a return of that queasy feeling he had known in the tower, Travis knew Manulito was speaking sense. They might have to open Pandora's box before the end of this campaign.

15

They camped another two days near the wrecked ship while Manulito prowled the haunted corridors and cabins in his space suit, planning his booby trap. At night he drew diagrams on pieces of bark and discussed the possibility of this or that device, sometimes lapsing into technicalities his companions could not follow. But Travis was well satisfied that Manulito knew what he was doing.

On the morning of the third day Nolan slipped into their midst. He was dust-grimed, his face gaunt, the signs of hard travel plain to read. Travis handed him the nearest canteen, and they watched him drink sparingly in small sips before he spoke.

"They come . . . with the girl—"

"You had trouble?" asked Jil-Lee.

"The Tatars had moved their camp, which was only wise, since the Russians must have had a line on the other one. And they are now farther to the west. But—" he wiped his lips with the back of his hand—"also we saw your towers, Fox. And that is a place of power!"

"No signs that the Russians are prowling there?"

Nolan shook his head. "To my mind the mists there conceal the towers from aerial view. Only one coming on foot could tell them from the natural crags of the hills."

Travis relaxed. Time still granted them a margin of grace. He glanced up to see Nolan smiling faintly.

"This maiden, she is a kin to the puma of the mountains," he announced. "She has marked Tsoay with her claws until he looks like the ear-clipped yearling fresh from the branding chute—"

"She is not hurt?" Travis demanded.

This time Nolan chuckled openly. "Hurt? No, we had much to do to keep her from hurting us, younger brother. That one is truly as she claims, a daughter of wolves. And she is also keen-witted, marking a return trail all the way, though she does not know that is as we wish. Did we not pick the easiest way back for just that reason? Yes, she plans to escape."

Travis stood up. "Let us finish this quickly!" His voice came out on a rough note. This plan had never had his full approval. Now he found it less and less easy to think about taking Kaydessa into the ship, allowing the emotional torment lurking there to work upon her. Yet he knew that the girl would not be hurt, and he had made sure he would be beside her within the globe, sharing with her the horror of the unseen.

A rattling of gravel down the narrow valley opening gave warning to those by the campfire. Manulito had already stowed the space suit in hiding. To Kaydessa they must have seemed reverted entirely to savagery.

Tsoay came first, an angry raking of four parallel scratches down his left cheek. And behind him Buck and Eskelta shoved the prisoner, urging her on with a show of roughness which did not descend to actual brutality. Her long braids had shaken loose, and a sleeve was torn, leaving one slender arm bare. But none of the fighting spirit had left her.

They thrust her out into the circle of waiting men and she planted her feet firmly apart, glaring at them all indiscriminately until she sighted Travis. Then her anger became hotter and more deadly.

"Pig! Rooter in the dirt! Diseased camel—" she shouted at him in English and then reverted to her own tongue, her voice riding up and down the scale. Her hands were tied behind her back, but there were no bonds on her tongue.

"This is one who can speak thunders, and shoot lightnings from her mouth," Buck commented in Apache. "Put her well away from the wood, lest she set it aflame."

Tsoay held his hands over his ears. "She can deafen a man when she cannot set her mark on him otherwise. Let us speedily get rid of her."

For all their jeering comments, their eyes held respect. Often in the past a defiant captive who stood up boldly to his captors had received more consideration than usual from Apache warriors; courage was a quality they prized. A Pinda-lick-o-yi such as Tom Jeffords, who rode into Cochise's camp and sat in the midst of his sworn enemies for a parley, won the friendship of the very chief he had been fighting. Kaydessa had more influence with her captors than she could dream of holding.

Now it was time for Travis to play his part. He caught the girl's shoulders and pushed her before him toward the wreck.

Some of the spirit seemed to have left her thin, tense body, and she went without any more fight. Only when they came into full view of the ship did she falter. Travis heard her breathe a gasp of surprise.

As they had planned, four of the Apaches—Jil-Lee, Tsoay, Nolan and Buck—fanned out toward the heights about the ship. Manulito had already gone to cover, to don the space suit and prepare for any accident.

Resolutely Travis continued to propel Kaydessa ahead. At the moment he did not know which was worse, to enter the ship expecting the fear to strike, or to meet it unprepared. He was ready to refuse to enter, not to allow the girl, sullenly plodding on under his compulsion, to face that unseen but potent danger.

Only the memory of the towers and the threat of the Russians finding and exploiting the treasure there kept him going. Eskelta went first, climbing to the tear. Travis cut the ropes binding Kaydessa's wrists and gave her a slight slap between the shoulders.

"Climb, woman!" His anxiety made that a harsh order and she climbed.

Eskelta was inside now, heading for the cabin which might reasonably be selected as a prison. They planned to get the girl as far as that point and then stage their act of being overcome by fear, allowing her to escape.

Stage an act? Travis was not two feet along that corridor before he knew that there would be little acting needed on his part. The thing which pervaded the ship did not attack sharply, rather it seeped into his mind and body as if he drew in poison with every breath, sent it racing along his veins with every beat of a laboring heart. Yet he could not put any name to his feelings, except an awful, weakening fear which weighted him heavier with every step he took.

Kaydessa screamed. Not this time in rage, but with such fervor that Travis lost his hold, staggered back to the wall. She whirled about, her face contorted, and sprang at him.

It was indeed like trying to fight a wildcat and after the first second or two he was hard put to protect his eyes, his face, his side, without injuring her in return. She scrambled over him, running for the break in the wall, and disappeared. Travis gasped, and started to crawl for the break. Eskelta loomed over him, pulled him up in haste.

They reached the opening but did not climb through. Travis was uncertain as to whether he could make that descent yet, and Eskelta was obeying orders in not venturing out too soon.

Below, the ground was bare. There was no sign of the Apaches, though they were in hiding there—and none of Kaydessa. Travis was amazed that she had vanished so quickly.

Still uneasy from the emanation within, they perched within the shadow of the break until Travis thought that the fugitive had a good five-minute start. Then he nodded a signal to Eskelta.

By the time they reached ground level Travis felt a warm wetness spreading under his shielding palm and he knew the wound had opened. He spoke a word or two in hot protest against that mishap, knowing it would keep him from the trail. Kaydessa must be covered all the way back across the pass, not only to be shepherded away from her people and toward the plains where she could be picked up by a Russian patrol, but also to keep her from danger. And he had planned from the first to be one of those shepherds.

Now he was about as much use as a trail-lame pony. However, he could send deputies. He thought out his call, and Nalik'ideyu's head appeared in a frame of bush.

"Go, both of you and run with her! Guard—!" He said the words in a whisper, thought them with a fierce intensity as he centered his gaze on the yellow eyes in the pointed coyote face. There was a feeling of assent, and then the animal was gone. Travis sighed.

The Apache scouts were subtle and alert, but the coyotes could far outdo any man. With Nalik'ideyu and Naginlta flanking her flight, Kaydessa would be well guarded. She would probably never see her guards or know that they were running protection for her.

"That was a good move," Jil-Lee said, coming out of concealment. "But what have you done to yourself?" He stepped closer, pulling Travis' hand away from his side. By the time Lupe came to report, Travis was again wound in a strapping bandage pulled tightly about his lower ribs, and reconciled to the fact that any trailing he would do must be well to the rear of the first party.

"The towers," he said to Jil-Lee. "If our plan works, we can catch part of the Russians here. But we still have their ship to take, and for that we need help which we may find at the towers. Or at least we can be on guard there if they return with Kaydessa on that path."

Lupe dropped down lightly from an upper ledge. He was grinning.

"That woman is one who thinks. She runs from the ship first as a rabbit with a wolf at her heels. Then she begins to think. She climbs—" He lifted one finger to the slope behind them. "She goes behind a rock to watch under cover. When Fox comes from the ship with Eskelta, again she climbs. Buck lets himself be seen, so she moves east, as we wish—"

"And now?" questioned Travis.

"She is keeping to the high ways; almost she thinks like one of the People on the war trail. Nolan believes she will hole up for the night somewhere above. He will make sure."

Travis licked his lips. "She has no food or water."

Jil-Lee's lips shaped a smile. "They will see that she comes upon both as if by chance. We have planned all of this, as you know, younger brother."

That was true. Travis knew that Kaydessa would be guided without her knowledge by the "accidental" appearance now and then of some pursuer—just enough to push her along.

"Then, too, she is now armed," Jil-Lee added.

"How?" demanded Travis.

"Look to your own belt, younger brother. Where is your knife?"

Startled, Travis glanced down. His sheath was empty, and he had not needed that blade since he had drawn it to cut meat at the morning meal. Lupe laughed.

"She had steel in her hand when she came out of that ghost ship."

"Took it from me while we struggled!" Travis was openly surprised. He had considered the frenzy displayed by the Tatar girl as an outburst of almost mindless terror. Yet Kaydessa had had wit enough to take his knife! Could this be another case where one race was less affected by a mind machine than the other? Just as the Apaches had not been governed by the Russian caller, so the Tatars might not be as sensitive to the Redax.

"She is a strong one, that woman—one worth many ponies." Eskelta reverted to the old measure of a wife's value.

"That is true!" Travis agreed emphatically and then was annoyed at the broadening of Jil-Lee's smile. Abruptly he changed the subject.

"Manulito is setting the booby trap in the ship."

"That is well. He and Eskelta will remain here, and you with them."

"Not so! We must go to the towers—" Travis protested.

"I thought," Jil-Lee cut in, "that you believed the weapons of the old ones too dangerous for us to use."

"Maybe they will be forced into our hands. But we must be sure the towers are not entered by the Russians on their way here."

"That is reasonable. But for you, younger brother, no trailing today, perhaps not tomorrow. If that wound opens again, you might have much bad trouble."

Travis was forced to accept that, in spite of his worry and impatience. And the next day when he did move on he had only the report that Kaydessa had sheltered beside a pool for the night and was doggedly moving back across the mountains.

Three days later Travis, Jil-Lee, and Buck came into the tower valley. Kaydessa was in the northern foothills, twice turned back from the west and the freedom of the outlaws by the Apache scouts. And only half an hour before, Tsoay had reported by mirror what should have been welcome news: the Russian helicopter was cruising as it had on the day they watched the hunters enter the uplands. There was an excellent chance of the fugitive's being sighted and picked up soon.

Tsoay had also spotted a party of three Tatars watching the helicopter. But after one wide sweep of the flyer they had taken to their ponies and ridden away at the fastest pace their mounts could manage in this rough territory.

On a stretch of smooth earth Buck scratched a trail,

and they studied it. The Russians would have to follow this route to seek the wrecked ship—a route covered by Apache sentinels. And following the chain of communication the result of the trap would be reported to the party at the towers.

The waiting was the most difficult; too many imponderables did not allow for unemotional thinking. Travis was down to the last shred of patience when word came on the second morning at the hidden valley that Kaydessa had been picked up by a Russian patrol—drawn out to meet them by the caller.

"Now—the tower weapons!" Buck answered the report with an imperative order to Travis. And the other knew he could no longer postpone the inevitable. And only by action could he blot out the haunting mental picture of Kaydessa once more drawn into the bondage she so hated.

Flanked by Jil-Lee and Buck, he climbed back through the tower window and faced the glowing pillar.

He crossed the room, put out both hands to the sleek pole, uncertain if the weird transport would work again. He heard the sharp gasp from the others as his body was sucked against the pillar and carried downward through the well. Buck followed him, and Jil-lee came last. Then Travis led the way along the underground corridor to the room with the table and the reader.

He sat down on the bench, fumbled with the pile of tape disks, knowing that the other two were watching him with almost hostile intentness. He snapped a disk into the reader, hoping he could correctly interpret the directions it gave.

He looked up at the wall before him. Three . . . four steps, the correct move—and then an unlocking . . .

"You know?" Buck demanded.

"I can guess—"

"Well?" Jil-Lee moved to the table. "What do we do?"

"This—" Travis came from behind the table, walked to the wall. He put out both hands, flattened his palms against the green-blue-purple surface and slid them slowly along. Under his touch, the material of the wall was cool and hard, unlike the live feel the pillar had. Cool until—

One palm, held at arm's length had found the right spot. He slid the other hand along in the opposite direction until his arms were level with his shoulders. His fingers were able now to press on those points of warmth. Travis tensed and pushed hard with all ten fingers.

16

At first, as one second and then two passed and there was no response to the pressure, Travis thought he had mistaken the reading of the tape. Then, directly before his eyes, a dark line cut vertically down the wall. He applied more pressure until his fingers were half numb with effort. The line widened slowly. Finally he faced a slit some eight feet in height, a little more than two in width, and there the opening remained.

Light beyond, a cold, gray gleam—like that of a cloudy winter day on Earth—and with it the chill of air out of some arctic wasteland. Favoring his still bandaged side, Travis scraped through the door ahead of the others, and came into the place of gray cold.

"Wauggh!" Travis heard that exclamation from Jil-Lee, could have echoed it himself except that he was too astounded by what he had seen to say anything at all.

The light came from a grid of bars set far above their heads into the native rock which roofed this storehouse, for storehouse it was. There were orderly lines of boxes, some large enough to contain a tank, others no bigger then a man's fist. Symbols in the same blue-green-purple lights of the outer wall shone from their sides.

"What—?" Buck began one question and then changed it to another: "Where do we begin to look?"

"Toward the far end." Travis started down the center aisle between rows of the massed spoils of another time and world—or worlds. The same tape which had given him the clue to the unlocking of the door, emphasized the importance of something stored at the far end, an object or objects which must be used first. He had wondered about that tape. A sensation of urgency, almost of despair, had come through the gabble of alien words, the quick sequence of diagrams and pictures. The message might have been taped under a threat of some great peril.

There was no dust on the rows of boxes or on the floor underfoot. A current of cold, fresh air blew at intervals down the length of the huge chamber. They could not see the next aisle across the barriers of stored goods, but the only noise was a whisper and the faint sounds of their own feet. They came out into an open space backed by the wall, and Travis saw what had been so important.

"No!" His protest was involuntary, but his denial loud enough to echo.

Six—six of them—tall, narrow cases set upright against the wall; and from their depths, five pairs of dark eyes staring back at him in cold measurement. These were the men of the ships—the men Menlik had dreamed of—their bald white heads, their thin bodies with the skin-tight covering of the familiar blue-green-purple. Five of them were here, alive—watching . . . waiting . . .

Five men—and six boxes. That small fact broke the spell in which those eyes held Travis. He looked again at the sixth box to his right. Expecting to meet another pair of eyes this time, he was disconcerted to face only emptiness. Then, as his gaze traveled downward, he saw what lay on the floor there—a skull, a tangle of bones, tattered material cobwebbed into dusty rags by time. Whatever had preserved five of the star men intact, had failed the sixth of their company.

"They are alive!" Jil-Lee whispered.

"I do not think so," Buck answered. Travis took another step, reached out to touch the transparent front of the nearest coffin case. There was no change in the eyes of the alien who stood within, no indication that if the Apaches could see him, he would be able to return their interest. The five stares which had bemused the visitors at first, did not break to follow their movements.

But Travis knew! Whether it was some message on the tape which the sight of the sleepers made clear, or whether some residue of the driving purpose which had set them there now reached his mind, was immaterial. He knew the purpose of this room and its contents, why it had been made and the reason its six guardians had been left as prisoners—and what they wanted from anyone coming after them.

"They sleep," he said softly.

"Sleep?" Buck caught him up.

"They sleep in something like deep freeze."

"Do you mean they can be brought to life again!" Jil-Lee cried.

"Maybe not now—it must be too long—but they were meant to wait out a period and be restored.

"How do you know that?" Buck asked.

"I don't know for certain, but I think I understand a little. Something happened a long time ago. Maybe it was a war, a war between whole star systems, bigger and worse than anything we can imagine. I think this planet was an outpost, and when the supply ships didn't come any more, when they knew they might be cut off for some length of time, they closed down. Stacked their supplies and machines here and then went to sleep to wait for their rescuers. . . ."

"For rescuers who never came," Jil-Lee said softly. "And there is a chance they could be revived even now?"

Travis shivered. "Not one I would want to take."

"No," Buck's tone was somber, "that I agree to, younger brother. These are not men as we know them, and I do not think they would be good *dalaanbiyat'i*—allies. They had *go'ndi* in plenty, these star men, but it is not the power of the People. No one but a madman or a fool would try to disturb this sleep of theirs."

"The truth you speak," Jil-Lee agreed. "But where in this," he turned his shoulder to the sleeping star men and looked back at the filled chamber—"do we find anything which will serve us here and now?"

Again Travis had only the scrappiest information to draw upon. "Spread out," he told them. "Look for the marking of a circle surrounding four dots set in a diamond pattern."

They went, but Travis lingered for a moment to look once more into the bleak and bitter eyes of the star men. How many planet years ago had they sealed themselves into those boxes? A thousand, ten thousand? Their empire was long gone, yet here was an outpost still waiting to be revived to carry on its mysterious duties. It was as if in Saxon-invaded Britain long ago a Roman garrison had been frozen to await the return of the legions. Buck was right; there was no common ground today between humans and these unknowns. They must continue to sleep undisturbed.

Yet when Travis also turned away and went back down the aisle, he was still aware of a persistent pull on him to return. It was as though those eyes had set locking cords to will him back to release the sleepers. He was glad to turn a corner, to know that they could no longer watch him plunder their treasury.

"Here!" That was Buck's voice, but it echoed so oddly across the big chamber that Travis had difficulty in deciding what part of the warehouse it was coming from. And Buck had to call several times before Travis and Jil-Lee joined him.

There was the circle-dot-diamond symbol shining on the side of a case. They worked it out of the pile, setting it in the open. Travis knelt to run his hands along the top. The container was an unknown alloy, tough, unmarked by the years—perhaps indestructible.

Again his fingers located what his eyes could not detect—the impressions on the edge, oddly shaped impressions into which his finger tips did not fit too comfortably. He pressed, bearing down with the full strength of his arms and shoulders, and then lifted up the lid.

The Apaches looked into a set of compartments, each holding an object with a barrel, a hand grip, a general resemblance to the sidearms of their own world and time, but sufficiently different to point up the essential strangeness. With infinite care Travis worked one out of the vise-support which held it. The weapon was light in weight, lighter than any automatic he had ever held. Its barrel was long, a good eighteen inches—the grip alien in shape so that it didn't fit comfortably into his hand, the trigger nonexistent, but in its place a button on the lower part of the barrel which could be covered by an outstretched finger.

"What does it do?" asked Buck practically.

"I'm not sure. But it is important enough to have a special mention on the tape." Travis passed the weapon along to Buck and worked another loose from its holder.

"No way of loading I can see," Buck said, examining the weapon with care and caution.

"I don't think it fires a solid projectile," Travis replied. "We'll have to test them outside to find out just what we do have."

The Apaches took only three of the weapons, closing the box before they left. And as they wriggled back through the crack door, Travis was visited again by that odd flash of compelling, almost possessive power he had experienced when they had lain in ambush for the Russian hunting party. He took a step or two forward until he was able to catch the edge of the reading table and steady himself against it.

"What is the matter?" Both Buck and Jil-Lee were

watching him; apparently neither had felt that sensation. Travis did not reply for a second. He was free of it now. But he was sure of its source; it had not been any backlash of the Russian caller! It was rooted here—a compulsion triggered to make the original intentions of the outpost obeyed, a last drag from the sleepers. This place had been set up with a single purpose: to protect and preserve the ancient rulers of Topaz. And perhaps the very presence here of the intruding humans had released a force, started an unseen installation.

Now Travis answered simply: "They want out. . . ."

Jil-Lee glanced back at the slit door, but Buck still watched Travis.

"They call?" he asked.

"In a way," Travis admitted. But the compulsion had already ebbed; he was free. "It is gone now."

"This is not a good place," Buck observed somberly. "We touch that which should not be held by men of our earth." He held out the weapon.

"Did not the People take up the rifles of the Pinda-lick-o-yi for their defense when it was necessary?" Jil-Lee demanded. "We do what we must. After seeing that," his chin indicated the slit and what lay behind it—"do you wish the Russians to forage here?"

"Still," Buck's words came slowly, "this is a choice between two evils, rather than between an evil and a good—"

"Then let us see how powerful this evil is!" Jil-Lee headed for the corridor leading to the pillar.

It was late afternoon when they made their way through the swirling mists of the valley under the archway giving on the former site of the outlaw Tatar camp. Travis sighted the long barrel of the weapon at a small bush backed by a boulder, and he pressed the firing button. There was no way of knowing whether the weapon was loaded except to try it.

The result of his action was quick—quick and terrifying.

There was no sound, no sign of any projectile . . . laser beam . . . or whatever might have issued in answer to his finger movement. But the bush—the bush was no more!

A black smear made a ragged outline of the extinguished branches and leaves on the rock which had stood behind. The earth might still enclose roots under a thin coating of ash, but the bush was gone!

"The breath of Naye'nezyani—powerful beyond belief!" Buck broke the horrified silence first. "In truth evil is here!"

Jil-Lee raised his gun—if gun it could be called—aimed at the rock with the bush silhouette plain to see and fired.

This time they were able to witness disintegration in progress, the crumble of the stone as if its substance was no more than sand lapped by river water. A pile of blackened rubble remained—nothing more.

"To use this on a living thing?" Buck protested, horror basing the doubt in his voice.

"We do not use it against living things," Travis promised, "but against the ship of the Russians—to cut that to pieces. This will open the shell of the turtle and let us at its meat."

Jil-Lee nodded. "Those are true words. But now I agree with your fears of this place, Travis. This is a devil thing and must not be allowed to fall into the hands of those who—"

"Will use it more freely than we plan to?" Buck wanted to know. "We reserve to ourselves that right because we hold our motives higher? To think that way is also a crooked trail. We will use this means because we must, but afterward . . ."

Afterward that warehouse must be closed, the tapes giving the entrance clue destroyed. One part of Travis fought that decision, right though he knew it to be. The towers were the menace he had believed. And what was more discouraging than the risk they now ran, was the belief that the treasure was a poison which could not be destroyed but which might spread from Topaz to Earth.

Suppose the Western Alliance had discovered that storehouse and explored its riches, would they have been any less eager to exploit them? As Buck had pointed out, one's own ideals could well supply reasons for violence. In the past Earth had been racked by wars of religion, one fanatically held opinion opposed to another. There was no righteousness in such struggles, only fatal ends. The Russians had no right to this new knowledge—but neither did they. It must be locked against the meddling of fools and zealots.

"Taboo—" Buck spoke that word with an emphasis they could appreciate. Knowledge must be set behind the invisible barriers of taboo, and that could work.

"These three—no more—we found no other weapons!" Jil-Lee added a warning suggestion.

"No others," Buck agreed and Travis echoed, adding:

"We found tombs of the space people, and these were left with them. Because of our great need we borrowed them, but they must be returned to the dead or trouble will follow. And they may only be used against the fortress of the Russians by us, who first found them and have taken unto ourselves the wrath of disturbed spirits."

"Well thought! That is an answer to give the People. The towers are the tombs of dead ones. When we return these they shall be taboo. We are agreed?" Buck asked.

"We are agreed!"

Buck tried his weapon on a sapling, saw it vanish into nothingness. None of the Apaches wanted to carry the strange guns against their bodies; the power made them objects of fear, rather than arms to delight a warrior. And when they returned to their temporary camp, they laid all three on a blanket and covered them up. But they could not cover up the memories of what had happened to bush, rock, and tree.

"If such are their small weapons," Buck observed that evening, "then what kind of things did they have to balance our heavy armament? Perhaps they were able to burn up worlds!"

"That may be what happened elsewhere," Travis replied. "We do not know what put an end to their empire. The capital-planet we found on the first voyage had not been destroyed, but it had been evacuated in haste. One building had not even been stripped of its furnishings." He remembered the battle he had fought there, he and Ross Murdock and the winged native, standing up to an attack of the ape-things while the winged warrior had used his physical advantage to fly above and bomb the enemies with boxes snatched from the piles. . . .

"And here they went to sleep in order to wait out some danger—time or disaster—they did not believe would be permanent," Buck mused.

Travis thought he would flee from the eyes of the sleepers throughout his dreams that night, but on the contrary he slept heavily, finding it hard to rouse when Jil-Lee awakened him for his watch. But he was alert when he saw a four-footed shape flit out of the shadows, drink water from the stream, and shake itself vigorously in a spray of drops.

"Naginlta!" he greeted the coyote. Trouble? He could have shouted that question, but he put a tight rein on his impatience and strove to communicate in the only method possible.

No, what the coyote had come to report was not trouble but the fact that the one he had been set to guard was headed back into the mountains, though others came with her—four others. Nalik'ideyu still watched their camp. Her mate had come for further orders.

Travis squatted before the animal, cupped the coyote's jowls between his palms. Naginlta suffered his touch with only a small whine of uneasiness. With all his power of mental suggestion, Travis strove to reach the keen brain served by the yellow eyes looking into his.

The others with Kaydessa were to be led on, taken to the ship. But Kaydessa must not suffer harm. When they reached a spot near-by—Travis thought of a certain rock beyond the pass—then one of the coyotes was to go ahead to the ship. Let the Apaches there know . . .

Manulito and Eskelta should also be warned by the sentry along the peaks, but additional alerting would not go amiss. Those four with Kaydessa—they must reach the trap!

"What was that?" Buck rolled out of his blanket.

"Naginlta—" The coyote sped back into the dark again. "The Russians have taken the bait, a party of at least four with Kaydessa are moving into the foothills, heading south."

But the enemy party was not the only one on the move. In the light of day a sentry's mirror from a point in the peaks sent another warning down to their camp.

Out in their mountain meadows the Tatar outlaws were on horseback, moving toward the entrance of the tower valley. Buck knelt by the blanket covering the alien weapons.

"Now what?"

"We'll have to stop them," Travis replied, but he had no idea of just how they would halt those determined Mongol horsemen.

17

There were ten of them riding on small, wiry steppe ponies—men and women both, and well armed. Travis recalled it was the custom of the Horde that the women fought as warriors when necessary. Menlik—there was no mistaking the flapping robe of their leader. And they were singing! The rider behind the shaman thumped with violent energy a drum fastened beside his saddle horn, its heavy boom, boom the same call the Apache had heard before. The Mongols were working themselves into the mood for some desperate effort, Travis deduced. And if they were too deeply under the Russian spell, there would be no arguing with them. He could wait no longer.

The Apache swung down from a ledge near the valley gate, moved into the open and stood waiting, the alien weapon resting across his forearm. If necessary, he intended to give a demonstration with it for an object lesson.

"Dar-u-gar!" The war cry which had once awakened fear across a quarter of Earth. Thin here, and from only a few throats, but just as menacing.

Two of the horsemen aimed lances, preparing to ride him down. Travis sighted a tree midway between them and pressed the firing button. This time there was a flash, a flicker of light, to mark the disappearance of a living thing.

One of the lancers' ponies reared, squealed in fear. The other kept on his course.

"Menlik!" Travis shouted. "Hold up your man! I do not want to kill!"

The shaman called out, but the lancer was already level with the vanished tree, his head half turned on his shoulders to witness the blackened earth where it had stood. Then he dropped his lance, sawed on the reins. A rifle bullet might not have halted his charge, unless it killed or wounded, but what he had just seen was a thing beyond his understanding.

The tribesmen sat their horses, facing Travis, watching him with the feral eyes of the wolves they claimed as forefathers, wolves that possessed the cunning of the wild, cunning enough not to rush breakneck into unknown danger.

Travis walked forward. "Menlik, I would talk—"

There was an outburst from the horsemen, protests from Hulagur and one or two of the others. But the shaman urged his mount into a walking pace toward the Apache until they stood only a few feet from each other—the warrior of the steppes and the Horde facing the warrior of the desert and the People.

"You have taken a woman from our yurts," Menlik said, but his eyes were more on the alien gun than on the man who held it. "Brave are you to come again into our land. He who sets foot in the stirrup must mount into the saddle; he who draws blade free of the scabbard must be prepared to use it."

"The Horde is not here—I see only a handful of people," Travis replied. "Does Menlik propose to go up against the Apaches so? Yet there are those who are his greater enemies."

"A stealer of women is not such a one as needs a regiment to face him."

Suddenly Travis was impatient of the ceremonious talking; there was so little time.

"Listen, and listen well, Shaman!" He spoke curtly now. "I have not got your woman. She is already crossing the mountains southward," he pointed with his chin—"leading the Russians into a trap."

Would Menlik believe him? There was no need, Travis decided, to tell him now that Kaydessa's part in this affair was involuntary.

"And you?" The shaman asked the question the Apache had hoped to hear.

"We," Travis emphasized that, "march now against those hiding behind in their ship out there." He indicated the northern plains.

Menlik raised his head, surveying the land about them with disbelieving, contemptuous appraisal.

"You are chief then of an army, an army equipped with magic to overcome machines?"

"One needs no army when he carries this." For the second time Travis displayed the power of the weapon he carried, this time cutting into shifting rubble an outcrop of cliff wall. Menlik's expression did not change, though his eyes narrowed.

The shaman signaled his small company, and they dismounted. Travis was heartened by this sign that Menlik was willing to talk. The Apache made a similar gesture, and Jil-Lee and Buck, their own weapons well in sight, came out to back him. Travis knew that the Tatar had no way of knowing that the three were alone; he well might have believed an unseen troop of Apaches were near-by and so armed.

"You would talk—then talk!" Menlik ordered.

This time Travis outlined events with an absence of word embroidery. "Kaydessa leads the Russians into a trap we have set beyond the peaks—four of them ride with her. How many now remain in the ship near the settlement?"

"There are at least two in the flyer, perhaps eight more in the ship. But there is no getting at them in there."

"No?" Travis laughed softly, shifted the weapon on his arm. "Do you not think that this will crack the shell of that nut so that we can get at the meat?"

Menlik's eyes flickered to the left, to the tree which was no longer a tree but a thin deposit of ash on seared ground.

"They can control us with the caller as they did before. If we go up against them, then we are once more gathered into their net—before we reach their ship."

"That is true for you of the Horde; it does not affect the People," Travis returned. "And suppose we burn out their machines? Then will you not be free?"

"To burn up a tree? Lightning from the skies can do that."

"Can lightning," Buck asked softly, "also make rock as sand of the river?"

Menlik's eyes turned to the second example of the alien weapon's power.

"Give us proof that this will act against their machines!"

"What proof, Shaman?" asked Jil-Lee. "Shall we burn down a mountain that you may believe? This is now a matter of time."

Travis had a sudden inspiration. "You say that the 'copter is out. Suppose we use that as a target?"

"That—that can sweep the flyer from the sky?" Menlik's disbelief was open.

Travis wondered if he had gone too far. But they needed to rid themselves of that spying craft before they dared to move out into the plain. And to use the destruction of the helicopter as an example, would be the best proof he could give of the invincibility of the new Apache arms.

"Under the right conditions," he replied stoutly, "yes."

"And those conditions?" Menlik demanded.

"That it must be brought within range. Say, below the level of a neighboring peak where a man may lie in wait to fire."

Silent Apaches faced silent Mongols, and Travis had a chance to taste what might be defeat. But the helicopter must be taken before they advanced toward the ship and the settlement.

"And, maker of traps, how do you intend to bait this one?" Menlik's question was an open challenge.

"You know these Russians better than we," Travis counterattacked. "How would you bait it, Son of the Blue Wolf?"

"You say Kaydessa is leading the Russians south; we have but your word for that," Menlik replied. "Though how it would profit you to lie on such a matter—" He shrugged. "If you do speak the truth, then the 'copter will circle about the foothills where they entered."

"And what would bring the pilot nosing farther in?" the Apache asked.

Menlik shrugged again. "Any manner of things. The Russians have never ventured too far south; they are suspicious of the heights—with good cause." His fingers, near the hilt of his tulwar, twitched. "Anything which might suggest that their party is in difficulty would bring them in for a closer look—"

"Say a fire, with much smoke?" Jil-Lee suggested.

Menlik spoke over his shoulder to his own party. There was a babble of answer, two or three of the men raising their voices above those of their companions.

"If set in the right direction, yes," the shaman conceded. "When do you plan to move, Apaches?"

"At once!"

But they did not have wings, and the cross-country march they had to make was a rough journey on foot. Travis' "at once" stretched into night hours filled with scrambling over rocks, and an early morning of preparations, with always the threat that the helicopter might not return to fly its circling mission over the scene of operations. All they had was Menlik's assurance that while any party of the Russian overlords was away from their well-defended base, the flyer did just that.

"Might be relaying messages on from a walkie-talkie or something like that," Buck commented.

"They should reach our ship in two days . . . three at the most . . . if they are pushing." Travis said thoughtfully. "It would be a help—if that flyer is a link in any com unit—to destroy it before its crew picks up and relays any report of what happens back there."

Jil-Lee grunted. He was surveying the heights above the pocket in which Menlik and two of the Mongols were piling brush. "There . . . there . . . and there . . ." The Apache's chin made three juts. "If the pilot swoops for a quick look, our cross fire will take out his blades."

They held a last conference with Menlik and then climbed to the perches Jil-Lee had selected. Sentries on lookout reported by mirror flash that Tsoay, Deklay, Lupe, and Nolan were now on the move to join the other three Apaches. If and when Manulito's trap closed its jaws on the Russians at the western ship, the news would pass and the Apaches would move out to storm the enemy fort on the prairie. And should they blast any caller the helicopter might carry, Menlik and his riders would accompany them.

There it was, just as Menlik had foretold: The wasp from the open country was flying into the hills. Menlik, on his knees, struck flint to steel, sparking the fire they hoped would draw the pilot to a closer investigation.

The brush caught, and smoke, thick and white, came first in separate puffs and then gathered into a murky pillar to form a signal no one could overlook. In Travis' hands the grip of the gun was slippery. He rested the end of the barrel on the rock, curbing his rising tension as best he could.

To escape any caller on the flyer, the Tatars had remained in the valley below the Apaches' lookout. And as the helicopter circled in, Travis sighted two men in its cockpit, one wearing a helmet identical to the one they had seen on the Russian hunter days ago. The Russians' long undisputed sway over the Mongol forces would make them overconfident. Travis thought that even if they sighted one of the waiting Apaches, they would not take warning until too late.

Menlik's brush fire was performing well and the flyer was heading straight for it. The machine buzzed the smoke once, too high for the Apaches to trust raying its blades. Then the pilot came back in a lower sweep which carried him only yards above the smoldering brush, on a level with the snipers.

Travis pressed the button on the barrel, his target the fast-whirling blades. Momentum carried the helicopter on, but at least one of the marksmen, if not all three, had scored. The machine plowed through the smoke to crack up beyond.

Was their caller working, bringing in the Mongols to aid the Russians trapped in the wreck?

Travis watched Menlik make his way toward the machine, reach the cracked cover of the cockpit. But in the shaman's hand was a bare blade on which the sun glinted. The Mongol wrenched open the sprung door, thrust inward with the tulwar, and the howl of triumph he voiced was as wordless and wild as a wolf's.

More Mongols flooding down . . . Hulagur . . . a woman . . . centering on the helicopter. This time a spear plunged into the interior of the broken flyer. Payment was being extracted for long slavery.

The Apaches dropped from the heights, waiting for Menlik to leave the wild scene. Hulagur had dragged out the body of the helmeted man and the Mongols were stripping off his equipment, smashing it with rocks, still howling their war cry. But the shaman came to the dying smudge fire to meet the Apaches.

He was smiling, his upper lip raised in a curve suggesting the victory purr of a snow tiger. And he saluted with one hand.

"There are two who will not trap men again! We believe you now, *andas*, comrades of battle, when you say you can go up against their fort and make it as nothing!"

Hulagur came up behind the shaman, a modern automatic in his hand. He tossed the weapon into the air, caught it again, laughing—disclaiming something in his own language.

"From the serpents we take two fangs," Menlik translated. "These weapons may not be as dangerous as yours, but they can bite deeper, quicker, and with more force than our arrows."

It did not take the Mongols long to strip the helicopter and the Russians of what they could use, deliberately smashing all the other equipment which had survived the wreck. They had accomplished one important move: The link between the southbound exploring party and the Russian headquarters—if that was the role the helicopter had played—was now gone. And the "eyes" operating over the open territory of the plains had ceased to exist. The attacking war party could move against the ship near the Russian settlement, knowing they had only controlled Mongol scouts to watch for. And to penetrate enemy territory under those conditions was an old, old game the Apaches had played for centuries.

While they waited for the signals from the peaks, a camp was established and a Mongol dispatched to bring up the rest of the outlaws and all extra mounts. Menlik carried to the Apaches a portion of the dried meat which had been transported Horde fashion—under the saddle to soften it for eating.

"We do not skulk any longer like rats or city men in dark holes," he told them. "This time we ride, and we shall take an accounting from those out there—a fine accounting."

"They still have other controllers," Travis pointed out.

"And you have that which is an answer to all their machines," blazed Menlik in return.

"They will send against us your own people if they can," Buck warned.

Menlik pulled at his upper lip. "That is also truth. But now they have no eyes in the sky, and with so many of their men away, they will not patrol too far from camp. I tell you, *andas*, with these weapons of yours a man could rule a world!"

Travis looked at him bleakly. "Which is why they are taboo!"

"Taboo?" Menlik repeated. "In what manner are these forbidden? Do you not carry them openly, use them as you wish? Are they not weapons of your own people?"

Travis shook his head. "These are the weapons of dead men—if we can name them men at all. These we took from a tomb of the star race who held Topaz when our world was only a hunting ground of wild men wearing the skins of beasts and slaying mammoths with stone spears. They are from a tomb and are cursed, a curse we took upon ourselves with their use."

There was a strange light deep in the shaman's eyes. Travis did not know who or what Menlik had been before the Red conditioner had returned him to the role of Horde shaman. He might have been a technician or scientist— and deep within him some remnants of that training could now be dismissing everything Travis said as fantastic superstition.

Yet in another way the Apache spoke the exact truth. There was a curse on these weapons, on every bit of knowledge gathered in that warehouse of the towers. As Menlik had already noted, that curse was power, the power to control Topaz, and then perhaps to reach back across the stars to Earth.

When the shaman spoke again his words were a half whisper. "It will take a powerful curse to keep these out of the hands of men."

"With the Russians gone or powerless," Buck asked, "what need will anyone have for them?"

"And if another ship comes from the skies—to begin all over again?"

"To that we shall have an answer, also, if and when we must find it," Travis replied. That could well be true . . . other weapons in the warehouse powerful enough to pluck a spaceship out of the sky, but they did not have to worry about that now.

"Arms from a tomb. Yes, this is truly dead men's magic. I shall say so to my people. When do we move out?"

"When we know whether or not the trap to the south is sprung," Buck answered.

The report came an hour after sunrise the next morning when Tsoay, Nolan, and Deklay padded into camp. The war chief made a slight gesture with one hand.

"It is done?" Travis wanted confirmation in words.

"It is done. The Pinda-lick-o-yi entered the ship eagerly. Then they blew it and themselves up. Manulito did his work well."

"And Kaydessa?"

"The woman is safe. When the Russians saw the ship, they left their machine outside to hold her captive. That mechanical caller was easily destroyed. She is now free and with the *mba'a* she comes across the mountains, Manulito and Eskelta with her also. Now—" he looked from his own people to the Mongols, "why are you here with these?"

"We wait, but the waiting is over," Jil-Lee said. "Now we go north!"

18

They lay along the rim of a vast basin, a scooping out of earth so wide they could not sight its other side. The bed of an ancient lake, Travis speculated, or perhaps even the arm of a long-dried sea. But now the hollow was filled with rolling waves of golden grass, tossing heavy heads under the flowing touch of a breeze with the exception of a space about a mile ahead where round domes—black, gray, brown—broke the yellow in an irregular oval around the globular silver bead of a spacer: a larger ship than that which had brought the Apaches, but of the same shape.

"The horse herd . . . to the west." Nolan evaluated the scene with the eyes of an experienced raider. "Tsoay, Deklay, you take the horses!"

They nodded, and began the long crawl which would take them two miles or more from the party to stampede the horses.

To the Mongols in those domelike yurts horses were wealth, life itself. They would come running to investigate any disturbance among the grazing ponies, thus clearing the path to the ship and the Russians there. Travis, Jil-Lee, and Buck, armed with the star guns, would spearhead that attack—cutting into the substance of the ship itself until it was a sieve through which they could shake out the enemy. Only when the installations it contained were destroyed, might the Apaches hope for any assistance from the Mongols, either the outlaw pack waiting well back on the prairie or the people in the yurts.

The grass rippled and Naginlta poked out a nose, parting stems before Travis. The Apache beamed an order, sending the coyotes with the horse-raiding party. He had seen how the animals could drive hunted split-horns; they would do as well with the ponies.

Kaydessa was safe, the coyotes had made that clear by the fact that they had joined the attacking party an hour earlier. With Eskelta and Manulito she was on her way back to the north.

Travis supposed he should be well pleased that their reckless plan had succeeded as well as it had. But when he thought of the Tatar girl, all he could see was her convulsed face close to his in the ship corridor, her raking nails raised to tear his cheek. She had an excellent reason to hate him, yet he hoped . . .

They continued to watch both horse herd and domes. There were people moving about the yurts, but no signs of life at the ship. Had the Russians shut themselves in there, warned in some way of the two disasters which had whittled down their forces?

"Ah—!" Nolan breathed.

One of the ponies had raised its head and was facing the direction of the camp, suspicion plain to read in its stance. The Apaches must have reached the point between the herd and the domes which had been their goal. And the Mongol guard, who had been sitting cross-legged, the reins of his mount dangling close to his hand, got to his feet.

"Ahhhuuuuu!" The ancient Apache war cry that had sounded across deserts, canyons, and southwestern plains to ice the blood, ripped just as freezingly through the honey-hued air of Topaz.

The horses wheeled, racing upslope away from the settlement. A figure broke from the grass, flapped his arms at one of the mounts, grabbed at flying mane, and pulled himself up on the bare back. Only a master horseman would have done that, but the whooping rider now drove the herd on, assisted by the snapping and snarling coyotes.

"Deklay—" Jil-Lee identified the reckless rider, "that was one of his rodeo tricks."

Among the yurts it was as if someone had ripped up a rotten log to reveal an ants' nest and sent the alarmed insects into a frenzy. Men boiled out of the domes, the majority of them running for the horse pasture. One or two were mounted on ponies that must have been staked out in the settlement. The main war party of Apaches skimmed silently through the grass on their way to the ship.

The three who were armed with the alien weapons had already tested their range by experimentation back in the hills, but the fear of exhausting whatever powered those barrels had curtailed their target practice. Now they snaked to the edge of the bare ground between them and the ladder hatch of the spacer. To cross that open space was to provide targets for lances and arrows—or the superior armament of the Russians.

"A chance we can hit from here." Buck laid his weapon across his bent knee, steadied the long barrel of the burner, and pressed the firing button.

The closed hatch of the ship shimmered, dissolved into a black hole. Behind Travis someone let out the yammer of a war whoop.

"Fire—cut the walls to pieces!"

Travis did not need that order from Jil-Lee. He was already beaming unseen destruction at the best target he could ask for—the side of the sphere. If the globe was armed, there was no weapon which could be depressed far enough to reach the marksmen at ground level.

Holes appeared, irregular gaps and tears in the fabric of the ship. The Apaches were turning the side of the globe into lacework. How far their fire penetrated into the interior they could not guess.

Movement at one of the holes, the chattering burst of machine-gun fire, spatters of soil and gravel into their faces; they could be cut to pieces by that! The hole enlarged, a scream . . . cut off . . .

"They will not be too quick to try that again," Nolan observed with cold calm from behind Travis' post.

Methodically they continued to beam the ship. It would never be space-borne again; there were neither the skills nor materials here to repair such damage.

"It is like laying a knife to fat," Lupe said as he crawled up beside Travis. "Slice, slice—!"

"Move!" Travis reached to the left, pulled at Jil-Lee's shoulder.

Travis did not know whether it was possible or not, but he had a heady vision of their combined fire power cutting the globe in half, slicing it crosswise with the ease Lupe admired.

They scurried through cover just as someone behind yelled a warning. Travis threw himself down, rolled into a new firing position. An arrow sang over his head; the Russians were doing what the Apaches had known they would—calling in the controlled Mongols to fight. The attack on the ship must be stepped up, or the Amerindians would be forced to retreat.

Already a new lacing of holes appeared under their concentrated efforts. With the gun held tight to his middle, Travis found his feet, zigzagged across the bare ground for the nearest of those openings. Another arrow clanged harmlessly against the fabric of the ship a foot from his goal.

He made it in, over jagged metal shards which glowed faintly and reeked of ozone. The weapons' beams had penetrated well past both the outer shell and the wall of insulation webbing. He climbed a second and smaller break into a corridor enough like those of the western ship to be familiar. The Russian spacer, based on the general plan of the alien derelict ship as his own had been, could not be very different.

Travis tried to subdue his heavy breathing and listen. He heard a confused shouting and the burr of what might be an alarm system. The ship's brain was the control cabin. Even if the Russians dared not try to lift now, that was the core of their communication lines. He started along the corridor, trying to figure out its orientation in relation to that all-important nerve center.

The Apache shoved open each door he passed with one shoulder, and twice he played a light beam on installations within cabins. He had no idea of their use, but the wholesale destruction of each and every machine was what good sense and logic dictated.

There was a sound behind. Travis whirled, saw Jil-Lee and beyond him Buck.

"Up?" Jil-Lee asked.

"And down," Buck added. "The Tatars say they have hollowed a bunker beneath."

"Separate and do as much damage as you can," Travis suggested.

"Agreed!"

Travis sped on. He passed another door and then backtracked hurriedly as he realized it had given on to an engine room. With the gun he blasted two long lines cutting the fittings into ragged lumps. Abruptly the lights went out; the burr of the alarms was silenced. Part of the ship, if not all, was dead. And now it might come to hunter and hunted in the dark. But that was an advantage as far as the Apaches were concerned.

Back in the corridor again, Travis crept through a curiously lifeless atmosphere. The shouting was stilled as if the sudden failure of the machines had stunned the Russians.

A tiny sound—perhaps the scrape of a boot on a ladder. Travis edged back into a compartment. A flash of light momentarily lighted the corridor; the approaching figure was using an electric torch. Travis drew his knife with one hand, reversed it so he could use the heavy hilt as a silencer. The other was hurrying now, on his way to investigate the burned-out engine cabin. Travis could hear the rasp of his fast breathing. Now!

The Apache had put down the gun, his left arm closed about a shoulder, and the Russian gasped as Travis struck with the knife hilt. Not clean—he had to hit a second time before the struggles of the man were over. Then, using his hands for eyes, he stripped the limp body on the floor of automatic and torch.

With the Russian's weapon in the front of his sash, the burner in one hand and the torch in the other, Travis prowled on. There was a good chance that those above might believe him to be their comrade returning. He found the ladder leading to the next level, began to climb, pausing now and then to listen.

Shock preceded sound. Under him the ladder swayed and the globe itself rocked a little. A blast of some kind must have been set off at or under the level of the ground. The bunker Buck had mentioned?

Travis clung to the ladder, waited for the vibrations to subside. There was a shouting above, a questioning. . . . Hurriedly he ascended to the next level, scrambled out and away from the ladder just in time to avoid the light from another torch flashed down the well. Again that call of inquiry, then a shot—the boom of the explosion loud in the confined space.

To climb into the face of that light with a waiting marksman above was sheer folly. Could there be another way up? Travis retreated down one of the corridors raying out from the ladder well. A quick inspection of the cabins along that route told him he had reached a section of living quarters. The pattern was familiar; the control cabin would be on the next level.

Suddenly the Apache remembered something: On each level there should be an emergency opening giving access to the insulation space between the inner and outer skins of the ship through which repairs could be made. If he could find that and climb up to the next level . . .

The light shining down the well remained steady, and there was the echoing crack of another shot. But Travis was far enough away from the ladder now to dare use his own torch, seeking the door he needed on the wall surface. With a leap of heart he sighted the outline—his luck was in! The Russian and Western ships were alike.

Once the panel was open he flashed his torch up, finding the climbing rungs and, above, the shadow outline of the next level opening. Securing the alien gun in his sash beside the automatic and holding the torch in his mouth, Travis climbed, not daring to think of the deep drop below. Four . . . five . . . ten rungs, and he could reach the other door.

His fingers slid over it, searching for the release catch. But there was no answering give. Balling his fist, he struck down at an awkward angle and almost lost his balance as the panel fell away beneath his blow. The door swung and he pulled through.

Darkness! Travis snapped on the torch for an instant, saw about him the relays of a com system, and gave it a full spraying as he pivoted, destroying the eyes and ears of the ship—unless the burnout he had effected below had already done that. A flash of automatic fire from his left, a searing burn along his arm an inch or so below the shoulder—

Travis' action was purely reflex. He swung the burner around, even as his mind gave a frantic No! To defend himself with automatic, knife, arrow—yes; but not this way. He huddled against the wall.

An instant earlier there had been a man there, a living, breathing man—one of his own species, if not of his own beliefs. Then because his own muscles had unconsciously obeyed warrior training, there was this. So easy— to deal death without really meaning to. The weapon in his hands was truly the devil gift they were right to fear. Such weapons were not to be put into the hands of men—any men—no matter how well intentioned.

Travis gulped in great mouthfuls of air. He wanted to throw the burner away, hurl it from him. But the task he could rightfully use it for was not yet done.

Somehow he reeled on into the control cabin to render the ship truly a dead thing and free himself of the heavy burden of guilt and terror between his hands. That weight could be laid aside; memory could not. And no one of his kind must ever have to carry such memories again.

The booming of the drums was like a pulse quickening the blood to a rhythm which bit at the brain, made a man's eyes shine, his muscles tense as if he held an arrow to bow cord or arched his fingers about a knife hilt. A fire blazed high and in its light men leaped and whirled in a mad dance with tulwar blades catching and reflecting the red gleam of flames. Mad, wild, the Mongols were drunk with victory and freedom. Beyond them, the silver globe of the ship showed the black holes of its death, which was also the death of the past—for all of them.

"What now?" Menlik, the dangling of amulets and charms tinkling as he moved, came up to Travis. There was none of the wild fervor in the shaman's face; instead, it was as if he had taken several strides out of the life of the Horde, was emerging into another person, and the question he asked was one they all shared.

Travis felt drained, flattened. They had achieved their purpose. The handful of Russian overlords were dead, their machines burned out. There were no controls here any more; men were free in mind and body. What were they to do with their freedom?

"First," the Apache spoke his own thoughts—"we must return these."

The three alien weapons were lashed into a square of Mongol fabric, hidden from sight, although they could not be so easily shut out of mind. Only a few of the others, Apache or Mongol, had seen them; and they must be returned before their power was generally known.

"I wonder if in days to come," Buck mused, "they will not say that we pulled lightning out of the sky, as did the Thunder Slayer, to aid us. But this is right. We must return them and make that valley and what it holds taboo."

"And what if another ship comes—one of *yours*?" Menlik asked shrewdly.

Travis stared beyond the Tatar shaman to the men about the fire. His nightmare dragged into the open . . . What if a ship did come in, one with Ashe, Murdock, men he knew and liked, friends on board? What then of his guardianship of the towers and their knowledge? Could he be as sure of what to do then? He rubbed his hand across his forehead and said slowly:

"We shall take steps when—or if—that happens—"

But could they, would they? He began to hope fiercely that it would not happen, at least in his lifetime, and then felt the cold bleakness of the exile they must will themselves into.

"Whether we like it or not," (was he talking to the others or trying to argue down his own rebellion?) "we cannot let what lies under the towers be known . . . found . . . used . . . unless by men who are wiser and more controlled than we are in our time."

Menlik drew his shaman's wand, twiddled it between his fingers, and beneath his drooping lids watched the three Apaches with a new kind of measurement.

"Then I say to you this: Such a guardianship must be a double charge, shared by my people as well. For if they suspect that you alone control these powers and their secret, there will be envy, hatred, fear, a division between us from the first—war . . . raids . . . This is a large land and neither of our groups numbers many. Shall we split apart fatally from this day when there is room for all? If these ancient things are evil, then let us both guard them with a common taboo."

He was right, of course. And they would have to face the truth squarely. To both Apache and Mongol any off-world ship, no matter from which side, would be a menace. Here was where they would remain and set roots. The sooner they began thinking of themselves as people with a common bond, the better it would be. And Menlik's suggestion provided a tie.

"You speak well," Buck was saying. "This shall be a thing we share. We are three who know. Do you be three also, but choose well, Menlik!"

"Be assured that I will!" the Tatar returned. "We start a new life here; there is no going back. But as I have said: The land is wide. We have no quarrel with one another, and perhaps our two peoples shall become one; after all, we do not differ too greatly. . . ." He smiled and gestured to the fire and the dancers.

Among the Mongols another man had gone into action, his head thrown back as he leaped and twirled, voicing a deep war cry. Travis recognized Deklay. Apache, Mongol—both raiders, horsemen, hunters, fighters when the need arose. No, there was no great difference. Both had been tricked into coming here, and they had no allegiance now for those who had sent them.

Perhaps clan and Horde would combine or perhaps they would drift apart—time would tell. But there would be the bond of the guardianship, the determination that what slept in the towers would not be roused—in their lifetime or many lifetimes!

Travis smiled a bit crookedly. A new religion of sorts, a priesthood with sacred and forbidden knowledge . . . in time a whole new life and civilization stemming from this night. The bleak cold of his early thought cut less deep. There was a different kind of adventure here.

He reached out and gathered up the bundle of the burners, glancing from Buck to Jil-Lee to Menlik. Then he stood up, the weight of the burden in his arms, the feeling of a greater weight inside him.

"Shall we go?"

To get the weapons back—that was of first importance. Maybe then he could sleep soundly, to dream of riding across the Arizona range at dawn under a blue sky with a wind in his face, a wind carrying the scent of piñon pine and sage, a wind which would never caress or hearten him again, a wind his sons and sons' sons would never know. To dream troubled dreams, and hope in time those dreams would fade and thin—that a new world would blanket out the old. Better so, Travis told himself with defiance and determination—better so!

Key Out of Time

1
Lotus World

There was a shading of rose in the pearl arch of sky, deepening to a rainbow tint of cloud. The lazy swells of the ocean held the same soft color, darkened with crimson veins where spirals of weed drifted. A rose world bathed in soft sunlight, knowing only gentle winds, peace, and—sloth.

Ross Murdock leaned forward over the edge of the rock ledge to peer down at a beach of fine sand, pale pink sand. Here and there sparkled the glitter of crystalline shells—or were those fluted ovals shells? Even the waves came in languidly. And the breeze which ruffled his hair and caressed his sun-browned, half-bare body, lightly stirred the growths which the Terran settlers called "trees" but which possessed long lacy fronds instead of true branches.

Hawaika—named for the old Polynesian paradise—a world seemingly without flaw except the subtle one of being too perfect, too welcoming, too wooing. Its long,

189

uneventful, unchanging days enticed forgetfulness, offered a life without effort. Except for the mystery . . .

Because this world was not the one pictured on the tape which had brought the human settlement team here. A map, a directing guide, a description all in one, that was the ancient voyage tape. Ross himself had helped to loot a storehouse on an unknown planet for a cargo of such tapes. Once they had been the space-navigation guides for a race or races who had ruled the star lanes ten thousand years ago in his own world's past, a civilization which had long since sunk back into dust.

Those tapes returned to Earth after their chance discovery, were studied, probed, deciphered by the best brains of his time, shared out by lot between already suspicious global powers, bringing into the exploration of space bitter rivalries and old hatreds.

Such a tape had landed their ship on Hawaika, a world of shallow seas and archipelagoes instead of true continents. The settlement team had had all the knowledge contained on that tape crowded into them, only to discover that much they had learned from it was false!

Of course, none of them had expected to discover the cities or the civilization the tape had projected as existing in that long-ago period. But no present island string that they had visited approximated those on the maps they had seen, and so far they had not found any trace that any intelligent beings had walked, built, or lived on these beautiful, slumberous atolls. So, what had happened to the Hawaika of the tape?

Ross's right hand rubbed across the ridged scars which disfigured his left one, to be carried for the rest of his life as a mark of his meeting with the star voyagers in the past of his own world. He had deliberately seared his own flesh to break their mental control over him. Then the battle had gone his way. But from it he had brought another scar—the unease of that old terror when Ross Murdock, outlaw by the conventions of his own era, Ross Murdock who considered himself exceedingly tough and made tougher yet by training for Time Agent sorties, had come up against a power he did not understand.

Now he breathed deeply of the wind—the smell of the sea, the scents of the land growths, strange but pleasant. So easy to relax, to drop into the soft, lulling swing of this world in which they had found no fault, no danger, no irritant. Yet, once those others had been here—the blue-suited, hairless ones he called "Baldies." And what had happened then . . . or afterward?

A black head, brown shoulders, slender body, broke the sleepy slip of the waves. A shimmering mask covered the face, flashing in the sun. Two hands freed a chin curved yet firmly set, a mouth made more for laughter than sternness, wide dark eyes. Karara Trehern of the Alii, once a lineage of divine chieftains in Hawaii, was an exceedingly pretty girl.

But Ross regarded her aloofly, with coldness which bordered on hostility, as she flipped her mask into its pocket on top of the gill-pack. Below his rocky perch she came to a halt, her feet slightly apart in the sand. There was an impish twist to her lips as she called:

"Why not come in? The water's fine."

"Perfect, like all the rest of this." Some of his impatience came out in the sour tone. "No luck, as usual?"

"As usual," Karara conceded. "If there ever was a civilization here, it's been gone so long we'll probably never find any traces. Why don't you just pick out a good place to set up that time-probe and try it blind?"

Ross scowled. "Because"—his patience was exaggerated to the point of insult—"we have only one peep-probe. Once it's set we can't tear it down easily for transport somewhere else, so we want to be sure there's something to look at beyond."

She began to wring the water out of her long hair. "Well, as far as we've explored . . . nothing. Come yourself next time. Tino-rau and Taua aren't particular; they like company."

Putting two fingers to her mouth, Karara whistled. Twin

heads popped out of the water, facing the shore and her. Projecting noses, mouths with upturned corners so they curved in a lasting pleasant grin at the mammals on the shore—the dolphin pair, mammals whose ancestors had chosen the sea, whistled back in such close counterfeit of the girl's signal that they could be an echo of her call. Years earlier their species' intelligence had surprised, almost shocked, men. Experiments, training, co-operation, had developed a tie which gave the water-limited race of mankind new eyes, ears, minds, to see, evaluate, and report concerning an element in which the bipeds were not free.

Hand in hand with that co-operation had gone other experiments. Just as the clumsy armored diving suits of the early twentieth century had allowed man to begin penetration into a weird new world, so had scuba equipment made him still freer in the sea. And now the gill-pack which separated the needed oxygen from the water made even that lighter burden of tanks obsolete. But there remained depths into which man could not descend outside a submarine whose secrets were closed to him. There the dolphins operated, in a partnership of minds, equal minds—though that last fact had been difficult for man to accept.

Ross's irritation, unjustified as he knew it to be, did not rest on Tino-rau or Taua. He enjoyed the hours when he buckled on gill-pack and took to the sea with those two ten-foot, black-and-silver escorts sharing the action. But Karara . . . Karara's presence was a different matter altogether.

The Agents' teams had always been strictly masculine. Two men partnered for an interlocking of abilities and temperaments, going through training together, becoming two halves of a strong and efficient whole. Before being summarily recruited into the Project, Ross had been a loner—living on the ragged edges of the law, an indigestible bit for the civilization which had become too ordered and "adjusted" to absorb his kind. But in the

Project he had discovered others like himself—men born out of time, too ruthless, too individualistic for their own age, but able to operate with ease in the dangerous paths of the Time Agents.

And when the time search for the wrecked alien ships had succeeded and the first intact ship found, used, duplicated, the Agents had come from forays into the past to be trained anew for travel to the stars. First there had been Ross Murdock, criminal. Then there had been Ross Murdock and Gordon Ashe, Time Agents. Now there was still Ross and Gordon and a quest as perilous as any they had known. Yet this time they had to depend upon Karara and the dolphins.

"Tomorrow"—Ross was still not sorting out his thoughts, though aware of prickly feelings sharp as embedded thorns—"I will come."

"Good!" If she recognized his hostility for what it was, that did not bother her. Once more she whistled to the dolphins, waved a casual farewell with one hand, and headed up the beach toward the base camp. Ross chose a more rugged path over the cliff.

Suppose they did not find what they sought near here? Yet the old taped map suggested that this was approximately the site starred upon it. Marking a city? A star port?

Ashe had volunteered for Hawaika, demanded this job after the disastrous Topaz affair when the team of Apache volunteers had been sent out too soon to counter what might have been a sneak settlement planted by Greater Russia. Ross was still unhappy over the ensuing months when only Major Kelgarries and maybe, in a lesser part, Ross had kept Gordon Ashe in the Project at all. That Topaz had been a failure was accepted when the settlement ship did not return. And that had added to Ashe's sense of guilt for having recruited and partially trained the lost team.

Among those dispatched over Ashe's vehement protests had been Travis Fox who had shared with Ashe and Ross the first galactic flight in an age-old derelict spaceship. Travis Fox—the Apache archaeologist—had he ever reached Topaz? Or would he and his team wander forever between worlds? Did they set down on a planet where some inimical form of native life or a Russian settlement had awaited them? The very uncertainty of their fate continued to ride Ashe.

So he insisted on coming out with the second settlement team, the volunteers of Samoan and Hawaiian descent, to carry on an even more exciting and hazardous exploration. Just as the Project had probed into the past of Earth, so would Ashe and Ross now attempt to discover what lay in the past of Hawaika, to see this world as it had been at the height of the galactic civilization, and so to learn what they could about their forerunners into space. And the mystery they had dropped into upon landing added to the necessity for those discoveries.

Their probe, if fortune favored them, might become a gate through time. The installation was a vast improvement over the kind of passage points they had first devised. Technical information had taken a vast leap forward after human engineers and scientists had had access to the tapes of the interstellar empire. Adaptations and shortcuts developed, so that a new hybrid technology came into use, woven from the knowledge and experimentation of two civilizations thousands of years apart in time.

If and when he or Ashe—or Karara and her dolphins—discovered the proper site, the two Agents could set up their own experiment. Both Ross and Ashe had had enough drill in the process. All they needed was the brick of discovery; then they could build their wall. But they must find some remainder of the past, some slight trace of ancient ruin upon which to center their peep-probe. And since landing here long days had flowed into weeks with no such discovery being made.

Ross crossed the ridge of rock which formed a cockscomb rise on the island's spine and descended to the village. As they had been trained, the Polynesian settlers adapted local products to their own heritage of building and tools. It was necessary that they live off the land, for their transport ship had had storage space only for a limited number of supplies and tools. After it took off to return home they would be wholly on their own for several years. Their ship, a silvery ball, rested on a rock ledge, its pilot and crew having lingered to learn the results of Ashe's search. Four days more and they would have to lift for home even if the Agents still had only negative results to report.

That disappointment was driving Ashe, the way that six months earlier his outrage and guilt over the Topaz affair had driven him. Karara's suggestion carried weight the longer Ross thought about it. With more swimmers hunting, there was just that much increased chance of turning up some clue. So far the dolphins had not reported any dangerous native sea life or any perils except the natural ones any diver always had at his shoulder under the waves.

There were extra gill-packs, and all of the settlers were good swimmers. An organized hunt ought to shake the Polynesians out of their present do-it-tomorrow attitude. As long as they had definite work before them—the unloading of the ship, the building of the village, all the labors incidental to the establishing of this base—they had shown energy and enthusiasm. It was only during the last couple of weeks that the languor which appeared part of the atmosphere here had crept up on them, so that now they were content to live at a slower and lazier pace. Ross remembered Ashe's comparison made the evening before, likening Hawaika to a legendary island on Earth where the inhabitants lived a drugged existence, feeding upon the seeds of a native plant. Hawaika was fast becoming a lotus land for humans.

"Through here, then westward . . ." Ashe hunched over the crate table in the mat-walled house. He did not look up as Ross entered. Karara's still damp head was bowed until those black locks, now sleeked to her round skull, almost touched the man's close-cropped brown hair. They were both studying a map as if they saw not lines on paper but the actual inlets and lagoons which that drawing represented.

"You are sure, Gordon, that this *is* the modern point to match the site on the tape?" The girl brushed back straying hair.

Ashe shrugged. There were tight lines about his mouth that had not been there six months ago. He moved jerkily, not with the fluid grace of those old days when he had faced the vast distance of time travel with unruffled calm and self-confidence to steady the novice Ross.

"The general outline of these two islands could stand for the capes on this—" He pulled a second map, this on transparent plastic, to fit over the first. The capes marked on the much larger body of land did slip over the modern islands with a surprising fit. Shattered and broken, the former land mass could have produced the groups of atolls and islets they now prospected.

"How long—" Karara mused aloud, "and why?"

Ashe shrugged. "Ten thousand years, five, two." He shook his head. "We have no idea. It's apparent that there must have been some world-wide cataclysm here to change the geography so much. We may have to wait on a return space flight to bring a 'copter or a hydroplane to explore farther." His hand swept beyond the boundaries of the map to indicate the whole of Hawaika.

"A year, maybe two, before we could hope for that," Ross cut in. "Then we'll have to depend on whether the Council believes this is important enough." The contrariness which spiked his tongue whenever Karara was present made him say that without thinking. Then a twitch of Ashe's lips brought home Ross's error. Gordon needed reassurance now, not a recitation of the various ways their mission could be doomed.

"Look here!" Ross came to the table, his hand sweeping past Karara, as he used his forefinger for a pointer. "We know that what we want could be easily overlooked, even with the dolphins helping us to check. This whole area's too big. And you know that it is certain that whatever might be down there would be hidden with sea growths. Suppose ten of us start out in a semi-circle from about here and go as far as this point, heading inland. Video-cameras here and here . . . comb the whole sector inch by inch if we have to. After all, we have plenty of time and manpower."

Karara laughed softly. "Manpower—always manpower, Ross? But there is woman-power, too. And we have perhaps even sharper sight. But this is a good idea, Gordon. Let me see—" she began to tell off names on her fingers, "PaKeeKee, Vaeoha, Hori, Liliha, Taema, Ui, Hono'ura—they are the best in the water. Me . . . you, Gordon, Ross. That makes ten with keen eyes to look, and always there are Tino-rau and Taua. We will take supplies and camp here on this island which looks so much like a finger crooked to beckon. Yes, somehow that beckoning finger seems to me to promise better fortune. Shall we plan it so?"

Some of the tight look was gone from Ashe's face, and Ross relaxed. This was what Gordon needed—not to be sitting in here going over maps, reports, reworking over and over their scant leads. Ashe had always been a field man. The settlement work had been a dismal chore for him.

When Karara had gone Ross dropped down on the bunk against the side wall.

"What *did* happen here, do you think?" Half was real interest in the mystery they had mulled over and over since they had landed on a Hawaika which diverged so greatly from the maps; the other half, a desire to keep Ashe thinking on a subject removed from immediate worries. "A nuclear war?"

"Could be. There are old radiation traces. But these aliens had, I'm sure, progressed beyond nuclear weapons. Suppose, just suppose, they could tamper with the weather, with the balance of the planet's crust? We don't know the extent of their powers, how they would use them. They had a colony here once, or there would have been no guide tape. And that is all we are sure of."

"Suppose"—Ross rolled over on his stomach, pillowed his head on his arms—"we could uncover some of that knowledge—"

The twitch was back at Ashe's lips. "That's the risk we have to run now."

"Risk?"

"Would you give a child one of those hand weapons we found in the derelict?"

"Certainly not!" Ross snapped, then saw the point. "You mean—*we* aren't to be trusted?"

The answer was plain to read in Ashe's expression.

"Then why this whole setup, this hunt for what might mean trouble?"

"The old pinch, the bad one. What if the Russians discover something first? They drew some planets in the tape lottery, remember. It's a seesaw between us—we advance here, they there. We have to keep up the race or lose it. They must be combing their stellar colonies for a few answers just as furiously as we are."

"So, we go into the past to hunt if we have to. Well, I think I could do without answers such as the Baldies would know. But I will admit that I would like to know what did happen here—two, five, ten thousand years ago."

Ashe stood up and stretched. For the first time he smiled. "Do you know, I rather like the idea of fishing off Karara's beckoning finger. Maybe she's right about that changing our luck."

Ross kept his face carefully expressionless as he got up to prepare their evening meal.

2
Lair of Mano-Nui

Just under the surface of the water the sea was warm, weird life showed colors Ross could name, shades he could not. The corals, the animals masquerading as plants, the plants disguised as animals which inhabited the oceans of Earth, had their counterparts here. And the settlers had given them the familiar names, though the crabs, the fish, the anemones, and weeds of the shallow lagoons and reefs were not identical with terrestrial creatures. There was just too much here, too much teeming life to attract one's eyes and divert one's attention. It was hard to keep focused on the job at hand—the search for what was not natural, for what had no normal place here.

As the land seduced the senses and bewitched the offworlder, so did the sea have its enchantment to pull one from duty. Ross resolutely skimmed by a forest of swaying lace which varied from a green which was almost black to a pale tint he could not truly identify. Among those waving fans lurked ghost-fish, finned swimmers

199

transparent enough so that one could see, through their pallid sides, the evidences of recently ingested meals.

The humans had begun their sweep-search a half hour ago, slipping overboard from a ferry canoe, heading in toward the checkpoint of the finger isle. They formed an arc of expert divers, men and girls so at home in the ocean that they should be able to make the discovery Ashe needed—if such did exist.

Mystery built upon mystery on Hawaika, Ross thought as he used his spear-gun to push aside a floating banner of weed in order to peer below its curtain. The native life of this world must always have been largely aquatic. The settlers had discovered only a few small animals on the islands.

The largest of these was the burrower, a creature not unlike a miniature monkey in that it had hind legs on which it walked erect and forepaws, well clawed for digging purposes, which it used with dexterity as a man used hands. Its body was hairless and it was able to assume, chameleonlike, the color of the soil and rocks where it denned. The head was set directly on its bowed shoulders without vestige of neck; and it had round bubbles of eyes near the top of its skull, a nose which was a single vertical slit, and a wide mouth fanged for crushing the shelled creatures on which it fed. All in all, to human eyes it was a vaguely repulsive creature, but as far as the settlers had been able to discover it was the highest form of land life. Smaller rodentlike things, the two species of wingless diving birds, and an odd assortment of reptiles and amphibians sharing the island were all the burrowers' prey.

A world of sea and islands, what type of native intelligent life had it once supported? Or had this been only a galactic colony, with no native population before the coming of the stellar explorers? Ross hovered above a dark pocket where the bottom had suddenly dipped into a saucer-shaped depression. The sea growth about the rim rippled in the water raggedly, but there was something about its general outline. . . .

Ross began a circuit of that hollow. Allowing for the distortion of the growths which had formed lumpy excrescences or raised turrets toward the surface—yes, allowing for those—this was decidedly something out of the ordinary! The depression was too regular, too even, Ross was certain of that. With a thrill of excitement he began a descent into the cup, striving to trace signs which would prove his suspicion correct.

How many years, centuries, had the slow coverage of the sea life gathered there, flourished, died, with other creatures to build anew on the remains? Now there was only a hint that the depression had other than a natural origin.

Anchoring with a one-handed grip on a spike of Hawaikan coral—smoother than the Terran species—Ross aimed the butt of his spear-gun at the nearest wall of the saucer, striving to reach into a crevice between two lumps of growth and so probe into what might lie behind. The spear rebounded; there was no breaking that crust with such a fragile tool. But perhaps he would have better luck lower down.

The depression was deeper than he had first judged. Now the light which existed in the shallows vanished. Red and yellow as colors went, but Ross was aware of blues and greens in shades and tints which were not visible above. He switched on his diving torch, and color returned within its beam. A swirl of weed, pink in the light, became darkly emerald beyond as if it possessed the chameleon ability of the burrowers.

He was distracted by that phenomenon, and so he transgressed the diver's rule of never becoming so absorbed in surroundings as to forget caution. Just when did Ross become aware of that shadow below? Was it when a school of ghost-fish burst unexpectedly between weed growths, and he turned to follow them with the torch? Then the outer edge of his beam caught the movement of a shape, a flutter in the water of the gloomy depths.

Ross swung around, his back to the wall of the saucer, as he aimed the torch down at what was arising

there. The light caught and held for a long moment of
horror something which might have come out of the night-
mares of his own world. Afterward Ross knew that the
monster was not as large as it seemed in that endless
minute of fear, perhaps no bigger than the dolphins.

He had had training in shark-infested seas on Earth,
been carefully briefed against the danger from such hunters
of the deep. But this thing he faced had only existed
before in the fairy tales of his race—it was a dragon
straight out of legend. His light beam exposed a scaled
head whose eyes gleamed with sullen hatred and whose
fanged mouth gaped in a horned muzzle. Its long,
undulating neck rose from the half-seen bulk of a mon-
strous body.

His spear-gun, the knife at his waist belt, neither were
protection against this! Yet to turn his back on that rising head was more than Ross could do. He pulled himself back against the wall of the saucer. The thing before
him did not rush to attack. Plainly it had seen him and
now it moved with the leisure of a hunter confident of
the hunt's eventual outcome. But the light appeared to
puzzle it and Ross kept the beam shining straight into
those evil eyes.

The shock of the encounter was wearing off; now Ross
edged his flipper into a crevice to hold him steady while
his hand went to the sonic-com at his waist. He tapped
out a distress call which the dolphins could relay to the
swimmers. The swaying dragon head paused, held rigid
on a stiff, scaled column in the center of the saucer. That
sonic vibration either surprised or bothered the hunter,
made it wary.

Ross tapped again. The belief that if he tried to escape,
he was lost, that only while he faced it so had he any
chance, grew stronger. The head was only inches below
the level of his flippered feet as he held to the weeds.

Again that weaving movement, the rise of head, a
tremor along the serpent neck, an agitation in the depths.
The dragon was on the move again. Ross aimed the light

directly at the head. The scales, as far as he could determine, were not horny plates but lapped, silvery ovals such as a fish possessed. And the underparts of the monster might even be vulnerable to his spear. But knowing the way a terrestrial shark could absorb the darts of that weapon and survive, Ross feared to attack except as a last resort.

Above and to his left there was a small hollow where some portion of the growths had been ripped away. If he could fit himself into that crevice, perhaps he could keep the dragon at bay until help arrived. Ross moved with all the skill he had. His hand closed upon the edge of the niche and he whirled himself up, just making it into that refuge as the head lashed at him wickedly. His suspicion that the dragon would attack anything on the run was well founded, and he knew he had no hope of winning to the surface above.

Now he stood in the crevice, facing outward, watching the head darting in the water. He had switched off the torch, and the loss of light appeared to bewilder the reptile for some precious seconds. Ross pulled as far back into the niche as he could, until the point of one shoulder touched a surface which was sleek, smooth, and cold. The shock of that contact almost sent him hurtling out again.

Gripping the spear before him in his right hand, Ross cautiously felt behind him with the left. His finger tips glided over a seamless surface where the growths had been torn or peeled away. Though he could not, or dared not, turn his head to see, he was certain that this was his proof that the walls of the saucer had been fashioned and placed there by some intelligent creature.

The dragon had risen, hovering now in the water directly before the entrance to Ross's hole, its neck curled back against its bulk. It had wide flippers moving to hold it poised. The body, sloping from a massive round of shoulders to a tapering rear, was vaguely familiar. If one provided a terrestrial seal with a gorgon head and scales in place of fur, the effect would be similar. But Ross was assuredly not facing a seal at this moment.

Slight movement of the flippers kept it as stabilized as if it sprawled on a supporting surface. With the neck flattened against the body, the head curved downward until the horn on its snout pointed the tip straight at Ross's middle. The man steadied his spear-gun. The dragon's eyes were its most vulnerable targets; if the creature launched the attack, Ross would aim for them.

Both man and dragon were so intent upon their duel that neither was conscious of the sudden swirl overhead. A sleek dark shape struck down, skimming across the humped-back ridge of the dragon. Some of the settlers had empathy with the dolphins to a high degree, but Ross's own powers of contact were relatively feeble.

Only now he was given an assurance of aid, and a suggestion to attack. The dragon head writhed, twisted as the reptile attempted to see above and behind its own length. But the dolphin was only a streak fast disappearing. And that writhing changed the balance the monster had maintained, pushing it toward Ross.

He fired too soon and without proper aim, so the dart snaked past the dragon's head. But the harpoon line half hooked about the neck and seemed to confuse the creature. Ross squirmed as far back as he could into his refuge and drew his knife. Against those fangs the weapon was an almost useless toy, but it was all he had.

Again the dolphin dived in attack on the monster, this time seizing the floating cord of the harpoon in its mouth and jerking the dragon even more off balance, pulling it away from Ross's niche and out into the center of the saucer.

There were two dolphins in action now, Ross saw, playing the dragon as matadors might play a bull, keeping the creature disturbed by their agile maneuvers. Whatever prey came naturally to the Hawaikan monster was not of this type, and the creature was not prepared to deal effectively with their teasing, dodging tactics. Neither had touched the beast, but they kept it constantly striving to get at them.

Though it swam in circles attempting to face its teasers, the dragon did not abandon the level before Ross's refuge, and now and then it darted its head at him, unwilling to give up its prey. Only one of the dolphins frisked and dodged above now as the sonic on Ross's belt vibrated against his lower ribs with its message warning to be prepared for further action. Somewhere above, his own kind gathered. Hurriedly he tapped in code his warning in return.

Two dolphins busy again, their last dive over the dragon pushing the monster down past Ross's niche toward the saucer's depths. Then they flashed up and away. The dragon was rising in turn, but coming to meet the Hawaikan creature was a ball giving off light, bringing sharp vision and color with it.

Ross's arm swung up to shield his eyes. There was a flash; such answering vibration carried through the waves that even his nerves, far less sensitive than those of the life about him, reacted. He blinked behind his mask. A fish floated by, spiraling up, its belly exposed. And about him growths drooped, trailed lifelessly through the water; while there was a now motionless bulk sinking to the obscurity of the depression's floor. A weapon perfected on Earth to use against sharks and barracuda had worked here to kill what could have been more formidable prey.

The man wriggled out of the niche, rose to meet another swimmer. As Ashe descended, Ross relayed his news via the sonic. The dolphins were already nosing into the depths in pursuit of their late enemy.

"Look here—" Ross gestured, guiding Ashe to the crevice which had saved him and aimed the torch beam into it. He had been right! There was a long groove in the covering built up by the growths; a vertical strip some six feet long, of a uniform gray, showed. Ashe touched the find and then gave the alert via the sonic code.

"We've found something!"

But what did they have? Even after an hour's exploration by the full company, Ashe's expert search with his knowledge of artifacts and ancient remains, they were still baffled. It would require labor and tools they did not have, to clear the whole of the saucer. They could be sure only of its size and shape, and the fact that its walls were of an unknown substance which the sea could cloak but not erode. The length of gray surface showed not the slightest pitting or time wear.

Down at its centermost point they found the dragon's den, an arch coated with growth. Before it sprawled the body of the creature. That was dragged aloft with the dolphins' aid, to be taken ashore for study. But the arch itself . . . was that part of some old installation?

Torches to the fore, they entered its shadow, only to remain baffled. Here and there were patches of the same gray showing in its interior. Ashe dug the butt of his spear-gun into the sand on the flooring to uncover another oval depression. But what it all signified or what had been its purpose, they could not guess.

"Set up the peep-probe here?" Ross asked.

Ashe's head moved in a slow negative. "Look farther . . . spread out," the sonic clicked.

Within a matter of minutes the dolphins reported new remains—two more saucers, each larger than the first, set in a line on the ocean floor, pointing directly to Karara's Finger Island. Cautiously explored, these were discovered to be free of any but harmless life; they stirred up no more dragons.

When the humans came ashore on Finger Island to rest and eat their midday meal one of the men paced along the beached dragon. Ashore it lost none of its frightening aspect. And seeing it, even beached and dead, Ross wondered at his luck in surviving the encounter without a scratch.

"I think that this one would be alone," PaKeeKee commented. "Where there is an eater of this size, there is usually only one."

"Mano-Nui!" The girl Taema shivered as she gave to this monster the name of the shark demon of her people. "Such a one is truly king shark in these waters! But why have we not sighted its like before? Tino-rau, Taua . . . they have not reported such—"

"Probably because, as PaKeeKee says, these things are rare," Ashe returned. "A carnivore of size would have to have a fairly wide hunting range, yet there's evidence that this thing has laired in that den for some time. Which means that it must have a defined hunting territory allowing no trespassing from others of its species."

Karara nodded. "Also it may hunt only at intervals, eat heavily, and lie quiet until that meal is digested. There are large snakes on Earth that follow that pattern. Ross was in its front yard when it came after him—"

"From now on"—Ashe swallowed a quarter of fruit— "we know what to watch for, and the weapon which will finish it off. Don't forget that!"

The delicate mechanisms of their sonics had already registered the vibrations which would warn of a dragon's presence, and the depth globes would then do the rest.

"Big skull, oversize for the body." PaKeeKee squatted on his heels by the head lying on the sand at the end of the now fully extended neck.

Ross had heretofore been more aware of the armament of that head, the fangs set in the powerful jaws, the horn on the snout. But PaKeeKee's comment drew his attention to the fact that the scale-covered skull did dome up above the eye pits in a way to suggest ample brain room. Had the thing been intelligent? Karara put that into words:

"Rule One?" She went over to survey the carcass.

Ross resented her half question, whether it was addressed to him or mere thinking aloud on her part.

Rule One: Conserve native life to the fullest extent. Humanoid form may not be the only evidence of intelligence.

There were the dolphins to prove that point right on Earth. But did Rule One mean that you had to let a monster nibble at you because it might just be a high type of alien intelligence? Let Karara spout Rule One while backed into a crevice under water with that horn stabbing at her mid-section!

"Rule One does not mean to forego self-defense," Ashe commented mildly. "This thing is a hunter, and you can't stop to apply recognition techniques when you are being regarded as legitimate prey. If you are the stronger, or an equal, yes—stop and think before becoming aggressive. But in a situation like this—take no chances."

"Anyway, from now on," Karara pointed out, "it could be possible to shock instead of kill."

"Gordon"—PaKeeKee swung around—"what have we found here—besides this thing?"

"I can't even guess. Except that those depressions were made for a purpose and have been there for a long time. Whether they were originally in the water, or the land sank, that we don't know either. But now we have a site to set up the peep-probe."

"We do that right away?" Ross wanted to know. Impatience bit at him. But Ashe still had a trace of frown. He shook his head.

"Have to make sure of our site, very sure. I don't want to start any chain reaction on the other side of the time wall."

And he was right, Ross was forced to admit, remembering what had happened when the galactics had discovered the Russian time gates and traced them forward to their twenty-first century source, ruthlessly destroying each station. The original colonists of Hawaika had been as giants to human pygmies when it came to technical knowledge. To use even a peep-probe indiscreetly near one of their outposts might bring swift and terrible retribution.

3
The Ancient Mariners

Another map spread out and this time pinned down with small stones on beach gravel.

"Here, here, and here—" Ashe's finger indicated the points marked in a pattern which flared out from three sides of Finger Island. Each marked a set of three under-sea depressions in perfect alliance with the land which, according to the galactic map, had once been a cape on a much larger land mass. Though the humans had found the ruins, if those saucers in the sea could be so termed, the remains had no meaning for the explorers.

"Do we set up here?" Ross asked. "If we could just get a report to send back. . . ." That might mean finally awakening the co-operation of the Project policy makers so that a flood of supplies and personnel would begin to head their way.

"We set up here," Ashe decided.

He had selected a point between two of the lines where a reef would provide them with a secure base. And once that decision was made, the humans went into action.

Two days to go, to install the peep-probe and take some shots before the ship had to clear with or without their evidence. Together Ross and Ashe floated the installation out to the reef, Ui and Karara helping to tow the equipment and parts, the dolphins lending pushing noses on occasion. The aquatic mammals were as interested as the human beings they aided. And in water their help was invaluable. Had dolphins developed hands, Ross wondered fleetingly, would they have long ago wrested control of their native world—or at least of its seas—from the human race?

All the humans worked with practiced ease, even while masked and submerged, to set the probe in place, aiming it landward at the check point of the Finger's protruding nail of rock. After Ashe made the final adjustments, tested each and every part of the assembly, he gestured them in.

Karara's swift hand movement asked a question, and Ashe's sonic code-clicked in reply: "At twilight."

Yes, dusk was the proper time for using a peep-probe. To see without risk of being sighted in return was their safeguard. Here Ashe had no historical data to guide him. Their search for the former inhabitants might be a long drawn-out process skipping across centuries as the machine adjusted to the different time eras.

"When were they here?" Back on shore Karara shook out her hair, spread it over her shoulders to dry. "How many hundred years back will the probe return?"

"More likely thousands," Ross commented. "Where will you start, Gordon?"

Ashe brushed sand from the page of the notebook he had steadied against one bent knee and gazed out at the reef where they had set the probe.

"Ten thousand years—"

"Why?" Karara wanted to know. "Why that exact figure?"

"We know that galactic ships crashed on Earth then. So their commerce and empire—if it was an empire—was far-flung at that time. Perhaps they were at the zenith of their civilization; perhaps they were already on the down slope. I do not think they were near the beginning. So that date is as good a starting place as any. If we don't hit what we're after, then we can move forward until we do."

"Do you think that there ever was a native population here?"

"Might have been."

"But without any large land animals, no modern traces of any," she protested.

"Of people?" Ashe shrugged. "Good answers for both. Suppose there was a world-wide epidemic of proportions to wipe out a species. Or a war in which they used forces beyond our comprehension to alter the whole face of this planet, which did happen—the alteration, I mean. Several things could have removed intelligent life. Then such species as the burrowers could have developed or evolved from smaller, more primitive types."

"Those ape-things we found on the desert planet." Ross thought back to their first voyage on the homing derelict. "Maybe they had once been men and were degenerating. And the winged people, they could have been less than men on their way up—"

"Ape-things . . . winged people?" Karara interrupted. "Tell me!"

There was something imperious in her demand, but Ross found himself describing in detail their past adventures, first on the world of sand and sealed structures where the derelict had rested for a purpose its involuntary passengers had never understood, and then of the humans' limited exploration of that other planet which might have been the capital world of a far-flung stellar empire. There they had made a pact with a winged people living in the huge buildings of a jungle-choked city.

"But you see"—the Polynesian girl turned to Ashe when

Ross had finished—"you did find them—these ape-things and the winged people. But here there are only the dragons and the burrowers. Are they the start or the finish? I want to know—"

"Why?" Ashe asked.

"Not just because I am curious, though I am that also, but because we, too, must have a beginning and an end. Did we come up from the seas, rise to know and feel and think, just to return to such beginning at our end? If your winged people were climbing and your ape-things descending"—she shook her head—"it would be frightening to hold a cord of life, both ends in your hands. Is it good for us to see such things, Gordon?"

"Men have asked that question all their thinking lives, Karara. There have been those who have said no, who have turned aside and tried to halt the growth of knowledge here or there, attempted to make men stand still on one tread of a stairway. Only there is that in us which will not stop, ill-fitted as we may be for the climbing. Perhaps we shall be safe and untroubled here on Hawaika if I do not go out to that reef tonight. By that action I may bring real danger down on all of us. Yet I can not hold back for that. Could you?"

"No, I do not believe that I could," she agreed.

"We are here because we are of those who must know—volunteers. And being of that temperament, it is in us always to take the next step."

"Even if it leads to a fall," she added in a low tone.

Ashe gazed at her, though her own eyes were on the sea where a lace of waves marked the reef. Her words were ordinary enough, but Ross straightened to match Ashe's stare. Why had he felt that odd instant of uneasiness as if his heart had fluttered instead of beating true?

"I know of you Time Agents," Karara continued. "There were plenty of stories about you told while we were in training."

"Tall tales, I can imagine, most of them." Ashe laughed, but his amusement sounded forced to Ross.

"Perhaps. Though I do not believe that many could be any taller than the truth. And so also I have heard of that strict rule you follow, that you must do nothing which might alter the course of history. But suppose, suppose here that the course of history could be altered, that whatever catastrophe occurred might be averted? If that was done, what would happen to our settlement in the here and now?"

"I don't know. That is an experiment which we have never dared to try, which we won't try—"

"Not even if it would mean a chance of life for a whole native race?" she persisted.

"Alternate worlds then, maybe." Ross's imagination caught up that idea. "Two worlds from a change point in history," he elaborated, noting her look of puzzlement. "One stemming from one decision, another from the alternate."

"I've heard of that! But, Gordon, if you could return to the time of decision here and you had it in your power to say, 'Yes—live!' or 'No—die!' to the alien natives, what would you do?"

"I don't know. But neither do I think I shall ever be placed in that position. Why do you ask?"

She was twisting her still damp hair into a pony tail and tying it so with a cord. "Because . . . because I feel . . . No, I can not really put it into words, Gordon. It is that feeling one has on the eve of some important event—anticipation, fear, excitement. You'll let me go with you tonight, please! I want to see it—not the Hawaika that is, but that other world with another name, the one they saw and knew!"

An instant protest was hot in Ross's throat, but he had no time to voice it. For Ashe was already nodding.

"All right. But we may have no luck at all. Fishing in time is a chancy thing, so don't be disappointed if we don't turn you up that other world. Now, I'm going to pamper these old bones for an hour or two. Amuse yourselves, children." He lay back and closed his eyes.

The past two days had wiped half the shadows from his lean, tanned face. He had dropped two years, three, Ross thought thankfully. Let them be lucky tonight, and Ashe's cure could be nearly complete.

"What do you think happened here?" Karara had moved so that her back was now to the wash of waves, her face more in the shadow.

"How do I know? Could be any of ten different things."

"And will I please shut up and leave you alone?" she countered swiftly. "Do you wish to savor the excitement then, explore a world upon world, or am I saying it right? We have Hawaika One which is a new world for us; now there is Hawaika Two which is removed in time, not distance. And to explore that—"

"We won't be exploring it really," Ross protested.

"Why? Did your agents not spend days, weeks, even months of time in the past on Earth? What is to prevent your doing the same here?"

"Training. We have no way of learning the drill."

"What do you mean?"

"Well, it wasn't as easy as you seem to think it was back on Earth," he began scornfully. "We didn't just stroll through one of those gates and set up business, say, in Nero's Rome or Montezuma's Mexico. An Agent was physically and psychologically fitted to the era he was to explore. Then he trained, and how he trained!" Ross remembered the weary hours spent learning how to use a bronze sword, the technique of Beaker trading, the hypnotic instruction in a language which was already dead centuries before his own country existed. "You learned the language, the customs, everything you could about your time and your cover. You were letter perfect before you took even a trial run!"

"And here you would have no guides," Karara said, nodding. "Yes, I can see the difficulty. Then you will just use the peep-probe?"

"Probably. Oh, maybe later on we can scout through a gate. We have the material to set one up. But it would be a strictly limited project, allowing no chance of being caught. Maybe the big brains back home can take peep-data and work out some basis of infiltration for us from it."

"But that would take years!"

"I suppose so. Only you begin to swim in the shallows, don't you—not by jumping off a cliff!"

She laughed. "True enough! However, even a look into the past might solve part of the big mystery."

Ross grunted and stretched out to follow Ashe's example. But behind his closed eyes his brain was busy, and he did not cultivate the patience he needed. Peep-probes were all right, but Karara had a point. You wanted more than a small window into a mystery, you wanted a part in solving it.

The setting of the sun deepened rose to red, made a dripping wine-hued banner of most of the sky, so that under it they moved in a crimson sea, looked back at an island where shadows were embers instead of ashes. Three humans, two dolphins, and a machine mounted on a reef which might not even have existed in the time they sought. Ashe made his final adjustments, and then pressed a button as they watched a monitor screen no larger than the palms of two hands.

Nothing, a dull gray nothing! Something must have gone wrong with their assembly work. Ross touched Ashe's shoulder. But now there were shadows gathering on the plate, thickening, to sharpen into a distinct picture.

It was still the sunset hour they watched. But somehow the colors were paler, less red and sullen than the ones about them in the here and now. And they were not seeing the isle toward which the probe had been aimed; they were looking at a rugged coastline where cliffs lifted well above the beach-strand. While on those cliffs— Ross had not realized Karara had reached out to grasp his arm until her nails bit into his flesh. And even then he was hardly aware of the pain. Because there was a building on the cliff!

Massive walls of native rock reared in outward defenses, culminating in towers. And from the high point of one tower the pointed tail of a banner cracked in the wind. There was a headland of rock reaching out, not toward them but to the north, and rounding that . . .

"War canoe!" Karara exclaimed, but Ross had another identification:

"Longboat!"

In reality, the vessel was neither one nor the other, not the double canoe of the Pacific which had transported warriors on raid from one island to another, or the shield-hung warship of the Vikings. But the humans were right in its purpose: That rakish, sharp-prowed ship had been fashioned for swift passage of the seas, for maneuverability as a weapon.

Behind the first nosed another and a third. Their sails were dyed by the sun, but there were devices painted on them, and the lines of those designs glittered as if they had been drawn with a metallic fluid.

"The castle!" Ashe's cry pulled their attention back to land.

There was movement along those walls. Then came a flash, a splash in the water close enough to the lead ship to wet her deck with spray.

"They're fighting!" Karara shouldered against Ross for a better look.

The ships were altering course, swinging away from land, out to sea.

"Moving too fast for sails alone, and I don't see any oars." Ross was puzzled. "How do you suppose . . ."

The bombardment from the castle continued but did not score any hits. Already the ships were out of range, the lead vessel off the screen of the peep as well. Then there was just the castle in the sunset. Ashe straightened up.

"Rocks!" he repeated wonderingly. "They were throwing rocks!"

"But those ships, they must have had engines. They

weren't just depending on sails when they retreated." Ross added his own cause for bewilderment.

Karara looked from one to the other. "There is something here you do not understand. What is wrong?"

"Catapults, yes," Ashe said with a nod. "Those would fit periods corresponding from the Roman Empire into the Middle Ages. But you're right, Ross, those ships had power of some kind to take them offshore that quickly."

"A technically advanced race coming up against a more backward one?" hazarded the younger man.

"Could be. Let's go forward some." The incoming tide was washing well up on the reef. Ashe had to don his mask as he plunged head and shoulders under water to make the necessary adjustment.

Once more he pressed the button. And Ross's gasp was echoed by one from the girl. The cliff again, but there was no castle dominating it, only a ruin, hardly more than rubble. Now, above the sites of the saucer depressions great pylons of silvery metal, flashing in the sunset, raked into the sky like gaunt, skeleton fingers. There were no ships, no signs of any life. Even the vegetation which had showed on shore had vanished. There was an atmosphere of stark abandonment and death which struck the humans forcibly.

Those pylons, Ross studied them. Something familiar in their construction teased his memory. That refuel planet where the derelict ship had set down twice, on the voyage out and on their return. That had been a world of metal structures, and he believed he could trace a kinship between his memory of those and these pylons. Surely they had no connection with the earlier castle on the cliff.

Once more Ashe ducked to reset the probe. And in the fast-fading light they watched a third and last picture. But now they might have been looking at the island of the present, save that it bore no vegetation and there was a rawness about it, a sharpness of rock outline now vanished.

Those pylons, were they the key to the change which

had come upon this world? What were they? Who had set them there? For the last Ross thought he had an answer. They were certainly the product of the galactic empire. And the castle . . . the ships . . . natives . . . settlers? Two widely different eras, and the mystery still lay between them. Would they ever be able to bring its key out of time?

They swam for the shore where Ui had a fire blazing and their supper prepared.

"How many years lying between those probes?" Ross pulled broiled fish apart with his fingers.

"That first was ten thousand year ago, the second," Ashe paused, "only two hundred years later."

"But"—Ross stared at his superior—"that means—"

"That there was a war or some drastic form of invasion, yes."

"You mean that the star people arrived and just took over this whole planet?" Karara asked. "But why? And those pylons, what were they for? How much later was that last picture?"

"Five hundred years."

"The pylons were gone, too, then," Ross commented. "But why—?" he echoed Karara's question.

Ashe had taken up his notebook, but he did not open it. "I think"—there was a sharp, grim note in his voice—"we had better find out."

"Put up a gate?"

Ashe broke all the previous rules of their service with his answer:

"Yes, a gate."

4
Storm Menace

"We have to know." Ashe leaned back against the crate they had just emptied. "Something was done here—in two hundred years—and then, an empty world."

"Pandora's box." Ross drew a hand across his forehead, smearing sweat and fine sand into a brand.

Ashe nodded. "Maybe we run that risk, loosing all the horrors of the aliens. But what if the Russians open the box first on one of their settlement worlds?"

There it was again, the old goad which prodded them into risks and recklessness. Danger ahead on both paths. Don't risk trying to learn galactic secrets, but don't risk your enemy's learning them either. You held a white-hot iron in both hands in this business. And Ashe was right, they had stumbled on something here which hinted that a whole world had been altered to suit some plan. Suppose the secret of that alteration was discovered by their enemies?

"Were the ship and castle people natives?" Ross wondered aloud.

"Just at a guess they were, or at least settlers who had been established here so long they had developed a local form of civilization which was about on the level of a feudal society."

"You mean because of the castle and the rock bombardment. But what about the ships?"

"Two separate phases of a society at war, perhaps a more progressive against a less technically advanced. American warships paying a visit to the Shogun's Japan, for example."

Ross grinned. "Those warships didn't seem to fancy their welcome. They steered out to sea fast enough when the rocks began to fall."

"Yes, but the ships could exist in the castle pattern; the pylons could not!"

"Which period are you aiming for first—the castle or the pylons?"

"Castle first, I think. Then if we can't pick up any hints, we'll take some jumps forward until we do connect. Only we'll be under severe handicaps. If we could only plant an analyzer somewhere in the castle as a beginning."

Ross did not show his surprise. If Ashe was talking on those terms, then he was intending to do more than just lurk around a little beyond the gate; he was really planning to pick up alien speech patterns, eventually assume an alien agent identity!

"Gordon!" Karara appeared between two of the lace trees. She came so hastily that the contents of the two cups she carried slopped over. "You must hear what Hori has to say—"

The tall Samoan who trailed her spoke quickly. For the first time since Ross had known him he was very serious, a frown line between his eyes. "There is a bad storm coming. Our instruments register it."

"How long away?" Ashe was on his feet.

"A day . . . maybe two . . ."

Ross could see no change in the sky, islands, or sea. They had had idyllic weather for the six weeks since their planeting, no sign of any such trouble in the Hawaikan paradise.

"It's coming," Hori repeated.

"The gate is half up," Ashe thought aloud, "too much of it set to be dismantled again in a hurry."

"If it's completed," Hori wanted to know, "would it ride out a storm?"

"It might, behind that reef where we have it based. To finish it would be a fast job."

Hori flexed his hands. "We're more brawn than brain in these matters, Gordon, but you've all our help, for what it's worth. What about the ship, does it lift on schedule?"

"Check with Rimbault about that. This storm, how will it compare to a Pacific typhoon?"

The Samoan shook his head. "How do we know? We have not yet had to face the local variety."

"The islands are low," Karara commented. "Winds and water could—"

"Yes! We'd better see Rimbault about a shelter if needed."

If the settlement had drowsed, now its inhabitants were busy. It was decided that they could shelter in the spaceship should the storm reach hurricane proportions, but before its coming the gate must be finished. The final fitting was left to Ashe and Ross, and the older agent fastened the last bolt when the waters beyond the reef were already wind ruffled, the sky darkening fast. The dolphins swam back and forth in the lagoon and with them Karara, though Ashe had twice waved her to the shore.

There was no sunlight left, and they worked with torches. Ashe began his inspection of the relatively simple transfer—the two upright bars, the slab of opaque material forming a doorstep between them. This was only a skeleton of the gates Ross had used in the past. But continual experimentation had produced this more easily transported installation.

Piled in a net were several supply containers ready for an exploring run—extra gill-packs, the analyzer, emergency rations, a medical kit, all the basics. Was Ashe going to try now? He had activated the transfer, the rods were glowing faintly, the slab they guarded having an eerie blue glimmer. He probably only wanted to be sure it worked.

What happened at that moment Ross could never find any adequate words to describe, nor was he sure he could remember. The disorientation of the pass-through he had experienced before; this time he was whirled into a vortex of feeling in which his body, his identity, were ripped from him and he lost touch with all stability.

Instinctively he lashed out, his reflexes more than his conscious will keeping him above water in the wild rage of a storm-whipped sea. The light was gone; here was only dark and beating water. Then a lightning flash ripped wide the heavens over Ross as his head broke the surface and he saw, with unbelieving eyes, that he was being thrust shoreward—not to the strand of Finger Island—but against a cliff where water pounded an unyielding wall of rock.

Ross comprehended that somehow he had been jerked through the gate, that he was now fronting the land that had been somewhere beneath the heights supporting the castle. Then he fought for his life to escape the hammer of the sea determined to crack him against the anvil of the cliff.

A rough surface loomed up before him, and he threw himself in that direction, embracing a rock, striving to cling through the backwash of the wave which had brought him there. His nails grated and broke on the stone, and then the fingers of his right hand caught in a hole, and he held with all the strength in his gasping, beaten body. He had had no preparation, no warning, and only the tough survival will which had been trained and bred into him saved his life.

As the water washed back, Ross strove to pull up farther on his anchorage, to be above the strike of the next wave. Somehow he gained a foot before it came. The mask of the gill-pack saved him from being smothered in that curling torrent as he clung stubbornly, resisting again the pull of the retreating sea.

Inch by inch between waves he fought for footing and stable support. Then he was on the surface of the rock, out of all but the lash of spray. He crouched there, spent and gasping. The thunder roar of the surf, and beyond it the deeper mutter of the rage in the heavens, was deafening, dulling his sense as much as the ordeal through which he had passed. He was content to cling where he was, hardly conscious of his surroundings.

Sparks of light along the shore to the north at last caught Ross's attention. They moved, some clustering along the wave line, a few strung up the cliff. And they were not part of the storm's fireworks. Men here—why at this moment?

Another bolt of lightning showed him the answer. On the reef fringe which ran a tongue of land into the sea hung a ship—two ships—pounded by every hammer wave. Shipwrecks . . . and those lights must mark castle dwellers drawn to aid the survivors.

Ross crawled across his rock on his hands and knees, wavered along the cliff wall until he was again faced with angry water. To drop into that would be a mistake. He hesitated—and now more than his own predicament struck home to him.

Ashe! Ashe had been ahead of him at the time gate. If Ross had been jerked through to this past, then somewhere in the water, on the shore, Gordon was here too! But where to find him . . .

Setting his back to the cliff and holding to the rough stone, Ross got to his feet, trying to see through the welter of foam and water. Not only the sea poured here; now a torrential rain fell into the bargain, streaming down about him, battering his head and shoulders. A chill rain which made him shiver.

He wore gill-pack, weighted belt with its sheathed tool

and knife, flippers, and the pair of swimming trunks which had been suitable for the Hawaika he knew; but his was a different world altogether. Dare he use his torch to see the way out of here? Ross watched the lights to the north, deciding they were not too unlike his own beam, and took the chance.

Now he stood on a shelf of rock pitted with depressions, all pools. To his left was a drop into a boiling, whirling caldron from which points of stone fanged. Ross shuddered. At least he had escaped being pulled into that!

To his right, northward, there was another space of sea, a narrow strip, and then a second ledge. He measured the distance between that and the one on which he perched. Staying where he was would not locate Ashe.

Ross stripped off his flippers, made them fast in his belt. Then he leaped and landed painfully, as his feet slipped and he skidded face down on the northern ledge.

As he sat up, rubbing a bruised and scraped knee, he saw lights advancing in his direction. And between them a shadow crawling from water to shore. Ross stumbled along the ledge hastening to reach that figure, who lay still now just out of the waves. Ashe?

Ross's limping pace became a trot. But he was too late; the other lights, two of them, had reached the shadow. A man—or at least a body which was humanoid—sprawled face down. Other men, three of them, gathered over the exhausted swimmer.

Those who held the torches were still partially in the dark, but the third stooped to roll over their find. Ross caught the glint of light on a metallic head covering, the glisten of wet armor of some type on the fellow's back and shoulders as he made quick examination of the sea's victim.

Then . . . Ross halted, his eyes wide. A hand rose and fell with expert precision. There had been a blade in that hand. Already the three were turning away from the man so ruthlessly dispatched. Ashe? Or some survivor of the wrecked ships?

Ross retreated to the end of the ledge. The narrow

stream of water dividing it from the rock where he had won ashore washed into a cave in the cliff. Dare he try to work his way into that? Masked, with the gill-pack, he could go under surface if he were not smashed by the waves against some wall.

He glanced back. The lights were very close to the end of his ledge. To withdraw to the second rock would mean being caught in a dead end, for he dared not enter the whirlpool on its far side. There was really no choice: stay and be killed, or try for the cave. Ross fastened on his flippers and lowered his body into the narrow stream. The fact that it was narrow and guarded on either side by the ledges tamed the waves a little, and Ross found the tug against him not so great as he feared it would be.

Keeping handholds on the rock, he worked along, head and shoulders often under the wash of rolling water, but winning steadily to the break in the cliff wall. Then he was through, into a space much larger than the opening, water-filled but not with a wild turbulence of waves.

Had he been sighted? Ross kept a handhold to the left of that narrow entrance, his body floating with the rise and fall of the water. He could make out the gleam of light without. It might be that one of those hunters had leaned out over the runnel of the cave entrance, was flashing his torch down into the water there.

Behind mask plate Ross's lips writhed into the snarl of the hunted. In here he would have the advantage. Let one of them, or all three, try to follow through that rock entrance and . . .

But if he had been sighted at the mouth of the lair, none of his trackers appeared to wish to press the hunt. The light disappeared, and Ross was left in the dark. He counted a hundred slowly and then a second hundred before he dared use his own torch.

For all its slit entrance this was a good-sized hideaway he had chanced upon. And he discovered, when he ventured to release his wall hold and swim out into its middle, the bottom arose in a slope toward its rear.

Moments later Ross pulled out of the water once more, to crouch shivering on a ledge only lapped now and then by wavelets. He had found a temporary refuge, but his good fortune did not quiet his fears. Had that been Ashe on the shore? And why had the swimmer been so summarily executed by the men who found him?

The ships caught on the reef, the castle on the cliff above his head . . . enemies . . . ship's crews and castle men? But the callous act of the shore patrol argued a state of war carried to fanatic proportions, perhaps interracial conflict.

He could not hope to explore until the storm was over. To plunge back into the sea would not find Ashe. And to be hunted along the shore by an unknown enemy was simply asking to die without achieving any good in return. No, he must remain where he was for the present.

Ross unhooked the torch from his belt and used it on this higher portion of the cave. He was perched on a ledge which protruded into the water in the form of a wedge. At his back the wall of the cave was rough with trails of weed festooned on its projections. The smell of fishy decay was strong enough to register as Ross pulled off his mask. As far as he could now see there was no exit except by sea.

A movement in the water brought his light flashing down into the dark flood. Then a sleek head arose in the path of that ray. Not a man swimming, but one of the dolphins!

Ross's exclamation of surprise was half gasp, half cry. The second dolphin showed for a moment and between the shadow of their bodies, just under the surface, moved a third form.

"Ashe!" Ross had no idea how the dolphins had come through the time gate, but that they had guided a human to safety he did not doubt at all. "Ashe!"

But it was not Ashe who came wading to the ledge where Ross waited with hand outstretched. He had been so sure of the other's identity that he blinked in complete bewilderment as his eyes met Karara's and she half stumbled, half reeled against him.

His arms about her shoulders steadied her, and her shivering body was close to his as she leaned her full weight upon him. Her hands made a feeble movement to her mask, and he pulled it off. Uncovered, her face was pale and drawn, her eyes now closed, and her breath came in ragged, tearing sobs which shook her even more.

"How did you get here?" Ross demanded even as he pushed her down on the ledge.

Her head moved slowly, in a weak gesture of negation.

"I don't know . . . we were close to the gate. There was a flash of light . . . then—" Her voice sealed up with a note of hysteria in it. "Then . . . I was here . . . and Taua with me. Tino-rau came . . . Ross, Ross . . . there was a man swimming. He got ashore; he was getting to his feet and—and they killed him!"

Ross's hold tightened; he stared into her face with fierce demand.

"Was it Gordon?"

She blinked, brought her hand up to her mouth, and wiped it back and forth across her chin. There was a small red trickle growing between her fingers, dripping down her arm.

"Gordon?" She repeated it as if she had never heard the name before.

"Yes, did they kill Gordon?"

In his grasp she was swaying back and forth. Then, realizing he was shaking her, Ross got himself under control.

But a measure of understanding had come into her eyes. "No, not Gordon. Where is Gordon?"

"You haven't seen him?" Ross persisted, knowing it was useless.

"Not since we were at the gate." Her words were less slurred. "Weren't you with him?"

"No. I was alone."

"Ross, where are we?"

"Better say—when are we," he replied. "We're through the gate and back in time. And we have to find Gordon!" He did not want to think of what might have happened out on the shore.

5
Time Wrecked

"Can we go back?" Karara was herself again, her voice crisp.

"I don't know." Ross gave her the truth. The force which had drawn them through the gate was beyond his experience. As far as he knew, there had never been such an involuntary passage by time gate, and what their trip might mean he did not know.

The main concern was that Ashe must have come through, too, and that he was missing. Just let the storm abate, and, with the dolphins' aid, Ross's chance for finding the missing agent was immeasurably better. He said so now, and Karara nodded.

"Do you suppose there is a war going on here?" She hugged her arms across her breast, her shoulders heaving in the torch light with shudders she could not control. The damp chill was biting, and Ross realized that was also dangerous.

"Could be." He got to his feet, switched the light from

229

the girl to the walls. That seaweed, could it make them some form of protective covering?

"Hold this—aim it there!" He thrust the torch into her hands and went for one of the loops of kelp.

Ross reeled in lines of the stuff. It was rank-smelling but only slightly damp, and he piled it on the ledge in a kind of nest. At least in the hollow of that mound they would be sheltered after a fashion.

Karara crawled into the center of the mass, and Ross followed her. The smell of the stuff filled his nose, was almost like a visible cloud, but he had been right, the girl stopped shivering, and he felt a measure of warmth in his own shaking body. Ross snapped off the torch, and they lay together in the dark, the half-rotten pile of weed holding them.

He must have slept, Ross guessed, when he stirred, raising his head. His body was stiff, aching, as he braced himself up on his hands and peered over the edge of their kelp nest. There was light in the cave, a pale grayish wash which grew stronger toward the slit opening. It must be day. And that meant they could move.

Ross groped in the weed, his hand falling on a curve of shoulder.

"Wake up!" His hoarse voice snapped the order.

There was a startled gasp in answer, and the mound beside him heaved as the girl stirred.

"Day out—" Ross pointed.

"And the storm—" she stood up, "I think it is over."

It was true that the level of water within the cave had fallen, that wavelets no longer lapped with the same vigor. Morning . . . the storm over . . . and somewhere Ashe!

Ross was about to snap his mask into place when Karara caught his arm.

"Be careful! Remember what I saw—last night they were killing swimmers!"

He shook her off impatiently. "I'm no fool! And with the packs on we do not have to surface. Listen—" he had another thought, one which would provide an excellent excuse for keeping her safely out of his company, reducing his responsibility for her, "you take the dolphins and try to find the gate. We'll want out as soon as I locate Ashe."

"And if you do not find him soon?"

Ross hesitated. She had not said the rest. What if he could not find Gordon at all? But he would—he had to!

"I'll be back here"—he checked his watch, no longer an accurate timekeeper, for Hawaika's days held an hour more than Earth's twenty-four, but the settlers kept the off-world measurement to check on work periods—"in, say, two hours. You should know by then about the gate, and I'll have some idea of the situation along the shore. But listen—" Ross caught her shoulder in a taut grip, pulled her around to face him, his eyes hot and almost angry as they held hers, "don't let yourself be seen—" He repeated the cardinal rule of Agents in new territory. "We don't dare risk discovery."

Karara nodded and he could see that she understood, was aware of the importance of that warning. "Do you want Tino-rau or Taua?"

"No, I'm going to search along the shore first. Ashe would have tried for that last night . . . was probably driven in the way we were. He'd go to ground somewhere. And I have this—" Ross touched the sonic on his belt. "I'll set it on his call; you do the same with yours. Then if we get within distance, he'll pick us up. Back here in two hours—"

"Yes." Karara kicked free of the weed, was already wading down to where the dolphins circled in the cave pool waiting for her. Ross followed, and the four swam for the open sea.

It could not be much after dawn, Ross thought, as he clung by one hand to a rock and watched Karara and the dolphins on their way. Then he paddled along the shore northward for his own survey of the coast. There was a rose cast in the sky, warming the silver along the far reaches of the horizon. And about him bobbed storm flotsam, so that he had to pick a careful way through floating debris.

On the reef one of the wrecked ships had vanished entirely. Perhaps it had been battered to death by the waves, ground to splinters against the rocks. The other still held, its prow well out of the now receding waves, jagged holes in its sides through which spurts of water cascaded now and then.

The wrack which had been driven landward was composed of planks, boxes, and containers rolled by the waves' force. Much of this was already free of the sea, and on the beach figures moved examining it. In spite of the danger of chance discovery, Ross edged along rocks, seeking a vantage point from which he could watch that activity.

He was flat against a sea-girt boulder, a swell of floating weed draped about him, when the nearest of the foraging parties moved into good view.

Men . . . at least they had the outward appearance of men much like himself, though their skin was dark and their limbs appeared disproportionately long and thin. There were two groups of them, four wearing only a scanty loincloth, busy turning over and hunting through the debris under the direction of the other two.

The workers had thick growths of hair which not only covered their heads, but down their spines and the outer sides of their thin arms and legs to elbow and knee. The hair was a pallid yellow-white in vivid contrast to their dark skins, and their chins protruded sharply, allowing the lower line of their faces to take on a vaguely disturbing likeness to an animal's muzzle.

Their overseers were more fully clothed, wearing not only helmets with a protective visor on their heads, but also breast- and back-plates molded to their bodies. Ross thought that these could not be solid metal since they adapted to the movements of the wearers.

Feet and legs were covered with dull red casings that combined shoe and leggings. They were armed with swords of an odd pattern; their points curved up so that the blade resembled a fishhook. Unsheathed, the blades were clipped to a waist belt by catches which glittered in the weak morning light as if gem set.

Ross could see little of their faces, for the beak visors overhung their features. But their skins were as dusky as those of the laborers, and their arms and legs of the same unusual length . . . men of the same race, he deduced.

Under the orders of the armed overseers the laborers were reducing the beach to order, sorting out the flotsam into two piles. Once they gathered about a find, and the sound of excited speech reached Ross as an agitated clicking. The armored men came up, surveyed the discovery. One of them shrugged, and clicked an order.

Ross caught only a half glimpse of the thing two of the workers dragged away. A body! Ashe . . . the human was about to move closer when he saw the green cloak dragging about the corpse. No, not Gordon, just another victim from the wrecks.

The aliens were working their way toward Ross, and perhaps it was time for him to go. He was pushing aside his well-arranged curtain of weed when he was startled by a shout. For a second he thought he might have been sighted, until resulting action on shore told him otherwise.

The furred workers shrank back against the mound to which they had just dragged the body. While the two guards took up a position before them, curved swords, snapped from their belt hooks, ready in their hands. Again that shout. Was it a warning or a threat? With the language barrier Ross could only wait to see.

Another party approached along the beach from the south. In the lead was a cloaked and hooded figure, so muffled in its covering of silver-gray that Ross had no idea of the form beneath. Silvery-gray—no, now that hue was deepening with blue tones, darkening rapidly. By the time the cloaked newcomer had passed the rock which sheltered the human the covering was a rich blue which seemed to glow.

Behind the leader were a dozen armed man. They wore the same beaked helmets, the supple encasing breast- and back-plates, but their leggings were gray. They, too, carried curved swords, but the weapons were still latched to their belts and they made no move to draw them in spite of the very patent hostility of the guards before them.

Blue cloak halted some three feet from the guards. The sea wind pulled at the cloak, wrapping it about the body beneath. But even so, the wearer remained well hidden. From under a flapping edge came a hand. The fingers, long and slender, were curled about an ivory-colored wand which ended in a knob. Sparks flashed from it in continuous flickering.

Ross clapped his hand to his belt. To his complete amazement the sonic disk he wore was reacting to those flashes, prickling sharply in perfect beat to their blink-blink. He cupped his scarred fingers over the disk as he waited to see what was going to happen, wondering if the holder of that wand might, in return, pick up the broadcast of the code set on Ashe's call.

The hand clasping the wand was not dusky-skinned but had much of the same ivory shade as the rod, so that to Ross the meeting between flesh and wand was hardly distinguishable. Now by one firm thrust the hand planted the rod into the sand, leaving it to stand sentinel between the two parties.

Retreating a step or two, the red-clad guards gave ground. But they did not reclasp their swords. Their attitude, Ross judged, was that of men in some awe of their opponent, but men urged to defiance, either by a belief in the righteousness of their cause, or strengthened by an old hatred.

Now the cloaked one began to speak—or was that speech? Certainly the flow of sound had little in common with the clicking tongue Ross had caught earlier. This trill of notes possessed the rise and fall of a chant or song which could have been a formula or greeting—or a warning. And the lines of warriors escorting the chanter stood to attention, their weapons still undrawn.

Ross caught his lower lip between his teeth and bit down on it. That chanting—it crawled into the mind, set up a pattern! He shook his head vigorously and then was shocked by that recklessness. Not that any of those on shore had glanced in his direction.

The chant ended on a high, broken note. It was followed by a moment of silence through which sounded only the wind and the beat of wave.

Then one of the laborers flung up his head and clicked a word or two. He and his fellows fell face down on the beach, cupping their hands to pour sand over their unkempt heads. One of the guards turned with a sharp yell to boot the nearest of the workers in the ribs.

But his companion cried out. The wand which had stood so erect when it was first planted, now inclined toward the working party, its sparks shooting so swiftly and with such slight break between that they were fast making a single beam. Ross jerked his hand from contact with the sonic; a distinct throb of pain answered that stepping up of the mysterious broadcast.

The laborers broke and ran, or rather crawled on their bellies until they were well away, before they got to their feet and pelted back down the strand. However, the guards were of sterner stuff. They were withdrawing all right, but slowly backing away, their swords held up before them as men might retreat before insurmountable odds.

When they were well gone the robed one took up the wand. Holding it out beyond, the cloaked leader of the second party approached the two piles of salvage the workers had heaped into rough order. There was a detailed inspection of both until the robed one came upon the body.

At a trilled order two of the warriors came up and laid out the corpse. When the robed one nodded they stood well back. The rod moved, the tip rather than the knobbed head being pointed at the body.

Ross's head snapped back. That bolt of light, energy, fire—whatever it was—issuing from the rod had dazzled him into momentary blindness. And a vibration of force through the air was like a blow.

When he was able to see once more there was nothing at all on the sand where the corpse had lain, nothing except a glassy trough from which some spirals of vapor arose. Ross clung to his rock support badly shaken.

Men with swords . . . and now this—some form of controlled energy which argued of technical development and science. Just as the cliff castle had bombarded with rocks ships sailing with a speed which argued engine power of an unknown type. A mixture of barbaric and advanced knowledge. To assess this, he needed more experience, more knowledge than he possessed. Now Ashe could . . .

Ashe!

Ross was jerked back to his own quest. The rod was quiet, no more sparks were flung from its knob. And under Ross's touch his sonic was quiet also. He snapped off the broadcast. If that device had picked up the flickering of the rod, the reverse could well be true.

The cloaked one chose from the pile of goods, and its escort gathered up the designated boxes, a small cask or two. So laden, the party returned south the way they had come. Ross allowed his breath to expel in a sigh of relief.

He worked his way farther north along the coast, watching other parties of the furred workers and their guards. Lines of the former climbed the cliff, hauling their spoil, their destination the castle. But Ross saw no sign of Ashe, received no answer to the sonic code he had reset once the strangers were out of distance. And he began to realize that his present search might well be fruitless, though he fought against accepting it.

When he turned back to the slit cave Ross's fear was ready to be expressed in anger, the anger of frustration over his own helplessness. With no chance of trying to penetrate the castle, he could not learn whether or not Ashe had been taken prisoner. And until the workers left the beach he could not prowl there hunting the grimmer evidence his mind flinched from considering.

Karara waited for him on the inner ledge. There was no sign of the dolphins and as Ross pulled out of the water, pushing aside his mask, her face in the thin light of the cave was deeply troubled.

"You did not find him," she made that a statement rather than a question.

"No."

"And I did not find it—"

Ross used a length of weed from the nest as a towel. But now he stood very still.

"The gate . . . no sign of it?"

"Just this—" She reached behind her and brought up a sealed container. Ross recognized one of the supply cans they had had in the cache by the gate. "There are others . . . scattered. Taua and Tino-rau seek them now. It is as if all that was on the other side was sucked through with us."

"You are sure you found the right place?"

"Is—is this not part of it?" Again the girl sought for something on the ledge. What she held out to him was a length of metal rod, twisted and broken at one end as if a giant hand had wrenched it loose from the installation.

Ross nodded dully. "Yes," his voice was harsh as if the words were pulled out of him against his will and against all hope—"that's part of a side bar. It—it must have been totally wrecked."

Yet, even though he held that broken length in his hands, Ross could not really believe the gate was gone. He swam out once more, heading for the reef where the dolphins joined him as guides. There was a second piece of broken tube, the scattered containers of supplies, that was all. They were wrecked in time as surely as those ships had been wrecked on the sea reef the night before!

Ross headed once again for the cave. Their immediate needs were of major importance now. The containers must be all gathered and taken into their hiding place, because upon their contents three human lives could depend.

He paused just at the entrance to adjust the net of containers he transported. And it was that slight chance which brought him knowledge of the intruder.

On the ledge Karara was heaping up the kelp of the nest. But to one side and on a level with the girl's head . . .

Ross dared not flash his torch, thus betraying his presence. Leaving the net hitched to the rock by its sling, he swam under water along the side of the cave by a route which should bring him out within striking distance of that hunched figure perching above to watch Karara's every move.

6
Loketh the Useless

The wash of waves covered Ross's advance until he came up against the wall not too far from the spy's perch. Whoever crouched there still leaned forward to watch Karara. And Ross's eyes, having adjusted to the gloom of the cavern, made out the outlines of head and shoulders. The next two or three minutes were critical ones for the human. He must emerge on the ledge in the open before he could attack.

Karara might almost have read his mind and given conscious help. For now she went out on the point of the ledge to whistle the dolphins' summons. Tino-rau's sleek head bobbed above water as he answered the girl with a bubbling squeak. Karara knelt and the dolphin came to butt against her outheld hand.

Ross heard a gasp from the watcher, a faint sound of movement. Karara began to sing softly, her voice rippling in one of the liquid chants of her own people, the dolphin interjecting a note or two. Ross had heard them at

239

that before, and it made perfect cover for his move. He sprang.

His grasp tightened on flesh, fingers closed about thin wrists. There was a yell of astonishment and fear from the stranger as the man jerked him from his perch to the ledge. Ross had his opponent flattened under him before he realized that the other had offered no struggle, but lay still.

"What is it?" Karara's torch beam caught them both. Ross looked down into a thin brown face not too different from his own. The wide-set eyes were closed, and the mouth gaped open. Though he believed the Hawaikan unconscious, Ross still kept hold on those wrists as he moved from the sprawled body. With the girl's aid he used a length of kelp to secure the captive.

The stranger wore a garment of glistening skintight material which covered body, legs, and feet, but left his lanky arms bare. A belt about his waist had loops for a number of objects, among them a hook-pointed knife which Ross prudently removed.

"Why, he is only a boy," Karara said. "Where did he come from?"

Ross pointed to the wall crevice. "He was up there, watching you."

Her eyes were wide and round. "Why?"

Ross dragged his prisoner back against the wall of the cave. After witnessing the fate of those who had swum ashore from the wreck, he did not like to think what motive might have brought the Hawaikan here. Again Karara's thoughts must have matched his, for she added:

"But he did not even draw his knife. What are you going to do with him?"

That problem already occupied Ross. The wisest move undoubtedly was to kill the native out of hand. But such ruthlessness was more than he could stomach. And if he could learn anything from the stranger—gain some knowledge of this new world and its ways—he would be twice winner. Why, this encounter might even lead to Ashe!

"Ross . . . his leg. See?" The girl pointed.

The tight fit of the alien's clothing made the defect clear; the right leg of the stranger was shrunken and twisted. He was a cripple.

"What of it?" Ross demanded sharply. This was no time for an appeal to the sympathies.

But Karara did not urge any modification of the bonds as he half feared she would. Instead, she sat back cross-legged, an odd, withdrawn expression making her seem remote though he could have put out his hand to touch her.

"His lameness—it could be a bridge," she observed, to Ross's mystification.

"A bridge—what do you mean?"

The girl shook her head. "This is only a feeling, not a true thought. But also it is important. Look, I think he is waking."

The lids above those large eyes were fluttering. Then with a shake of the head, the Hawaikan blinked up at them. Blank bewilderment was all Ross could read in the stranger's expression until the alien saw Karara. Then a flood of clicking speech poured from his lips.

He seemed utterly astounded when they made no answer. And the fluency of his first outburst took on a pleading note, while the expectancy of his first greeting faded away.

Karara spoke to Ross. "He is becoming afraid, very much afraid. At first, I think, he was pleased . . . happy."

"But why?"

The girl shook her head. "I do not know; I can only feel. Wait!" Her hand rose in imperious command. She did not rise to her feet, but crawled on hands and knees to the edge of the ledge. Both dolphins were there, raising their heads well out of the water, their actions expressing unusual excitement.

"Ross!" Karara's voice rang loudly. "Ross, they can understand him! Tino-rau and Taua can understand him!"

"You mean, they understand this language?" Ross found

that fantastic, awesome as the abilities of the dolphins were.

"No, his mind. It's his mind, Ross. Somehow he thinks in patterns they can pick up and read! They do that, you know, with a few of us, but not in the same way. This is more direct, clearer! They're so excited!"

Ross glanced at the prisoner. The alien had wriggled about, striving to raise his head against the wall as a support. His captor pulled the Hawaikan into a sitting position, but the native accepted that aid almost as if he were not even aware of Ross's hands on his body. He stared with a kind of horrified disbelief at the bobbing dolphin heads.

"He is afraid," Karara reported. "He has never known such communication before."

"Can they ask him questions?" demanded Ross. If this odd mental tie between Terran dolphin and Hawaikan did exist, then there was a chance to learn about this world.

"They can try. Now he only knows fear, and they must break through that."

What followed was the oddest four-sided conversation Ross could have ever imagined. He put a question to Karara, who relayed it to the dolphins. In turn, they asked it mentally of the Hawaikan and conveyed his answer back via the same route.

It took some time to allay the fears of the stranger. But at last the Hawaikan entered wholeheartedly into the exchange.

"He is the son of the lord ruling the castle above." Karara produced the first rational and complete answer. "But for some reason he is not accepted by his own kind. Perhaps," she added on her own, "it is because he is crippled. The sea is his home, as he expresses it, and he believes me to be some mythical being out of it. He saw me swimming, masked, and with the dolphins, and he is sure I change shape at will."

She hesitated. "Ross, I get something odd here. He does know, or thinks he knows, creatures who can appear and disappear at will. And he is afraid of their powers."

"Gods and goddesses—perfectly natural."

Karara shook her head. "No, this is more concrete than a religious belief."

Ross had a sudden inspiration. Hurriedly he described the cloaked figure who had driven the castle people from the piles of salvage. "Ask him about that one."

She relayed the question. Ross saw the prisoner's head jerk around. The Hawaikan looked from Karara to her companion, a shade of speculation in his expression.

"He wants to know why you ask about the Foanna? Surely you must well know what manner of beings they are."

"Listen—" Ross was sure now that he had made a real discovery, though its importance he could not guess, "tell him we come from where there are no Foanna. That we have powers and must know of their powers."

If he could only carry on this interrogation straight and not have to depend upon a double translation! And could he even be sure his questions reached the alien undistorted?

Wearily Ross sat back on his heels. Then he glanced at Karara with a twinge of concern. If he was tired by their roundabout communication, she must be doubly so. There was a droop to her shoulders, and her last reply had come in a voice hoarse with fatigue. Abruptly he started up.

"That's enough—for now."

Which was true. He had to have time for evaluation, to adjust to what they had learned during the steady stream of questions passed back and forth. And in that moment he was conscious of his hunger, just as his voice was paper dry from lack of drink. The canister of supplies he had left by the cave entrance . . .

"We need food and drink." He fumbled with his mask, but Karara motioned him back from the water.

"Taua brings . . . Wait!"

The dolphin trailed the net of containers to them. Ross unscrewed one, pulled out a bulb of fresh water. A second box yielded the dry wafers of emergency rations.

Then, after a moment's hesitation, Ross crossed to the prisoner, cut his wrist bonds, and pressed both a bulb and a wafer into his hold. The Hawaikan watched the humans eat before he bit into the wafer, chewing it with vigor, turning the bulb around in his fingers with alert interest before he sucked at its contents.

As Ross chewed and swallowed, mechanically and certainly with no relish, he fitted one fact to another to make a picture of this Hawaikan time period in which they were now marooned. Of course, his picture was based on facts they had learned from their captive. Perhaps he had purposely misled them or fogged some essentials. But could he have done that in a mental contact? Ross would simply have to accept everything with a certain amount of cautious skepticism.

Anyway, there were the Wreckers of the castle—petty lordlings setting up their holds along the coasts, preying upon the shipping which was the lifeblood of this island-water world. The humans had seen them in action last night and today. And if the captive's information was correct, it was not only the storm's fury which brought the waves' harvest. The Wreckers had some method of attracting ships to crack up on their reefs.

Some method of attraction . . . And that force which had pulled them through the time gate; could there be a connection? However, there remained the Wreckers on the cliff. And their prey, the seafarers of the ocean, with an understandably deep enmity between them.

Those two parties Ross could understand and be prepared to deal with, he thought. But there remained the Foanna. And, from their prisoner's explanation, the Foanna were a very different matter.

They possessed a power which did not depend upon swords or ships or the natural tools and weapons of men. No, they had strengths which were unearthly, to give them superiority in all but one way—numbers. Though the Foanna had their warriors and servants, as Ross had seen on the beach, they, themselves, were of another race—

a very old and dying race of which few remained. How many, their enemies could not say, for the Foanna had no separate identities known to the outer world. They appeared, gave their orders, levied their demands, opposed or aided as they wished—always just one or two at a time—always so muffled in their cloaks that even their physical appearances remained a mystery. But there was no mystery about their powers. Ross gathered that no Wrecker lord, no matter how much a leader among his own kind, how ambitious, had yet dared to opposed actively one of the Foanna, though he might make a token protest against some demand from them.

And certainly the captive's description of those powers in action suggested a supernatural origin of Foanna knowledge, or at least its application. But Ross thought that the answer might be that they possessed the remnants of some almost forgotten technical know-how, the heritage of a very old race. He had tried to learn something of the origin of the Foanna themselves, wondering if the robed ones could be from the galactic empire. But the answer had come that the Foanna were older than recorded time, that they lived in the great citadel before the race of the humans' prisoner had risen from very primitive savagery.

"What do we do now?" Karara broke in upon Ross's thoughts as she refastened the containers.

"These slaves that the Wreckers take upon occasion . . . Maybe Ashe . . ." Ross was catching at very fragile straws; he had to. And the stranger had said that able-bodied men who swam ashore relatively uninjured were taken captive. Several had been the night before.

"Loketh."

Ross and Karara looked around. The prisoner put down the water bulb, and one of his hands made a gesture they could not mistake; he pointed to himself and repeated that word, "Loketh."

The man touched his own chest. "Ross Murdock."

Perhaps the other was as impatient as he with their

roundabout method of communication and had decided to try and speed it up. The analyzer! Ashe had included the analyzer with the equipment by the gate. If Ross could find that . . . why, then the major problem could be behind them. Swiftly he explained to Karara, and with a vigorous nod of assent she called to Taua, ordering the rest of the salvage material from the gate be brought to them.

"Loketh." Ross pointed to the youth. "Ross." That was himself. "Karara." He indicated the girl.

"Rosss." The alien made a clicking hiss of the first name. "Karara—" He did better with the second.

Ross carefully unpacked the box Taua had located. He had only slight knowledge of how the device worked. It was intended to record a strange language, break it down into symbols already familiar to the Time Agents. But could it also be used as a translator with a totally alien tongue? He could only hope that the rough handling of its journey through the gate had not damaged it and that the experiment might possibly work.

Putting the box between them, he explained what he wanted; and Karara took up the miniature recorder, speaking slowly and distinctly the same liquid syllables she had used in the dolphin song. Ross clicked the control box when she was finished, and watched the small screen. The symbols which flashed there had meaning for him right enough; he could translate what she had just taped. The machine still worked to that extent.

Now he pushed the box into place before Loketh and made the visibly reluctant Hawaikan take the recorder from Karara. Then through the dolphin link Ross passed on definite instructions. Would it work as well to translate a stellar tongue as it had with languages past and present of his own planet?

Reluctantly Loketh began to talk to the recorder, at first in a very rapid mumble and then, as there was no frightening response, with less speed and more confidence. Symbol lines formed on the screen, and some of them made sense! Ross was elated.

"Ask him: Can one enter the castle unseen to check on the slaves?"

"For what reason?"

Ross was sure he had read those symbols correctly.

"Tell him—that one of our kind may be among them."

Loketh did not reply so quickly this time. His eyes, grave and measuring, studied Ross, then Karara, then Ross again.

"There is a way . . . discovered by this useless one."

Ross did not pay attention to the odd adjective Loketh chose to describe himself. He pressed to the important matter.

"Can and will he show me that way?"

Again that long moment of appraisal on the part of Loketh before he answered. Ross found himself reading the reply symbols aloud.

"If you dare, then I will lead."

7
Witches' Meat

He might be recklessly endangering all of them, Ross knew. But if Ashe was immured somewhere in that rock pile over their heads, then the risk of trusting Loketh would be worth it. However, because Ross was chancing his own neck did not mean that Karara need be drawn into immediate peril too. With the dolphins at her command and the supplies, scanty as those were, she would have a good chance to hide here safely.

"Holding out for what?" she asked quietly after Ross elaborated on this subject, thus bringing him to silence.

Because her question was just. With the gate gone the humans were committed to this time, just as they had earlier been committed to Hawaika when on their home world they had entered the spaceship for the take-off. There was no escape from the past, which had become their present.

"The Foanna," she continued, "these Wreckers, the sea people—all at odds with one another. Do we join any, then their quarrels must also become ours."

Taua nosed the ledge behind the girl, squeaked a demand for attention. Karara looked around at Loketh; her look was as searching as the one the native had earlier turned on her and Ross.

"He"—the girl nodded at the Hawaikan—"wishes to know if you trust him. And he says to tell you this: Because the Shades chose to inflict upon him a twisted leg he is not one with those of the castle, but to them a broken, useless thing. Ross, I gather he thinks we have powers like the Foanna, and that we may be supernatural. But because we did not kill him out of hand and have fed him, he considers himself bound to us."

"Ritual of bread and salt . . . could be." Though it might be folly to match alien customs to ones on Earth, Ross thought of that very ancient pact on his own world. Eat a man's food, become his friend, or at least declare a truce between you. Stiff taboos and codes of behavior marked nations on Earth, especially warrior societies, and the same might be true here.

"Ask him," Ross told Karara, "what is the rule for food and drink between friends or enemies!" The more he could learn of such customs the better protection he might be able to weave for them.

Long moments for the relay of that message, and then Loketh spoke into the recorder of the analyzer, slowly, with pauses, as if trying to make sure Ross understood every word.

"To give bread into the hands of one you have taken in battle, makes him your man—not as a slave to labor, but as one who draws sword at your bidding. When I took your bread I accepted you as cup-lord. Between such there is no betrayal, for how may a man betray his lord? I, Loketh, am now a sword in your hands, a man in your service. And to me this is doubly good, for as a useless one I have never had a lord, nor one to swear to. Also, with this Sea Maid and her followers to listen to thoughts, how could any man speak with a double tongue were he one who consorted with the Shadow and wore the Cloak of Evil?"

"He's right," Karara added. "His mind is open; he couldn't hide his thoughts from Taua and Tino-rau even if he wished."

"All right, I'll accept that." Ross glanced about the ledge. They had piled the containers at the far end. For Karara to move might be safe. He said so.

"Move where?" she asked flatly. "Those men from the castle are still hunting drift out there. I don't think anyone knows of this cave."

Ross nodded to Loketh. "He did, didn't he? I wouldn't want you trapped here. And I don't want to lose those supplies. What is in those containers may be what saves us all."

"We can sink those over by the wall, weight them down in a net. Then, if we have to move, they will be ready. Do not worry—that is my department." She smiled at him with a slightly mocking lift of lips.

Ross subsided, though he was irritated because she was right. The management of the dolphin team and sea matters were her department. And while he resented her reminder of that point he could not deny the justice of her retort.

In spite of his crippled leg, Loketh displayed an agility which surprised Ross. Freed from his ankle bonds, he beckoned the man back to the very niche where he had hidden to watch Karara. Up he swung into that and in a second had vanished from sight.

Ross followed, to discover it was not a niche after all but the opening of a crevice, leading upward as a vent. And it had been used before as a passage. There was no light, but the native guided Ross's hands to the hollow climbing holds cut into the stone. Then Loketh pushed past and went up the crude ladder into the dark.

It was difficult to judge either time or distance in this black tube. Ross counted the holds for some check. His agent training made one part of his mind sharply aware of such things; the need for memorizing a passage which led into the enemy's territory was apparent. What the purpose of this slit had originally been he did not know, but strongholds on Earth had had their hidden ways in and out for use in times of siege, and he was beginning to believe that these aliens had much in common with his own kind.

He had reached twenty in his counting and his senses, alerted by training and instinct, told him there was an opening not too far above. But the darkness remained so thick it fell in tangible folds about his sweating body. Ross almost cried out as fingers clamped about his wrist when he reached for a new hold. Then urged by that grasp, he was up and out, sprawling into a vertical passage. Far ahead was a gray of faint light.

Ross choked and then sneezed as dust puffed up from between his scrabbling hands. The hold which had been on his wrist shifted to his shoulder, and with a surprising strength Loketh hauled the man to his feet.

The passage in which they stood was a slit extending in height well above their heads, but narrow, not much wider than Ross's shoulders. Whether it was a natural fault or had been cut he could not tell.

Loketh was ahead again, his rocking limp making the outline of his body a jerky up-and-down shadow. Again his speed and agility amazed the man. Loketh might be lame, but he had learned to adapt to his handicap very well.

The light increased and Ross marked slits in the walls to his right, no wider than the breadth of his two fingers. He peered out of one and was looking into empty air while below he heard the murmur of the sea. This way must run in the cliff face above the beach.

A click of impatient whisper drew him on to join Loketh. Here was a flight of stairs, narrow of tread and very steep. Loketh turned back and side against these to climb, his outspread hand flattened on the stone as if it possessed adhesive qualities to steady him. For the first time his twisted leg was a disadvantage.

Ross counted again—ten, fifteen of those steps, bringing them once more into darkness. Then they emerged from a well-like opening into a circular room. A sudden and dazzling flare of light made Ross shade his eyes. Loketh set a pale but glowing cone on a wall shelf, and the man discovered that the burst of light was only relative to the dark of the passage; indeed it was very weak illumination.

The Hawaikan braced his body against the far wall. The strain of his effort, whatever its purpose, was easy to read in the contorted line of his shoulders. Then the wall slid under Loketh's urging, a slow move as if the weight of the slab he strove to handle was almost too great for his slender arms, or else the need for caution was intensified here.

They now fronted a narrow opening, and the light of the cone shone only a few feet into the space. Loketh beckoned to Ross and they went on. Here the left wall was cut in many places emitting patches of light in a way which bore no resemblance to conventional windows. It was like walking behind a pierced screen which followed no logical pattern in cutaway portions. Ross gazed out and gasped.

He was standing above the center core of the castle, and the life below and beyond drew his attention. He had seen drawings reproducing the life of a feudal castle. This resembled them and yet, as Ross studied the scene closer, the differences between Earth's past and this became more distinct.

In the first place there were those animals—or were they animals?—being hooked up to a cart. They had six limbs, walking on four, holding the remaining two folded under their necks. Their harness consisted of a network fitted over their shoulders, anchored to the folded limbs. Their grotesque heads, bobbing and weaving on lengthy necks, their bodies, were sleekly scaled. Ross was startled by a resemblance he traced to the sea dragon he had met in the future of this world.

But the creatures were subject to the men harnessing them. And the activity in other respects . . . Ross had to fight a wayward and fascinated interest in all he could see, force himself to concentrate on learning what might be pertinent to his own mission. But Loketh did not allow him to watch for long. Instead, his hand on the man's arm urged the other down the gallery behind the screen and once more into the bulk of the fortress.

Another narrow way ran through the thickness of the walls. Then a patch of light, not that of outer day, but a reddish gleam from an opening waist high. There Loketh went awkwardly to his good knee, motioning Ross to follow his example.

What lay below was a hall furnished with a barbaric rawness of color and glitter. There were long strips of brightly hued woven stuff on the walls, touched here and there with the sparkling glints of jewels. And set at intervals among the hangings were oval objects perhaps Ross's height on which were designs and patterns picked out in paint and metal. Maybe the stylized representation of native plants and animals.

The whole gave an impression of clashing color, just as the garments of those gathered there were garish in turn.

There were three Hawaikans on the two-step dais. All wore robes fitting tightly to the upper portion of their bodies, girded to their waists with elaborate belts, then falling in long points to floor level, the points being finished off with tassels. Their heads were covered with tight caps formed from interlaced decorated strips that glittered as they moved. And the mixture of colors in their apparel was such as to offend human eyes with their harsh clash of shade against shade.

Drawn up below the dais were two rows of guards. But the reason for the assembly baffled Ross, since he could not understand the clicking speech.

There came a hollow echoing sound as from a gong. The three on the dais straightened, turned their attention to the other end of the hall. Ross did not need Loketh's gesture to know that something of importance was about to begin.

Down the hall was a somber note in the splash of clashing color. The man recognized the gray-blue robe of the Foanna. There were three of the robed ones this time, one slightly in advance of the other two. They came at a gliding pace as if they swept along above that paved flooring, not by planting feet upon it. As they halted below the dais the men there rose.

Ross could read their reluctance to make that concession in the slowness of their movements. They were plainly being compelled to render deference when they longed to refuse it. Then the middle one of the castle lords spoke first.

"Zahur—" Loketh breathed in Ross's ear, his pointed finger indicating the speaker.

Ross longed vainly for the ability to ask questions, a chance to know what was in progress. That the meeting of the two Hawaikan factions was important he did not doubt.

There was an interval of silence after the castle lord finished speaking. To the man this spun on and on and he sensed the mounting tension. This must be a showdown, perhaps even a declaration of open hostilities between Wreckers and the older race. Or perhaps the pause was a subtle weapon of the Foanna, used to throw a less-sophisticated enemy off balance, as a judo fighter might use an opponent's attack as part of his own defense.

When the Foanna did make answer it came in the singsong of chanted words. Ross felt Loketh shiver, felt the crawl of chill along his own spine. The words—if those were words and not just sounds intended to play upon the mind and emotions of a listener—cut into one. Ross wanted to close his ears, thrust his fingers into them to drown out that sound, yet he did not have the power to raise his hands.

It seemed to him that the men on the dais were swaying now as if the chant were a rope leashed about them, pulling them back and forth. There was a clatter; one of the guards had fallen to the floor and lay there, rolling, his hands to his head.

A shout from the dais. The chanting reached a note so high that Ross felt the torment in his ears. Below, the lines of guards had broken. A party of them were heading for the end of the hall, making a wide detour around the Foanna. Loketh gave a small choked cry; his fingers tightened on Ross's forearm with painful intensity as he whispered.

What was about to happen meant something important. To Loketh or to him? Ashe! Was this concerned with Ashe? Ross crowded against the opening, tried to see the direction in which the guards had disappeared.

The wait made him doubly impatient. One of the men on the dais had dropped on the bench there, his head forward on his hands, his shoulders quivering. But the one Loketh had identified as Zahur still fronted the Foanna spokesman, and Ross gave tribute to the strength of will which kept him there.

They were returning, the guards, and herded between their lines three men. Two were Hawaikans, their bare dark bodies easily identifiable. But the third—Ashe! Ross almost shouted his name aloud.

The human stumbled along and there was a bandage above his knee. He had been stripped to his swimming trunks, all his equipment taken from him. There was a dark bruise on his left temple, the angry weal of a lash mark on neck and shoulder.

Ross's hands clenched. Never in his life had he so desperately wanted a weapon as he did at that moment. To spray the company below with a machine gun would have given him great satisfaction. But he had nothing but the knife in his belt and he was as cut off from Ashe as if they were in separate cells of some prison.

The caution which had been one of his inborn gifts and which had been fostered by his training, clamped down on his first wild desire for action. There was not the slightest chance of his doing Ashe any good at the present. But he had this much—he knew that Gordon was alive and that he was in the aliens' hands. Faced by those facts Ross could plan his own moves.

The Foanna chant began again, and the three prisoners moved; the two Hawaikans turned, set themselves on
either side of Ashe, and gave him support. Their actions
had a mechanical quality as if they were directed by a
will beyond their own. Ashe gazed about him at the
Wreckers and the robed figures. His awareness of them
both suggested to Ross that if the natives had come under
the control of the Foanna, the human resisted their
influence. But Ashe did not try to escape the assistance
of his two fellow prisoners, and he limped with their aid
back down the hall, following the Foanna.

Ross deduced that the captives had been transferred from
the lord of the castle to the Foanna. Which meant Ashe
was on his way to another destination. Ross and Loketh
swiftly returned to the sea cave.

"You have found Gordon!" Karara read his news from
his face.

"The Wreckers had him prisoner. Now they've turned
him over to the Foanna—"

"What will *they* do with him?" the girl demanded of
Loketh.

His answer came roundabout as usual as the native
squatted by the analyzer and clicked his answer into it.

"They have claimed the wreck survivors for tribute. Your
companion will be witches' meat."

"Witches' meat?" repeated Ross, uncomprehending.

Then Karara drew a ragged breath which was a gasp
of horror.

"Sacrifice! Ross, he must mean they are going to use
Gordon for a sacrifice."

Ross stiffened and then whirled to catch Loketh by the
shoulders. The inability to question the native directly was
an added disaster now.

"Where are they taking him? Where?" He began that
fiercely, and then forced control on himself.

Karara's eyes were half closed, her head back; she was
manifestly aiming that inquiry at the dolphins, to be translated to Loketh.

Symbols burned on the analyzer screen.

"The Foanna have their own fortress. It can be entered best by sea. There is a boat . . . I can show you, for it is my own secret."

"Tell him—yes, as soon as we can!" Ross broke out. The old feeling that time was all-important worried at him. Witches' meat . . . witches' meat . . . the words were sharp as a lash.

8
The Free Rovers

Twilight made a gray world where one could not trace
the true meeting of land and water, sea and sky. Surely
the haze about them was more than just the normal dusk
of coming night.

Ross balanced in the middle of the skiff as it bobbed
along the swell of waves inside a barrier reef. To his mind
the craft carrying the three of them and their net of
supplies was too frail, rode too high. But Karara paddling
in the bow, Loketh at the stern seemed to be content,
and Ross could not, for pride's sake, question their com-
petency. He comforted himself with the knowledge that
no agent was able to absorb every primitive skill, and
Karara's people had explored the Pacific in outrigger canoes
hardly more stable than their present vessel, navigating
by currents and stars.

Smothering his feeling of helplessness and the slow
anger that roused in him, the man busied himself with
study of a sort. They had had the longer part of the day

258

in the cave before Loketh would agree to venture out of hiding and paddle south. Aided by Loketh, Ross used the analyzer to learn what he could of the native tongue.

Now he possessed a working vocabulary of clicked words, he was able to follow Loketh's speech so that translation through the dolphins was not necessary except for complicated directions. Also, he had a more detailed briefing of the present situation on Hawaika.

Enough to know that they might be embarking on a mad venture. The citadel of the Foanna was distinctly forbidden ground, not only for Loketh's people but also for the Foanna's Hawaikan followers who lived and worked in an outer ring of fortification. Those natives were, Ross gathered, a hereditary corps of servants and warriors, born to that status and not recruited from the native population at large. As such, they were armored by the "magic" of their masters.

"If the Foanna are so powerful," Ross had demanded, "why do you go with us against them?" To depend so heavily on the native made him uneasy.

The Hawaikan looked to Karara. One of his hands raised; his fingers sketched a sign toward the girl.

"With the Sea Maid and her magic I do not fear." He paused before adding, "Always has it been said of me— and to me—that I am a useless one, fit only to do women's tasks. No word weaver shall ever chant my battle deeds in the great hall of Zahur. I who am Zahur's true son can not carry my sword in any lord's train. But now you offer me one of the great to-be-remembered quests. If I go, so may I prove that I am a man, even if I go limpingly. There is nothing the Foanna can do to me which is worse than what the Shadow has already done. Choosing to follow you I may stand up to face Zahur in his own hall, show him that the blood of his House has not been drained from my veins because I walk crookedly!"

There was such bitter fire, not only in the sputtering rush of Loketh's words, but in his eyes and the wry twist of his lips, that Ross believed him. The human no longer had any doubts that the castle outcast was willing to brave the unknown terrors of the Foanna keep, not only because he was bound to aid Ross, but because he saw in this venture a chance to gain what he had never had, a place in his warrior culture.

Shut off from the normal life of his people, he had early turned to the sea. His twisted leg had not proved a handicap in the water, and he stated with confidence that he was the best swimmer in the castle. Not that the men of his father's following had taken greatly to the sea, which they looked upon merely as a way of preying upon the true sea rovers.

The reef on which the ships had been wrecked was a snare of sorts—first by the whim of nature when wind and current piled up the trading ships there. Then, Ross was startled when Loketh elaborated on a later development of that trap.

"So Zahur returned from his meeting and set up a great magic among the rocks, according to the spells he was taught. Now ships are drawn there so the wrecks have been many and Zahur becomes an even greater lord with many men coming to take sword oath under him."

"This magic," asked Ross, "of what manner is it and where did Zahur obtain it?"

"It is fashioned so—" Loketh sketched two straight lines in the air, "not curved as a sword. And the color of water under a storm sky, both rods being as tall as a man. There was much care to set them in place, that was done by a man of Glicmas."

"A man of Glicmas?"

"Glicmas is now the high lord of the Iccio. He is blood kin to Zahur, yet Zahur must take sword oath to send to Glicmas a fourth of all his sea-gleanings for a year in payment for this magic."

"And Glicmas, where did he get it? From the Foanna?"

Loketh made an emphatic denial of that. "No, the Foanna have spoken out against their use, making even greater ill feeling between the Old Ones and the coast people. It is said that Glicmas saw a great wonder in the sky and followed it to a high place of his own country. A mountain broke in twain and a voice issued forth from the rent, calling that the lord of the country come and stand to hear it. When Glicmas did so he was told that the magic would be his. Then the mountain closed again and he found many strange things upon the ground. As he uses them they make him akin to the Foanna in power. Some he gives to those who are his blood kin, and together they will be great until they close their fists not only upon the sea rovers, but upon the Foanna also. This they have come to believe."

"But you do not?" Karara asked then.

"I do not know, Sea Maid. The time is coming when perhaps they shall have their chance to prove how strong is their magic. Already the Rovers gather in fleets as they never did before. And it seems that they, too, have found a new magic, for their ships fly through the water, depending no longer on wind-filling sails, or upon strong arms of men at long paddles. There is a struggle before us. But that you must know, being who and what you are, Sea Maid."

"And what do you think I am? What do you think Ross is?"

"If the Foanna dwell on land and hold old knowledge and power beyond our reckoning in their two hands," he replied, "then it is possible that the same could have roots in the sea. It is my belief that you are of the Shades, but not the Shadow. And this warrior is also of your kind—but perhaps in different degree, putting into action your desires and wishes. Thus, if you go up against the Foanna, you shall be well matched, kind to kind."

Nice to be so certain of that, Ross thought. He did not share Loketh's confidence on that subject.

"The Shades . . . the Shadow . . ." Karara persisted. "What are these, Loketh?"

An odd expression crossed the Hawaikan's face. "Are

those not known to you, Sea Maid? Indeed, then you are of a breed different from the people of land. The Shades are those of power who may come to the aid of men should it be their desire to influence the future. And the Shadow . . . the Shadow is That Which Ends All—man, hope, good. To Which there is no appeal, and Which holds a vast and enduring hatred for that which has life and full substance."

"So Zahur has this new magic. Is it the gift of Shades or Shadow?" Ross brought them back to the subject which had sparked in him a small warning signal.

"Zahur prospers mightily." Loketh's answer was ambiguous.

"And so the Shadow could not provide such magic?" the man pushed.

But before the Hawaikan had a chance to answer, Karara added another question:

"But you believe that it did?"

"I do not know. Only the magic has made Zahur a part of Glicmas, and Glicmas is now perhaps a part of that which spoke from the mountain. It is not well to accept gifts which tie one man to another unless there is from the first a saying of how deep that bond may run."

"I think you are wise in that, Loketh," Karara said.

But the uneasiness had grown in Ross. Alien powers, out of a mountain heart, passed from one lord to another. And on the other hand the Rovers' sudden magic in turn, lending their ships wings. The two facts balanced in an odd way. Back on Earth there had been those sudden and unaccountable jumps in technical knowledge on the part of the enemy, jumps which had set in action the whole Time Travel service of which he had become a party. And these jumps had not been the result of normal research; they had come from the looting of derelict spaceships wrecked on his world in the far past.

Could driblets of the same stellar knowledge have been here deliberately fed to warring communities? He asked

Loketh about the possibility of space-borne explorers. But to the Hawaikan that was a totally foreign conception. The stars, for Loketh, were the doorways and windows of the Shades, and he treated the suggestion of space travel as perhaps natural to those all-powerful specters, but certainly not for beings like himself. There was no hint that Hawaika had been openly visited by a galactic ship. Though that did not bar such landings. The planet was, Ross thought, thinly populated. Whole sections of the interiors of the larger islands were wilderness, and this world must be in the same state of only partial occupation as his own earth had been in the Bronze Age when tribes on the march had fanned out into virgin wilderness, great forests, and steppes unwalked by man before their coming.

Now as he balanced in the canoe and tried to keep his mind off the queasiness in his middle and the insecurity of the one thickness of sea-creature hide stretched over a bone framework which made up the craft between his person and the water, Ross still mulled over what might be true. Had the galactic invaders for their own purposes begun to meddle here, leaking weapons or tools to upset what must be a very delicate balance of power? Why? To bring on a conflict which would occupy the native population to the point of exhaustion or depopulation? So they could win a world for their own purposes without effort or risk on their part? Such cold-blooded fishing in deliberately troubled waters fitted very well with the behavior of the Baldies as he had known them on Earth.

And he could not set aside that memory of this very coast as he had seen it through the peep, the castle in ruins, tall pylons reaching from the land into the sea. Was this the beginning of that change which would end in the Hawaika of his own time, empty of intelligent life, shattered into a loose network of islands?

"This fog is strange." Karara's words startled Ross to return to the here and now.

The haze he had been only half conscious of when they had put out from the tiny secret bay where Loketh kept his boat, was truly a fog, piling up in soft billows and cutting down visibility with speed.

"The Foanna!" Loketh's answer was sharp, a recognition of danger. "Their magic—they hide their place so! There is trouble, trouble on the move!"

"Do we land then?" Ross did not ascribe the present blotting out of the landscape to any real manipulation of nature on the part of the all-powerful Foanna. Too many times the reputations of "medicine men" had been so enhanced by coincidence. But he did doubt the wisdom of trying to bore ahead blindly in this murk.

"Taua and Tino-rau can guide us," Karara reminded him. "Throw out the rope, Ross. What is above water will not confuse them."

He moved cautiously, striving to adapt his actions to the swing of the boat. The line was ready coiled to hand and he tossed the loose end overboard, to feel the cord jerk taut as one of the dolphins caught it up.

They were being towed now, though both paddlers reinforced the forward tug with their efforts. The curtain gathering above the surface of the water did not hamper the swimmers beneath its surface, and Ross felt relief. He turned his head to speak to Loketh.

"How near are we?"

The mist had thickened to the point that, close as the native was, the lines of his body blurred. His clicking answer seemed distorted, too, almost as if the fog had altered not only his form but his personality.

"Maybe very soon now. We must see the sea gate before we are sure."

"And if we aren't able to see that?" challenged Ross.

"The sea gate is above and below the water. Those who obey the Sea Maid, who are able to speak thought to thought, will find it if we can not."

But they were never to reach that goal. Karara gave warning: "There are ships about."

Ross knew that the dolphins had told her. He demanded in turn: "What kind?"

"Larger, much larger than this."

Then Loketh broke in: "A Rover Raider—three of them!"

Ross frowned. He was the cripple here. The other two, with their ability to communicate with the dolphins, were the sighted, he the blind. And he resented his handicap in a burst of bitterness which must have colored his tone as he ordered, "Head inshore—now!"

Once on land, even in the fog, he felt that they had the advantage in any hide-and-seek which might ensue with this superior enemy force. But afloat he was help-less and vulnerable, a state Ross did not accept easily.

"No," Loketh returned as sharply. "There is no place to land along the cliff."

"We are between two of the ships," Karara reported.

"Your paddles—" Ross schooled his voice to a whis-per, "hold them—don't use them. Let the dolphins take us on. In the fog, if we make no sound, we may get by the ships."

"Right!" Karara agreed, and he heard an assenting grunt from Loketh.

They were moving very slowly. Strong as the dolphins were, they dared not expend all their strength on tow-ing the skiff too fast. Ross thought furiously. Perhaps the sea could be their way of escape if the need arose. He had no idea why raiding ships were moving under the cover of fog into the vicinity of the Foanna citadel. But his knowledge of tactics led him to guess that this impending visit was not anticipated by the Foanna, nor was it a friendly one. And, as veteran seamen who should normally be wary of fog as thick as this, the Rovers them-selves must have a driving reason, or some safeguard which led them here now.

But dared the three spill out of their boat, trust to their swimming ability and that of the dolphins, and invade the Foanna sea gate so? Could they use the coming Rover attack as a cover for their own invasion of the hold? Ross considered that the odds in their favor were beginning to look better.

He whispered his idea and began to prepare their gear. The boat was still headed for the shore the three could not see. But they could hear sounds out of the white cotton wall which told them how completely they were boxed in by the raiders; creaks, whispers, noises Ross could not readily identify, carried across the waves.

Before leaving the cave and beginning this voyage they had introduced Loketh to the use of the gill-pack, made him practice in the depths of the cave pool with one of the extras drawn through the gate among the supplies. Now all three were equipped with the water aid, and they could be gone in the sea before the trap closed.

"The supply net—" Ross warned Karara. A moment or two later there was a small bump against the skiff at his left hand. He cautiously raised the collection of containers and eased the burden into the water, knowing that one of the dolphins would take charge of it.

However, he was not prepared for what happened next. Under him the boat lurched first one way and then the other in sharp jerks as if the dolphins were trying to spill them into the sea. Ross heard Karara call out, her voice thin and frightened:

"Taua! Tino-rau! They have gone mad! They will not listen!"

The boat raced in a zigzag path. Loketh clutched at Ross, striving to steady him, to keep the boat on an even keel.

"The Foanna—!" Just as Loketh cried out, Karara plunged over the prow of the boat, whether by design or chance Ross did not know.

And then the craft whirled about, smashed side against side with a dark bulk looming out of the fog. Above, Ross heard cries, knew that they had crashed against one of the raiders. He fought to retain his balance, but he had been knocked to the bottom of the boat against Loketh and they struggled together, unable to move during a precious second or two.

Out of the air over their heads dropped a mass of waving strands which enveloped both of them. The stuff was adhesive, slimy. Ross let out a choked cry as the lines tightened about his arms and body, pinioning him.

Those tightened, wove a net. Now he was being drawn up out of the plunging skiff, a helpless captive. His flailing legs, still free of the slimy cords, struck against the side of the larger ship. Then he swung in, over the well of the deck, thudded down on that surface with bruising force, unable to understand anything except that he had been taken prisoner by a very effective device.

Loketh dropped beside him. But Karara was not brought in, and Ross held to that small bit of hope. Had she made it to freedom by dropping into the water before the Rovers netted them? He could see men gathering about him, masked and distorted in the fog. Then he was rolled across the deck, boosted over the edge of a hatch and knew an instant of terror as he fell into the depth below.

How long was he unconscious? It could not have been very long, Ross decided, as he opened his eyes on dark, heard the small sounds of the ship. He lay very still, trying to remember, to gather his wits before he tried to flex his arms. They were held tight to his sides by strands which no longer seemed slimy, but were wrinkling as they dried. There was an odor from them which gagged him. But there was no loosening of those loops despite his struggles, which grew more intense as his strength returned. And at last he lay panting, knowing there was no easy way of escape from here.

9
Battle Test

Babble of speech, cries, sounded muffled to Ross, made a mounting clamor on the deck. Had the raiders' ship been boarded? Was it now under attack? He strove to hear and think through the pain in his head, the bewilderment.

"Loketh?" He was certain that the Hawaikan had been dumped into the same hold.

The only answer was a low moan, a mutter from the dark. Ross began to inch his way in that direction. He was no seaman, but during that worm's progress he realized that the ship itself had changed. The vibration which had carried through the planks on which he lay was stilled. Some engine shut off; one portion of his mind put that into familiar terms. Now the vessel rocked with the waves, did not bore through them.

Ross brought up against another body.

"Loketh!"

"Ahhhhh . . . the fire . . . the fire—!" The half-intelligible answer held no meaning for the human. "It burns in my head . . . the fire—"

The rocking of the ship rolled Ross away from his fellow prisoner toward the opposite side of the hold. There was a roar of voice, bull strong above the noise on deck, then the sound of feet back and forth there.

"The fire . . . ahhh—" Loketh's voice rose to a scream.

Ross was now wedged between two abutments he could not see and from which his best efforts could not free him. The pitching of the ship was more pronounced. Remembering the two vessels he had seen pounded to bits on the reef, Ross wondered if the same doom loomed for this one. But that disaster had occurred during a storm. And, save for the fog, this had been a calm night, the sea untroubled.

Unless—maybe the shaking his body had received during the past few moments had sharpened his thinking—unless the Foanna had their own means of protection at the sea gate and this was the result. The dolphins . . . What had made Tino-rau and Taua react as they did? And if the Rover ship was out of control, it would be a good time to attempt escape.

"Loketh!" Ross dared to call louder. "Loketh!" He struggled against the drying strands which bound him from shoulder to mid thigh. There was no give in them.

More sounds from the upper deck. Now the ship was answering to direction again. Ross heard sounds he could not identify, and the ship no longer rocked so violently. Loketh moaned.

As far as Ross could judge, they were heading out to sea.

"Loketh!" He wanted information; he must have it! To be so ignorant of what was going on was unbearable frustration. If they were now prisoners in a ship leaving the island behind . . . The threat of that was enough to set Ross struggling with his bonds until he lay panting with exhaustion.

"Rossss?" Only a Hawaikan could make that name a hiss.

"Here! Loketh?" But of course it was Loketh.

"I am here." The other's voice sounded oddly weak as if it issued from a man drained by a long illness.

"What happened to you?" Ross demanded.

"The fire . . . the fire in my head—eating . . . eating . . ." Loketh's reply came with long pauses between the words.

The human was puzzled. What fire? Loketh had certainly reacted to something beyond the unceremonious handling they had received as captives. This whole ship had reacted. And the dolphins . . . But what fire was Loketh talking about?

"I did not feel anything," he stated to himself as well as to the Hawaikan.

"Nothing burning in your head? So you could not think—"

"No."

"It must have been the Foanna magic. Fire eating so that a man is nothing, only that which fire feeds upon!"

Karara! Ross's thoughts flashed back to those few seconds when the dolphins had seemed to go crazy. Karara had then called out something about the Foanna. So the dolphins must have felt this, and Karara, and Loketh. Whatever *it* was. But why not Ross Murdock?

Karara possessed an extra, undefinable sense which gave her contact with the dolphins. Loketh had a mind which those could read in turn. But such communication was closed to Ross.

At first that realization carried with it a feeling of shame and loss. That he did not have what these others possessed, a subtle power beyond the body, a part of mind, was humbling. Just as he had felt shut out and crippled when he had been forced to use the analyzer instead of the sense the others had, so did he suffer now.

Then Ross laughed shortly. All right, sometimes insensitivity could be a defense as it had at the sea gate. Suppose his lack could also be a weapon? He had not been knocked out as the others appeared to be. But for the bad luck of having been captured before the raiders had succumbed, Ross could, perhaps, have been master of this ship by now. He did not laugh now; he smiled sardonically at his own grandiose reaction. No use thinking about what might have been, just file this fact for future reference.

A creaking overhead heralded the opening of the hatch. Light lanced down into the cubby, and a figure swung over and down a side ladder, coming to stand over Ross, feet apart for balancing, accommodating to the swing of the vessel with the ease of long practice.

Thus Ross came face to face with his first representative of the third party in the Hawaikan tangle of power—a Rover.

The seaman was tall, with a heavier development of shoulder and upper arms than the landsmen. Like the guards he wore supple armor, but this had a pearly hue that shimmered with opaline lines. His head was bare except for a broad, scaled band running from the nape of his neck to the mid-point of his forehead, a band supporting a sharply serrated crest not unlike the erect fin of some Terran fish.

Now as he stood, fists planted on hips, the Rover presented a formidable figure, and Ross recognized in him the air of command. This must be one of the ship's officers.

Dark eyes surveyed Ross with interest. The light from the deck focused directly across the raider's shoulder to catch the human in its full glare, and Ross fought the need for squinting. But he tried to give back stare for stare, confidence for self-confidence.

In Earth's past more than one adventurer's life had been saved simply because he had the will and nerve enough to face his captors without any display of anxiety. Such bravado might not hold here and now, but it was the only weapon Ross had to hand and he used it.

"You—" the Rover broke the silence first, "you are not of the Foanna—" He paused as if waiting an answer—denial or protest. Ross provided neither.

"No, not of the Foanna, nor of the scum of the coast either." Again a pause.

"So, what manner of fish has come to the net of Torgul?" He called an order aloft. "A rope here! We'll have this fish and its fellow out—"

Loketh and Ross were jerked up to the outer deck, dumped into the midst of a crowd of seamen. The Hawaikan was left to lie but, at a gesture from the officer, Ross was set on his feet. He could see the nature of his bonds now, a network of dull gray strands, shriveled and stinking, but not giving in the least when he made another try at moving his arms.

"Ho—" The officer grinned. "The fish does not like the net! You have teeth, fish. Use them, slash yourself free."

A murmur of applause from the crew answered that mild taunt. Ross thought it time for a countermove.

"I see you do not come too close to those teeth." He used the most defiant words his limited Hawaikan vocabulary offered.

There was a moment of silence, and then the officer clapped his hands together with a sharp explosion of sound.

"You would use your teeth, fish?" he asked and his tone could be a warning.

This was going it blind with a vengeance, but Ross took the next leap in the dark. He felt as he often did in tight quarters, that some impenetrable core far within was supplying him with the right words, the fortunate guess.

"On which one of you?" He drew his lips tight, displaying those same teeth, wondering for one startled moment if he should take the Rover's query literally.

"Vistur! Vistur!" More than one voice called.

One of the crew took a step or two forward. Like Torgul, he was tall and heavy, his over-long arms well muscled. There were scars on his forearms, the seam of one up his jaw. He looked to be a very tough fighting man, one who was judged so by peers as seasoned and dangerous.

"Do you choose to prove your words on Vistur, fish?" Again the officer had a formal note in his question, as if this was all part of some ceremony.

"If he meets with me as he stands—no other weapons." Ross flashed back.

Now he had another reaction from them. There were some jeers, a sprinkling of threats as to Vistur's intentions. But Ross also noted that two or three of them had gone silent and were eyeing him in a new and more searching fashion. And Torgul was one of those.

Vistur laughed. "Well said, fish. So shall it be."

Torgul's hand came out, palm up, facing Ross. In its hollow was a small object the human could not see clearly. A new weapon? Only the officer made no move to touch it to Ross, the hand merely moved in a series of waves in mid-air. Then the Rover spoke.

"He carries no unlawful magic."

Vistur nodded. "He's no Foanna. And what need have I to fear the spells of any coast crawler? I am Vistur!"

Again the yells of his supporters arose in hearty answer. The statement held more complete and quiet confidence than any wordy boast.

"And I am Ross Murdock!" He matched the Rover tone for tone. "But does a fish swim with its fins bound to its sides? Or does Vistur fear a free fish too greatly to face one?"

His taunt brought the result Ross wanted. The ties were cut from behind, to flutter down as withered, useless strings. Ross flexed his arms. Tight as those thongs had been they had not constricted circulation, and he was ready to meet Vistur. The human did not doubt that the Rover champion was a formidable fighter, but he had not had Time Agent training courses. Every trick of unarmed fighting known on his own world had been pounded into Ross long ago. His hands and feet could be as deadly weapons as any crook-bladed sword—or gun—provided he could get close enough to use them properly.

Vistur stripped off his weapon belt, put to one side

his helmet, showing that under it his hair was plaited into a braid coiled around the crown of his head to provide what must be extra padding for that strangely narrowed helm. Then he peeled off his armor, peeled it literally indeed, catching the lower edge of the scaled covering with his hands and pulling it up and over his head and shoulders as one might skin off a knitted garment. Now he stood facing Ross, wearing little more than the human's swimming trunks.

Ross had dropped his belt and gill-pack. He moved into the circle the crew had made. From above came a strong light, centering from a point on the mainmast and giving him good sight of his opponent.

Vistur was being urged to make a quick end of the reckless challenger, his supporters shouting directions and encouragement. But if the Rover had confidence, he also possessed the more valuable trait of caution in the face of the unknown. He outweighed, apparently outmatched Ross, but he did not rush in rashly as his backers wished him to.

They circled, Ross studying every move of the Rover's muscles, every slight fraction of change in the other's balance. There would be something to telegraph an attack from the other. For he intended to fight purely in defense.

The charge came at last as the crew grew impatient and yelled their impatience to see the prisoner taught a lesson. But Ross did not believe it was that which sent Vistur at him. The Hawaikan simply thought he knew the best way to take the human.

Ross ducked so that a hammer blow merely grazed him. But his stiffened hand swept sidewise in a judo chop. Vistur gave a whooping cry and went to his knees and Ross swung again, sending the Rover flat to the deck. It had been quick but not so vicious as it might have been. He had no desire to kill or even disable Vistur for more than a few minutes. His victim would carry a couple of aching bruises and perhaps a hearty respect for a new mode of fighting from this encounter. He could have as easily been dead had either of those blows landed other than where Ross chose to plant them.

"Ahhhh—"

Ross swung around, setting his back to the foot of the mast. Had he guessed wrong? With their chosen champion down, would the crew now rush him? He had gambled on the element of fair play which existed in Earth's primitive warrior societies after a man-to-man challenge. But he could be wrong. Ross waited, tense. Just let one of them pull a weapon, and it could be his end.

Two of them were aiding Vistur to his feet. The Rover's breath whistled in and out of him with that same whooping, and both of his hands rose unsteadily to his chest. The majority of his fellows stared from him to the slighter human as if unable to believe the evidence of their eyes.

Torgul gathered up from the deck the belt and gill-pack Ross had shed in preparation for the fight. He turned the belt around over his forearm until the empty knife sheath was uppermost. One of the crew came forward and slammed back into its proper place the long diver's knife which had been there when Ross was captured. Then the Rover offered belt and gill-pack to Ross. The human relaxed. His gamble had paid off; by the present signs he had won his freedom.

"And my swordsman?" As he buckled on the belt Ross nodded to Loketh still lying bound where they had pushed him at the beginning of the fight.

"He is sworn to you?" Torgul asked.

"He is."

"Loose the coast rat then," the Rover ordered. "Now—tell me, stranger, what manner of man are you? Do you come from the Foanna, after all? You have a magic which is not our magic, since the Stone of Phutka did not reveal it on you. Are you from the Shades?"

His fingers moved in the same sign Loketh had once made before Karara. Ross gave his chosen explanation.

"I am from the sea, Captain. As for the Foanna, they

are no friend to me, since they hold captive in their keep one who is my brother-kin."

Torgul stared him up and down. "You say you are from the sea. I have been a Rover since I was able to stumble on my two feet across a deck, after the manner and custom of my people, yet I have never seen your like before. Perhaps your coming means ill to me and mine, but by the Law of Battle, you have won your freedom on this ship. I swear to you, however, stranger, that if ill comes from you, then the Law will not hold, and you shall match your magic against the Strength of Phutka. That you shall discover is another thing altogether."

"I will swear any oath you desire of me, Captain, that I have no ill toward you and yours. There is only one wish I hold: to bring him whom I seek out from the Foanna hold before they make him witches' meat."

"That will be a task worthy of any magic you may be able to summon, stranger. We have tasted this night of the power of the sea gate. Though we went in under the Will of Phutka, we were as weeds whirled about on the waves. Who enters that gate must have more force than any we now know."

"And you, too, then have a score to settle with the Foanna?"

"We have a score against the Foanna, or against their magic," Torgul admitted. "Three ships—one island fair-ing—are gone as if they never were! And those who went with them are of our fleet-clan. There is the work of the Shadow stretching dark and heavy across the sea, new come into these waters. But there remains nothing we can do this night. We have been lucky to win to sea again. Now, stranger, what shall we do with you? Or will you take to the sea again since you name it as home?"

"Not here," Ross countered swiftly. He must gain some idea of where they might be in relation to the island, how far from its shore. Karara and the dolphins—what had happened to them?

"You took no other prisoners?" Ross had to ask.

"There were more of you?" Torgul countered.

"Yes." No need to say how many, Ross decided.

"We saw no others. You . . . all of you—" the Captain rounded on the still-clustered crew, "get about your work! We must raise Kyn Add by morning and report to the council."

He walked away and Ross, determined to learn all he could, followed him into the stern cabin. Here again the man was faced with barbaric splendor in carvings, hangings, a wealth of plate and furnishing not too different from the display he had seen in the Wreckers' castle. As Ross hesitated just within the doorway Torgul glanced back at him.

"You have your life and that of your man, stranger. Do not ask more of me, unless you have that within your hands to enforce the asking."

"I want nothing, save to be returned to where you took me, Captain."

Torgul smiled grimly. "You are of the sea, you yourself said that. The sea is wide, but it is all one. Through it you must have your own paths. Take any you choose. But I do not risk my ship again into what lies in wait before the gates of the Foanna."

"Where do you go then, Captain?"

"To Kyn Add. You have your own choice, stranger— the sea or our fairing."

There would be no way of changing the Rover's decision, Ross thought. And even with the gill-pack he could not swim back to where he had been taken. There were no guideposts in the sea. But a longer acquaintance with Torgul might be helpful.

"Kyn Add then, Captain." He made the next move to prove equality and establish himself with this Rover, seating himself at the table as one who had the right to share the Captain's quarters.

10
Death at Kyn Add

The hour was close to dawn again and a need for sleep weighted Ross's eyelids, was a craving as strong as hunger. Still restlessness had brought him on deck, sent him to pacing, alert to this vessel and its crew.

He had seen the ships of the Earth's Bronze Age traders—small craft compared to those of his own time, depending upon oarsmen when the wind failed their sails, creeping along coasts rather than venturing too far into dangerous seas, sometimes even tying up at the shore each night. There had been other ships, leaner, hardier. Those had plunged into the unknown, touching lands beyond the sea mists, sailed and oared by men plagued by the need to learn what lay beyond the horizon.

And here was such a ship, taut, well kept, larger than the Viking longboats Ross had watched on the tapes of the Project's collection, yet most like those far-faring craft. The prow curved up in a mighty bowsprit where there was the carved likeness of the sea dragon Ross had fought in the Hawaika of his own time. The eyes of that monster flashed with a regular blink of light which the human did not understand. Was it a signal or merely a device to threaten a possible enemy?

There were sails, now furled as this ship bored on, answering to the steady throb of what could only be an engine. And his puzzlement held. A Viking longboat powered by motor? The mixture was incongruous.

The crew were uniform as to face. All of them wore the flexible pearly armor, the skull-strip helmets. Though there were individual differences in ornaments and the choice of weapons. The majority of the men did carry curve-pointed swords, though those were broader and heavier than those he had seen ashore. But several had axes with sickle-shaped heads, whose points curved so far back that they nearly met to form a circle.

Spaced at regular intervals on deck were boxlike objects fronting what resembled gun ports. And smaller ones of the same type were on the raised deck at the stern and mounted in the prow, their muzzles, if the square fronts might be deemed muzzles, flanking the blinking dragon head. Catapults of some type? Ross wondered.

"Rosss—" His name was given the hiss Loketh used, but it was not the Wrecker youth who joined him now at the stern of the ship. "Ho . . . that was strong magic, that fighting knowledge of yours!"

Vistur rubbed his chest reminiscently. "You have big magic, sea man. But then you serve the Maid, do you not? Your swordsman has told us that even the great fish understand and obey her."

"Some fish," qualified Ross.

"Such fish as that, perhaps?" Vistur pointed to the curling wake of foam.

Startled, Ross stared in that direction. Torgul's command was the centermost in a trio of ships, and those cruised in a line, leaving three trails of troubled wave behind them. Coming up now to port in the comparative calm between two wakes was a dark object. In the limited light

Ross could be sure of nothing save that it trailed the ships, appeared to rest on or only lightly in the water, and that its speed was less than that of the vessels it doggedly pursued.

"A fish—that?" Ross asked.

"Watch!" Vistur ordered.

But the Hawaikan's sight must have been keener than the human's. Had there been a quick movement back there? Ross could not be sure.

"What happened?" He turned to Vistur for enlightenment.

"As a salkar it leaps now and than above the surface. But that is no salkar. Unless, Ross, you who say you are from the sea have servants unlike any finned one we have drawn in by net or line before this day."

The dolphins! Could Tino-rau or Taua or both be in steady pursuit of the ships? But Karara . . . Ross leaned against the rail, stared until his eyes began to water from the strain of trying to make out the nature of the black blot. No use, the distance was too great. He brought his fist down against the wood, trying to control his impatience. More than half of him wanted to burst into Torgul's quarters, demand that the Captain bring the ship about to pick up or contact that trailer or trailers.

"Yours?" again Vistur asked.

Ross had tight rein on himself now. "I do not know. It could well be."

It could well be also that the smart thing would be to encourage the Rovers to believe that he had a force of sea dwellers much larger than the four Time castaways. The leader of an army—or a navy—had more prestige in any truce discussion than a member of a lost scouting party. But the thought that the dolphins could be trailing held both promise and worry—promise of allies, and worry over what had happened to Karara. Had she, too, disappeared after Ashe into the hold of the Foanna?

The day did not continue to lighten. Though there was no cottony mist as had enclosed them the night before, there was an odd muting of sea and sky, limiting vision. Shortly Ross was unable to sight the follower or followers. Even Vistur admitted he had lost visual contact. Had the blot been hopelessly outdistanced, or was it still dogging the wakes of the Rover ships?

Ross shared the morning meal with Captain Torgul, a round of leathery substance with a salty, meaty flavor, and a thick mixture of what might be native fruit reduced to a tart paste. Once before he had tasted alien food when in the derelict spaceship it had meant eat or starve. And this was a like circumstance, since their emergency ration supplies had been lost in the net. But though he was apprehensive, no ill effects followed. Torgul had been uncommunicative earlier; now he was looser of tongue, volunteering that they were almost to their port—the fairing of Kyn Add.

The human had no idea how far he might question the Hawaikan, yet the fuller his information the better. He discovered that Torgul appeared willing to accept Ross's statement that he was from a distant part of the sea and that local customs differed from those he knew.

Living on and by the sea the Rovers were quick-witted, adaptive, with a highly flexible though loose-knit organization of fleet-clans. Each of these had control over certain islands which served them as "fairings," ports for refitting and anchorage between voyages, usually ruggedly wooded where the sea people could find the raw material for their ships. Colonies of clans took to the sea, not in the slim, swift cruisers like the ship Ross was now on, but in larger, deeper vessels providing living quarters and warehouses afloat. They lived by trade and raiding, spending only a portion of the year ashore to grow fast-sprouting crops on their fairing islands and indulge in some manufacture of articles the inhabitants of the larger and more heavily populated islands were not able to duplicate.

Their main article of commerce was, however, a sea-dwelling creature whose supple and well-tanned hide formed their defensive armor and served manifold other uses. This could only be hunted by men trained and fearless enough to brave more than one danger Torgul did not explain in detail. And a cargo of such skins brought enough in trade to keep a normal-sized fleet-clan for a year.

There was warfare among them. Rival clans tried to jump each other's hunting territories, raid fairings. But until the immediate past, Ross gathered, such encounters were relatively bloodless affairs, depending more upon craft and skillful planning to reduce the enemy to a position of disadvantage in which he was forced to acknowledge defeat, rather than ruthless battle of no quarter.

The shore-side Wrecker lords were always considered fair game, and there was no finesse in Rover raids upon them. Those were conducted with a cold-blooded determination to strike hard at an ancient foe. However, within the past year there had been several raids on fairings with the same blood-bath result of a foray on a Wrecker port. And, since all the fleet-clans denied the sneak-and-strike, kill-and-destroy tactics which had finished those Rover holdings, the seafarers were divided in their opinion as to whether the murderous raids were the work of Wreckers suddenly acting out of character and taking to the sea to bring war back to their enemies, or whether there was a rogue fleet moving against their own kind for some purpose no Rover could yet guess.

"And you believe?" Ross asked as Torgul finished his résumé of the new dangers besetting his people.

Torgul's hand, its long, slender fingers spidery to human eyes, rubbed back and forth across his chin before he answered:

"It is very hard for one who has fought them long to believe that suddenly those shore rats are entrusting themselves to the waves, venturing out to stir us with their swords. One does not descend into the depths to kick a salkar in the rump; not if one still has his wits safely encased under his skull braid. As for a rogue fleet . . .

what would turn brother against brother to the extent of slaying children and women? Raiding for a wife, yes, that is common among our youth. And there have been killings over such matters. But not the killing of a woman—never of a child! We are a people who have never as many women as there are men who wish to bring them into the home cabin. And no clan has as many children as they hope the Shades will send them."

"Then who?"

When Torgul did not answer at once Ross glanced at the Captain, and what the human thought he saw showing for an instant in the other's eyes was a revelation of danger. So much so that he blurted out:

"You think that I—we—"

"You have named yourself of the sea, stranger, and you have magic which is not ours. Tell me this in truth: Could you not have killed Vistur easily with those two blows if you had wished it?"

Ross took the bold course. "Yes, but I did not. My people kill no more wantonly than yours."

"The coast rats I know, and the Foanna, as well as any man may know their kind and ways, and my people—But you I do not know, sea stranger. And I say to you as I have said before, make me regret that I suffered you to claim battle rights and I shall speedily correct that mistake!"

"Captain!"

That cry had come from the cabin door behind Ross. Torgul was on his feet with the swift movements of a man called many times in the past for an instant response to emergency.

The human was close on the Rover's heels as they reached the deck. A cluster of crewmen gathered on the port side near the narrow bow. That odd misty quality this day held provided a murk hard to pierce, but the men were gesturing at a low-riding object rolling with the waves.

That was near enough for even Ross to be able to

distinguish a small boat akin to the one in which he, Karara, and Loketh had dared the sea gate of the Foanna.

Torgul took up a great curved shell hanging by a thong on the mainmast. Setting its narrow end to his lips, he blew. A weird booming note, like the coughing of a sea monster, carried over the waves. But there was no answer from the drifting boat, no sign it carried any passenger.

"Hou, hou, hou—" Torgul's signal was re-echoed by shell calls from the other two cruisers.

"Heave to!" the Captain ordered. "Wakti, Zimmon, Yoana—out and bring that in!"

Three of the crew leaped to the railing, poised there for a moment, and then dived almost as one into the water. A rope end was thrown, caught by one of them. And then they swam with powerful strokes toward the drifting boat. Once the rope was made fast the small craft was drawn toward Torgul's command, the crewmen swimming beside it. Ross longed to know the reason for the tense expectancy of the men around him. It was apparent the skiff had some ominous meaning for them.

Ross caught a glimpse of a body huddled within the craft. Under Torgul's orders a sling was dropped, to rise, weighted with a passenger. The human was shouldered back from the rail as the limp body was hurried into the Captain's cabin. Several crewmen slid down to make an examination of the boat itself.

Their heads came up, their eyes searched along the rail and centered on Ross. The hostility was so open the human braced himself to meet those cold stares as he would a rush from a challenger.

A slight sound behind sent Ross leaping to the right, wanting to get his back against solid protection. Loketh came up, his limp making him awkward so that he clutched at the rail for support. In his other hand was one of the hooked swords bared and ready.

"Get the murderers!" Someone in the back line of the massing crew yipped that.

Ross drew his diver's knife. Shaken at this sudden

change in the crew's attitude, he was warily on the defensive. Loketh was beside him now and the Hawaikan nodded to the sea.

"Better go there," he cried. "Over before they try to gut you!"

"Kill!" The word shrilled into a roar from the Rovers. They started up the deck toward Ross and Loketh. Then someone leaped between, and Vistur fronted his own comrades.

"Stand away—" One of the others ran forward, thrusting at the tall Rover with a stiffened out-held arm to fend him out of their path.

Vistur rolled a shoulder, sending the fellow shunting away. He went down while two more, unable to halt, thudded on him. Vistur stamped on an outstretched hand and sent a sword spinning.

"What goes here!" Torgul's demand was loud enough to be heard. It stopped a few of the crew and two more went down as the Captain struck out with his fists. Then he was facing Ross, and the chill in his eyes was the threat the others had voiced.

"I told you, sea stranger, that if I found you were a danger to me or mine, you would meet the Justice of Phutka!"

"You did," Ross returned. "And in what way am I now a danger, Captain?"

"Kyn Add has been taken by those who are not Wreckers, not Rovers, not those who serve the Foanna—but strangers out of the sea!"

Ross could only stare back, confused. And then the full force of his danger struck home. Who these raiding sea strangers could be, he had no idea, but that he was now condemned out of his own mouth was true and he realized that these men were not going to listen to any argument from him in their present state of mind.

The growl of the crew was that of a hungry animal. Ross saw the wisdom in Loketh's choice. Far better chance the open sea than the mob before them.

But his time for choice had passed. Out of nowhere whirled a lacy gray-white net, slapping him back against a bulkhead to glue him there. Ross tried to twist loose, got his head around in time to see Loketh scramble to the top of the rail, turn as if to launch himself at the men speeding for the now helpless human. But the Hawaikan's crippled leg failed him and he toppled back overside.

"No!" Again Torgul's shout halted the crew. "He shall take the Black Curse with him when he goes to meet the Shadow—and only one can speak that curse. Bring him!"

Helpless, reeling under their blows, dragged along, Ross was thrown into the Captain's cabin, confronted by a figured braced up by coverings and cushions in Torgul's own chair.

A woman, her face a drawn death's head of skin pulled tight upon bone, yet a fiery inner strength holding her mind above the suffering of her body, looked at the human with narrowed eyes. She nursed a bandaged arm against her, and now and then her mouth quivered as if she could not altogether control some emotion or physical pain.

"Yours is the cursing, Lady Jazia. Make it heavy to bear for him as his kind has laid the burden of pain and remembering on all of us."

She brought her good hand up to her mouth, wiping its back across her lips as if to temper their quiver. And all the time her eyes held upon Ross.

"Why do you bring me this man?" Her voice was strained, high. "He is not of those who brought the Shadow to Kyn Add."

"What—?" Torgul began and then schooled his voice to a more normal tone. "Those were from the sea?" He was gentle in his questioning. "They came out of the sea, using weapons against which we had no defense?"

She nodded. "Yes, they made very sure that only the dead remained. But I had gone to the Shrine of Phutka, since it was my day of duty, and Phutka's power threw its shade over me. So I did not die, but I saw—yes, I saw!"

"Not those like me?" Ross dared to speak to her directly.

"No, not those like you. There were few . . . only so many—" She spread out her five fingers. "And they were all of one like as if born in one birth. They had no hair on their heads, and their bodies were of this hue—" She plucked at one of the coverings they had heaped around her; it was a lavender-blue mixture.

Ross sucked in his breath, and Torgul was fast to pounce upon the understanding he read in the human's face.

"Not your kind—but still you know them!"

"I know them," Ross agreed. "They are the enemy!"

The Baldies from the ancient spaceships, that wholly alien race with whom he had once fought a desperate encounter on the edge of an unnamed sea in the far past of his own world. The galactic voyagers were here—and in active, if secret, conflict with the natives!

11
Weapon from the Depths

Jazia told her story with an attention to time and detail which amazed Ross and won his admiration for her breed. She had witnessed the death and destruction of all which was her life, and yet she had the wit to note and record mentally for possible future use all that she had been able to see of the raiders.

They had come out of the sea at dawn, walking with supreme confidence and lack of any fear. Axes flung when they did not reply to the sentries' challenges had never touched them, and a bombardment of heavier missiles had been turned aside. They proved invulnerable to any weapon the Rovers had. Men who made suicidal rushes to use sword or battle ax hand-to-hand had fallen, before they were in striking distance, under spraying tongues of fire from tubes the aliens carried.

Rovers were not fearful or easily cowed, but in the end

they had fled from the five invaders, gone to ground in their halls, tried to reach their beached ships, only to die as they ran and hid. The slaughter had been remorseless and entire, leaving Jazia in the hill shrine as the only survivor. She had hidden for the rest of the day, seen the killing of a few fugitives, and that night had stolen to the shore, launched one of the ship's boats which was in a cove well away from the main harbor of the fairing, heading out to sea in hope of meeting the homing cruisers with her warning.

"They stayed there on the island?" Ross asked. That point of her story puzzled him. If the object of that murderous raid had been only to stir up trouble among the Hawaikan Rovers, perhaps turning one clan against the other, as he had deduced when he had listened to Torgul's report of similar happenings, then the star men should have withdrawn as soon as their mission was complete, leaving the dead to call for vengeance in the wrong direction. There would be no reason to court discovery of their true identity by lingering.

"When the boat was asea there were still lights at the fairing hall, and they were not our lights, nor did the dead carry them," she said slowly. "What have those to fear? They can not be killed!"

"If they are still there, that we can put to the test," Torgul replied grimly, and a murmur from his officers bore out his determination.

"And lose all the rest of you?" Ross retorted coldly. "I have met these before; they can will a man to obey them. Look you—" He slammed his left hand flat on the table. The ridges of scar tissue were plain against his tanned skin. He knew no better way of driving home the dangers of dealing with the star men than providing this graphic example. "I held my own hand in fire so that the hurt of it would work against their pull upon my thoughts, against their willing that I come and be easy meat for their butchering."

Jazia's fingers flicked out, smoothed across his old scars lightly as she gazed into his eyes.

"This, too, is true," she said slowly. "For it was also pain of body which kept me from their last snare. They stood by the hall and I saw Prahad, Okun, Mosaji, come out to them to be killed as if they were in a hold net and were drawn. And there was that which called me also so that I would go to them though I called upon the Power of Phutka to save. And the answer to that plea came in a strange way, for I fell as I went from the shrine and cut my arm on the rocks. The pain of that hurt was as a knife severing the net. Then I crawled for the wood and that calling did not come again—"

"If you know so much about them, tell us what weapons we may use to pull them down!" That demand came from Vistur.

Ross shook his head. "I do not know."

"Yet," Jazia mused, "all things which live must also die sooner or later. And it is in my mind that these have also a fate they dread and fear. Perhaps we may find and use it."

"They came from the sea—by a ship, then?" Ross asked. She shook her head.

"No, there was no ship; they came walking through the breaking waves as if they had followed some road across the sea bottom."

"A sub!"

"What is that?" Torgul demanded.

"A type of ship which goes under the waves, not through them, carrying air within its hull for the breathing of the crew."

Torgul's eyes narrowed. One of the other captains who had been summoned from the two companion cruisers gave a snort of disbelief.

"There are no such ships—" he began, to be silenced by a gesture from Torgul.

"We know of no such ships," the other corrected. "But then we know of no such devices as Jazia saw in operation either. How does one war upon these under-the-seas ships, Ross?"

The human hesitated. To describe to men who knew nothing of explosives the classic way of dealing with a sub via depth charges was close to impossible. But he did his best.

"Among my people one imprisons in a container a great power. Then the container is dropped near the sub and—"

"And how," broke in the skeptical captain, "do you know where such a ship lies? Can you see it through the water?"

"In a way—not see, but hear. There is a machine which makes for the captain of the above-seas ship a picture of where the sub lies or moves so that he may follow its course. Then when he is near enough he drops the container and the power breaks free—to also break apart the sub."

"Yet the making of such containers and the imprisoning of the power within them," Torgul said, "this is the result of a knowledge which is greater than any save the Foanna may possess. You do not have it?" His conclusion was half statement, half question.

"No. It took many years and the combined knowledge of many men among my people to make such containers, such a listening device. I do not have it."

"Why then think of what we do not have?" Torgul's return was decisive. "What *do* we have?"

Ross's head came up. He was listening, not to anything in that cabin, but to a sound which had come through the port just behind his head. There—it had come again! He was on his feet.

"What—?" Vistur's hand hovered over the ax at his belt. Ross saw their gaze centered on him.

"We may have reinforcements now!" He was already on his way to the deck.

He hurried to the rail and whistled, the thin, shrill summons he had practiced for weeks before he had ever begun this fantastic adventure.

A sleek dark body broke water and the dolphin grin was exposed as Tino-rau answered his call. Though Ross's communication powers with the two finned scouts was very far from Karara's, he caught the message in part and swung around to face the Rovers who had crowded after him.

"We have a way now of learning more about your enemies."

"A boat—it comes without sail or oars!" One of the crew pointed.

Ross waved vigorously, but no hand replied from the skiff. Though it came steadily onward, the three cruisers its apparent goal.

"Karara!" Ross called.

Then side by side with Tino-rau were two wet heads, two masked faces showing as the swimmers trod water— Karara and Loketh.

"Drop ropes!" Ross gave that order as if he rather than Torgul commanded. And the Captain himself was one of those who moved to obey.

Loketh came out of the sea first and as he scrambled over the rail he had his sword ready, looking from Ross to Torgul. The human held up empty hands and smiled.

"No trouble now."

Loketh snapped up his mask. "So the Sea Maid said the finned ones reported. Yet before, these thirsted for your blood on their blades. What magic have you worked?"

"None. Just the truth has been discovered." Ross reached for Karara's hand as she came nimbly up the rope, swung her across the rail to the deck where she stood unmasked, brushing back her hair and looking around with a lively curiosity.

"Karara, this is Captain Torgul," Ross introduced the Rover commander who was staring round-eyed at the girl. "Karara is she who swims with the finned ones, and they obey her." Ross gestured to Tino-rau. "It is Taua who bring the skiff?" he asked the Polynesian.

She nodded. "We followed from the gate. Then Loketh came and said that . . . that . . ." She paused and then added, "But you do not seem to be in danger. What has happened?"

"Much. Listen—this is important. There is trouble at an island ahead. The Baldies were there; they murdered the kin of these men. The odds are they reached there by some form of sub. Send one of the dolphins to see what is happening and if they are still there . . ."

Karara asked no more questions, but whistled to the dolphin. With a flip of tail Tino-rau took off.

Since they could make no concrete plan of action, the cruiser captains agreed to wait for Tino-rau's report and to cruise well out of sight of the fairing harbor until it came.

"This belief in magic," Ross remarked to Karara, "has one advantage. The natives seem able to take in their stride the fact the dolphins will scout for us."

"They have lived their lives on the sea; for it they must have a vast respect. Perhaps they know, as did my people, that the ocean has many secrets, some of which are never revealed except to the forms of life which claim their homes there. But, even if you discover this Baldy sub, what will the Rovers be able to do about it?"

"I don't know—yet." Ross could not tell why he clung to the idea that they could do anything to strike back at the superior alien force. He only knew that he was not yet willing to relinquish the thought that in some way they could.

"And Ashe?"

Yes, Ashe . . .

"I don't know." It hurt Ross to admit that.

"Back there, what really happened at the gate?" he asked Karara. "All at once the dolphins seemed to go crazy."

"I think for a moment or two they did. You felt nothing?"

"No."

"It was like a fire slashing through the head. Some protective device of the Foanna, I think."

A mental defense to which he was not sensitive. Which meant that he might be able to breach that gate if none of the others could. But he had to be there first. Suppose, just suppose Torgul could be persuaded that this attack on the gutted Kyn Add was useless. Would the Rover commander take them back to the Foanna keep? Or with the dolphins and the skiff could Ross himself return to make the try?

That he could make it on his own, Ross doubted. Excitement and will power had buoyed him up throughout the past Hawaikan day and night. Now fatigue closed in, past his conditioning and the built-in stimulant of rations eaten earlier to enclose him in a groggy haze. He had been warned against this reaction, but that was just another item he had pushed out of his conscious mind. The last thing he remembered now was seeing Karara move through a fuzzy cloud.

Voices argued somewhere beyond, the force of that argument carried more by tone than any words Ross could understand. He was pulled sluggishly out of a slumber too deep for any dream to trouble, and lifted heavy eyelids to see Karara once again. There was a prick in his arm— or was that part of the unreality about him?

"—four—five—six—" she was counting, and Ross found himself joining in:

"—seven—eight—nine—ten!"

On reaching "ten" he was fully awake and knew that she had applied the emergency procedure they had been drilled in using, giving him a pep shot. When Ross sat up on the narrow bunk there was a light in the cabin and no sign of day outside the porthole. Torgul, Vistur, the two other cruiser captains, all there . . . and Jazia.

Ross swung his feet to the deck. A pep-shot headache was already beginning, but would wear off soon. There was, however, a concentration of tension in the cabin, and something must have driven Karara to use the drug.

"What is it?"

Karara fitted the medical kit into the compact carrying case.

"Tino-rau has returned. There *is* a sub in the bay. It emits signals on a shoreward beam."

"Then they are still there." Ross accepted the dolphin's report without question. Neither of the scouts would make a mistake in those matters. Energy is being beamed shoreward—power for some type of unit the Baldies were using? Suppose the Rovers could find a way of cutting off the power.

"The Sea Maid has told us that this ship sits on the bottom of the harbor. If we could board it—" began Torgul.

"Yes!" Vistur brought his fist down against the end of the bunk on which the human still sat, jarring the dull, drug-borne pain in Ross's head. "Take it—then turn it against its crew!"

There was an eagerness in all Rover faces. For that was a game the Hawaikan seafarers understood: Take an enemy ship and turn its armament against its companions in a fleet. But that plan would not work here. Ross had a healthy respect for the technical knowledge of the galactic invaders. Of course he, Karara, even Loketh might be able to reach the sub. Whether they could then board her was an entirely different matter.

Now the Polynesian girl shook her head. "The broadcast there—Tino-rau rates it as lethal. There are dead fish floating in the bay. He had warning at the reef entrance. Without a shield, there will be no way of getting in."

"Might as well wish for a depth bomb," Ross began and then stopped.

"You have thought of something?"

"A shield—" Ross repeated her words. It was so wild this thought of his, and one which might have no chance of working. He knew almost nothing about the resources of the invaders. Could that broadcast which protected the sub and perhaps activated the weapons of the invaders ashore be destroyed? A wall of fish—sea life herded in there as a shield . . . wild, yes, even so wild it might work. Ross outlined the idea, speaking more to Karara than to the Rovers.

"I do not know," she said doubtfully. "That would need many fish, too many to herd and drive—"

"Not fish," Torgul cut in, "salkars!"

"Salkars?"

"You have seen the bow carving on this ship. That is a salkar. Such are larger than a hundred fish! Salkars driven in . . . they might even wreck this undersea ship with their weight and anger."

"And you can find these salkars near-by?" Ross began to take fire. That dragon which had hunted him—the bulk of the thing was well above any other sea life he had seen here. And to its ferocity he could give testimony.

"At the spawning reefs. We do not hunt at this season which is the time for the taking of mates. Now, too, they are easily angered so they will even attack a cruiser. To slay them at present is a loss, for their skins are not good. But they would be ripe for battle were they to be disturbed."

"And how would you get them from the spawning reefs to Kyn Add?"

"That is not too difficult; the reef lies here." Torgul drew lines with the point of his sword on the table top. "And here is Kyn Add. Salkars have a great hunger at this time. Show them bait and they will follow; especially will they follow swimming bait."

There were a great many holes in the plan which had only a halfway chance of working. But the Rovers seized upon it with enthusiasm, and so it was set up.

Perhaps some two hours later Ross swam toward the land mass of Kyn Add. Gleams of light pricked on the shore well to his left. Those must mark the Rover settlement. And again the human wondered why the invaders had remained there. Unless they knew that there had been three cruisers out on a raid and for some reason they were determined to make a complete mop-up.

Karara moved a little to his right, Taua between them, the dolphin's super senses their guide and warning. The swiftest of the cruisers had departed, Loketh on board to communicate with Tino-rau in the water. Since the male dolphin was the best equipped to provide a fox for salkar hounds, he was the bait for this weird fishing expedition.

"No farther!" Ross's sonic pricked a warning against his body. Through that he took a jolt which sent him back, away from the bay entrance.

"On the reef." Karara's tapped code drew him on a new course. Moments later they were both out of the water, though the wash of waves over their flippered feet was constant. The rocks among which they crouched were a rough harborage from which they could see the shore as a dark blot. But they were well away from the break in the reef through which, if their outlandish plan succeeded, the salkars would come.

"A one-in-a-million chance!" Ross commented as he put up his mask.

"Was not the whole Time Agent project founded on just such chances?" Karara asked the right question. This was Ross's kind of venture. Yes, one-in-a-million chances had been pulled off by the Time Agents. Why, it had been close to those odds against their ever finding what they had first sought along the back trails of time—the wrecked spaceships.

Just suppose this could be a rehearsal for another attack? If the salkars could be made to crack the guard of the Baldies, could they also be used against the Foanna gate? Maybe . . . But take one fight at a time.

"They come!" Karara's fingers gripped Ross's shoulder. Her hand was hard, bar rigid. He could see nothing, hear nothing. That warning must have come from the dolphins. But so far their plan was working; the monsters of the Hawaikan sea were on their way.

12
Baldies

"Ohhhh!" Karara clutched at Ross, her breath coming in little gasps, giving vent to her fear and horror. They had not known what might come from this plan; certainly neither had foreseen the present chaos in the lagoon.

Perhaps the broadcast energy of the enemy whipped the already vicious-tempered salkars into this insane fury. But now the moonlit water was beaten into foam as the creatures fought there, attacking each other with a ferocity neither human had witnessed before.

Lights gleamed along the shore where the alien invaders must have been drawn by the clamor of the fighting marine reptiles. Somewhere in the heights above the beach of the lagoon a picked band of Rovers should now be making their way from the opposite side of Kyn Add under strict orders not to go into attack unless signaled. Whether the independent sea warriors would hold to that command was a question which had worried Ross from the first.

Tino-rau and Taua in the waters to the seaward of the reef, the two humans on that barrier itself, and between them and the shore the wild melee of maddened salkars. Ross started. The sonic warning which had been pulsing steadily against his skin cut off sharply. The broadcast in the bay had been silenced! This was the time to move, but no swimmer could last in the lagoon itself.

"Along the reef," Karara said.

That would be the long way round, Ross knew, but the only one possible. He studied the cluster of lights ashore. Two or three figures moved there. Seemingly the attention of the aliens was well centered upon the battle still in progress in the lagoon.

"Stay here!" he ordered the girl. Adjusting his mask, Ross dropped into the water, cutting away from the reef and then turning to swim parallel with it. Tino-rau matched him as he went, guiding Ross to a second break in the reef, toward the shore some distance from where the conflict of the salkars still made a hideous din in the night.

The human waded in the shallows, stripping off his flippers and snapping them to his belt, letting his mask swing free on his chest. He angled toward the beach where the aliens had been. At least he was better armed for this than he had been when he had fronted the Rovers with only a diver's knife. From the Time Agent supplies he had taken the single hand weapon he had long ago found in the armory of the derelict spaceship. This could only be used sparingly, since they did not know how it could be recharged, and the secret of its beam still remained secret as far as human technicians were concerned.

Ross worked his way to a curtain of underbrush from which he had a free view of the beach and the aliens. Three of them he counted, and they were Baldies, all right—taller and thinner than his own species, their bald heads gray-white, the upper dome of their skulls overshadowing the features on their pointed chinned faces.

They all wore the skintight blue-purple-green suits of the
space voyagers—suits which Ross knew of old were insulated and protective for their wearers, as well as a medium
for keeping in touch with one another. Just as he, wearing
one, had once been trailed over miles of wilderness.

To him, all three of the invaders looked enough alike
to have been stamped out from one pattern. And their
movements suggested that they worked or went into action
with drilled precision. They all faced seaward, holding
tubes aimed at the salkar-infested lagoon. There was no
sound of any explosion, but green spears of light struck
at the scaled bodies plunging in the water. And where
those beams struck, flesh seared. Methodically the trio
raked the basin. But, Ross noted, those beams which had
been steady at his first sighting, were now interrupted
by flickers. One of the Baldies upended his tube, rapped
its butt against a rock as if trying to correct a jamming.
When the alien went into action once again his weapon
flashed and failed. Within a matter of moments the other
two were also finished. The lighted rods pushed into the
sand, giving a glow to the scene, darkened as a fire might
sink to embers. Power fading?

An ungainly shape floundered out of the churned water,
lumbered over the shale of the beach, its supple neck outstretched, its horned nose down for a gore-threatening charge.
Ross had not realized that the salkars could operate out of
what he thought was their natural element, but this wild-
eyed dragon was plainly bent on reaching its tormentors.

For a moment or two the Baldies continued to front
the creature, almost, Ross thought, as if they could not
believe that their weapons had failed them. Then they
broke and ran back to the fairing which they had taken
with such contemptuous ease. The salkar plowed along
in their wake, but its movements grew more labored the
farther it advanced, until at last it lay with only its head
upraised, darting it back and forth, its fanged jaws well
agape, voicing a coughing howl.

Its plaint was answered from the water as a second

of its kind wallowed ashore. A terrible wound had torn skin and flesh just behind its neck; yet still it came on, hissing and bubbling a battle challenge. It did not attack its fellow; instead it dragged its bulk past the first comer, on its way after the Baldies.

The salkars continued to come ashore, two more, a third, a fourth, mangled and torn—pulling themselves as far as they could up the beach. To lie, facing inland, their necks weaving, their horned heads bobbing, their cries a frightful din. What had drawn them out of their preoccupation of battle among themselves into this attempt to reach the aliens, Ross could not determine. Unless the intelligence of the beasts was such that they had been able to connect the searing beams which the Baldies had turned on them so tellingly with the men on the beach, and had responded by striving to reach a common enemy.

But no desire could give them the necessary energy to pull far ashore. Almost helplessly beached, they continued to dig into the yielding sand with their flippers in a vain effort to pursue the aliens.

Ross skirted the clamoring barrier of salkars and headed for the fairing. A neck snapped about; a head was lowered in his direction. He smelled the rank stench of reptile combined with burned flesh. The nearest of the brutes must have scented the human in turn, as it was now trying vainly to edge around to cut across Ross's path. But it was completely outclassed on land, and the man dodged it easily.

Three Baldies had fled this way. Yet Jazia had reported five had come out of the sea to take Kyn Add. Two were missing. Where? Had they remained in the fairing? Were they now in the sub? And that sub—what had happened to it? The broadcast had been cut off; he had seen the failure of the weapons and the shore lights. Might the sub have suffered from salkar attack? Though Ross could hardly believe that the beasts could wreck it.

He was traveling blindly, keeping well under cover of such brush as he could, knowing only that he must head inland. Under his feet the ground was rising, and he recalled the nature of this territory as Torgul and Jazia had pictured it for him. This had to be part of the ridge wall of the valley in which lay the buildings of the fairing. In these heights was the Shrine of Phutka where Jazia had hidden out. To the west now lay the Rover village, so he had to work his way left, downhill, in order to reach the hole where the Baldies had gone to ground. Ross made that progress with the stealth of a trained scout.

Hawaika's moon, triple in size to Earth's companion, was up, and the landscape was sharply clear, with shadows well defined. The glow, weird to human eyes, added to the effect of being abroad in a nightmare, and the bellowing of the grounded salkars continued a devils' chorus.

When the Rovers had put up the buildings of their fairing, they had cleared a series of small fields radiating outward from these structures. All of these were now covered with crops almost ready to harvest. The grain, if that Earth term could be applied to this Hawaikan product, was housed in long pods which dipped from shoulder-high bushes. And the pods were well equipped with horny projections which tore. A single try at making his way into one of those fields convinced Ross of the folly of such an advance. He sat back to nurse his scratched hands and survey the landscape.

To go down a very tempting lane would be making himself a clear target for anyone in those buildings ahead. He had seen the flamers of the Baldies fail on the beach, but that did not mean the aliens were now weaponless.

His best chance, Ross decided, was to circle north, come back down along the bed of a stream. And he was at the edge of that watercourse when a faint sound brought him to a frozen halt, weapon ready.

"Rosss—"

"Loketh!"

"And Torgul and Vistur."

This was the party from the opposite side of the island,

gone expertly to earth. In the moonlight Ross could detect no sign of their presence, yet their voices sounded almost beside him.

"They are in there, in the great hall." That was Torgul. "But no longer are there any lights."

"Now—" An urgent exclamation drew their attention.

Light below. But not the glow of the rods Ross had seen on the beach. This was the warm yellow-red of honest fire, bursting up, the flames growing higher as if being fed with frantic haste.

Three figures were moving down there. Ross began to believe that there were only this trio ashore. He could sight no weapons in their hands, which did not necessarily mean that they were unarmed. But the stream ran close behind the rear wall of one of the buildings, and Ross thought its bed could provide cover for a man who knew what he was doing. He pointed out as much to Torgul.

"And if their magic works and you are drawn out to be killed?" The Rover captain came directly to the point.

"That is a chance to be taken. But remember . . . the magic of the Foanna at the sea gate did not work against me. Perhaps this won't either. Once, earlier, I won against it."

"Have you then another hand to give to the fire as your defense?" That was Vistur. "But no man has the right to order another's battle challenge."

"Just so," returned Ross sharply. "And this is a thing I have long been trained to do."

He slid down into the stream bed. Approaching from this angle, the structures of the fairing were between him and the fire. So screened he reached a log wall, got to his feet, and edged along it. Then he witnessed a wild scene. The fire raged in great, sky-touching tongues. And already the roof of one of the Rover buildings smoldered. Why the aliens had built up such a conflagration, Ross could not guess. A signal designed to reach some distance?

He did not doubt there was some urgent purpose. For the three were dragging in fuel with almost frenzied haste, bringing out of the Rover buildings bales of cloth to be ripped apart and whirled into the devouring flames, furniture, everything movable which would burn.

There was one satisfaction. The Baldies were so intent upon this destruction that they kept no watch save that now and then one of them would run to the head of the path leading to the lagoon and listen as if he expected a salkar to come pounding up the slope.

"They're . . . they're rattled!" Ross could hardly believe it. The Baldies who had always occupied his mind and memory as practically invincible supermen were acting like badly frightened primitives! And when the enemy was so off balance you pushed—you pushed hard.

Ross thumbed the button on the grip of the strange weapon. He sighted with deliberation and fired. The blue figure at the top of the path wilted, and for a long moment neither of his companions noted his collapse. Then one of them whirled and started for the limp body, his colleague running after him. Ross allowed them to reach his first victim before he fired the second and third time.

All three lay quiet, but still Ross did not venture forth until he had counted off a dozen seconds. Then he slipped forward keeping to cover until he came up to the bodies.

The blue-clad shoulder had a flaccid feel under his hand as if the muscles could not control the flesh about them. Ross rolled the alien over, looked down in the bright light of the fire into the Baldy's wide-open eyes. Amazement— the human thought he could read that in the dead stare which answered his intent gaze—and then anger, a cold and deadly anger which chilled into ice.

"Kill!"

Ross slewed around, still down on one knee, to face the charge of a Rover. In the firelight the Hawaikan's eyes were blazing with fanatical hatred. He had his hooked sword ready to deliver a finishing stroke. The human blocked with a shoulder to meet the Rover's knees, threw him back. Then Ross landed on top of the fighting crewman, trying to pin the fellow to earth and avoid that recklessly slashing blade.

"Loketh! Vistur!" Ross shouted as he struggled.

More of the Rovers appeared from between the buildings, bearing down on the limp aliens and the two fighting men. Ross recognized the limping gait of Loketh using a branch to aid him into a running scuttle across the open.

"Loketh—here!"

The Hawaikan covered the last few feet in a dive which carried him into Ross and the Rover. "Hold him," the human ordered and had just time enough to throw himself between the Baldies and the rest of the crew. There was a snarling from the Rovers; and Ross, knowing their temper, was afraid he could not save the captives which they considered, fairly, their legitimate prey. He must depend upon the hope that there were one or two cooler heads among them with enough authority to restrain the would-be avengers. Otherwise he would have to beam them into helplessness.

"Torgul!" he shouted.

There was a break in the line of runners speeding for him. The big man lunging straight across could only be Vistur; the other, yelling orders, was Torgul. It would depend upon how much control the Captain had over his men. Ross scrambled to his feet. He had clicked on the beamer to its lowest frequency. It would not kill, but would render its victim temporarily paralyzed; and how long that state would continue Ross had no way of knowing. Tried on laboratory animals on Earth, the time had varied from days to weeks.

Vistur used the flat side of his war ax, clapping it against the foremost runners, setting his own bulk to impose a barrier. And now Torgul's orders appeared to be getting through, more and more of the men slacked, leaving a trio of hotheads, two of whom Vistur sent reeling with his fists.

The Captain came up to Ross. "They are alive then?" He leaned over to inspect the Baldy the human had rolled on his back, assessing the alien's frozen stare with thoughtful measurement.

"Yes, but they can not move."

"Well enough." Torgul nodded. "They shall meet the Justice of Phutka after the Law. I think they will wish that they had been left to the boarding axes of angry men."

"They are worth more alive than dead, Captain. Do you not wish to know why they have carried war to your people, how many of them there may yet be to attack— and other things? Also—" Ross nodded at the fire now catching the second building, "why have they built up that blaze? Is it a signal to others of their kind?"

"Very well said. Yes, it would be well for us to learn such things. Nor will Phutka be jealous of the time we take to ask questions and get answers, many answers." He prodded the Baldy with the toe of his sea boot. "How long will they remain so? Your magic has a bite in it."

Ross smiled. "Not my magic, Captain. This weapon was taken from one of their own ships. As to how long they will remain so—that I do not know."

"Very well, we can take precautions." Under Torgul's orders the aliens were draped with capture nets like those Ross and Loketh had worn. The sea-grown plant adhered instantly, wet strands knitting in perfect restrainers as long as it was uncut.

Having seen to that, Torgul ordered the evacuation of Kyn Add.

"As you say," he remarked to Ross, "that fire may well be a signal to bring down more of their kind. I think we have had the Favor of Phutka in this matter, but the prudent man stretches no favor of that kind too far. Also," he looked about him—"we have given to Phutka and the Shades our dead; there is nothing for us here now but hate and sorrow. In one day we have been broken from a clan of pride and ships to a handful of standardless men."

"You will join some other clan?" Karara had come with Jazia to stand on the stone ledge chipped to form a base for a column bearing a strange, brooding-eyed head looking seaward. The Rover woman was superintending the freeing of the head from the column.

At the human girl's question the Captain gazed down into the dreadful chaos of the valley. They could yet hear the roars of the dying salkars. The reptiles that had made their way to land had not withdrawn but still lay, some dead now, some with weaving heads reaching inland. And the whole of the fairing was ablaze with fire.

"We are now blood-sworn men, Sea Maid. For such there is no clan. There is only the hunting and the kill. With the magic of Phutka perhaps we shall have a short hunt and a good kill."

"There . . . now . . . so . . ." Jazia stepped back. The head which had faced the sea was lowered carefully to a wide strip of crimson-and-gold stuff she had brought from Torgul's ship. With her one usable hand the Rover woman drew the fabric about the carving, muffling it except for the eyes. Those were large ovals deeply carved, and in them Ross saw a glitter. Jewels set there? Yet, he had a queer, shivery feeling that something more than gems occupied those sockets—that he had actually been regarded for an instant of time, assessed and dismissed.

"We go now." Jazia waved and Torgul sent men forward. They lifted the wrapped carving to a board carried between them and started downslope.

Karara cried out and Ross looked around.

The pillar which had supported the head was crumbling away, breaking into a rubble which cascaded across the stone ledge. Ross blinked—this must be an illusion, but he was too tired to be more than dully amazed as he became one of the procession returning to the ships.

13
The Sea Gate of the Foanna

Ross raised a shell cup to his lips but hardly sipped the fiery brew it contained. This was a gesture of ceremony, but he wanted a steady head and a quick tongue for any coming argument. Torgul, Afrukta, Ongal—the three commanders of the Rover cruisers; Jazia, who represented the mysterious Power of Phutka; Vistur and some other subordinate officers; Karara; himself, with Loketh hovering behind: a council of war. But summoned against whom?

The human had come too far afield from his own purpose—to reach Ashe in the Foanna keep. And to further his own plans was a task he doubted his ability to perform. His attack on the Baldies had made him too important to the Rovers for them to allow him willingly to leave them on a quest of his own.

"These star men"—Ross set down the cup, tried to choose the most telling words in his limited Hawaikan vocabulary—"possess weapons and powers you can not dream of, that you have no defense against. But at Kyn Add we were lucky. The salkars attacked their sub and halted the broadcast powering their flamers. Otherwise we could not have taken them, even though we were many against their few. Now you talk of hunting them in their own territory—on land and in the mountains where they have their base. That would be folly akin to swimming barehanded to front a salkar."

"So—then we must sit and wait for them to eat us up?" flared Ongal. "I say it is better to die fighting with one's blade wet!"

"Do you not also wish to take at least one of the enemy with you when you fight to that finish?" Ross countered. "These could kill you before you came in blade range."

"You had no trouble with that weapon of yours," Afrukta spoke up.

"I have told you—this weapon was stolen from them. I have only one and I do not know how long it will continue to serve me, or whether they have a defense against it. Those we took were naked to any force, for their broadcast had failed them. But to smash blindly against their main base would be the act of madmen."

"The salkars opened a way for us—" That was Torgul.

"But we can not move a pack of those inland to the mountains," Vistur pointed out reasonably.

Ross studied the Captain. That Torgul was groping for a plan and that it had to be a shrewd one, the human guessed. His respect for the Rover commander had been growing steadily since their first meeting. The cruiser-raiders had always been captained by the most daring men of the Rover clans. But Ross was also certain that a successful cruiser commander must possess level-headed intelligence and be a strategist of parts.

The Hawaikan force needed a key which would open the Baldy base as the salkars had opened the lagoon. And all they had to aid them was a handful of facts gained from their prisoners.

The picklock to the captives' minds had been produced by the dolphins. Just as Tino-rau and Taua had formed a bridge of communication between Karara and Loketh, so did they read and translate the thoughts of the galactic invaders. For the Baldies, among their own kind, were telepathic, vocalizing only to give orders to inferiors.

Their capture by these primitive "inferiors" had delivered the first shock, and the mind-probes of the dolphins had sent the "supermen" close to the edge of insanity. To accept an animal form as an equal had been shattering.

But the star men's thoughts and memories had been winnowed at last and the result spread before this impromptu council. Rovers and humans were briefed on the invaders' master plan for taking over a world. Why they desired to do so even the dolphins had not been able to discover; perhaps they themselves had not been told by their superiors.

It was a plan almost contemptuous in its simplicity, as if the galactic force had no reason to fear effective opposition. Except in one direction—one single direction.

Ross's fingers tightened on the shell cup. Had Torgul reached that conclusion yet, the belief that the Foanna could be their key? If so, they might be able to achieve their separate purposes in one action.

"It would seem that they are wary of the Foanna," he suggested, alert to any telltale response from Torgul. But it was Jazia who answered the human's half question.

"The Foanna have a powerful magic; they can order wind and wave, man and creature—if so be their will. Well might these killers fear the Foanna!"

"Yet now they move against them," Ross pointed out, still eyeing Torgul.

The Captain's reply was a small, quiet smile.

"Not directly, as you have heard. It is all a part of their plan to set one of us against the other, letting us fight many small wars and so use up our men while they take no risks. They wait the day when we shall be exhausted and then they will reveal themselves to claim all they wish. So today they stir up trouble between the Wreckers and the Foanna, knowing that the Foanna are few. Also they strive in turn to anger us by raids, allowing us to believe that either the Wreckers or Foanna have attacked. Thus—" he held up his left thumb, made a pincers of right thumb and forefinger to close upon it, "they hope to catch the Foanna, between Wreckers and Rovers. Because the Foanna are those they reckon the most dangerous they move against them now, using us and weakening our forces into the bargain. A plan which is clever, but the plan of men who do not like to fight with their own blades."

"They are worse than the coast scum, these cowards!" Ongal spat.

Torgul smiled again. "That is what they believe we will say, kinsman, and so underrate them. By our customs, yes, they are cowards. But what care they for our judgments? Did we think of the salkars when we used them to force the lagoon? No, they were only beasts to be our tools. So now it is the same with us, except that we know what they intend. And we shall not be such obedient tools. If the Foanna are our answer, then—" He paused, gazing into his cup as if he could read some shadowy future there.

"If the Foanna are the answer, then what?" Ross pushed.

"Instead of fighting the Foanna, we must warn, cherish, try to ally ourselves with them. And do all that while we still have time!"

"Just how do we do these things?" demanded Ongal. "The Foanna you would warn, cherish, claim as allies, are already our enemies. Were we not on the way to force their sea gate only days ago? There is no chance of seeking peace now. And have the finned ones not learned from the women-killers that already there is an army of Wreckers camped about the citadel to which these sons of the Shadow plan to lend certain weapons? Do we throw away three cruisers—all we have left—in a hopeless fight? That is the counsel of despair."

"There is a way—my way," Ross seized the opening. "In the Foanna citadel is my sword-lord, to whose service I am vowed. We were on our way to attempt his freedom when your ship picked us out of the waves. He is learned beyond me in the dealing with strange peoples, and if the Foanna are as clever as you say, they will already have discovered that he is not just a slave they claimed from Lord Zahur."

There it was in the open, his own somewhat tattered hope that Ashe had been able to impress his captors with his knowledge and potential. Trained to act as contact man with other races, there was a chance that Gordon had saved himself from whatever fate had been planned for the prisoners the Foanna had claimed. If that happened, Ashe could be their opening wedge in the Foanna stronghold.

"This also I know: That which guards the gate—which turns your minds whirling and sent you back from your raid—does not affect me. I may be able to win inside and find my clansman, and in that doing treat with the Foanna."

The Baldy prisoners had not underestimated the attack on the Foanna citadel. As the Rover cruisers beat in under the cover of night the fires and torches of both besieged and besiegers made a wild glow across the sky. Only on the sea side of the fortress there was no sign of involvement. Whatever guarded the gate must still be in force.

Ross stood with his feet well apart to balance his body against the swing of the deck. His suggestion had been argued over, protested, but at last carried with the support of Torgul and Jazia, and now he was to make his try. The sum of the Rovers' and Loketh's knowledge of the sea gate had been added for his benefit, but he knew that this venture must depend upon himself alone. Karara, the dolphins, and the Hawaikans, were all too sensitive to the barrier.

Torgul moved in the faint light. "We are close; our power is ebbing. If we advance, we shall be drifting soon."

"It is time then." Ross crossed to the rope ladder, but another was there before him. Karara perched on the rail. He regarded her angrily.

"You can't go."

"I know. But we are still safe here. Just because you are free of one defense of the gate, Ross, do not believe that makes it easy."

He was stung by her assumption that he could be so self-assured.

"I know my business."

Ross pushed past her, swinging down the rope ladder, pausing only above water level to snap on flippers, make sure of the set of his weighted belt, and slide his gill-mask over his face. There was a splash beside him as the net containing spare belt, flippers, and mask hit the water and he caught at it. These could provide Ashe's escape from the fortress.

The lights on the shore made a wide arc of radiance across the sea. As Ross headed toward the wave-washed coast he began to hear shouting and other sounds which made him believe that the besiegers were in the midst of an all-out assault. Yet those distant fires and rocket-like blasts into the sky had a wavery blur. And Ross, effortlessly cleaving the water, surfaced now and then to spot film curling up from the surface of the sea between the two standing rock pillars which marked the sea gate.

He was startled by a thunderous crack, rending the air above the small bay. Ross pulled to one of the pillars, steadied himself with one hand against it. Those twists of film rising from the surging surface were thickening. More tendrils grew out from parent stems to creep along above the waves, raising up sprouts and branches in turn. A wall of mist was building between gate and shore.

Again a thunderclap overhead. Involuntarily the human ducked. Then he turned his face up to the sky, striving to see any evidence of storm. What hung there sped the growth of the fog on the water. Yet where the fog was gray-white, it was a darkness spouting from the highest

point of the citadel. Ross could not explain how he was
able to see one shade of darkness against equal dusk,
but he did—or did he only sense it? He shook his head,
willing himself to look away from the finger. Only it was
a finger no longer; now it was a fist aimed at the stars
it was fast blotting out. A fist rising to the heavens before
it curled back, descended to press the fortress and its
surroundings into rock and earth.

Fog curled about Ross, spilled outward through the sea
gates. He loosed his grip on the pillar and dived, swimming on through the gap with the fortress of the Foanna
before him.

There was a jetty somewhere ahead; that much he knew
from Torgul's description. Those who served the Foanna
sometimes took sea roads and they had slim, fast cutters for such coastwise travel. Ross surfaced cautiously,
to discover there was no visibility to wave level. Here
the mist was thick, a smothering cover so bewildering
he was confused as to direction. He ducked below again
and flippered on.

Was his confusion born of the fog, or was it also in
his head? Did he, after all, have this much reaction to
the gate defense? Ross ducked that suspicion as he had
ducked the moist blanket on the surface. He had come
from the gate, which meant that the jetty must lie—there!

A few moments later Ross had proof that his sense of
direction had not altogether failed him, when his shoulder grazed against a solid obstruction in the water and
his exploring touch told him that he had found one of
the jetty piles. He surfaced again and this time he heard
not a thunder roll but the singsong chanting of the
Foanna.

It was loud, almost directly above his head, but since
the cotton mist held he was not afraid of being sighted.
The chanter must be on the jetty. And to Ross's right
was a dark bulk which he thought was one of the cutters.
Was a sortie by the besieged being planned?

Then, out of the night, came a dazzling beam, well

above the level of Ross's head where he clung to the piling. It centered on the cutter, slicing into the substance of the vessel with the ease of steel piercing clay. The chanting stopped on mid-note, broken by cries of surprise and alarm. Ross, pressing against the pile, received a jolt from his belt sonic.

There must be a Baldy sub in the basin inside the gate. Perhaps the flame beam now destroying the cutter was to be turned on the walls of the keep in turn.

Foanna chant again, low and clear. Splashes from the water as those on the jetty cast into the sea objects Ross could not define. His body jerked, his mask smothered a cry of pain. About his legs and middle, immersed in the waves, there was a cold so intense that it seared. Fear goaded him to pull up on one of the under beams of the pier. He reached that refuge and rubbed his icy legs with what vigor he could summon.

Moments later he crept along toward the shore. The energy ray had found another target. Ross paused to watch a second cutter sliced. If the counter stroke of the Foanna would rout the invaders, it had not yet begun to work.

The net holding the extra gear brought along in hopes of Ashe's escape weighed the human down, but he would not abandon it as he felt his way from one foot- and hand-hold to the next. The waves below gave off an icy exudation which made him shiver uncontrollably. And he knew that as long as that effect lasted he dared not venture into the sea again.

Light . . . along with the cold, there was a phosphorescence on the water—white patches floating, dipping, riding the waves. Some of them gathered under the pier, clustering about the pilings. And the fog thinned with their coming, as if those irregular blotches absorbed and fed upon the mist. Ross could see now he had reached the land end of the jetty. He clipped his flippers to his belt, pulled on over his feet the covers of salkar-hide Torgul had provided.

Save for his belt, his trunks, and the gill-pack, Ross's

body was bare and the cold caught at him. But, sling-
ing the carry net over his shoulder, he dropped to the
damp sand and stood listening.

The clamor of the attack which had carried all the way
offshore to the Rover cruisers had died away. And there
were no more claps of thunder. Instead, there was now
a thick wash of rain.

No more fire rays as he faced seaward. And the fog
was lifting, so Ross could distinguish the settling cutters,
their bows still moored to the jetty. There was no
movement there. Had those on the pier fled?

Dot . . . dash . . . dot . . .

Ross did not drop the net. But he crouched back in
the half protection of the piling. For an agonizing moment
he froze so, waiting.

Dot . . . dash . . . dot . . .

Not the prickle induced by the enemy installations, it
was a real coded call picked up by his sonic, and one
he knew.

Don't rush, he told himself sharply—play it safe. By
rights only two people in this time and place would know
that call. And one would have no reason to use it. But—
a trap? This could be a trap. Awe of the Foanna powers had touched him a little in spite of his off-world
skepticism. He could be lured now by someone using
Ashe's call.

Ross stripped for action after a fashion, bundling the
net and its contents into a hollow he scooped behind a
pile well above water level. The alien hand weapon he
had left with Karara. But he had his diver's knife and
his two hands which, by training, could be, and had been,
deadly weapons.

With the sonic against the bare skin of his middle
where it would register strongest and knife in hand, Ross
moved into the open. The floating patches did not supply much light, but he was certain the call had come
from the jetty.

There was movement there—a flash or two. And the

sonic? Ross had to be sure, very sure. The broadcast was certainly stronger when he faced in that direction. Dared he come into the open? Perhaps in the dark he could cut Ashe away from his captors so they could swim for it together.

Ross clicked a code reply. Dot . . . dot . . . dot . . .

The answer was quick, imperative: "Where?"

Surely no one but Ashe could have sent that! Ross did not hesitate.

"Be ready—escape."

"No!" Even more imperative. "Friends here . . ."

Had he guessed rightly? Had Ashe established friendly relations with the Foanna? But Ross kept to the caution which had been his defense and armor so long. There was one question he thought only Ashe could answer, something out of the past they had shared when they had made their first journey into time disguised as Beaker traders of the Bronze Age. Deliberately he tapped that question.

"What did we kill in Britain?"

Tensely he waited. But when the reply came it did not pulse from the sonic under his fingers; instead, a well-remembered voice called out of the night.

"A white wolf." And the words were English.

"Ashe!" Ross leaped forward, climbed toward the figure he could only dimly see.

14
The Foanna

"Ross!" Ashe's hands gripped his shoulders as if never intending to free him again. "Then you did come through—"

Ross understood. Gordon Ashe must have feared that he was the only one swept through the time door by that freak chance.

"And Karara and the dolphins!"

"Here—now?" In this black bowl of the citadel bay Ashe was only a shadow with voice and hands.

"No, out with the Rover cruisers. Ashe, do you know the Baldies are on Hawaika? They've organized this whole thing—the attack here—trouble all over. Right now they have one of their subs out there. That's what cut those cutters to pieces. Five days ago five of them wiped out a whole Rover fairing, just five of them!"

"Gordoon." Unlike the hissing speech of the Hawaikans, this new voice made a singing, lilting call of Ashe's name. "This is your swordsman in truth?" Another shadow drew near them, and Ross saw the flutter of cloak edge.

"This is my friend." There was a tone of correction in Ashe's reply. "Ross, this is the Guardian of the sea gate."

"And you come," the Foanna continued, "with those who gather to feast at the Shadow's table. But your Rovers will find little loot to their liking—"

"No." Ross hesitated. How did one address the Foanna? He had claimed equality with Torgul. But that approach was not the proper one here; instinct told him that. He fell back on the complete truth uttered simply. "We took three of the Baldy killers. From them we learned they move to wipe out the Foanna first. For you," he addressed himself to the cloaked shape, "they believe to be a threat. We heard that they urged the Wreckers to this attack and so—"

"And so the Rovers come, but not to loot? Then they are something new among their kind." The Foanna's reply was as chill as the sea bay's water.

"Loot does not summon men who want a blood price for their dead kin!" Ross retorted.

"No, and the Rovers are believers in the balance of hurt against hurt," the Foanna conceded. "Do they also believe in the balance of aid against aid? Now that is a thought upon which depends much. Gordoon, it would seem that we may not take to our ships. So let us return to council."

Ashe's hand was on Ross's arm guiding him through the murk. Though the fog which had choked the bay had vanished, thick darkness remained and Ross noted that even the fires and flares were dimmed and fewer. Then they were in a passage where a very faint light clung to the walls.

Robed Foanna, three of them, moved ahead with that particular gliding progress. Then Ashe and Ross, and bringing up the rear, a dozen of the mailed guards. The passageway became a ramp. Ross glanced at Ashe. Like the Foanna, the Time Agent wore a cloak of gray, but his did not shift color from time to time as did those of the Hawaikan enigmas. And now Gordon shoved back its folds, revealing supple body armor.

Questions gathered in Ross. He wanted to know—needed desperately to know—Ashe's standing with the Foanna. What had happened to raise Gordon from the status of captive in Zahur's hold to familiar companionship with the most dreaded race on this planet?

The ramp's head faced blank wall with a sharp-angled turn to the right of a narrower passage. One of the Foanna made a slight sign to the guards, who turned with drilled precision to march off along the passage. Now the other Foanna held out their wands.

What a moment earlier had been unbroken surface showed an opening. The change had been so instantaneous that Ross had not seen any movement at all.

Beyond that door they passed from one world to another. Ross's senses, already acutely alert to his surroundings, could not supply him with any reason by sight, sound, or smell for his firm conviction that this hold was far more alien than the Wrecker castle or the Rover ships had been. Surely the Foanna were not the same race, perhaps not even the same species as the other native Hawaikans.

Those robes which he had seen both silver gray and dark blue, now faded, pearled, thinned, until each of the three still gliding before him were opalescent columns without definite form.

Ashe's grasp fell on Ross's arm once more, and his whisper reached the younger man thinly. "They are mistresses of illusion. Be prepared not to believe all that you see."

Mistresses—Ross caught that first. Women, or at least female then. Illusion, yes, already he was convinced that here his eyes could play tricks on him. He could hardly determine what was robe, what was wall, or if more than shades of shades swept before him.

Another blank wall, then an opening, and flowing through it to touch him such a wave of alienness that Ross felt he was buffeted by a storm wind. Yet as he hesitated before it, reluctant in spite of Ashe's hold to go ahead, he also knew that this did not carry with it the cold hostility he had known while facing the Baldies. Alien—yes. Inimical to his kind—no.

"You are right, younger brother."

Spoken those words—or forming in his mind?

Ross was in a place which was sheer wonder. Under his feet dark blue the blue of Earth's sky at dusk—caught up in it twinkling points of light as if he strode, not equal with stars, but above them! Walls—were there any walls here? Or shifting, swaying blue curtains on which silvery lines ran to form symbols and words which some bemused part of his brain almost understood, but not quite.

Constant motion, no quiet, until he came to a place where those swaying curtains were stilled, where he no longer strode above the sky but on soft surface, a mat of gray living sod where his steps released a spicy fragrance. And there he really saw the Foanna for the first time.

Where had their cloaks gone? Had they tossed them away during that walk or drift across this amazing room, or had the substance which had formed those coverings flowed away by itself? As Ross looked at the three in wonder he knew that he was seeing them as not even their servants and guards ever viewed them. And yet was he seeing them as they really were or as they wished him to see them?

"As we are, younger brother, as we are!" Again an answer which Ross was not sure was thought or speech.

In form they were humanoid, and they were undoubtedly women. The muffling cloaks gone, they wore sleeveless garments of silver which were girded at the waist with belts of blue gems. Only in their hair and their eyes did they betray alien blood. For the hair which flowed and wove about them, cascading down shoulders, rippling about their arms, was silver, too, and it swirled, moved as if it had a separate life of its own. While their eyes . . . Ross looked into those golden eyes and was lost for seconds until panic awoke in him, forcing him after sharp struggle to look away.

Laughter? No, he had not heard laughter. But a sense of amusement tinged with respect came to him.

"You are very right, Gordoon. This one is also of your kind. He is not witches' meat." Ross caught the distaste, the kind of haunting unhappiness which colored those words, remnants of an old hurt.

"These are the Foanna," Ashe's voice broke more of the spell. "The Lady Ynlan, the Lady Yngram, the Lady Ynvalda."

The Foanna—these three only?

She whom Ashe had named Ynlan, whose eyes had entrapped and almost held what was Ross Murdock, made a small gesture with her ivory hand. And in that gesture as well as in the words witches' meat the human read the unhappiness which was as much a part of this room as the rest of its mystery.

"The Foanna are now but three. They have been only three for many weary years, oh man from another world and time. And soon, if these enemies have their way, they will not be three—but none!"

"But—" Ross was still startled. He knew from Loketh that the Wreckers had deemed the Foanna few in number, an old and dying race. But that there were only three women left was hard to believe.

The response to his unspoken wonder came clear and determined. "We may be but three; however, our power remains. And sometimes power distilled by time becomes the stronger. Now it would seem that time is no longer our servant but perhaps among our enemies. So tell us this tale of yours as to why the Rovers would make one with the Foanna—tell us all, younger brother!"

Ross reported what he had seen, what Tino-rau and Taua had learned from the prisoners taken at Kyn Add.

And when he had finished, the three Foanna stood very still, their hands clasped one to the other. Though they were only an arm's distance from him, Ross had the feeling they had withdrawn from this time and world. So complete was their withdrawal that he dared to ask Ashe one of the many questions which had been boiling inside him.

"Who are they?" But Ross knew he really meant: What are they?

Gordon Ashe shook his head. "I don't really know— the last of a very old race which possesses powers and knowledge different from any we have believed in for centuries. We have heard of witches. In the modern day we discount the legends about them. The Foanna bring those legends alive. And I promise you this—if they turn those powers loose"—he paused—"it will be such a war as this world, perhaps any world has never seen!"

"That is so." The Foanna had returned from the place to which they had withdrawn. "And this is also the truth or one face of the truth. The Rovers are right in their belief that we have kept some measure of balance between one form of change and another on this world. If we were as many as we once were, then against us these invaders could not move at all. But we are three only and also—do we have the right to evoke disaster which will strike not only the enemy but perhaps recoil upon the innocent? There has been enough death here already. And those who are our servants shall no longer be asked to face battle to keep an empty shell inviolate. We would see with our own eyes these invaders, probe what they would do. There is ever change in life. If a pattern grows too set, then the race caught in it may wither and die. Maybe our pattern has been too long in its old design. We shall make no decision until we see in whose hands the future may rest."

Against such finality of argument there was no appeal. These could not be influenced by words.

"Gordoon, there is much to be done. Do you take with

you this younger brother and see to his needs. When all is in readiness we shall come."

One minute Ross had been standing on the carpet of living moss. Then . . . he was in a more normal room with four walls, a floor, a ceiling, and light which came from rods set in the corners. He gasped.

"Stunned me, too, the first time they put me through it," he heard Ashe say. "Here, get some of this inside you, it'll steady your head."

There was a cup in his hand, a beautifully carved, rose-red container shaped in the form of a flower. Somehow Ross brought it to his lips with shaking hands, gulped down a good third of its contents. The liquid was a mixture of tart and sweet, cooling his mouth and throat, but warming as it went down, and that glow spread through him.

"What—how did they do that?" he demanded.

Ashe shrugged. "How do they do the hundred and one things I have seen happen here? We've been teleported. How it's done I don't know any more than I did the first time it happened. Simply a part of the Foanna 'magic' as far as spectators are concerned." He sat down on a stool, his long legs stretched out before him. "Other worlds, other ways—even if they are confounded strange ones. As far as I know, there's no reason for their power to work, but it does. Now, have you seen the time gate? Is it in working order?"

Ross put down the now empty cup and sat down opposite Ashe. As concisely as he could, he outlined the situation with a quick summary of all that had happened to him, Karara, and the dolphins since they had been sucked through the gate. Ashe asked no questions, but his expression was that of the Agent Ross had known, evaluating and listing all the younger man had to report. When the other was through he said only two words:

"No return."

So much had happened in so short a time that Ross's initial shock at the destruction of the gate had faded, been well overlaid by all the demands made upon his resources, skill, and strength. Even now, the fact Ashe voiced seemed of little consequence balanced against the struggle in progress.

"Ashe—" Ross rubbed his hands up and down his arms, brushing away grains of sand, "remember those pylons with the empty seacoast behind them? Does that mean the Baldies are going to win?"

"I don't know. No one has ever tried to change the course of history. Maybe it is impossible even if we dared to try." Ashe was on his feet again, pacing back and forth.

"Try what, Gordoon?"

Ross jerked around, Ashe halted. One of the Foanna stood there, her hair playing about her shoulders as if some breeze felt only by her stirred those long strands.

"Dare to try and change the course of the future," Ashe explained, accepting her materialization with the calm of one who had witnessed it before.

"Ah, yes, your traveling in time. And now you think that perhaps this poor world of ours has a choice as to which overlords it will welcome? I do not know either, Gordoon, whether the future may be altered nor if it be wise to try. But also . . . well, perhaps we should see our enemy before we are set in any path. Now, it is time that we go. Younger brother, how did you plan to leave this place when you accomplished your mission?"

"By the sea gate. I have extra swimming equipment cached under the jetty."

"And the Rover ships await you at sea?"

"Yes."

"Then we shall take your way, since the cutters are sunk."

"There is only one extra gill-pack—and that Baldy sub is out there, too!"

"So? Then we shall try another road, though it will sap our power temporarily." Her head inclined slightly to the left as if she listened. "Good! Our people are now in the passage which will take them to safety. What those outside will find here when they break in will be of little aid to their plans. Secrets of the Foanna remain secrets past others' prying. Though they shall try, oh, how they shall try to solve them! There is knowledge that only certain types of minds can hold and use, and to others it remains for all time unlearnable. Now—"

Her hand reached out, flattened against Ross's forehead.

"Think of your Rover ship, younger brother, see it in your mind! And see well and clearly for me."

Torgul's cruiser was there; he could picture with details he had not thought he knew or remembered. The deck in the dark of the night with only a shaded light at the mast. The deck . . .

Ross gave a choked cry. He did not see this in his mind; he saw it with his eyes! His hand swung out in an involuntary gesture of repudiation and struck painfully against wood. He was on the cruiser!

A startled exclamation from behind him—then a shout. Ashe, Ashe was here and beyond him three cloaked figures, the Foanna. They had their own road indeed and had taken it.

"You . . . Rosss—" Vistur fronted them, his face a mixture of bewilderment and awe. "The Foanna—" said in a half whisper, echoed by crewmen gathering around, but not too close.

"Gordon!" Karara elbowed her way between two of the Hawaikans and ran across the deck. She caught the Agent's both hands as if to assure herself that he was alive and there before her. Then she turned to the three Foanna.

There was an odd expression on the Polynesian girl's face, first of measurement with some fear, and then of dawning wonder. From beneath the cloak of the middle Foanna came the rod of office with its sparking knob. Karara dropped Ashe's hands, took a tentative step forward and then another. The knob was directly before her, breast high. She brought up both hands, cupping them about the knob, but not touching it directly. The sparks it emitted could have been flashing against her flesh, but Karara displayed no awareness of that. Instead, she lifted both hands farther, palm up and cupped, as if she carried some invisible bounty, then flattened them, loosing what she held.

There was a sigh from the crewmen; Karara's gesture had been confident, as if she knew just what she was doing and why. And Ross heard Ashe draw a deep breath also as the human girl turned, allying herself with the Foanna.

"These Great Ones stand in peace," she said. "It is their will that no harm comes to this ship and those who sail in her."

"What do the Great Ones want of us?" Torgul advanced but not too near.

"To speak concerning those who are your prisoners."

"So be it." The Captain bowed. "The Great Ones' will is our will; let it be as they wish."

15
Return to the Battle

Ross lay listening to the even breathing from across the cabin. He had awakened in that quick transference from sleep to consciousness which was always his when on duty, but he made no attempt to move. Ashe was still sleeping.

Ashe, whom he thought or had thought he knew as well as one man could ever know another, who had taken the place of family for Ross Murdock the loner. Years— two . . . four of them now since he had made half of that partnership.

His head turned, though he could not see that lean body, that quiet, controlled face. Ashe still looked the same, but . . . Ross's sense of loss was hurt and anger mingled. What had they done to Gordon, those three? Bewitched? Tales humans had accepted as purest fantasy for centuries came into his mind. Could it be that his own world once had its Foanna?

Ross scowled. You couldn't refute their "magic," call

it by what scientific name you wished—hypnotism . . . teleporting. They got results, and the results were impressive. Now he remembered the warning the Foanna themselves had delivered hours earlier to the Rovers. There were limits to their abilities; because they were forced to draw on mental and physical energy, they could be exhausted. Thus, they had barriers, too.

Again Ross considered the subject of barriers. Karara had been able to meet the aliens, if not mind-to-mind, then in a closer way even than Ashe. The talent which tied her to the dolphins had in turn been a bond with the Foanna. Ashe and Karara could enter that circle, but not Ross Murdock. Along with his new separation from Ashe came that feeling of inferiority to bite on, and the taste was sour.

"This isn't going to be easy."

So Ashe was awake.

"What can they do?" Ross asked in return.

"I don't know. I don't believe that they can teleport an army into Baldy headquarters the way Torgul expects. And it wouldn't do such an army much good to get there and then be outclassed by the weapons the Baldies might have," Ashe said.

Ross had a moment of warmth and comfort; he knew that tone of old. Ashe was studying the problem, willing to talk out difficulties as he always had before.

"No, outright assault isn't the answer. We'll have to know more about the enemy. One thing puzzles me: Why have the Baldies suddenly stepped up their timing?"

"What makes you think they have?"

"Well, according to the accounts I've heard, it's been about three or four planet years here since some off-world devices have been infiltrating the native civilization—"

"You mean such things as those attractors set up on the reef at Zahur's castle?" Ross remembered Loketh's story.

"Those, and other things. The refinements added to the engine power on these ships . . . Torgul said they spread from Rover fleet to fleet; no one's sure where they started. The Baldies began slowly, but they are speeding up now—those fairing attacks have all been recent. And this assault on the Foanna citadel blew up almost overnight on a flimsy excuse. Why the quick push after the slow beginning?"

"Maybe they decided the natives are easy pushovers and they no longer have to worry about any real opposition," Ross suggested.

"Could be. Self-confidence becoming arrogance when they didn't uncover any opponent strong enough to matter. Or else, they may be spurred by some need with a time limit. If we knew the reason for those pylons, we might guess their motives."

"Are you going to try to change the future?"

"That sounds arrogant, too. Can we if we wish to? We never dared to try it on Earth. And the risk may be worse than all our fears. Also, the choice is not ours."

"There's one thing I don't understand," Ross said. "Why did the Foanna walk out of the citadel and leave it undefended for their enemies? What about their guards? Did they just leave them too?" He was willing to make the most of any flaw in the aliens' character.

"Most of their people had already escaped through underground ways. The rest left when they knew the cutters had been sunk," Ashe returned. "As to why they deserted the citadel, I don't know. The decision was theirs."

There—up with the barrier between them again. But Ross refused to accept the cutoff this time, determined to pull Ashe back into the familiar world of the here and now.

"That keep could be a trap, about the best on this planet!" the idea was more than just a gambit to attract Ashe's attention, it was true! A perfect trap to catch Baldies.

"Don't you see," Ross sat up, slapped his feet down on the deck as he leaned forward eagerly. "Don't you see . . . if the Baldies know anything at all about the Foanna, and I'm betting they do and want to learn all they can, they'll visit the citadel. They won't want to depend on second- and third-hand reports of the place, especially ones delivered by primitives such as the Wreckers. They had a sub there. I'll bet the crew are in picking over the loot right now!"

"If that's what they're hunting"—there was amusement in Ashe's tone—"they won't find much. The Foanna have better locks than their enemies have keys. You heard Ynlan before we left—any secrets left will remain secrets."

"But there's bait—bait for a trap!" argued Ross.

"You're right!" To the younger man's joy Ashe's enthusiasm was plain. "And if the Baldies could be led to believe that what they wanted was obtainable with just a little more effort, or the right tools—"

"The trap could net bigger catch than just underlings!" Ross's thought matched Ashe's. "Why, it might even pull in the VIP directing the whole operation! How can we set it up, and do we have time?"

"The trap would have to be of Foanna setting; our part would come after it was sprung." Ashe was thoughtful again. "But it is the only move which we can make at present with any hope of success. And it will only work if the Foanna are willing."

"Have to be done quickly," Ross pointed out.

"Yes, I'll see." Ashe was a dark figure against the thin light of the companionway as he slid back the cabin door. "If Ynvalda agrees . . ." As he went out Ross was right behind him.

The Foanna had been given, by their own choice, quarters on the bow deck of the cruiser where sailcloth had been used to form a tent. Not that any of the awe-stricken Rovers would venture too near them. Ashe reached for the flap of the fabric and a lilting voice called:

"You seek us, Gordoon?"

"This is important."

"Yes, it is important, for the thought which brings you both has merit. Enter then, brothers!"

The flap was looped aside and before them was a swirling of mist? . . . light? . . . sheets of pale color? Ross could not have described what he saw—save if the Foanna were there, he could not distinguish them from the rippling of their hair, the melting film of their robes.

"So, younger brother, you think that which was our home and our treasure box has now become a trap for the confounding of those who believe we are a threat to them?"

Somehow Ross was not surprised that they knew about his idea before he had said a word, before Ashe had given any explanations. Their near-omniscience was only a small portion of their other talents.

"Yes."

"And why do you believe so? We swear to you that the coast folk can not be driven into those parts of the castle which mean the most, any more than our sea gate can be breached unless we will it so."

"Yet I swam through the sea gate, and the sub was there also." Ross knew again a flash of—was it pleasure?—at being able to state this fact. There *were* chinks in the Foanna defenses.

"Again the truth. You have that within you, younger brother, which is both a lack and a shield. True also that this underseas ship entered after you. Perhaps it has a shield as part of it; perhaps those from the stars have their own protection. But they can not reach the heart of what they wish, not unless we open the doors for them. It is your belief, younger brother, that they still strive to force such doors?"

"Yes. Knowing there is something to be learned, they will try for it. They will not dare not to." Ross was very certain on that point. His encounters with the Baldies had not led to any real understanding. But the way they had wiped out the line of Russian time stations made him sure that they dealt thoroughly with any situation they considered a threat.

From the prisoners taken at Kyn Add they had learned

the invaders believed that the Foanna were their enemies here, even though the Old Ones had not repulsed them or their activities. Therefore, it followed that, having taken the stronghold, the Baldies would endeavor to rip open every one of its secrets.

"A trap with good bait—"

Ross wondered which one of the Foanna said that. To see nothing but the swirls of mist-color, listen to disembodied voices from it, was disconcerting. Part of the stage dressing, he decided, for building their prestige with the other races with whom they dealt. Three women alone would have to buttress their authority with such trappings.

"Ah, younger brother, indeed you are beginning to understand us!" Laughter, soft but unmistakable.

Ross frowned. He did not feel the touch-go-touch of mental communication which the dolphins used. But he did not doubt that the Foanna read his thoughts, or at least a few of them.

"Some of them," echoed from the mist. "Not all—not as your older brother's or the maiden whose mind meets with ours. With you, younger brother, it is a thought here, a thought there, and only our intuition to connect them into a pattern. But now, there is serious planning to be done. And, knowing this enemy, you believe they will come to search for what they can not find. So you would set a trap. But they have weapons beyond your weapons, have they not, younger brother? Brave as are these Rover kind, they can not use swords against flame, their hands against a killer who may stand apart and slay. What remains, Gordoon? What remains in our favor?"

"You have your weapons, too," Ashe answered.

"Yes, we have our weapons, but long have they been used only in one pattern, and they are attuned to another race. Did our defenses hold against you, Gordoon, when you strove to prove that you were as you claimed to be? And did another repulse younger brother when he dared the sea gate? So can we trust them in turn against these other strangers with different brains? Only at the testing shall we know, and in such learning perhaps we shall also be forced to eat the sourness of defeat. To risk all may be to lose all."

"That may be true," Ashe assented.

"You mean the sight you have had into our future says that this happens? Yes, to stake all and to lose—not only for ourselves, but for all others here—that is a weighty decision to make, Gordoon. But the trap promises. Let us think on it for a space. Do you also consult with the Rovers if they wish to take part in what may be desperate folly."

Torgul paced the afterdeck, well away from the tent which sheltered the Foanna, but with his eyes turning to it as Ross explained what might be a good attack.

"Those women-killers would have no fear of Foanna magic, rather would they come to seek it out? It would be a chance to catch leaders in a trap?"

"You have heard what the prisoners said or thought. Yes, they would seek out such knowledge and we would have this chance to capture them—"

"With what?" Torgul demanded. "I am not Ongal to argue that it is better to die in pursuit of blood payment than to take an enemy or enemies with me! What chance have we against their powers?"

"Ask that of them!" Ross nodded toward the still silent tent.

Even as he spoke the three cloaked Foanna emerged, pacing down to mid-ship where Torgul and his lieutenants, Ross and Ashe came to meet them.

"We have thought on this." The lilting half chant which the Foanna used for ordinary communication was a song in the dawn wind. "It was in our minds to retreat, to wait out this troubling of the land, since we are few and that which we hold within us is worth the guarding. But now, what profit such guardianship when there may be none to whom we may pass it after us? And if you have seen the truth, elder brother"—the cowled heads swung to Ashe—"then there may be no future for any of us.

But still there are our limitations. Rover," now they spoke directly to Torgul, "we can not put your men within the citadel by desiring—not without certain aids which lie sealed there now. No, we, ourselves, must win inside bodily and then . . . then, perhaps, we can pull tight the lines of our net!"

"To run a cruiser through the gate—" Torgul began.

"No, not a ship, Captain. A handful of warriors in the water can risk the gate, but not a ship."

Ashe broke in, "How many gill-packs do we have?"

Ross counted hurriedly. "I left one cached ashore. But there's mine and Karara's and Loketh's—also two more—"

"To pass the gates," that was the Foanna, "we ourselves shall not need your underwater aids."

"You," Ross said to Ashe, "and I with Karara's pack—"

"For Karara!"

Both the men looked around. The Polynesian girl stood close to the Foanna, smiling faintly.

"This venture is mine also," she spoke with conviction. "As it is Tino-rau's and Taua's. Is that not so, Daughters of the Alii of this world?"

"Yes, Sea Maid. There are weapons of many sorts, and not all of them fit into a warrior's hand or can be swung with the force of a man's arm and shoulder. Yes, this venture is yours, also, sister."

Ross's protests bubbled unspoken; he had to accept the finality of the Foanna decree. It seemed now that the make-up of their task force depended upon the whims of the three rather than the experience of those trained to such risks. And Ashe was apparently willing to accept their leadership.

So it was an odd company that took to the water just as dawn colored the sky. Loketh had clung fiercely to his pack, insisted that he be one of the swimmers, and the Foanna accepted him as well. Ross and Ashe, Loketh, and Baleku, a young under officer of Ongal's, accorded the best swimmer of the fleet, Karara and the dolphins. And with them those three others, shapes sliding smoothly through the water, as difficult to define in this new element as they had been in their tent. Before them frisked the dolphins. Tino-rau and Taua played about the Foanna in an ecstatic joy and when all were in the sea they shot off shoreward.

That sub within the sea gate, had it unleashed the same lethal broadcast as the one at Kyn Add? But the dolphins could give warning if that were so.

Ross swam easily, Ashe next, Loketh on his left, Baleku a little behind and Karara to the fore as if in vain pursuit of the dolphins—the Foanna well to the left. An odd invasion party, even odder when one totaled up the risks which might lie ahead.

There was no mist or storm this morning to hide the headlands where the Foanna citadel stood. And the promontories of the sea gate were starkly clear in the growing light. The same drive which always was a part of Ross when he was committed to action sustained him now, though he was visited by a small prick of doubt when he though that the leadership did not lie with Ashe but with the Foanna.

No warning of any trouble ahead as they passed between the mighty, sea-sunk bases of the gate pillars. Ross depended upon his sonic, but there was no adverse report from the sensitive recorder. The terrible chill of the water during the night attack had been dissipated, but here and there dead sea things floated, being torn and devoured by hunters of the waves.

They were well past the pillars when Ross was aware that Loketh had changed place in the line, spurting ahead. After him went Baleku. They caught up with Karara, flashed past her.

Ross looked to Ashe, on to the Foanna, but saw nothing to explain the action of the two Hawaikans. Then his sonic beat out a signal from Ashe.

"Danger . . . follow the Foanna . . . left."

Karara had already changed course to head in that direction. Ahead of her he could see Loketh and Baleku both still bound for the mid-point of the shore where the jetty and the sunken cutters were. Ashe passed before him, and Ross reluctantly followed orders.

A shelf of rock reached out from the cliff wall, under it a dark opening. The Foanna sought this without hesitation, Ashe, Karara, and Ross following. Moments later they were out of the water where footing sloped back and up. Below them Tino-rau and Taua nosed the rise, their heads lifting out of the water as they "spoke." And Karara hastened to reply.

"Loketh . . . Baleku . . ." Ross began when he caught a mental stroke of anger so deadly that it was a chill lance into his brain. He faced the Foanna, startled and a little frightened.

"They will not come—now." A knob-crowned wand stretched out in the air, pointing to the upper reaches of the slope. "Nor can any of their blood—unless we win."

"What is wrong?" Ashe asked.

"You were right, very right, men out of time! These invaders are not to be lightly dismissed. They have turned one of our own defenses against us. Loketh, Baleku, all of their kind, can be made into tools for a master. They belong to the enemy now."

"And we have failed so early?" Karara wanted to know.

Again that piercing thrust of anger so vivid that it was no mere emotion but seemed a tangible force.

"Failed? No, not yet have we even begun to fight! You were very right; this is such an evil as must be faced and fought, even if we lose all in battle! Now we must do that which none of our own race has done for generations—we must open three locks, throw wide the Great Door, and seek out the Keeper of the Closed Knowledge!"

Light, a sharp ray sighting from the tip of the wand. And the Foanna following that beam, the three humans coming after . . . into the unknown.

16
The Opening of the Great Door

It was not the general airlessness of the long-closed passage which wore on Ross's nerves, made Karara suddenly reach out and clasp fingers about the wrists of the two men she walked between; it was a crushing sensation of age, of a toll of years so long, so heavy, as to make time itself into a thick flood which tugged at their bodies, mired their feet as they trudged after the Foanna. This sense of age, of a dead and heavy past, was so stifling that all three humans breathed in gasps.

Karara's breaths became sobs. Yet she matched her pace to Ashe and Ross, kept going. Ross himself had little idea of their surroundings, but one small portion of his brain asked answerless questions. The foremost being: Why did the past crush in on him here? He had traveled time, but never before had he been beaten with the feel of countless dead and dying years.

"Going back—" That hoarse whisper came from Ashe, and Ross thought he understood.

"A time gate!" He was eager to accept such an explanation. Time gates he could understand, but that the Foanna used one . . .

"Not our kind," Ashe replied.

But his words had pulled Ross out of a spell which had been as quicksand about him. And he began to fight back with a determination not to be sucked into what filled this place. In spite of Ross's efforts, his eyes could supply him with no definite impression of where they were. The ramp had led them out of the sea, but where they walked now, linked hand to hand, Ross could not say. He could see the glimmer of the Foanna; turning his head he could see his companions as shadows, but all beyond that was utter dark.

"Ahhhh—" Karara's sobs gave way to a whisper which was half moan. "This is a way of gods, old gods, gods who never dealt with men! It is not well to walk the road of the gods!"

Her fear lapped to Ross. He faced that emotion as he had faced so many different kinds of fear all his life. Sure, he felt that pressure on him, not the pressure of past centuries now—but a power beyond his ability to describe.

"Not our gods!" Ross put his stubborn defiance into words, more as a shield against his own wavering. "No power where there is no belief!" From what half-forgotten bit of reading had he dredged that knowledge? "No being without belief!" he repeated.

To his vast amazement he heard Ashe laugh, though the sound bordered on hysteria.

"No belief, no power," the older man replied. "You've speared the right fish, Ross! No gods of ours dwell here, Karara, and whatever power does has no rights over us. Hold to that, girl, hold that!"

> "Ah, ye forty thousand gods,
> Ye gods of sea, of sky, of woods,
> Of mountains, of valleys,

Ye assemblies of gods,
Ye elder brothers of the gods that are,
Ye gods that once were,
Ye that whisper. Ye that watch by night,
Ye that show your gleaming eyes,
Come down, awake, stir,
Walk this road, walk this road!"

She was singing, first softly and then more strongly, the liquid words of her own tongue repeated in English as if what she strove to call she would share with her companions. Now there was triumph in her singing and Ross found himself echoing her, "Walk this road!" as a demand.

It was still there, all of it, the crushing weight of the past, and that which brooded within that past, which had reached out for them, to possess or to alter. Only they were free of that reaching now. And they could see too! The fuzzy darkness was lighter and there were normal walls about them. Ross put out his free hand and rubbed finger tips along rough stone.

Once more their senses were assaulted by a stealthy attack from beyond the bounds of space and time as the walls fell away and they came out into a wide space whose boundaries they could not see. Here that which brooded was strong, a mighty weight poised aloft to strike them down.

"Come down, awake, stir. . . ." Karara's pleading sank again to a whisper, her voice sounded hoarse as if her mouth were dry, her words formed by a shrunken tongue, issued from a parched throat.

Light spreading in channels along the floor, making a fiery pattern—patterns within patterns, intricate designs within designs. Ross jerked his eyes away from those patterns. To study them was danger, he knew without being warned. Karara's nails bit into his flesh and he welcomed that pain; it kept him alert, conscious of what was Ross Murdock, holding him safely apart from something greater than he, but entirely alien.

The designs and patterns were lines on a pavement. And now the three Foanna, swaying as if yielding to unseen winds, began to follow those patterns with small dancing steps. But the humans remained where they were, holding to one another for the sustaining strength their contact offered.

Back, forth, the Foanna danced—and once more their cloaks vanished or were discarded, so their silver-bright figures advanced, retreated, weaving a way from one arabesque to another. First about the outer rim and then in, by spirals and circles. No light except the crimson glowing rivulets on the floor, the silver bodies of the Foanna moving back and forth, in and out.

Then, suddenly, the three dancers halted, huddled together in an open space between the designs. And Ross was startled by the impression of confusion, doubt, almost despair wafted from them to the humans. Back across the patterned floor they came, their hands clasped even as the humans stood together, and now they fronted the three out of time.

"Too few . . . we are too few . . ." she who was the mid one of the trio said. "We can not open the Great Door."

"How many do you need?" Karara's voice was no longer parched, frightened. She might have traveled through fear to a new serenity.

Why did he think that, Ross wondered fleetingly. Was it because he, too, had had the same release?

The Polynesian girl loosed her grip on her companions' hands, taking a step closer to the Foanna.

"Three can be four—"

"Or five." Ashe moved up beside her. "If we suit your purpose."

Was Gordon Ashe crazy? Or had he fallen victim to whatever filled this place? Yet it was Ashe's voice, sane, serene, as Ross had always heard it. The younger Agent wet his lips; it was his turn to have a dry mouth. This was not his game; it could not be. Yet he summoned voice enough to add in turn:

"Six—"

When it came the Foanna answer was a warning:

"To aid us you must cast aside your shields, allow your identities to become one with our forces. Having done so, it may be that you shall never be as you are now but changed."

"Changed . . ."

The word echoed, perhaps not in the place where they stood, but in Ross's head. This was a risk such as he had never taken before. His chances in the past had been matters of action where his own strength and wits were matched against the problem. Here, he would open a door to forces he and his kind should not meet—expose himself to danger such as did not exist on the plane where weapons and strength of arm could decide victory or defeat.

And this was not really his fight at all. What did it matter to humans ten thousand years or so in the future what happened to Hawaikans in this past? He was a fool; they were all fools to become embroiled in this. The Baldies and their stellar empire—if that ever had existed as the humans surmised—was long gone before his breed entered space.

"If you accomplish this with our aid," said Ashe, "will you be able to defeat the invaders?"

Again a lengthening moment of silence before the Foanna replied:

"We can not tell. We only know that there is a force laid up here, set behind certain gates in the far past, upon which we may call for some supreme effort. But this much we also know: The Evil of the Shadow reaches out from here now, and where that darkness falls men will no longer be men but things in the guise of men who obey and follow as mindless creatures. As yet this shadow of the Shadow is a small one. But it will spread, for that is the nature of those who have spawned it. They have chanced upon and corrupted a thing we know. Such power feeds upon the will to power. Having turned it to their bidding, they will not be able to resist using it, for it is so easy to do and the results exult the nature of those who employ it.

"You have said that you and those like you who travel the time trails fear to change the past. Here the first steps have been taken to alter the future, but unless we complete the defense it will be ill for all of us."

"And this is your only weapon?" Ashe asked once more.

"The only one strong enough to stand against that which is now unleashed."

In the pavement the fiery lines were bright and glowing. Even when Ross shut his eyes, parts of those designs were still visible against his eyelids.

"We don't know how." He made a last feeble protest on the side of prudence. "We couldn't move as you did."

"Apart, no—together, yes."

The silvery figures were once more swaying, the mist which was their hair flowing about them. Karara's hands went out, and the slender fingers of one of the Foanna lifted, closed about firm, brown human flesh. Ashe was doing the same!

Ross thought he cried out, but he could not be sure, as he watched Karara's head begin to sway in concert with her Foanna partner, her black hair springing out from her shoulders to rival the rippling strands of the alien's. Ashe was consciously matching steps with the companion who also drew him along a flowing line of fire.

In this last instant Ross realized the time for retreat was past—there was no place left to go. His hands went out, though he had to force that invitation because in him there was a shrinking horror of this surrender. But he could not let the others go without him.

The Foanna's touch was cool, and yet it seemed that flesh met his flesh, fingers as normal as his met fingers in that grasp. And when that hold was complete he gave a small gasp. For his horror was wiped away; he knew in its place a burst of energy which could be disciplined to use as a weapon or a tool in concentrated and complicated action. His feet so . . . and then so . . . Did those directions flow without words from the Foanna's fingers to his and then along his nerves to his brain? He only knew which was the proper next step, and the next, and the next, as they wove their way along the pattern lines, with their going adding a necessary thread to a design.

Forward four steps, backward one—in and out. Did Ross actually hear that sweet thrumming, akin to the lilting speech of the Foanna, or was it a throbbing in his blood? In and out . . . What had become of the others he did not know; he was aware only of his own path, of the hand in his, of the silvery shape at his side to whom he was now tied as if one of the Rover capture nets enclosed them both.

The fiery lines under his feet were smoking, tendrils rising and twisting as the hair of the Foanna rippled and twisted. And the smoke clung, wreathed his body. They moved in a cocoon of smoke, thicker and thicker, until Ross could not even see the Foanna who accompanied him, was only assured of her presence by the hand which grasped his.

And a small part of him clung desperately to the awareness of that clasp as an anchorage against what might come, a tie between the world of reality and the place into which he was passing.

How did one find words to describe this? Ross wondered with that part of him which remained stubbornly Ross Murdock, Time Agent. He thought that he did not see with his eyes, hear with his ears but used other senses his own kind did not recognize nor acknowledge.

Space . . . not a room . . . a cave—anything made by normal nature. Space which held something.

Pure energy? His mind strove to give name to that which was nameless. Perhaps it was that spark of memory and consciousness which gave him that instant of "Seeing." Was it a throne? And on it a shimmering figure? He was regarded intently, measured, and—set aside.

There were questions or a question he could not hear, and perhaps an answer he would never be able to understand. Or had any of this happened at all?

Ross crouched on a cold floor, his head hanging, drained of energy, of all that feeling of power and well-being he had had when they had begun their dance across the symbols. About him those designs still glowed dully. When he looked at them too intently his head ached. He could almost understand, but the struggle was so exhausting he winced at the effort.

"Gordon—?"

There was no clasp on his hand; he was alone, alone between two glowing arabesques. That loneliness struck at him with the sharpness of a blow. His head came up; frantically he stared about him in search of his companions. "Gordon!" His plea and demand in one was answered:

"Ross?"

On his hands and knees, Ross used the rags of his strength to crawl in that direction, stopping now and then to shade his eyes with his hands, to peer through the cracks between his fingers for some sight of Ashe.

There he was, sitting quietly, his head up as if he were listening, or striving to listen. His cheeks were sunken; he had the drained, worn look of a man strained to the limit of physical energy. Yet there was a quiet peace in his face. Ross crawled on, put out a hand to Ashe's arm as if only by touching the other could he be sure he was not an illusion. And Ashe's fingers came up to cover the younger man's in a grasp as tight as the Foanna's hold had been.

"We did it; together we did it," Ashe said. "But where— why—?"

Those questions were not aimed at him, Ross knew. And at that moment the younger man did not care where they had been, what they had done. It was enough that his terrible loneliness was gone, that Ashe was here.

Still keeping his hold on Ross, Ashe turned his head and called into the wilderness of the symbol-glowing space about them, "Karara?"

She came to them, not crawling, not wrung almost dry of spirit and strength, but on her two feet. About her shoulders her dark hair waved and spun—or was it dark now? Along those strands there seemed to be threaded motes of light, giving a silvery sheen which was a faint echo of the Foanna's tresses. And was it only his bemused and bewildered sight, Ross wondered, or had her eyes turned golden?

Karara smiled down at them and held out her hands, offering one to each. When they took them Ross knew again that surge of energy he had felt when he had followed the Foanna into the maze dance.

"Come! There is much to do."

He could not be mistaken; her voice held the singing lilt of the Foanna. Somehow she had crossed some barrier to become a paler, perhaps a lesser, but still a copy of the three aliens. Was this what they had meant when they warned of a change which might come to those who followed them into the ritual of this place?

Ross looked from the girl to Ashe with searching intensity. No, he could see no outward change in Gordon. And he felt none within himself.

"Come!" Some of Karara's old impetuousness returned as she tugged at them, urging them to their feet and drawing them with her. She appeared to know where they must go, and both men followed her guidance.

Once more they came out of the weird and alien into the normal, for here were the rock walls of a passage running up at an angle which became so steep they were forced to pull along by handholds hollowed in the walls.

"Where are we going?" Ashe asked.

"To cleanse." Karara's answer was ambiguous, and she sped along hardly touching the handholds. "But hurry!"

They finished their climb and were in another corridor where patches of sunlight came through a pierced wall to dazzle their eyes. This was similar to the way which had run beside the courtyard in Zahur's castle.

Ross looked out of the first opening down into a courtyard. But where Zahur's had held the busy life of a castle, this was silent. Silent, but not deserted. There were men below, armed, helmed. He recognized the uniform of the Wrecker warriors, saw one or two who wore the gray of the Foanna servants. They stood in lines, unmoving, without speech among themselves, men who might have been frozen into immobility and arranged so for some game in which they were the voiceless, willing pieces.

And their immobility was a thing to arouse fear. Were they dead and still standing?

"Come!" Karara's voice had sunk to a whisper and her hand pulled at the men.

"What—?" began Ross.

Ashe shook his head. Those rows below drawn up as if in order to march, unliving rows. They could not be alive as the humans knew life!

Ross left his vantage point, ready to follow Karara. But he could not blot from his mind the picture of those lines, nor forget the terrible blankness which made their faces more inhuman, more frighteningly alien than those of the Foanna.

17
Shades Against Shadow

The corridor ended in a narrow slit of room, and the wall before them was not the worked stone of the citadel but a single slab of what appeared to be glass curdled into creamy ridges and depressions.

Here were the Foanna, their robes once more cloaking them. Each held, point out, one of the rods. They moved slowly but with the precise gestures of those about a demanding and very important task as they traced each depression in the wall before them with the wand points. Down, up, around . . . as their feet had moved to cover each line.

"Now!"

The wands pointed to the floor. The Foanna moved equidistant from one another. Then, as one, the rods were lifted vertically, brought down together with a single loud tap.

On the wall the blue lines they had traced with such care darkened, melted. The glassy slab shivered, shattered, fell outward in a lace of fragments. So the narrow room became a balcony above a large chamber.

Below a platform ran the full length of that hall, and on it were mounted a line of oval disks. These had been turned to different angles and each reflected light, a ray beam directed at them from a machine whose metallic casing, projecting antennae, was oddly out of place here.

Once more the three staffs of the Foanna raised as one in the air. This time, from the knobs held out over the hall blazed, not the usual whirl of small sparks, but strong beams of light—blue light darkening as it pierced downward until it became thrusting lines of almost tangible substance.

When those blue beams struck the nearest ovals they webbed with lines which cracked wide open. Shattered bits tinkled down to the platform. There was a stir at the end of the hall where the machine stood. Figures ran into plain sight. Baldies! Ross cried out a warning as he saw those star men raise weapon tubes aimed at the perch on which the Foanna stood.

Fire crackling with the speed and sound of lightning lashed up at the balcony. The lances of light met the spears of dark, and there was a flash which blinded Ross, a sound which split open the whole world.

The human's eyes opened, not upon darkness but on dazzling light, flashes of it which tore over him in great sweeping arcs. Dazed, sick, he tried to press his prone body into the unyielding surface on which he lay. But there was no way of burrowing out of this wild storm of light and clashing sound. Now under him the very fabric of the floor rocked and quivered as if it were being shaken apart into rubble.

All the will and ability to move was gone. Ross could only lie there and endure. What had happened, he did not know save that what raged about him now was a warring of inimical forces, perhaps both feeding on each other even as they strove for mastery.

The play of rays resembled sword blades crossing, fencing. Ross threw his arm over his eyes to shut out the intolerable brilliance of that thrust and counter. His body tingled and winced as the whirlwind of energy clashed and reclashed. He was beaten, stupid, as a man pinned down too long under a heavy shelling.

How did it end? In one terrific thunderclap of sound and blasting power? And when did it end—hours . . . days later? Time was a thing set apart from this. Ross lay in the quiet which his body welcomed thirstily. Then he was conscious of the touch of wind on his face, wind carrying the hint of sea salt.

He opened his eyes and saw above him a patch of clouded sky. Shakily he levered himself up on his elbows. There were no complete walls any more, just jagged points of masonry, broken teeth set in a skull's jawbone. Open sky, dark clouds spattering rain.

"Gordon? Karara?" Ross's voice was a thin whisper. He licked his lips and tried again:

"Gordon!"

Had there been an answering whimper? Ross crawled into a hollow between two fallen blocks. A pool of water? No, it was the cloak of one of the Foanna spread out across the flooring in this fragment of room. Then Ross saw that Ashe was there, the cloaked figured braced against his shoulder as he half supported, half embraced the Foanna.

"Ynvalda!" Ashe called that with an urgency which was demanding. Now the Foanna moved, raising an arm in the cloak's flowing sleeve.

Ross sat back on his heels.

"Ross—Ashe?" He turned his head. Karara stood here, then came forward, planting her feet with care, her hands outstretched, her eyes wide and unseeing. Ross pulled himself up and went to her, finding that the once solid floor seemed to dip and sway under him, until he, too, must balance and creep. His hands closed on her shoulders and he pulled her to him in mutual support.

"Gordon?"

"Over there. You all right."

"I think so." Her voice was weak. "The Foanna . . . Ynlan . . . Ynvalda—" Steadying herself against him, she tried to look around.

The place which had once been a narrow room, then a balcony, was now a perch above stomach-turning space. The hall of the oval mirrors was gone, having disappeared into a hollow the depths of which were veiled by a vapor which boiled and bubbled as if, far below, some huge caldron hung above a blazing fire.

Karara cried out and Ross drew her back from that drop. He was clearer-headed now and looked about for some way down from this doubtful perch. Of the other two Foanna there was no sign. Had they been sucked up and out in the inferno they had created with their unleashing of energy against the Baldies' installation?

"Ross—look!" Karara's cry, her upflung arm directed his attention aloft.

Under the sullen gathering of the storm a sphere arose as a bubble might seek the surface of a pool before breaking. A ship—a Baldy ship taking off from the ruined citadel! So some of the enemy had survived that trial of strength!

The globe was small, a scout used for within-atmosphere exploration, Ross judged. It arose first, and then moved inland, fleeing the gathering storm, to be out of sight in moments. Inland, where the mountain base of the invaders was reputed to be. Retreating? Or bound to gather reinforcements?

"Baldies?" Karara asked.

"Yes."

She wiped her hand across her face, smearing dust and grime on her cheeks. As raindrops pattered about them, Ross drew the girl with him into the alcove where Ashe sheltered with the Foanna. The cowled alien was sitting up, her hand still gripping one of the wands, now a half-melted ruin.

Ashe glanced at them as if for the first time he remembered they might be there.

"Baldy ship just took off inland," Ross told him. "We didn't see either of the other Foanna."

"They have gone to do what is to be done," Ashe's companion replied. "So some of the enemy fled. Well, perhaps they have learned one lesson, not to meddle with others' devices. Ahh, so much gone which will never come again! Never again—"

She held up the half-melted wand, turning it back and forth before her, before she cast it away. It flew out, up, then dropped into the caldron of the hall which had been. A gust of rain, cold, chilling the lightly clad humans, swept across them.

The Foanna was helped to her feet by Ashe. For a moment she turned slowly, giving a lingering look to the ruins. Then she spoke: "Broken stone holds no value. Take hands, my brothers, my sister, it is time we go hence."

Karara's hand in Ross's right, Ashe's in his left, and both linked to Ynvalda in turn. Then—they were indeed elsewhere, in a courtyard where bodies lay flaccid under the drenching downpour of the rain. And moving among those bodies were the two other Foanna, bending to examine one man after another. Perhaps over one in three they so inspected they held consultation before a wand was used in tracing certain portions of the body between them. When they were finished, that man stirred, moaned, showed signs of life once more.

"Rosss—!" From behind a tumbled wall crept a Hawaikan who did not wear the guard armor of the others. Gill-pack, flippers, diver's belt, had been stripped from him. There was a bleeding gash down the side of his face, and he held his left arm against his body, supported by his right hand.

"Baleku!"

The Rover pulled himself up to his feet and stood swaying. Ross reached him quickly to catch him as he slumped forward.

"Loketh?" he asked.

"The women-killers took him." Somehow the Rover got that out as Ross half supported, half led him to where the Foanna were gathering those they had been able to revive. "They wanted to learn"—Baleku was obviously making a great effort to tell his story—"about . . . about where we came from . . . where we got the packs."

"So now they will know of us, or will if they get the story out of Loketh." Ashe worked with Ross to splint the Rover's broken arm. "How many of them were here, Baleku?"

The Rover's head moved slowly from side to side. "I do not know in truth. It is—was—like a dream. I was in the water swimming through the sea gate. Then suddenly I was in another place where those from the stars waited about me. They had our packs and belts and these they showed us, demanding to know whereof these were. Loketh was like one deep in sleep and they left him so when they questioned me. Then there came a great noise and the floor under us shook, lightning flashed through the air. Two of the women-killers ran from the room and all of them were greatly excited. They took up Loketh and carried him away, with him the packs and other things. And I was left alone, though I could not move— as if they had left me in a net I could not see.

"More and more were the flashes. Then one of those slayers of women stood in the doorway. He raised his hand, and my feet were free, but I could not move otherwise than to follow after him. We came along a hall and into this court where men stood unstirring, although stones fell from the walls upon some of them and the ground shook—"

Baleku's voice grew shriller, his words ran together. "The one who pulled me after him by his will—he cried out and put his hands to his head. Back and forth he ran, bumping into the standing men, and once running into a wall as if he were blinded. And then he was gone and I was alone. There was more falling stone and one struck my shoulder so I was thrown to the ground. There I lay until you came."

"So few—out of many so few—" One of the Foanna stood beside them, her cloak streaming with the falling rain. "And for these"—she faced the lines of those they had not revived—"there was no chance. They died as helplessly as if they went into a meeting of swords with their arms bound to their sides! Evil have we wrought here."

Ashe shook his head. "Evil has been wrought here, Ynlan, but not by your seeking. And those who died here helplessly may be only a small portion of those yet to be sacrificed. Have you forgotten the slaughter at Kyn Add and those other fairings where women and children were also struck down to serve some purpose we do not even yet know?"

"Lady, Great One—" Baleku struggled to sit up and Ross slipped an arm behind him in aid. "She for whom I made a bride-cup was meat for them at Kyn Add, along with many others. If these slayers are not put to the sword's edge, there will be other fairings so used. And these Shadow ones possess a magic to draw men to them helplessly to be killed. Great One, you have powers; all men know that wind and wave obey your call. Do you now use your magic! It is better to fall with a power we know, than answer such spells as those killers have netted about the men here!"

"This is one weapon which they shall not use again." Ynvalda rose from a stone block where she had been sitting. "And perhaps in its way it was one of the most dangerous. But in defeating it we have by so much weakened ourselves also. And the strong place of these star men lies not on the coast, but inland. They will be warned by those who fled this place. Wind and wave, yes, those have served our purpose in the past. But now perhaps we have found that which our power will not best! Only—for this"—her gesture was for the ruins of the citadel and the dead—"there shall be a payment exacted—to the height of our desire!"

Whether the Foanna did have any control over the storm

winds or not, the present deluge appeared not to accommodate them. The dazed, injured survivors of the courtyard were brought to shelter in some of the underground passages.

There appeared to be no other reminders of the Wrecker force which had earlier besieged the keep than those survivors. But within hours some of those who had served the Foanna for generations returned. And the Foanna themselves opened the sea gates so that the Rover cruisers anchored in the small bay below their ruined walls.

A small force, and one ill-equipped to go up against the Baldies. Some five star men's bodies had been found in the citadel, but the ship had gone off to warn their base. To Ross's thinking the advantage still lay with the invaders.

But the Hawaikans refused to accept the idea that the odds were against them. As soon as the storm blew out its force Ongal's cruiser headed northwest to other clan fairings where the Rovers could claim kinship. And Afrukta sailed on the same errand south. While some of the Wreckers were released to carry the warning to their lords. Just how great a force could be gathered through such means and how effective it would be, was a question to make the humans uneasy.

Karara disappeared with the Foanna into the surviving inner cliff-burrows below the citadel. But Ashe and Ross remained with Torgul and his officers, striving to bring organization out of the chaos about them.

"We must know just where their lair lies," Torgul stated the obvious. "The mountains you believe, and they can fly in sky ships to and from that point. Well"—he spread out a chart—"here are the mountains on this island, running so. An army marching hither could be sighted from sky ships. Also, there are many mountains. Which is the one or ones we must seek? It may take many tens of days to find that place, while they will always know where we are, watch us from above, prepare for our coming—"

Again Ross mentally paid tribute to the Captain's quick grasp of essentials.

"You have a solution, Captain?" Ashe asked.

"There is the river—here—" Torgul said reflectively. "Perhaps I think in terms of water because I am a sailor. But here it does run, and for this far along it our cruisers may ascend." He pointed with his finger tip. "This lies, however, in Glicma's land, and he is now the mightiest of the Wrecker lords, his sword always drawn against us. I do not believe that we could talk him into—"

"Glicmas!" Ross interrupted. They both looked at him inquiringly, and he repeated Loketh's story of the Wrecker lord who had had dealings with a "voice from the mountain" and so gained the wrecking devices to make him the dominant lord of the district.

"So!" Torgul exclaimed. "That is the evil of this Shadow in the mountains! No, under those circumstances I do not think we shall talk Glicmas into furthering any raid against those who have made him great over his fellows. Rather will he turn against us in their cause."

"And if we do not use the cruisers up the river"—Ashe conned the map—"then perhaps a small party or parties working overland could strike the stream here, nearer to the uplands."

Torgul frowned at the map. "I do not think so. Even small parties moving in that direction would be sighted by Glicmas's people. The more so if they headed inland. He will not wish to share his secrets with others."

"But, say—a party of Foanna."

The Captain glanced up swiftly to favor Ashe with a keen regard. "Then he would not dare. No, I am sure he would not dare to interfere. Not yet has he risen high enough to turn the hook of his sword against them. But would the Foanna do so?"

"If not the Foanna, then others wearing like robes," Ashe said slowly.

"Others wearing like robes?" repeated Torgul. Now his frown was heavy. "No man would take on the guise of the Foanna; he would be blasted by their power for so doing. If the Foanna will lead us in their persons, then we shall follow gladly, knowing that their magic will be with us."

"There is also this," Ross broke in. "The Baldies have the gill-packs they took from Baleku and Loketh, and they have Loketh. They will want to learn more about us. We hoped that the citadel would provide bait to draw them and it did. That our plan for a trap there was spoiled was ill fortune. But I am sure that if the Baldies believe we are coming to them, they will hold off an all-out attack against our march, hoping to gather us in intact. They'd risk that."

Ashe nodded. "I agree. We are the unknown they must solve now. And this much I am sure of—the future of this world and her people balances on a very narrow line of choice. It is my hope that such a choice is still to be made."

Torgul smiled thinly. "We live in perilous times when the Shades require our swords to go up against the Shadow!"

18
World in Doubt?

The day was dully overcast as all days had been since they had begun this skulk-and-march penetration into the mountain territory. Ross could not accept the idea that the Foanna might actually command wind and wave, storm and sun, as the Hawaikans firmly believed, but the gloomy weather *had* favored them so far. And now they had reached the last breathing point before they took the plunge into the heart of the enemy country. About the way in which they were to make that plunge, Ross had his own plan. One he did not intend to share with either Ashe or Karara. Though he had had to outline it to the one now waiting here with him.

"This is still your mind, younger brother?"

He did not turn his head to look at the cloaked figure. "It is still my mind!" Ross could be firm on that point.

The human backed out of the vantage place from which he had been studying the canyonlike valley cupping the

Baldy spaceship. Now he got to his feet and faced Ynlan, his own gray cloak billowing out in the wind to reveal the Rover scale armor underneath.

"You can do it for me?" he asked in turn. During the past days the Foanna had admitted that the weird battle within the citadel had weakened and limited their "magic." Last night they had detected a force barrier ahead and to transport the whole party through that by teleporting was impossible.

"Yes, you alone. Then my wand would be drained for a space. But what can you do within their hold, save be meat for their taking?"

"There can not be too many of them left there. That's a small ship. They lost five at the citadel, and the Rovers have three prisoners. No sign of the scout ship we know they have—so more of them must be gone in it. I won't be facing an army. And what they have in the way of weapons may be powered by installations in the ship. A lot of damage done there. Or even if the ship lifted—" He was not sure of what he could do; this was a venture depending largely on improvisation at the last moment.

"You propose to send off the ship?"

"I don't know whether that is possible. No, perhaps I can only attract their attention, break through the force shield so the rest may attack."

Ross knew that he must attempt this independent action, that in order to remain the Ross Murdock he had always been, he must be an actor not a spectator.

The Foanna did not argue with him now. "Where—?" Her long sleeve rippled as she gestured to the canyon. Dull as the skies were overhead, there was light here— too much of it for his purpose as the ground about the ship was open. To appear there might be fatal.

Ross was grasped by another and much more promising idea. The Foanna had transported them all to the deck of Torgul's cruiser after asking him to picture it for her mentally. And to all outward appearances the Baldy ship

before them now was twin to the one which had taken
him once on a fantastic voyage across a long-vanished
stellar empire. Such a ship he knew!

"Can you put me in the ship?"

"If you have a good memory of it, yes. But how know
you these ships?"

"I was in one once for many days. If these are alike,
then I know it well!"

"And if this is unlike, to try such may mean your
death."

He had to accept her warning. Yet outwardly this ship
was a duplicate. And before he had voyaged on the derelict he had also explored a wrecked freighter on his own
world thousands of years before his own race had evolved.
There was one portion of both ships which had been
identical—save for size—and that part was the best for
his purpose.

"Send me—here!"

With closed eyes, Ross produced a mental picture of
the control cabin. Those seats which were not really seats
but webbing support swinging before banks of buttons
and levers; all the other installations he had watched, studied, until they were as known to him as the plate bulkheads of the cabin below in which he had slept. Very
vivid, that memory. He felt the touch of the Foanna's cool
fingers on his forehead—then it was gone. He opened his
eyes.

No more wind and gloom, he stood directly behind the
pilot's web-sling, facing a viewscreen and rows of controls, just as he had stood so many times in the derelict. He had made it! This was the control cabin of the
spacer. And it was alive—the faint thrumming in the air,
the play of lights on the boards.

Ross pulled the cowl of his Foanna cloak up over his
head. He had had days to accustom himself to the bulk
of the robe, but still its swathings were sometimes a
hindrance rather than a help. Slowly he turned. There
were no Baldies here, but the well door to the lower level

was open, and from it came small sounds echoing up the communication ladder. The ship was occupied.

Not for the first time since he had started on this venture Ross wished for more complete information. Doubtless several of those buttons or levers before him controlled devices which could be the greatest aid to him now. But which and how he did not know. Once in just such a cabin he had meddled and, in activating a long-silent installation, had called the attention of the Baldies to their wrecked ship, to the humans looting it. Only by the merest chance had the vengeance of the stellar space-men fallen then on the Russian investigators and not on his own people.

He knew better than to touch anything before the pilot's station, but the banks of controls to one side were concerned with the inner well-being of the ship—and they tempted him. To go it blind was, however, more of a risk than he dared take. There was one future precaution for him.

From a very familiar case beside the pilot's seat Ross gathered up a collection of disks, sorted through them hastily for one which bore a certain symbol on its covering. There was only one of those. Slapping the rest back into their container, Ross pressed a button on the control board.

Again his guess paid off! Another disk was exposed as a small panel slid back. Ross clawed that out of the holder, put in its place the one he had found. Now, if his choice had been correct, the crew who took off in this ship, unless they checked their route tape first, would find themselves heading to another primitive planet and not returning to base. Perhaps exhaustion of fuel might ground them past hope of ever regaining their home port again. Next to damaging the ship, which he could not do, this was the best thing to assure that any enemy leaving Hawaika would not speedily return with a second expeditionary force.

Ross dropped the route disk he had taken out into a

pocket on his belt, to be destroyed when he had the chance. Now he catfooted across the deck to look into the well and listen.

The walls glowed with a diffused light. From here he could count at least four levels under him, with perhaps another. The bottom two ought to be supplies and general storage. Then the engine room, tech labs above, and next to the control cabin the living quarters.

Through the fabric of the ship, shivering up his body from the soles of his feet, he could feel the vibration of engines at work. One such must control the force field which ringed this canyon, perhaps even powered the weapons the invaders could turn against any assault.

Ross whirled about, his Foanna cloak in a wide swing. There was one control which he knew. Yes, again the board was the same as the one he was familiar with. His hand plunged out and down, raking the lever from one measure point to the very end of the slit in which it moved. Then he planted himself with his back to the wall. Whoever came up the well hunting the cause for the failure would be facing the other way. Ross crouched a little, pushing the cape well back on his shoulders to free his arms. There was a feline suppleness in his stance just as a jungle cat might wait the coming of its prey.

What he heard was a shout below, the click of footgear on the rungs of the level ladder. Ross's lips drew back in a snarl which was also feline. He thought that would do it! Spacemen were ultra-sensitive to any failure in air flow.

White-skinned head, bare of any hair, thin shoulders a little hunched under the blue-green-lavender stuff of the Baldies' uniform . . . Head turning now so that the eyes could see the necessary switch. An exclamation from the alien and—

But the Baldy never had a chance to complete that turn or look behind him. Ross sprang and struck with the side of his hand. The hairless head snapped forward. His hands already hooked in the other's armpits, the human heaved the alien up and over onto the deck of the control cabin. It was only when he was about to bind his captive that Ross discovered the Baldy was dead. A blow calculated to stun the alien had been too severe. Breathing a little faster, the human rolled the body back and hoisted it into the navigator's swing-seat, fastening it with the take-off belts. One down—how many left?

He had little time to wonder, for before he could reach the well once again there was a call from below—sharp and demanding. Ross searched his victim, but the Baldy was unarmed.

Again a shout. Then silence—too complete a silence. How could they have guessed trouble so quickly? Unless, unless the Baldies' mental communication had been at work . . . they might even now know their fellow was dead.

But not how he died. Ross was prepared to grant the Baldies superhuman abilities, but he did not see how they could know what had happened here. They could only suspect danger, not know the form it had taken. And sooner or later one of them must come to adjust the switch. This could be a duel of patience.

Ross squatted at the edge of the well, trying to make his ears supply him with hints of what might be happening below. Had there been an alteration in the volume of vibration? He set his palm flat to the deck, tried to deduce the truth. But he could not be sure. That there had been some slight change he was certain.

They could not wait much longer without making an attempt to reopen the air-supply regulator, or could they? Again Ross was hampered by lack of information. Perhaps the Baldies did not need the same amount of oxygen his own kind depended upon. And if that were true, Ross could be the first to suffer in playing a waiting game. Well, air was not the only thing he could cut off from here, though it had been the first and most important to his mind. Ross hesitated. Two-edged weapons cut in both directions. But he had to force a countermove from them. He pulled another switch. The control cabin, the whole of the ship, was plunged into darkness.

No sound from below this time. Ross pictured the interior layout of the ships he had known. Two levels down to reach the engine room. Could he descend undetected? There was only one way to test that—try it.

He pulled the Foanna cloak about him, was several rungs down on the ladder when the glow in the walls came on. An emergency switch? With a forward scramble, Ross swung into one of the radiating side corridors. The sliding-door panels along it were all closed; he could detect no sounds behind them. But the vibration in the ship's walls had returned to its steady beat.

Now Ross realized the folly of his move. He was more securely trapped here than he had been in the control cabin. There was only one way out, up or down the ladder, and the enemy could have that under observation from below. All they would need to do was to use a flamer or a paralyzing ray such as the one he had turned over to Ashe several days ago.

Ross inched along to the stairwell. A faint pad of movement, a shadow of sound from the ladder. Someone on the way up. Could they mentally detect him, know him for an alien intruder by the broadcast of his thoughts? The Baldies had a certain respect for the Foanna and might desire to take one alive. He drew the robe about him, used it to muffle his figure completely as the true wearers did.

But the figure pulling painfully up from rung to rung was no Baldy. The lean Hawaikan arms, the thin Hawaikan face, drawn of feature, painfully blank of expression—Loketh—under the same dread spell as had held the warriors in the citadel courtyard. Could the aliens be using this Hawaikan captive as a defense shield, moving up behind him?

Loketh's head turned, those blank eyes regarded Ross. And their depths were troubled, recognition of a sort returning. The Hawaikan threw up one hand in a beseeching gesture and then went to his knees in the corridor.

"Great One! Great One!" The words came from his lips in a breathy hiss as he groveled. Then his body went flaccid, and he sprawled face down, his twisted leg drawn up as if he would run but could not.

"Foanna!" The one word came out of the walls themselves, or so it seemed.

"Foanna—the wise learn what lies before them when they walk alone in the dark." The Hawaikan speech was stilted, accented, but understandable.

Ross stood motionless. Had they somehow seen him through Loketh's eyes? Or had they been alerted merely by the Hawaikan's call? They believed he was one of the Foanna. Well, he would play that role.

"Foanna!" Sharper this time, demanding. "You lie in our hand. Let us clasp the fingers tightly and you shall be naught."

Out of somewhere the words Karara had chanted in the Foanna temple came to Ross—not in her Polynesian tongue but in the English she had repeated. And softening his voice to his best approximation of the Foanna singsong Ross sang:

> "Ye forty thousand gods,
>   Ye gods of sea, of sky—of stars," he improvised.
> "Ye elders of the gods that are,
>   Ye gods that once were,
>   Ye that whisper, ye that watch by night,
>   Ye that show your gleaming eyes."

"Foanna!" The summons was on the ragged edge of patience. "Your tricks will not move our mountains!"

"Ye gods of mountains," Ross returned, "of valleys, of Shades and not the Shadow," he wove in the beliefs of this world, too. "Walk now this world, between the stars!" His confidence was growing. And there was no use in remaining pent in this corridor. He would have to chance that they were not prepared to kill summarily one of the Foanna.

Ross went to the well, went down the ladder slowly, keeping his robe about him. Here at the next level there was a wider space about the opening, and three door panels. Behind one must be those he sought. He was buoyed up by a curious belief in himself, almost as if wearing this robe did give him in part the power attributed to the Foanna.

He laid his hand on the door to his right and sent it snapping back into its frame, stepped inside as if he entered here by right.

There were three Baldies. To his eyes they were all superficially alike, but the one seated on a control stool had a colder arrogance in his expression, a pitiless half smile which made Ross face him squarely. He longed for one of the Foanna staffs and the ability to use it. To spray that energy about this cabin might reduce the Baldy defenses to nothing. But now two of the paralyzing tubes were trained on him.

"You have come to us, Foanna, what have you to offer?" demanded the commander, if that was his rank.

"Offer?" For the first time Ross spoke. "There is no reason for the Foanna to make any offer, slayer of women and children. You have come from the stars to take, but that does not mean we choose to give."

He felt it now, that inner pulling, twisting in his mind, the willing which was their more subtle weapon. Once they had almost bent him with that willing because then he had worn their livery, a spacesuit taken from the wrecked freighter. Now he did not have that chink in his defense. And all that stubborn determination to be himself alone resisted the influence with a fierce inner fire.

"We offer life to you, Foanna, freedom of the stars. These other dirt creepers are nothing to you, why take you weapons in their cause? You are not of the same race."

"Nor are you!" Ross's hands moved under the envelope of the robe, unloosing the two hidden clasps which held it. That bank of controls before which the commander sat—to silence that would cause trouble. And he depended upon Ynlan. The Rovers should now be massed at either end of the canyon waiting for the force field to fail and let them in.

Ross steadied himself, poised for action. "We have something for you, star men—" he tried to hold their attention with words, "have you not heard of the power of the Foanna—that they can command wind and wave? That they can be where they were not in a single movement of the eyelid? And this is so—behold!"

It was the oldest trick in the world, perhaps on any planet. But because it was so old maybe it had been forgotten by the aliens. For, as Ross pointed, those heads did turn for an instant.

He was in the air, the robe gathered in his arms wide spread as bat wings. And then they crashed in a tangle which bore them all back against the controls. Ross strove to enmesh them in the robe, using the pressure of his body to slam them all on the buttons and levers of the board. Whether that battering would accomplish his purpose, he could not tell. But that he had only these few seconds torn out of time to try, he knew, and determined to use them as best he could.

One of the Baldies had slithered down to the floor and another was aiming strangely ineffectual blows at him. But the third had wriggled free to bring up a paralyzer. Ross slewed around, dragging the alien he held across his body just as the other fired. But though the fighter went limp and heavy in Ross's hold, the human's own right arm fell to his side, his upper chest was numb, and his head felt as if one of the Rover's boarding axes had clipped it. Ross reeled back and fell, his left hand raking down the controls as he went. Then he lay on the cabin floor and saw the convulsed face of the commander above him, a paralyzer aiming at his middle.

To breathe was an effort Ross found torture to endure. The red haze in his head filled all the world. Pain—he strove to flee the pain but was held captive in it. And always the pressure on him kept that agony steady.

"Let . . . be . . ." He wanted to scream that. Perhaps he had, but the pressure continued. Then he forced his eyes open. Ashe—Ashe and one of the Foanna bending over him, Ashe's hands on his chest, pressing, relaxing, pressing again.

"It is good—" He knew Ynvalda's voice. Her hand rested lightly on his forehead and from that touch Ross drew again the quickening of body and spirit he had felt on the dancing floor.

"How—?" He began and then changed to—"Where—?" For this was not the engine room of the spacer. He lay in the open, with sweet, rain-wet wind filling his starved lungs now without Ashe's force aid.

"It is over," Ashe told him, "all over—for now."

But not until the sun reached the canyon hours later and they sat in council, did Ross learn all the tale. Just as he had made his own plan for reaching the spacer, so had Ashe, Karara, and the dolphins worked on a similar attempt. The river running deep in those mountain gorges had provided a road for the dolphins and they found beneath its surface an entrance past the force barrier.

"The Baldies were so sure of their superiority on this primitive world they set no guards save that field," Ashe explained. "We slipped through five swimmers to reach the ship. And then the field went down, thanks to you."

"So I did help—that much." Ross grinned wryly. What had he proven by his sortie? Nothing much. But he was not sorry he had made it. For the very fact he had done it on his own had eased in part that small ache which was in him now when he looked at Ashe and remembered how it had once been. Ashe might be—always would be—his friend, but the old tight-locking comradeship of the Project was behind them, vanished like the time gate.

"And what will you do with them?" Ross nodded toward the captives, the three from the ship, two more taken from the small scouting globe which had homed to find their enemies ready for them.

"We wait," Ynvalda said, "for those on the Rover ship to be brought hither. By our laws they deserve death."

The Rovers at that council nodded vigorously, all save Torgul and Jazia. The Rover woman spoke first.

"They bear the Curse of Phutka heavy on them. To live under such a curse is worse than a clean, quick dying. Listen, it has come upon me that better this curse not only eat them up but be carried by them to rot those who sent them—"

Together the Foanna nodded. "There has been enough of killing," said Ynlan. "No, warriors, we do not say this because we shrink from rightful deaths. But Jazia speaks the truth in this matter. Let these depart. Perhaps they will bear that with them which will convince their leaders that this is not a world they may squeeze in their hands as one crushes a ripe quaya to eat its seeds. You believe in your cursing, Rovers, then let the fruit of it be made plain beyond the stars!"

Was this the time to speak of the switched tapes, Ross wondered. No, he did not really believe that the Rover curse or their treatment of the captives would, either one, influence the star leaders. But, if the invaders did not return to their base, their vanishing might also work to keep another expedition from invading Hawaikan skies. Leave it to chance, a curse, and time . . .

So it was decided.

"Have we won?" Ross asked Ashe later.

"Do you mean, have we changed the future? Who can answer that? They may return in force, this may have been a step which was taken before. Those pylons may still stand in the future above a deserted sea and island. We shall probably never know."

That was also their own truth. For them also there had been a substitution of journey tapes by Fate, and this was now their Hawaika. Ross Murdock, Gordon Ashe, Karara Trehern, Tino-rau, Taua—five humans forever lost in time— in the past with a dubious future. Would this be the barren, lotus world, or another now? Yes, no—either. They had found their key to the mystery out of time, but they could not turn it, and there was no key to the gate which had ceased to exist. Grasp tight the present. Ross looked about him. Yes, the present, which might be very satisfying after all . . .